David Black is the author of the *Harry Gilmour* series of novels set in the Royal Navy submarine service during the Second World War. He also wrote *All the Freshness of the Morning*, a fictionalised account of President John F Kennedy's epic wartime service as skipper of the US Navy torpedo boat PT109 during the Solomons' campaign against the Japanese in the South Pacific. Black is a former UK national newspaper journalist and TV documentary producer. He now lives in Argyll and writes full time.

SEE YOU AT THE BAR

The Fifth Harry Gilmour Novel

DAVID BLACK

LUME BOOKS

LUME BOOKS

This edition published in 2021 by Lume Books
30 Great Guildford Street,
London, SE1 0HS

ISBN 978-1-83901-346-1

Typeset using Atomik ePublisher from Easypress Technologies

www.lumebooks.co.uk

To my mate, John

Author's Note

Readers of the previous Harry Gilmour novels will have noticed that I have consistently sought to set my hero's story against actual events, and the general course of the Second World War as it unfolded.

However, the last third of *See You at the Bar* marks a complete departure from that approach.

The British campaign in the Dodecanese in late 1943, as described here, is a total fiction.

While British forces did indeed launch a campaign into the Greek islands, for broadly the reasons I ascribe, the actual strategic decisions, and tactical events bear no resemblance whatsoever to the story I have written. Nor is there an island called Thirios, which I also invented for the purpose of my narrative.

Just thought I'd better clear that up.

David Black

My technical adviser is Captain Iain D. Arthur OBE RN, who is a former Captain (S) of the Devonport Flotilla of the Royal Navy Submarine Service

One

Harding was still marvelling at the stench of the head bandito, lying there in the long grass, his arse in the air, his bare feet in front of Harding's nose. He stared sullenly at the heap, its lines picked out in the pale wash of a quarter moon. I mean to say, how could he, Lieutenant Miles Harding RN, the navigating officer of one of His Majesty's submarines, possibly be persuaded to think of this specimen as being anything so romantic as a partisan?

That, however, was exactly the word the creature had used to introduce himself to Captain Gilmour. No, it just wasn't on. Not with that droopy moustache of his, randomly clotted with uneaten food, or the once-gaudy silk waistcoat, now faded to the colour of dried blood that stretched across a hairy belly peeking over his rope-tied waistband. This was a cut-throat straight out of Hollywood central casting. Even in HMS *Scourge's* wardroom, with all the competition from the reek of diesel and thirty-odd sailors' bodies, the beast had managed to smell like a dead goat. So, not surprising really, out here in the clean sea air of a Sicilian clifftop, he continued to smell like a dead goat.

That, and the fact that this desperado had sat on the very banquette where Harding and his fellow officers ate their meals and had demanded the lolly up front, before either he or the rest of his gang ashore were prepared to even bestir themselves in any direction. It all tended to undermine his claim to be fighting only for the freedom of Italy.

There was scuffling in the not-quite-darkness, and elbowing himself into view out of the tussock came the blacked-up face of that evilly bland corporal that had been giving Harding the creeps since Algiers.

'Sir!' he hissed, but not at him. Harding missed the rest of what was being murmured. For the corporal was addressing another shapeless lump of shadow that Harding knew was Second Lieutenant Ewan Pettifer, whose regimental badge said he was Duke of Cornwall's Light Infantry and his shoulder flash, a commando. All very dashing, except that Pettifer's overall presence reeked of a languid repose that told a different truth about him.

Harding hadn't been to the same public school as him, but he might as well have been; he knew the type. Entitled, indolent and usually indifferent to the sufferings of others, especially ones he had power over. A rotter in other words. Oh, how Harding hated a rotter. He pushed himself up into a crouch and shouldered his way past the Italian brigand to slump by the corporal, whereupon he began prodding him none too gently in the ribs. The corporal spun, with murder in his eyes, until he saw who was beside him.

'You were saying, Corporal?' whispered Harding, as if he'd just joined a drawing-room chat.

Back in *Scourge's* wardroom, Captain Gilmour had been very specific about who was now going to be in charge of the landing party about to go ashore, and it hadn't been Mister one-pipper Pettifer. Neither Pettifer, his NCO thug, nor indeed any of the commandos had been too pleased about that and had persistently made their feelings clear through lots of little acts of insubordination.

The corporal shut up immediately then looked at the dirt before replying, like he was bored, 'I wiz just tellin' Mr Pettifer...'

'Well, you're telling me now,' said Harding, like he was talking to a wayward child. All of it in whispers. The Italian brigand rolled onto his back and began chewing on a stalk of tussock, bored. Harding had the impression the rest of their band – the other commandos and the 'partisans' stretching down the slope behind him – were doing much the same.

The corporal began to recount what he'd seen in his swift reconnaissance of the villa. 'Nice place,' he said, talking a tone or so louder, like he knew now there were no Jerries close enough to hear him, 'very flash. No' fer the likes o' us...' a pause, '...and no' exactly bristlin' wi' impregnable defences as ye might think would befit a Jerry field marshal's bunker.'

Harding thinking, *I don't need a travelogue*, and knowing the little bastard was just showing off how cool under duress he could be. But Harding said nothing, wondering only how he could make his own expression seem cool and unruffled, through all the face-blackening, in the dark. Two could play, etc.

Directly in their path, apparently, was a swimming pool – which was full – and a summer house off to the side. Two Jerry soldiers were inside the summer house, one snoring, the other listening to a radio; a commercial radio playing maudlin popular songs, all of them, 'in Eyetie', said the corporal. Then there was a terrace then the villa proper, with big glass doors. There was another Jerry walking round the villa, 'Paying more attention to smokin' his gasper and scratchin' his arse than guardin' the place,' the corporal added. Otherwise, no other sign of life. That was the good news. The bad news was there were two Jerry halftracks at the bottom of the drive, about two hundred and fifty yards beyond, and scant cover in between; just a scatter of little rock-walled shrubberies, no more. 'The tracks are those Hanomag jobs,' said the corporal. 'One's got a half dozen or so infantry lounging around it, tabbin' it and pickin' their noses. And the other has a triple twenty millimetre AA strapped to its back.'

Pettifer rearranged his buttocks on the ground to get comfy. 'Interesting, Corporal McLucas,' he said then, with a languorous crane of his neck, to Harding, he said, 'What's your plan, sir.'

'Wait here,' said Harding, who then stood up suddenly and walked directly towards the pool. This caused a minor stir among the spread-out raiding party, but Harding wasn't looking back to notice. Although he was smirking to himself over how his just jumping up like that had probably, at last, bestirred Pettifer out of his too-cool-for-school langour. But he'd only done it because he could see how the low summer house masked him from the villa and the drive. He was up to its wall in fewer than a couple of dozen strides. He could hear the music from the radio now and even the muffled snoring. The terrace beyond was clear. He waited, the big Webley revolver still snug in his webbing holster. Fat lot of good he was going to do with that up against Jerry armed with a 20mm anti-aircraft triple-mount!

The guard walking the outside of the villa appeared on the terrace. Even though it was in shadow, the moon made his outline clear, and the flare from his cigarette stood out like a lighthouse every time he drew on it. Plod, plod, shuffle, shuffle; he covered the terrace, and as he came to the end, the little beacon of light that was his cigarette went arcing through the air into the nearest shrubbery. The Jerry stopped and lit another one and then was off again, disappearing round the corner. Harding checked his watch. Time passed. He looked over to where he knew his team was hidden. You couldn't tell. He was impressed.

Over ten minutes elapsed before the Jerry reappeared; Harding could hear him crunching on gravel. He checked his watch again. *Strange*, he thought. The terrace was stone-flagged; *why the crunching?* When he leaned out to check, he almost shit himself. The Jerry was walking directly towards him; it was only the fact that he was squinting as he blew out a huge lungful of smoke that he didn't see Harding's big head jerking back behind the cover of the summer house gable.

'Jesus Christ!' Harding hissed to himself. He thought about fumbling out the Webley, but if he even farted now, the Jerry would hear him. He stood frozen. A clump of boots and lots of crashing and voices, and none of them too good-natured either.

'Verschiebung!'… 'Du bist dran!'… 'Schweine!'

Then the shouting stopped, and the language became more amiable-sounding. There was a clatter of a tin mug, pouring and the smell of coffee. A bit of chat, and then more shuffling and Harding heard a different Jerry crunching over the gravel; a lighter man. He wasn't grinding the pebbles to dust. Harding peeked, much more discreetly, and he saw the back of a battledress and forage cap and a rifle dangling from its shoulder strap, receding towards the villa. He checked his watch and then turned and strode purposefully back towards Pettifer, Cpl McLucas and all the gang.

When he plonked down beside Pettifer, the soldier was speechless with rage. 'What…!?' was all he managed to hiss before Harding told him to, 'Shut up!' in the most *sotto voce* of tones. 'Get your men, and come with me,' said Harding, who then grabbed the bandito's shoulder hard and said, jabbing at the ground with his other hand, 'Stare qui a guardare!'

Captain Gilmour, who could speak Italian, had armed Harding in advance with a few key phrases for handling their 'partisan' friends, like 'stay here and watch'. Also, in his new-gained repertoire was 'come with me', 'don't shoot the prisoners', 'run like hell'; that sort of thing.

Harding stood up and began striding back towards the villa. Pettifer gawped after him momentarily then realised he'd better get moving too. The corporal and the four other British soldiers followed. The little group soon realised that Harding was walking like he belonged here. And that he was leading them in a loop round the back of the summer house so that they'd be approaching the villa up the drive. All six of them fell into step.

Pettifer caught up with Harding. 'So we're just going to walk up and knock on the door?'

'Don't be stupid,' said Harding, with out breaking his stride. 'We'd wake whoever's inside. Why d'you think those Jerries have the radio turned down? There's folk in there trying to get a good night's sleep. We're just going to let ourselves in. And we've...' he paused to look at his watch again, '... just less than seven minutes to do it... before our strolling Jerry comes back around.'

One of the German soldiers, perched up on the Hanomag's triple AA mount noticed the figures moving up the drive between the summer house and the villa. Five shadows, obviously soldiers, marching in line, and an officer out front. All he thought was, good job they hadn't wandered up to that shack to say hello, he hadn't realised there were so many of the buggers in there, there wouldn't have been enough of their schnapps to go round.

Harding put his hand on the French windows' handle... and turned it. The door opened.

His heart could start beating again.

Pettifer said in his ear, 'How did you know it would be unlocked?'

Harding said, 'It's a secret.'

They were in a sprawling art-deco lounge. Completely dark. Just the barest splash of moonlight through the huge window showed the scatter of low sofas and tables. The only illumination inside came from a corridor that led off from the far wall; it picked out the spill of some night light from somewhere down its length. The other men were crowding in behind. Harding walked across the middle of the room towards the corridor. Cpl McLucas was right behind him, unslinging his Thompson gun.

They had gone only halfway down the corridor when a slight, bare-footed figure in shirttails and a Luftwaffe forage cap suddenly appeared at the far end. He said something like, '…wer bist du?' But more in incredulity than alarm. Harding marched purposefully towards him, stopping only when he gauged he would still be in shadow, and began haranguing the man. Loud, but not exactly shouting.

'Non sparare i prigionieri!' he accused him… *don't shoot the prisoners…* The spindly little Jerry was transfixed; he plainly didn't understand the language of his ally, so he did the only thing he could think of in the face of obvious authority. He snapped to attention.

'Stare qui a guardare!' said Harding, sounding even more annoyed. The only effect he had was to make the German airman stand even more rigidly to attention and splutter something guttural, very loud, obviously hoping that would atone for whatever it was he was doing wrong.

'Eseguire come l'inferno!' said Harding. *Run like hell!* Barked in the timeless, international tones of someone used to command, berating the commanded. The Jerry didn't run, however, he just made himself more rigid and jutted his chin higher thus demonstrating total compliance, so that he didn't notice McLucas stepping forward and hitting him square on the jaw with the butt of his Thompson gun. The little chap went down like a sack of potatoes, blood and teeth splattering the pale walls.

Pettifer and his commandos spread out through the house at a breathless run; the only sound the light slap of their plimsolls on the marble floor. Harding hefted the fallen little Jerry and dragged him into a small cloakroom-cum-toilet. The Jerry was woozy now, coming round. Harding sat him on the toilet pan and began gently wiping away the blood from his face with a cloth from the sink. As the Jerry's eyes focused on him, Harding made a 'zip-it' gesture across his mouth. The Jerry's eyes were fixed on him, wide with terror. He obviously thought he was about to get his throat cut. Harding dabbed a bit more then used the soap bar to properly clean the gash along the Jerry's bottom lip. The little chap now looked more confused than scared, thought Harding. He smiled at him and winked.

One of Pettifer's men was at Harding's elbow. 'Sir,' he said. 'Mr Pettifer says you need to come and see this.'

'Watch him,' said Harding. Suddenly, the little Jerry was looking down the barrel of the commando's Thompson gun, his eyes now back to goggling in fright. Harding said, 'Where is Mr Pettifer?'

'Round the corner, second on the right. Can't miss it. The light's on.'

Harding gave the commando a backward look, then he eyed the Jerry, still perched on the toilet. 'Non sparare i prigionieri!' he said.

The commando gave him a funny look, obvious, even through his blackened features. 'Huh?' he said.

'Don't shoot the prisoners,' said Harding in his best 'it's a joke' voice. The commando looked blank. 'He's harmless,' said Harding and then sped off.

It was a big room with a big table in the middle. The table and one wall were adorned with maps. Sicily mainly, but one of the toe of Italy and the Straits of Messina and others of the western Mediterranean, North Africa and the Sicilian Channel.

Pettifer was sitting on the edge of the table, one foot up on one of the numerous chairs around it, with his finger hooked through the pistol guard of a Walther, dangling it insouciantly. In front of him, sitting back on a huge, winged easy chair, was an aristocratic-looking middle-aged officer in his shirt sleeves and no boots. Beside him was a small table with an open bottle of cognac and a big, half-full balloon glass, its contents glittering in the light from a standard lamp behind him. There was an open book, fallen on the floor, and a uniform jacket draped over one of the chair wings. To Harding, it looked as if the man had just been awakened from a nap; a slightly drunken nap.

'This chap's a Luftwaffe oberst,' said Pettifer without preamble. 'A full colonel. According to the flashes on his jacket. And at a guess from the other flashes, a staff officer to boot. Who doesn't haben sie English. Eh, cock? Neinen gesprechensie?' This last to the seated German, whose expression had now composed itself from dazed to that of a man sitting through a rather boring church sermon, despite having to listen to the atrocities being committed against his language by this camouflaged thug who'd just crashed in from nowhere.

'Put the gun down, Lieutenant Pettifer,' said Harding. 'Remember what Captain Gilmour told us… "Non sparare i prigionieri!"…'

In the end, it hadn't been necessary for the oberst to say anything for them to learn everything they needed to know.

Once Harding had sponged him a bit more and stuck a mug of brandy in his hand, it had been Ulrich, the little gefreiter – Jerry rank for an Aircraftman First Class, apparently – that had blabbed. It was amazing how much you could learn by just waving your arms about; that and the ever-present threat of violence, of course. In fact, he proved to be a veritable treasure trove: He was Oberst Von Puttkamer's batman. And Oberst Von Puttkamer was one of Field Marshal Kesselring's chief intelligence officers; and yes, Field Marshal Kesselring, the big cheese, Hitler's man on the spot for the new Thousand Year Reich's entire southern flank, *had* been here but he wasn't now. And no, he didn't know when or even if he was expected back.

But to make up for it, here was the table full of documents with title stamps such as *Intelligenz-Bewertung* and *Auftrag der Schlacht*.

'Schlacht? That's Jerry for "battle", isn't it?' Pettifer had said, and Harding agreed.

'*Auftrag der Schlacht?* It's just lists and lists of units,' Pettifer had observed. 'Hundreds of them. *Für die Luftwaffe?* And *für Panzer-Grenadier-Regiment* this? And for *Fallschirmjäger-battlaion* that? It's Jerry's full order of battle. Must be.'

This put a different complexion entirely on the matters at hand. And just as well, thought Harding. He had been of one mind with his captain when he'd heard what their initial orders had been, back when Captain Gilmour had finally spilled the beans to HMS *Scourge's* crew as to why they had a sub full of commandos, a huge weapons cache and all those bloody explosives and were heading for the north coast of Sicily on another of those cloak-and-dagger missions so unbeloved of the service.

They were to put the commandos ashore near some fancy villa a dozen or so miles east of Palermo where *Generalfeldmarschall* Albert Kesselring, Commander-in-Chief South was – according to 'intelligence' – having a lie-down. And the objective of the mission was for the commandos to murder him.

That hadn't gone down too well with the rest of the crew. It wasn't that Jack – your average lower deck sailor – had any inherent squeamishness about killing Jerries. Far from it. There were probably more than a few aboard *Scourge* who would be happy to tell you they enjoyed it. But only in a good, clean fight. Murder was something altogether different as far as Jack was concerned. And aboard *Scourge*, this wasn't just a hypothetical feeling. There had been a patrol in the Dodecanese, under Bertie Bayliss, their former CO, that the whole boat preferred not to talk about.

Then circumstances had changed.

The commando three-pipper who should have been in charge of the landing party, Captain Tony di Marco – latterly Eighth Battalion, the Argyll & Sutherland Highlanders and now Combined Operations – had come down with 'flu en route. And without Captain Tony, whose family owned a third-generation ice cream parlour on Montague Street, Rothesay, capital of the island of Bute, the whole op was kiboshed. Because Tony was a fluent Italian speaker, and his skills were to be key to liaising with a band of Sicilian partisans who were going to guide his team to the villa, suppress any armed guards while Tony slit Kesselring's throat and then the partisans were to spirit the assassins back to the beach for rescue by *Scourge* before melting into the Sicilian hinterland to await further rewards after the upcoming Allied invasion had stormed ashore.

'Bugger, Captain Tony's second in command,' Ewan Pettifer had said while listening to Captain Tony cough and sneeze as he writhed and sweated in the grip of a fever in Captain Gilmour's bunk. Captain Tony had been very keen on the idea of murdering Kesselring, despite Captain Gilmour's strongly expressed misgivings. But whichever way you looked at it, a coughing, sneezing, delirious CO, was not going to be an effective leader of a clandestine operation behind enemy lines, where speed, clarity of thought and keeping quiet would be essential. With Captain Tony out of the picture, it should have been a no-go. But Captain Gilmour had come up with an alternative plan; one in which the operation still went ahead, but didn't involve murdering the wretched Nazi Field Marshal. They were going to nab him instead.

The fact that Kesselring wasn't here, however, didn't have to mean the op was a total wash-out, thought Harding, and he said so to Pettifer, who agreed. They were going to nab Von Puttkamer instead and all the bumpf strewn across the villa's large dining table and in the box files surrounding it. However, in order for their efforts to be worthwhile, both British officers also agreed there were two other things they had to do. Since Harding was insistent that no one was going to be allowed to slit poor little Ulrich's throat, they were going to have to nab him too; and for the barrow loads of document intelligence to still be relevant after they'd nabbed it, Jerry was going to have to believe they'd been destroyed.

'We have to get that cut-throat Dandolo in here now,' said Harding, referring to their smelly 'partisan' leader. Dandolo's personal hygiene was another thing that Harding and Pettifer agreed on.

A commando was dispatched to summon Snr Dandolo. The other commandos also peeled off on their missions; and right there, the war, and all its absence of morality and mercy, resumed.

One of the commandos sneaked out and shoved his commando dagger into the brain stem of the guard on walk-round duty, while the other two sneaked back to the summer house and did the two Jerries in there likewise. It was all very, quick, silent and brutal, like they'd been trained to do. One of the bodies was dragged back and was dressed in the oberst's uniform.

Dandolo's men were relieved of three of the demolition charges from the stack that had formed part of the US Navy gift package to their new partisan allies, and had been carried here by *Scourge*. Two of the charges were attached to the villa's load-bearing walls; the other was attached to the very modern, large steel cylinder out back, that was full of propane gas for heating and cooking.

The commandos started stuffing documents and maps into pillowcases, and Pettifer led the partisans carrying the BARs – Browning Automatic Rifles, another gift from the US Navy – to the edge of the driveway. Here, he shoved them into a little impromptu gun line. 'I fire,' he said, pointing at his own Thompson, 'then you,' pointing at his little gaggle of gangsters. 'Three bursts,' he told them, counting with his fingers and mimicking firing, '…and then you eseguire come l'inferno! You run! Capeachy? Run!'

When he got back to the villa, it was just Harding left there. He was sloshing paraffin over the floor in the dark. 'Ready,' said Pettifer, grinning. Harding couldn't help but notice that the man had lost all that louche indifference that had been rubbing him up since the young subaltern had first deigned to disport himself on *Scourge's* wardroom banquettes. The type Harding had remembered from his public school days, and not fondly, appeared to have gone, while the battlefield Pettifer seemed to be shaping up to be an entirely different creature.

'Well then,' said Harding, 'I'll pop the timers on the wall charges, and you do the propane tank…'

'And fire my starting gun,' Pettifer interrupted, un-shouldering his Thompson and brandishing it. He then snapped briefly, and comically, to attention, snapped off a salute and said, 'Aye, aye, sir!' But not mocking, having fun.

'See you on the beach, then,' said Harding, grinning too, now, and then both men peeled off.

Harding was already running on sand when he heard the rapid, tell-tale *rat-at-tat* of the Thompson gun from up the hill. There was a brief pause in which he wondered if anything at all had actually happened, and then all hell had broken loose.

Deep down inside he knew it would be prudent of him to be scared, but he couldn't stop grinning as he sprinted, he just couldn't help himself. The ninety minutes or so it had taken to get into that villa, grab their man – not the right man admittedly, but an important one anyway – load their booty and see it all on its way to the beach to be picked up by *Scourge*, easily qualified as the most exciting, exhilarating and downright bloody marvellous of his life. They'd all been wrong-footed by what they'd discovered up there on the clifftop, but he'd kept his head and devised another plan, on the run; he'd kept the momentum of the op going. No standing about thumb-sucking while the minutes dripped away. He had acted.

Now, at the ripe old age of twenty-five, Harding had long ago learned that plans never usually worked out, but by God, this one was looking bloody good so far! The fact that it had in large part depended on a mob of half-cut Eyetie irregulars running away had probably a lot to do with it... but hey!

And there, in the lapping waves, were the two folbots, held by two of Pettifer's commandos, and if he squinted really hard, out there in the night, on the fine line between the darkness of the water and the sky, was *Scourge*.

The steady thump of the 20mms echoed out to him and then reflected in the lapping waves, the false sunrise of the propane going up and quickly after, the bang.

*

Even in the darkness of *Scourge's* bridge, his captain, Lt Harry Gilmour DSO, DSC, RNVR could tell how pleased Harding was with himself, now that he had, at last, got him back aboard. Behind them, down on the casing, that commando subaltern was supervising the collapsing of the folbots – those flimsy canvas-and-frame kayaks Combined Ops seemed to love so much – as his boat crept back out to sea again, half astern together on her diesels, not even bothering to go to her quiet electric motors because the bangs and flashes from the headland told Harry that Jerry was still busy in a firefight with an empty villa. No one was looking their way or listening over the *thump, thump* of the 20mms and the persistent chatter of small-arms fire.

Harry had no idea what had happened back there, but no doubt he'd soon find out. That it had turned out well, however, there was no doubt, judging from the grin still splitting Harding's face. It was as if someone had just a rammed an inverted coat hanger in his mouth. With the flames still flickering from the burning villa on the headland, even a chap with night vision as terrible as Harry Gilmour's couldn't miss it.

'Well, Mr Harding, you look like you've been having a jolly time,' said Harry.

'Bloody right, sir!' said Harding.

Two

He's still just a bloody kid, thought Shrimp. Yes, there were lines tightening about the eyes, and the set of the jaw and the mouth was a lot harder. And that stillness about him, that air of composure you never ordinarily see in the young. What age was he now? Twenty-three? Twenty-four?

Harry Gilmour. One of his battle-hardened captains. The CO of a 670-ton S-class submarine, dispatcher-to-the-deep of God knows how many thousand tons of Axis shipping now, with some thirty-six men under his command and thirteen torpedoes at his disposal to fire at the enemy wherever he could find them. And here he was back on Malta. When he shouldn't have been.

'This is by way of a more detailed examination of the night of the ninth, tenth and the days leading up to it and since,' said Shrimp, still sitting back in his new chair, tapping a pencil on the big legal pad before him on the desk. 'As you can imagine, Mr Gilmour, C-in-C Mediterranean is going to want a lot more detail than the bare bones we signalled last night.'

'Indeed, sir,' said Harry, trying to look bright-eyed despite the cargo of brandy he'd taken on board... last night.

'And Mr Wincairns' friends are also taking an interest,' added Shrimp.

18

George Wincairns, a roly-poly sort of chap in a cobbled-together uniform of no service or unit Harry had ever seen or heard of, beamed familiarly at him from the corner. Harry knew him of old. He'd been on Malta for some time now. No one knew exactly what he did though. Some said he was some kind of 'Information Officer', although he was more frequently to be seen hanging around places where anyone connected with public relations should've been decidedly *persona non grata* – like the island's main ops room and the main signals 'hole'.

And so they began. Shrimp – Captain George Simpson RN, the Captain S of the Tenth Submarine Flotilla – took Harry over the hurdles: could he be specific about his orders for this op? Who gave them? What exactly was the mission? Why had he arbitrarily decided to vary those orders? And more importantly, why had he decided to return to Malta and not to Algiers where his boat had been temporarily detached to Twelfth Flotilla?

For Harry, the great temptation was to dissemble. But he knew he mustn't. For there were going to be the statements from the two pongo officers, di Marco and Pettifer, that had to tally with his. *Just tell it straight, Harry, and don't elaborate*, he told himself.

What Harry didn't know about was the signal from the CO of the Twelfth Flotilla back in Algiers that had arrived since, that Shrimp had read with furrowed brow, a signal that Harry was going to have to explain, eventually.

As for the other man in the room, George Wincairns, nobody ever knew what George Wincairns knew, and if they were wise, they didn't bother wondering.

'Start at the beginning,' said Shrimp.

So Harry began, surprised at how little nerves he felt. It would be good to finally get the story out there, although he was under no illusions that this little gathering was *not* the place to fully reveal how poisoned the waters were that he was swimming in.

Harry told how he'd been ordered to a meeting ashore in Algiers. The summons had come in the form of a written order from, 'Staff Officer, Operations: Twelfth Flotilla' and handed to him at the door of the pokey little wardroom of the Twelfth's depot ship, HMS *Ellan Vannin,* by a petty officer writer. He'd been summoned to a meeting. Usually, these notes were informal, jokey even, for a skipper returning from patrol, dashed off by a flotilla CO, grateful, at least, to have got his boat back. Not this one. It had been curt and to the point, not that Harry had been expecting anything like bonhomie. Especially after the post-patrol interview he'd just given right after *Scourge* had come in – with the Twelfth's Captain S, Captain Charles Bonalleck VC, DSO and Bar, RN, the famous Bonny Boy – when Captain Bonalleck had called into question Lt Gilmour's 'zeal', and 'diligence' and noted his 'tendency to interpret your orders in an apparent effort to justify what can only be described as a lack of fighting spirit in the face of the enemy'. Even so, a summons to an operational meeting, he'd have expected one of those to at least come from his Captain S and not just the SOO. This was his CO sending a message that he was keeping an eye on him.

Harry, however, decided now was not the time to mention Captain S12's verbal assessment of him, even though it ended up having considerable bearing on Harry's subsequent decisions, because that would have involved going into all the painful details of that previous patrol. The whole dodgy set-up for it, the orders that took no account of the tactical picture at sea, the signals and intelligence – vital signals and intelligence – that had not been passed on and the terrible conclusion he'd been driven to confront, the only one that made any sense when you'd stacked up all the evidence, that the Captain S12 had been trying to kill him. Instead, he just stuck to his storyline.

The meeting the SOO's summons had referred to had been ashore, Harry told Shrimp and Wincairns, at an address he didn't recognise.

'Can't miss it,' he remembered a US Army MP telling him. 'It's one of them big fancy French shacks. Got a big sign outside says, "*Mediterranean Theater of Operations, United States Army*". It's where Ike lives.'

Ike – General Dwight D Eisenhower, the US Army officer who was now supreme commander for the whole of the Med – which had turned out to be ironic in a way as most of the American officers in the meeting had been US Navy.

It had been all very informal; there had been a US Army one-star general presiding, having come out from behind the cover of his desk to sit with everyone in the room on easy chairs. With one other exception, everybody else had been in blue.

And that was when Harry first learned that they wanted *his* boat to carry a team of *British* commandos to a beach just east of Palermo and drop them ashore so they could murder Field Marshal Albert Kesselring. Oh, and while you're at it, could you also drop off this not-inconsiderable cache of arms and explosives… and cash… to a team of waiting Italian partisans eager to help us kick Jerry off of Sicily when the time comes in the not-too-distant future.

The plan had all been thought out and written down on flipcharts and was spelled out to the room by a pointer-waving, spindly, myopic US Army major in a most immaculate uniform. Harry had noticed the uniform – in fact, all their uniforms – because as only one of two British servicemen in the room, he compared very unfavourably in his ill-fitting shirt and shorts, which he'd been forced to scrounge from HMS *Ellan Vannin's* slops room. Because what kit he'd had left these days had been back here on Malta, in the Lazaretto's wardroom – the kit that is, that had survived all the bombing.

The US Army major, nor indeed any of the others in that room, hadn't looked like they'd seen much bombing, if any, in their careers. But Harry didn't mention any of that to Shrimp or Wincairns either.

'So this was an American op?' asked Shrimp.

Before Harry could answer, Wincairns said, 'Oh, no. No. It's all under AFHQ these days… Allied Forces Headquarters. We're all in it, friends together, George.'

Shrimp winced slightly at the familiarity.

'Yes, sir. All the other officers in the room were US Navy, commanders mainly,' said Harry. 'And apart from Captain Bonalleck and myself, the only other British representative was a civilian.'

'Who?' said Shrimp.

'Ah…' said Harry, his eyes resting on Wincairns, who merely smiled like an innocent babe before filling the gap in the conversation.

'Oh, I don't think we need bother about him,' said Wincairns. 'Probably just some FO Johnny sent there so as he could fill in all the colour for Winston. You know how he loves to hear about all our behind-the-enemy-lines japes.'

'I don't know, sir,' said Harry. 'He didn't speak and wasn't introduced.'

'And the reason they'd picked on a British boat for this… operation… was because?' asked Shrimp.

'According to one of their commanders, S12 and I were there because the US Navy doesn't have any boats in the Med, sir…' said Harry.

'…and our Combined Ops chaps are more experienced at this sort of stuff than theirs,' Shrimp finished for him.

And then Harry started relating the jeep ride back to *Ellan Vannin* with Captain Bonalleck.

'He told me this job, this mission to kill the German Field Marshal, was not only vital to winning the war, but to the future of the Anglo–American alliance,' recounted Harry. 'He was very emphatic. I'd better return with evidence of a corpse, or not return at all, were more or less his exact words.'

Harry didn't mention the sneer with which Bonalleck's pep talk had been delivered, the, 'See if you can do as you're told this time, Gilmour,' line with which they parted at the gangway.

Shrimp listened closely, but there was still no answer to the question uppermost in his mind: where had the British authorisation for this op come from?

Then they were onto the prep for the op, the commandos coming aboard and the weapons cache, all delivered by a very efficient detail of US Navy sailors, busy as bees in their dainty little white 'Dixie' caps, who had made no effort to hide their wrinkled noses on encountering the operational squalor aboard HMS *Scourge* as she got ready for yet another war patrol. The boat had been over a year in continuous action, if you counted her time under Bertie Bayliss, and no matter how much Izal they used on every return, the reek of the old tub had never gotten any sweeter.

Folbots and an inflatable, to carry their cargo ashore, had gone down the torpedo loading hatch, watched by Harry and Sam Bridger, the Commander S12. Bridger, all big blonde hair and beard, his brow uncharacteristically scrunched and his arms folded. He'd asked Harry for a look at his C-in-C Mediterranean Fleet confirmation signal for the op. But there hadn't been one. If there had been, both men knew it should have passed across Sam Bridger's desk.

Vice-Admiral Henry Harwood might have been new in the job as C-in-C, back there in Alexandria, but he'd still have wanted to approve the use of one of his boats by an Allied power on such an unusual mission. It wasn't just that, however, that had been making Sam Bridger uncomfortable. He knew all about *Scourge's* last patrol, and you couldn't miss the stuff going on between young Gilmour and their boss, Captain Charles 'the Bonny Boy' Bonalleck. And he hadn't liked it.

But again, Harry said nothing of this in his narrative. Nor did he mention the undertone of friction between *Scourge's* crew and the commandos on the run across to Sicily, especially between Second Lt Pettifer and the wardroom. Harry just stuck to the story.

And then Captain di Marco had come down with the sniffles.

'According to the orders, Captain di Marco was key to the op, sir,' said Harry. 'He could speak Italian, and he was to do all the liaison work with the people ashore who were to guide his party to and from the villa, and who were looking for their reward in the form of the arms cache and a considerable sum of money to help them in their struggle. But Captain di Marco had quickly become incapacitated. He was coughing and sneezing, and by the time we were round the corner and off Cape Zafferano, he had a temperature of a hundred and four and was practically raving. So we had to think again.'

And Harry, in his head, was back sitting at his wardroom table in the tiny the little alcove off *Scourge's* main passage, being challenged on his own boat by that smug, lugubrious Subaltern Pettifer, going on about 'my orders are my orders… sir.'

Harry knew all about orders; he had his own. But they'd been blown out the water by di Marco's flu, or whatever lurgy it had been that had poleaxed the bastard.

However, there were other matters on Harry's mind – like the Bonny Boy's malevolent intent against him and his boat and what would happen to both him and his crew if they returned to Algiers without even trying to complete their mission.

Because he knew, as far as the Bonny Boy was concerned, *Scourge* had failed to complete her previous mission. That she had never stood a chance of doing so hadn't mattered to the Bonny Boy, in fact, Harry was now convinced that was why he, in particular, had been sent in the first place.

That last patrol had been to a stretch of coast astride the Franco–Spanish border, one along which Axis blockade runners routinely ferried vital iron ore for the Jerry war machine. And something Harry had never heard of until then. Before ordering Harry to go in and disrupt the trade, before informing him that a successful patrol in those waters would shorten the war, the Bonny Boy had assured him that the original minefields covering the passage were no longer a threat – blown away by storm and current. The path to glory was now clear.

But the mines had still been there.

The Bonny Boy had lied to him.

He'd also failed to mention the system of safe-conduct ships: neutral vessels allowed to trade with the Axis powers, guaranteed safe passage by the Allies because they also carried medicines, food parcels and other life-giving supplies for Allied prisoners of war and interned civilians, ships that routinely passed through this new patrol billet the Bonny Boy had assigned to *Scourge*. That Harry had learned of such ships had happened only by accident, and a signal alerting all Allied units to the impending passage of one such ship, right through the middle of Harry's billet, had only been thrust under his nose while he was in the process of attacking said ship. Oh, the signal had been sent in plenty of time, but Captain Bonalleck hadn't deigned to pass it on. If *Scourge* had sunk her… Harry felt sick every time he thought of the international furore that would have resulted, of the blackening of his personal reputation and that of the Royal Navy, to have sunk a neutral merchantman, sailing under a safe-conduct pass from the British government. And of the malignant smile that would've been on the Bonny Boy's face.

No wonder the Bonny Boy had been furious on *Scourge's* return; his plans had all gone awry. However, if Harry returned again, having failed to carry out another mission, well… There were always other ways to destroy the name of an officer who consistently failed to press home his attacks.

So, Harry was buggered if he wasn't going to press home this one. But since Plan A had all but fallen apart, he was going to do it his way, and that way wasn't going to involve either him or his crew in cold-blooded murder, even if the 'target' was an enemy field marshal. If all that mattered was depriving the enemy of their theatre commander, then kidnapping would work just as well, and wouldn't that provide an even bigger propaganda coup? Even a junior RNVR two-ringer like him could see the potential of marching a Nazi big shot into the Tower, alive and well, for the world's newsreel cameras. Much better than having shots of the big Jerry lying in his bed, unarmed, drenched in gore and very dead being flashed around the world, to fanfares of outrage by Josef Goebbels.

So that's why he'd told Second Lt Pettifer, rather forcefully, that he was on Captain Gilmour's boat, and that Captain Gilmour was in charge of this op now. And there was a new plan. And if Second Lt Pettifer was refusing to co-operate, 'well, we can all turn around and go home, and you can explain to your bosses why you decided to throw away the best chance we're ever likely to have of nabbing one of Hitler's most senior henchmen.'

Pettifer hadn't had an answer to that.

But that was all backstory that Harry had no intention of troubling Shrimp and Wincairns with. He completely failed to mention that his new plan had been to kidnap, not murder, and since the way he was telling the story made it look like the decision to nab the Jerry intelligence officer had been taken on the spot, he was happy to let that stand. There'd be too much to explain if he didn't. All that stuff would just have to remain between him and the uppity subaltern; after all, it looked like Second Lt Pettifer was going to emerge from the whole bizarre saga with considerable credit, *so let's just hold our noses and let that one pass downstream*, he'd thought to himself.

'It was out the question I was going to leave the boat, of course,' said Harry, back at his narrative, 'even though I am an Italian speaker.' It was time to explain to Shrimp and Wincairns exactly what his new plan had been and how he was going to execute it. 'So if the op was to go ahead, the Italians had to come to me so as I could explain what was going to be required of them.'

Wincairns asked, 'Why was it out the question? Why not decide to lead the team ashore yourself, seeing as you speak Italian? Then you'd have been on the spot if circumstances had changed.'

'Not with us jammed up against the enemy's coast, Mr Wincairns,' said Harry. 'I am *Scourge's* captain. The boat is my responsibility, first and foremost. Mine.'

Harry then described the band of cut-throats Pettifer had brought back aboard, sullen at the inconvenience of being bounced around in folbots and soaked into the bargain, just to be lectured at by an officer as young as this one, albeit in their own language, but with an accent that was an atrocity in itself.

'I don't know who our American friends back in Algiers imagined they were dealing with,' Harry had said. 'But these so-called partisans looked more like mafia gangsters than Guiseppe Garibaldi.'

Little laughs all round. And then they were onto Harding's report of the action ashore; how Kesselring hadn't been there, but his intelligence officer had, along with all that lovely paperwork.

'So now we come to your decision to disobey a direct order from Twelfth Flotilla's Captain S... to return to Algiers on completion of the op,' said Shrimp. 'You didn't. You went the long way round Sicily and ended up here, at Malta. Even though you must've known the gravity of the decision you took. The extreme peril you placed your boat in, by leaving your designated billet. Why?'

Why, indeed?

Harry had thought long and hard on that one. Of course he knew the peril he'd be in. Any submarine leaving its patrol billet, for whatever reason, automatically becomes a target for its own side's anti-submarine forces. In war, that's the rule. Every submarine is the enemy unless you hold a docket saying otherwise.

But how could he explain the real reason to these men? How could he explain that to the real navy, the one run by grown-ups with a war to win and with scant patience to waste on a pipsqueak lieutenant with fantasies about a senior officer with an Ahab complex, supposedly out to kill him?

'The waters between Sicily and the Tunisian ports were crawling with Italian A/S, sir, as I'm sure you're aware,' said Harry, brows knitted as if reflecting on a decision that had been difficult to take. 'I knew from the intelligence reports I'd read that another convoy was in the offing. It's a narrow corridor, and the only one they have left to channel their supplies to what's left of the Afrika Korps, so they were patrolling it tightly, sir. Very tightly. So, I decided that with the wealth of intelligence we'd bagged, it would've been a shame for our side to lose it just because *Scourge's* luck ran out to some Regia Marina corvette, sir.'

Shrimp smiled. So did Wincairns. Harry formed the opinion neither had believed him, even for a second. But neither of them said a word.

To fill the silence, Harry added, 'Also, from reading all the intelligence briefs, I knew we had nothing immediately north of Sicily. No RAF or Fleet Air Arm up there and nothing from Twelfth or Tenth Flotillas indicating we had any boats on patrol. So, I, eh, decided to risk it, sir.'

After another few moments of deliberative quiet, Shrimp got up, fetched a bottle of brandy from one of his filing cabinets and began filling tumblers for the three of them. For breaking his patrol billet, Harry knew that Shrimp had every justification for relieving him of command right here, right now, with immediate effect, which was why he was holding his breath. Except Shrimp was smiling now, not scowling. He raised his glass and said, 'Bottoms up, Captain Gilmour. It was indeed quite a bag you brought home.'

'Especially the Herr Oberst,' added Wincairns, raising his glass too. 'Oh, they are *very* excited about that back in Cairo and at Eighth Army.'

*

'Your man, Harding,' Wincairns had asked airily, later, while they were sitting outside Harry's favourite café, still there on the promenade in Sliema, a survivor of the bombing. 'Why, when there was no Kesselring to kill, did he not just plug the next best thing instead?'

'The Jerry colonel, you mean?' said Harry, vaguely.

'Yes,' said Wincairns. 'Kidnapping him strikes me as quite a departure from the script. Were you angry? Did you consider he'd exceeded his remit? A spot of over-interpretation in the orders department?'

'No,' said Harry, but he wasn't really paying attention, too busy thinking to himself about what Wincairns had just told him previously: the piece of 'news' that had been dangled so as he'd go for a drink with

Wincairns in the first place, instead of straight along to the Lazaretto's wardroom; 'news' that Wincairns insisted he should hear from him first before someone blurted it: that Katty Kadzow had gone and that he'd probably never seen her again.

'Of course, maybe you didn't actually order Lieutenant Harding to do any execution,' mused Wincairns, sipping the cheap rot-gut the café still sold, despite the lifting of the siege. It was a lovely day – hot, everything blue from the sea to the sky with only the rubble still lying about everywhere, bulldozed into piles, and the wire entanglements along the beach below to show there was still a war on.

Harry looked up, paying attention again. 'He used his initiative,' he said, 'and decided not to commit a war crime. So no, I wasn't angry.'

'Excellent,' said Wincairns, clapping his hands. 'Glad to hear it. No charges or official incriminations flying around then, to attract attention to a very tidy piece of work, Mr Gilmour. I commend you on the decisions made by you and your crew, from a purely selfish point of view, of course. Not only do you stumble on intelligence gold, but your junior also makes it look like you never grabbed it in the first place. Very nice. And when you bring it back, you bring it back to Monty, not Ike. Oh, I know I said we're all in this together… share and share alike… and I'm sure Ike would've been very generous with its contents. But this way, we don't have to wonder, do we, eh? Very nice. We are all very pleased with you, Mr Gilmour.'

Which Wincairns knew not to be true. Twelfth Flotilla's Captain S hadn't been at all pleased with Harry. Wincairns knew this because he got to see all signals zinging their way to, from and across the entire Mediterranean theatre. It was part of his job. Even though no one knew what his actual job was. So when that absolute corker dropped – the one Captain Bonalleck had fired off to Shrimp on learning where his missing submarine had ended up – Wincairns had made a note. He'd said nothing at the time, of course; he never did when little warning lights flashed.

The only thing this 'Bonny Boy' character hadn't accused young Gilmour of was interfering with the Princesses Elizabeth and Margaret. There was obviously something amiss between the two of them, personally. Some bad blood with a long-nurtured reek to it. Except that Wincairns had known young Gilmour for some time, and his reputation as a fighting sailor. None of the ravings in the signal made any sense. Quite the opposite when you considered what Gilmour had just pulled off. But it did prove one thing: the Bonny Boy had no idea what *Scourge* had come back with, which was good. In the meantime, Wincairns was sure Captain Simpson could prevail upon some of his own higher-ups to tell this Bonny Boy character to put a sock in it.

Also, from this last little chat it was obvious now Gilmour wasn't going to go all officious over folk not obeying orders, which meant there should be no noisy fallout from the op from this end. And as long as that remained the state of play, Wincairns didn't care.

In fact, Wincairns really did suspect Harry had ordered his navigating officer not to murder Kesselring, even if he had been there, that kidnapping had always been his plan. Some people might have thought that overly squeamish, but Wincairns didn't; he called it smart. He'd remember that about young Gilmour. He'd even felt a slight twinge for the lad, having had to tell him his exotic night-club singer squeeze had gone and married a USAAF supply major while he'd been away.

Three

Scourge was heading out into the Ionian Sea on a steady course, pointed directly at the island of Cephalonia, three hundred miles to the north-east. They were running at a handy twelve knots, but the water streaming over *Scourge's* casing looked oily and viscous, so she felt sluggish beneath her captain's feet. Storms, really big ones, were rare in any part of the Med in June, but obviously, nobody had told this one coming.

They'd sailed from Malta just over two hours ago, with the glass already falling fast, but not as fast as it had fallen in last half hour. Harry was on the bridge, with Harding as watchkeeper and two lookouts doing their best to scan a dark horizon that even Harry could see was thickening with big, black banks of cloud heading their way. Even as he was standing there, he could feel the deck plates beneath his feet begin to rise and fall in a steadily building wave.

He gazed into the wall of impenetrable night. The sky wouldn't start to lighten for several hours yet, so *Scourge* really had to keep going on the surface if she was to keep to her timetable. Because she had a date, halfway up the Adriatic, which it had been impressed upon Harry *Scourge* had to keep. It was the reason they had sailed, intentionally, into the teeth of this oncoming dirty weather.

Harry wondered how the main package they were carrying would fare once they'd entered the tempest, whether its scrawny frame would be worth delivering. He could see 'the package' right now, sitting there in the PO's mess, hunched over his piping hot tin mug of Ky as if the steam from it was the only heat keeping him alive. Staff Sergeant Willie Reynolds. Gaunt, pale and looking terminally dazed since he'd come aboard – one hand for his satchel of code books and the other for his beret, which he couldn't keep on his head on account of all that unruly blonde tow exploding everywhere, like a burst sofa. Why on earth hadn't he had a haircut first? Probably because he had to spend all his time looking after all that bloody radio kit he was also lugging with him.

There was another item attached, but he was an altogether more robust package: Corporal George Hibbert, a short, wiry, and as it quickly became apparent, eternally cheerful Royal Marine, who was always spruce, polite and self-effacing to the point of being practically invisible. He was Reynolds' 'assistant', or in other words, go-fer and bodyguard. On his second look at Hibbert, Harry suspected that much more lurked beneath his affable, easy-going surface, and that here was a man you wouldn't want to get on the wrong side of.

Thuddudd!

Harry felt that one up through his sea boots; *Scourge* coming off the crest of the last wave with a particularly heavy belly flop. It was the thing you noticed about filthy weather in the Med. For a sea supposedly as tranquil as it was compact, when it turned, it became a short, nasty little maelstrom – no long rolling seas to stretch you out. It was *bam! bam!* till you were punch drunk, and a wind pushing each wave higher with scant troughs between so that the crests toppled on you as often as they lifted you.

Which was why he'd had his chat with Mr Petrie, the warrant engineer, about what they'd do when this bastard really got going if they were going to keep running on the surface. Harry squinted across a wide, dark waste of water that was becoming increasingly spume-streaked even as he watched. Funny thing about the sea; it could be vast and empty, but it could cocoon you too. Here they were in the middle of a war – a terrible war engulfing nearly the whole world – wherever the hands stood on the clock or at whatever angle stood the sun or moon in the sky, somewhere there was disintegration, suffering, death across all of Europe, Russia, the Far East, the Pacific. But right now, on their little cockleshell – a speck with not even a gull or a star for company, all alone in the teeth of a storm – life was exhilarating. He was clinging to the bridge screen as they climbed and bucked and shouldered wave crests aside in welters of spray and wind – warm wind, not the knifing you got in the North Sea or Atlantic – here he really *was*. Not really thinking about anything – not the war, nor the Bonny Boy, or Katty running off with a Yank, or even the defaulters' list his boat had accumulated from her stay in Algiers, that he still hadn't worked through – just alive in the moment, enjoying himself here, on this little patch of water, right now, plunging deep into enemy waters, on their way to contribute their own little penny's worth to the whole bloody conflagration, and he was having fun.

Within an hour, the storm was upon them. Right back to when he used to crew on rich men's yachts, Harry had loved it when it came on to blow. He never got sick, but not all his crew shared his constitution. And he shuddered a silly-grinned shudder when he thought how quickly it would be getting squalid down below. He especially felt for poor Staff Sgt Reynolds. Most of the time, the crew would be there to help, for Jack was usually the most compassionate of creatures when they had aboard as guests those not fortunate enough to be sailors; until you got a really good blow. Then all their care and attention went into holding on themselves, and their solicitousness ended up in the scuppers along with the contents of their own guts. Not all sailors were 'good' sailors, not even the experienced ones.

Farrar, the Jimmy, had already ordered the 'birdbath' shipped – a device like a child's paddling pool, fashioned out of canvas, that sat beneath the lower conning tower hatch to trap all the seawater that came flooding down every time a wave broke over the bridge, except that it never quite managed all of the water so that everyone in the control room knew they were in for a drenching, just as if they'd been upstairs on watch.

Not that anyone cared about the drenching, but water getting into the boat's electrics and instruments was another matter, a real danger if the drain from the birdbath wasn't channelling the water into the bilges fast enough. Because you couldn't just shut the conning tower hatch – that was how the diesels sucked down the air to fuel their combustion chambers. Shut the hatch, and her two 1900 horsepower diesels would have had all the air out the boat in a matter of seconds.

But in a storm like this one was shaping up to be, you were definitely going to get big green ones coming over, so big you were going to *have* to shut the hatch. Which was why Harry had agreed a scheme with Petrie for him to have a stoker permanently watching the engine room barometer for the second it started to move – which it would, rapidly, if the hatch was shut – and then he'd automatically shut down the diesels and either clutch in the electric motors or wait one and then immediately blast in high-pressure air to blow-start the whole shebang again. There'd be no bothering with the engine room telegraph, wasting seconds ringing back acknowledgements.

Down below, from the bounce and clang of his deck plates, Warrant Engineer Petrie was already expecting the first yell from the stoker to 'stop together!'.

On the bridge, Harry had clipped on his safety harness to stop himself being washed overboard and ordered Harding and one of the lookouts below. So it was just him and Leading Seaman Frear left to mind the shop. Not that they were ever likely to see anything in this; the entire Italian battlefleet could probably have passed within a mile of them and they'd have been none the wiser.

The walls of water, with only the streaked foam and residue of phosphorescence picking out their height, were coming faster and furiouser now. In a matter of mere minutes, Harry watched as it all passed from being a joyride to something far more serious.

Scourge was shouldering the sea as it rolled in on her at angle, just behind the starboard fore-planes, so she was corkscrewing, at times wildly. The sea state had become so bad, it was now no longer safe to continue on a heading that cut across the waves. *Scourge* was in danger of rolling so far beyond acceptable limits that serious damage must inevitably occur. Altering into the run of the sea was now the only option. He leaned into the voicepipe and called a course change to starboard. His order was heard through a welter of water coming down the pipe that soaked the helmsman below.

On the bridge right then, if you could have seen Harry's face through the plaster of spray and his chin tucked into his Ursula suit, you would have seen a rueful grin as he reflected on the quiet complacence he'd been feeling a mere half an hour ago, as he'd been absently contemplating this man he'd become, the certain smug pride he'd been feeling that here he was exercising command at sea in wartime, aboard one of His Majesty's submarines. Whereas the only feeling he was conscious of right now was fright. And bloody right too. It was getting pretty damned hairy! Which was another funny old thing about the sea – how it put you in your place whenever it felt like it.

Scourge was forced to run far to the east-south-east during the night in order to keep her head into the seas. She was well away from where she should have been for a nice, quiet, submerged daylight run through the Straits of Otranto and into the Adriatic. Daylight now had revealed a vast, spume-streaked waste, with sea and sky leached of all colour. The wind had abated and the wave crests were less scrunched together so that the boat felt like she was riding them instead of being thrown, violently, from one to the other.

Harry had opted to not dive at dawn, as would have been standard operating procedure. He'd decided to stay surfaced for a while yet, finding it hard to imagine any Regia Aeronautica pilots would've been keen to get airborne in all this, let alone to fly through it to this dead-end corner of the Ionian Sea.

The main reason was the state of the boat. She had emerged from the storm with a bit of a bashing, and the crew had taken a bit of a bashing too. Two dislocated shoulders, six sailors with bruised or cracked ribs, and there was an urgent necessity to begin pumping bilges because of all the vomit sloshing around in them.

Also, they'd been pumping amps out of the batteries all through the night. Although *Scourge* had sailed from Malta with a full charge, she'd had to go to motors on numerous occasions during the storm, the conning tower hatch having to be firmly shut to stop waves flooding the control room. That had burned amps at a hell of a rate. They had also been depleting their HP air tanks. Every time he had to start the diesels again, Mr Petrie had to fire yet another blast of HP just to get the crankshaft turning. And he'd had to do it a lot. Also, seawater had shorted out the main blower which meant that in order to maintain full buoyancy, the ballast tanks had required frequent blasts of HP air too, further draining this precious commodity. Which was making Mr Petrie concerned because having full HP air bottles wasn't just a luxury. That was what you used to blow the water out your ballast tanks when you wanted to surface.

So every time he started the diesels, he had to parcel out the power, not only to turn the propellers and drive the boat but to recharge the batteries and power the pumps that recharged the HP air bottles too.

Mr Petrie hadn't said anything, he never would, but Harry had the sense he was thinking this young skipper was flogging the poor old boat harder than was wise.

When the sun was well up, they could no longer avoid diving. Below now, Harry sat with Mr Petrie's scribbled calculations before him on the wardroom table, and Mr Petrie sat watching him, cradling a cup of coffee which Harry had ordered the wardroom steward to load with a shot of brandy. Mr Petrie had smeared his face clean before coming for'ard from the engine room, but it was still the usual impassive wall beneath the same greasy watch cap. Harry was glad his first lieutenant, Nick Farrar was on watch in the control room, sparing him any furrow-browed disapproval over Mr Petrie's overalls and the oily mess they were making of the wardroom banquettes. The only sound was navigator Miles Harding's light snoring from the curtained bunk across the passage.

The calculations were all to do with how long it was going to take to get the batteries and the HP air bottles fully recharged.

'There's no answer to it,' said Harry. 'We're just going to have to skulk about for a day getting everything topped off before we go for the straits.'

Enough flogging, he was saying to Mr Petrie. Mr Petrie acknowledged the gesture with a brief nod.

A chart of the Ionian Sea was spread over the table, and Harry sketched an imaginary circle on it about a hundred miles west-nor'-west of Zante. He told Mr Petrie this was where he intended to surface at nightfall and start all the charging they'd need to get all the dials pointing in the right direction. To the north, the fifty-mile gap between Italy and the coast of Albania was definitely a submarine choke point and well patrolled by the Italians, even at night. So they'd need to keep well clear to do all this charging. Then it would be a matter of a last-minute surface dash before dawn so as to close the Straits of Otranto before diving for the run through. Mr Petrie nodded again. But all Harry was thinking now was *delay, delay, delay*. He was never going to make his rendezvous at the top of the Adriatic now. It was like fate was conspiring to confirm all the bad things he imagined the Bonny Boy must be saying about him, how he could never just obey orders, never get anything right.

Mr Petrie took his figures and went aft again, and Harry sat back gazing into space. He could have done with a game of uckers to take his mind off everything. But Farrar was on watch, Harding was out for the count and young Tom McCready, his RNVR sub lieutenant, was for'ard overseeing the re-securing of the stores stacked around the torpedo reload racks after the buffeting they'd taken.

McCready was his new guns'n'torps officer now since the Bonny Boy had taken Powell off him and sent him off to be Jimmy on another boat. Lt Jeremy Powell RN had deserved the promotion, but by God he missed him. Life had been so much smoother with four officers under him, not just three.

The euphoria he'd felt earlier, battering into the start of the storm, had evaporated. As had the relief that he'd finally made it out of the Bonny Boy's clutches. *Scourge's* return to Algiers after that last patrol had been like sailing down Alice's rabbit hole. Captain Bonalleck hadn't bothered to come on deck to welcome *Scourge* back from engaging the enemy. Only his deputy, Cdr Sam Bridger had been there with a friendly wave. That wasn't right. It was the sort of thing crews couldn't help but notice. And when Harry had stepped into the 'Captain S' office on *Ellann Vanin* to deliver his patrol report, Captain Bonalleck had actually made him stand while *he'd* delivered a vicious, forensic bollocking. Before he'd even heard the report's details. Making one of his flotilla COs stand after returning from patrol? *And* bollocking him? It was… unheard of, even if Lt Gilmour *had* made a balls-up. Everybody made balls-ups. At least he'd brought his boat back safe. There'd always be another patrol.

And then, nothing. Smiles all round, drinks in the wardroom, no mention of past patrols or of any bollockings. As if nothing had happened. Harry remembered the unreality. Everybody had known about that bollocking. Christ, they'd probably heard it. How the Captain S had accused Gilmour to his face of deliberately 'failing' to follow orders. But that wasn't all. To make matters worse, the scuttlebutt was that there hadn't been any 'orders' in the first place, at least not written ones. An atmosphere permeated the flotilla. There was this overwhelming sense that the world had somehow stopped being as it should be. The other flotilla officers were twitchy, everybody was walking on eggshells. Something was definitely 'up'. And if that wasn't enough, the eternally laughing and joking Sam Bridger was always looking pensive every time he saw Harry.

The crew were 'off' too. They'd hardly been trotted up when the defaulters' list had been opened for business. All the usual nonsense – brawling with depot ship crew and lads off other boats keen to intrude on their personal grief that the Captain S had it in for them, drunkenness, and one usually demure leading torpedoman who'd kept losing his cap every time he'd stepped onto a gangway. You weren't allowed to let your cap go over the wall, even if it was only the wind to blame; there was a charge for that.

'And then there's our dexterous friend, Leading Seaman Cross,' Lt Harding had added when presenting Harry with the latest list. 'He's had a busy night.'

'Red' Cross, the helmsman who'd helped him put the torpedoes through that tiny harbour gap at Monte Carlo.

'Oh God,' said Harry. 'What's he done now?' Sighing, because Cross was becoming as dab a hand at trouble, as he was at conning the boat.

'Oh, the usual,' said Harding, unable to suppress a wry grin. 'Drunk and uncatchable.'

Harry didn't want to think about it anymore. He started folding the chart.

*

Two hundred-odd miles behind him, back on Malta, Captain Simpson, the S10, was staring at paperwork on his own desk: two signals, one from C-in-C Mediterranean Fleet and the other from the Admiralty in London. The first was seeking 'clarification and comment' on an attached signal from Captain S12. On the face of it, the language of S12's signal was dry and cold, but in naval context, the bloody thing was practically hysterical. It was a litany of accusations against Lt Harris John Gilmour RNVR, officer commanding HMS *Scourge*, so long and laborious that they just blended into noise before his eyes. Apart from the conclusion, that this officer should be put before a court martial. No wonder C-in-C Med wanted a 'clarification and comment' from Lt Gilmour's current CO.

Except the second signal said that Shrimp was no longer Harry's current CO; it was appointing him Commodore, Western Approaches, and ordering him to Londonderry to command all the North Atlantic convoy escorts based there. He stared at both signals. The first was confirmation enough, if it had been needed, of Shrimp's early instincts that he should be getting *Scourge* and her 'hot potato' skipper well out of the way, quick time. Which was why he'd packed him off on that cloak-and-dagger op, all the way up the Adriatic, with all that haste he hadn't needed.

In the usual run of things, he'd have assigned *Scourge* to one of those the COPP teams he'd been saddled with, shuttling them back and forth to the Sicilian beaches in preparation for the Operation Husky landings. The COPPs – Combined Operations Pilotage Parties – were back and forward every night, charting potential landing grounds for the landing craft, with the subs carrying them, having to close with the enemy coast to launch and collect their canoes – all highly risky stuff. But as the boats involved were all operating close to base, they were eminently recallable. And Shrimp hadn't wanted *Scourge* recallable, her crew here to be questioned, at least not until he'd worked out what had really led to Harry's decision to withdraw to Malta after that last patrol and not obey S 12's orders to return to Algiers.

The second signal made it imperative that he do that now, and quickly. That was when he had his idea.

Chief Petty Officer Gault. Shrimp knew him from way back on the China Station. In fact, had been good friends with him in the way relatively junior officers could be with their senior rates in the trade. The reason he was thinking about him now was because Shrimp had had him sitting right there, opposite him, a mere couple of weeks ago – Gault straight off the cruiser that had brought him to Malta, clutching his orders appointing him HMS *Talbot's* boatswain, *Talbot* being the official name of Tenth Flotilla's 'stone frigate' base.

And because Shrimp also remembered that Gault had been aboard the unfortunate *Pelorus* when she'd been rammed and sunk by a British merchant ship early in the war, along with a certain Sub Lt Harry Gilmour, and that their boat had been commanded at the time by the legendary Bonny Boy Bonalleck. There was no doubt in Shrimp's mind that it was wrong to do what he was thinking – just not done, un-naval, beyond every custom, against all norms of discipline and command – but Shrimp was going to do it anyway. He was going to get his old friend and shipmate up here, pour him a glass of brandy and ask him outright if he had any idea what the bloody hell was going on between that old bastard Bonalleck and one of the best young submarine COs in the Med.

Four

'I was thinking we might as well use the time to rig for Sunday service,' said Harry, sprawled out on the wardroom banquette, cradling his cup of coffee. 'Then I can tell the crew where we're taking Sergeant Reynolds and his radios. Let them know the reason we're crashing the Adriatic, then give them a sing-song to take their mind off it. What d'you think?'

Harding sat up and leaned over the far end of the wardroom table. He'd been reading *The Mayor of Casterbridge* by Thomas Hardy before Harry had interrupted him, Harry thinking as he contemplated Harding's choice of book that really the chap was never done confounding him.

'Um, no,' said Harding. 'It's not Sunday, sir.'

'I *know* that,' said Harry, 'but as I'm the captain, I'll say it is.'

'That ERA, whatshisname, the one that does all the God bits… McKay. He won't like it, so neither will the crew.'

McKay was indeed the ERA who did 'all the God bits'. A gloomy West Highland caricature of a man, who every week would methodically draw up the order of the service, with two hymns and two gaps for Harry, the captain, to deliver a 'reading', and make his 'any other comments', which was the bit where Harry filled everybody in on what was going on in the war in general and on the boat in particular. Really, it was only the last bit that anybody was interested in, and the service just an excuse. But that was the way Jack liked it, it made it look less like a crew of grown men needing pep talks. And it kept at bay McKay's comic tendencies to lapse into old testament doom-saying – or so the word was from the engine room. Especially as everybody knew that that kind of talk on a boat could easily end in bad joss, and nobody found *that* comic.

'Just get Nick to tell the cox'n, sir,' said Harding. 'It'll be round the boat before you've sat down again and save you interrupting everybody's sleep.' And with that, Harding leaned back and lifted up his book.

'Hmmn,' said Harry as he thought about better ways to keep the crew up to speed on what was up. Keeping the crew informed, making them feel part of everything that was going on was important. If you knew where you were going, who was supposed to be doing what and *why* it was important, it meant you were free to concentrate on the *really* important things. And everybody knew what they were on a submarine.

And then he started reflecting on Harding and how little he knew about him. Nothing, if he was just to go on what Harding had told him, apart from he'd been to some minor public school and then to Britannia Royal Naval College, Dartmouth at the age of sixteen. Oh, and that he was almost eighteen months older than Harry.

Of his origins, however, it had been Farrar who had told him that the young Miles came from a landed family down Wiltshire way – not much land though. And they didn't farm it, the tenants did that. So not that much money either. There were siblings, but Farrar wasn't sure as to their gender or how many.

Professionally speaking, of Harding's work as navigator, what could Harry say? He made it look easy, and Harry, no mean navigator himself, knew it wasn't. Apart from that, Harding appeared to be a supremely self-contained young man, fleet of thought with the odd flash of insight that left you wondering how much more was in there that he wasn't giving away. And, of course, he could be very, very funny.

Harry was smiling to himself as he remembered Harding leaning breathless on the bridge that night after he'd come scrambling back aboard from kidnapping their Luftwaffe Colonel and his trembling little airman, his face split by the most ecstatic grin.

Behind him, the evidence of Harding's and his team's handiwork had still been unfolding – flames from the villa's gas tank were leaping over the horizon of the cliff and the *bump! bump! bump!* from the Jerry 20mm was still going off.

'And you're last off the beach,' Harry had said to him, before delivering his bollocking. About how RN navigators weren't as expendable as pongos and certainly not as replaceable. And Harding answering him back. Actually arguing with him.

'I was simply ensuring the op succeeded, sir,' he'd said. 'It's sort of a Royal Navy tradition, sir.'

Harry hadn't been able to believe the cheek. 'Are you arguing with me, Lieutenant Harding?' he said, very softly, deciding not to add, '… on my own bridge… with the boat engaging the enemy…?' Because it was self-evident, and he shouldn't have to.

'Absolutely not, sir!' A suddenly realising Harding had blurted after he'd managed to control his look of horror. 'No, sir. Never, sir. Sorry, sir. Don't know what came over me, sir. Must've had a rush of…'

'…shite to the brain?' Harry had offered. One of Harding's frequent phrases when describing a miscreant rating's motivations. 'Do shut up, Miles,' he'd then added, smiling.

Later, he asked Harding, almost as an afterthought, 'Your little Ulrich, why didn't you or Pettifer just kill him along with the rest of Jerry "other ranks"? Why'd you bring him off?'

And Harding, looking like the question hadn't occurred to him, said, 'Well, I suppose he'd just sort of already surrendered by the time Pettifer's lot got round to doing the chopping. And poor Ulrich, he was so terrified and obviously harmless by then, it just wouldn't have been sporting. I mean, he's hardly the master race, is he, sir? It would've been like drowning puppies. Very… eh… un-British, sir.'

'And here was I thinking that you were a bit of a hooligan, Miles,' said Harry smiling.

Harding, not smiling, said, 'Sir, I wish to register, forcefully, that I strongly resent your use of the words, "…a bit of…".'

Looking back, Harry remembered a totally unexpected urge to give his navigator a big, bloke hug, without really knowing why. Later, it turned out, it must have been because of his amazement at Harding's perspicacity, because of how things turned out, how Ulrich, still alive, had shown his gratitude by proving such a useful reference point for all the lies Oberst Von Puttkamer had tried to put over on the interrogation teams. *Funny how things can turn out,* Harry thought.

Just before the change of watch, with *Scourge* at sixty feet, just edging towards the Straits of Otranto at a mere two knots to conserve batteries, Harry told Farrar to spread the word about where they were going and why, and he also told him, since nobody had anything better to do, he'd start whittling down the defaulters' list and see how many he could get through before nightfall, and they'd have to surface for their final dash to be off the straits' entrance by dawn the following day.

'Not all of them merit the captain's table, sir,' said Farrar, who struck Harry as becoming more and more punctilious with each passing day.

'I know,' said Harry, 'but I'm in the mood to put the fear of God up them.'

Algiers had been their first run ashore in a port of plenty for some considerable time, and the *Scourges* had not acquitted themselves well. Just because Algiers had well-stocked bars, unlike the Malta they'd come from, it had been no excuse for all the brawling that had gone on. That was the judgement of their captain. So there he'd sat, cap on, in all his glory at the head of the wardroom table, punishment book before him as Ainsworth marched each one up… 'Attenshun! Off cap! Stand at ease!'

Each one the same, usual story of rolling about some drinking den floor knocking lumps out of some other tub's matelots, or pongos or Yanks. He'd managed to work through four of the cases before he had to quit and go to diving stations and start their dash through the straits.

They'd stood and taken their bollockings and their stoppages of leave or rum like proper chaps, but it was only the smart ones who, when they got back to their messes, worked out that the punishments they'd received would all have expired by the time they'd got back from patrol. They filled in their messmates on how the land lay: the skipper was pissed off with them, but not that pissed off as long as they'd learned their lesson.

*

Scourge went through the Straits of Otranto, right down the middle, at a depth of two hundred and fifty feet, coming out the other end about halfway through the middle watch, with Brindisi lying about thirty-odd miles astern of her and the port of Durrës in Albania about seventy miles off the starboard beam.

All day and into the night, Biddle had been giving everyone a running commentary on the criss-crossings of Italian anti-submarine patrols above – mostly those destroyer escort types they called torpedo boats, all about a thousand tons and two hundred and fifty feet-plus, with their three or four 3.9 inch gun mounts and their quarter decks all choked with depth-charge racks. All pinging away with their echo-sounders, or passively listening with their hydrophones and then chucking off the odd depth charge here or there – their favourite tactical ruse, apparently, to see what they could scare up but which only ever served to let you know where they were and to keep away.

None of them had shown any signs they'd even suspected *Scourge* was passing through. So Harry decided they'd come up to use the remaining hours of darkness to air the boat, cram on a few more amps and generally see what was about. Biddle did an all-round Asdic search from sixty feet: nothing. Harry then ordered them up to twenty-seven feet and got Farrar to do the same through the periscope, as his night vision was better: nothing. So up they went, rising on an even keel, barely making a froth on the surface, and Harry had followed up the lookouts into the balmy, almost caressing night air. The first thing Harry saw was the riot of stars, but the first thing he heard was the alert voice of the port lookout, 'Searchlights! Bearing red one seven zero! Panning the horizon, sir. Really low down.'

Even Harry could see them now, a long way off – long needles of light swinging out and back in the immaculate darkness and not even remotely looking for them. It was like a dramatic visual display to welcome them, the way Hollywood cinemas always seemed to herald the release of their latest big star attraction. It made Harry smile at the thought of it, even though he knew it was almost certainly just some bored escort sweeping the surface to see if it could catch a periscope.

It was Farrar's watch. He joined Harry on the bridge, having already resigned himself to the fact he was going to have to spend another turn upstairs with the skipper watching him. They exchanged pleasantries about the evening, and Harry read his mood. God, sometimes the Jimmy could be a real old woman.

'How many defaulters left to flog at the grating,' said Harry, just to lighten the mood.

Farrar, his binoculars stuck to his face, scanning a horizon Harry could not make out, took a second to reply, 'Two sir,' he said, then realising that his pause could've been construed as the dumb insolence it was, he began to be a little more chatty. 'One's more of the same, but the second one's Leading Seaman Cross, sir. It's more serious.'

Harding had more or less implied the same earlier, without giving any details. Cross. He liked Cross, but… and he sighed, 'What's he done now?'

Farrar lowered his bins. Finally submitting to the fact he was going to have to humour the skipper, even though they were running on the surface in enemy waters.

'It appears it all started with him getting into it with a mob of ratings off another boat, in some wine shop off the Corniche,' Farrar began. 'The shore patrol arrived, and he ducked out. They couldn't catch him. He made it back to *Ellan Vannin* and managed to bluff his way past the regulating POs before heading down to the lower mess deck where he resumed drinking beer. The shore patrol turned up, gave the officer of the watch Cross's description, and they all set off to apprehend him. When he saw them coming through the door, he scattered all manner of kit in their way, tables, chairs, and he started throwing beer bottles willy-nilly. In the mayhem, he managed to make it onto the upper deck and down onto the trotted-up boats…'

'Full beer bottles, Number One?' asked Harry.

'Empty ones, sir, as I understand it.'

'Thank God for that!' said Harry. 'At least he was still in possession of his faculties.'

Farrar smiled patiently, then continued, 'He landed on HMS *Tobermory* and ran along her casing, chased by one of the shore patrol. There appears to be some dispute here as to exactly what happened next. Did the shore patrol fall into the water, or did Cross throw him? No matter… for Cross then disappeared down *Tobermory's* open torpedo loading hatch, leading the remaining SPs and *Ellan Vannin's* regulating POs to assume he was part of *Tobermory's* crew. A verbal altercation then ensued between them and *Tobermory's* officer of the watch over whether they should be permitted to come aboard and search the boat. In the ensuing chaos, Cross somehow managed to make it back aboard *Scourge*.'

Harry sighed, 'And he's being charged with what?'

'Late on watch, sir,' said Farrar. 'He was supposed to have presented himself on board for harbour watch duties twenty minutes before all those events occurred, sir.' Farrar paused. 'Neither the depot ship's regulating POs, nor the SPs have a confirmed identification on Leading Seaman Cross, sir. So I thought it better to restrict the charges to the one immediately at hand until you have decided how you wish to proceed. Although I am led to understand there are suspicions that the man they are after is indeed a *Scourge*, if you'll pardon the pun, sir.'

'Ha, ha,' said Harry, flatly, then he sighed. 'Honestly, they're worse than children sometimes. We'll do Cross and the other one after the start of the afternoon watch. I'm going below now, Number One. Suddenly I feel quite tired.'

Scourge dived just before first light, still holding her 315 degrees heading. Working with Harding, Harry had plotted a course and speed to bring them to the north coast of the island of Vis, just off the coast of Yugoslavia at two hours before sunset on the following day.

As the boat crept up the Adriatic at sixty feet, Biddle, then one of his back-up Asdic men, kept up a steady running commentary on all the HE, they were picking up in the water: HE being the Asdic shorthand for the hydrophone effects generated by any passing ship's screws. There were half a dozen or more prime targets blithely cruising by, not in convoy, entirely un-escorted in this backwater to the war, blissfully unaware of the Royal Navy submarine crossing their tracks with never a whisper of her presence. From time to time, when they'd picked up a particularly juicy-sounding contact, Harry would go and sit in the Asdic cubby and listen on the spare headset as yet another potential target slipped away over the horizon. For *Scourge* was under strict orders not to engage any enemy shipping until she had delivered her cargo safely into the hands of the Yugoslav partisans. It made sense. The last thing anyone wanted was to have the whole bloody sea alerted, with aircraft and A/S vessels scooting about everywhere when what you really needed was everything to be all peace and quiet so as you could go creeping inshore on the surface to drop your men off and get away again without anyone suspecting what you'd been up to.

After the watch changed at midday, Harry set up his desk and quickly disposed of the first defaulter – stoppage of all shore leave for ten days. *Scourge* would likely have as much as another two weeks at sea after his punishment expired. But the rating took it seriously and solemnly swore his future conduct would be exemplary, sir.

Then came Cross.

The charge was read out, and Harry asked him how he pled.

'Guilty, sir.'

Harry gave him a brief lecture on the essentialness of punctuality when it came to presenting himself for duty, fairness to fellow crew, safety of the boat etc. And then he sentenced him to ten days stoppage of spirits and said, 'Dismissed.'

The look on Cross's face was abject. He plainly didn't understand what had just happened – or not happened, more likely. But it was more than that. Harry let Ainsworth lead him away, then called for the wardroom steward.

'Windass! Be a good chap and bring me two piping hot coffees. And put a gulper of rum in each,' he said. Then he took his cap off, leant out the wardroom and called, 'Pass the word for Leading Seaman Cross!'

Cross, when he arrived back at the wardroom, snapped to attention before the table and was about to salute when he noticed his skipper was bare-headed. His face immediately became a picture of confusion.

'Sit down, Cross,' said Harry as Windass arrived with two mugs. 'Two coffees with, sir!' said Windass, plonking them down and drawing Cross a sideways look. 'And take your cap off, Cross,' added Harry, catching the poor sailor halfway to obeying the first order and pitching him into an even further confusion of movement.

Harry let him compose himself before saying, 'Well, this is a right bloody mess, Red. What the hell were you thinking of?' Before the lad could answer, Harry said, 'Have a drink of that,' gesturing to one of the tin mugs.

Cross raised it to his lips and immediately smelled the rum.

'Sir?' he said, looking confused again, 'I'm under stoppage of...'

'Just drink it, Red,' said Harry. 'I'm the captain and I said so.'

'Aye, aye, sir,' he said and complied and immediately looked all the better for doing so.

At length, Harry said, 'I know about all your antics. And the hue and cry that's following you. You're a good submariner, Red. A credit to this boat. So why are you conducting yourself this way? Are you *trying* to get yourself returned to general service? Do you *miss* being a skimmer?'

'Oh no, sir!' It came out more like an anguished howl than a statement.

'I'm sorry, sir. I don't know... sometimes... something happens... it's like I can't help it. I am going to do better, sir. Honest, sir. I will, sir. Please don't... This is the first time I've ever been good at anything, sir. Being a helmsman, on *Scourge*, sir. Being a submariner. Please don't...'

'Oh take another belt of your coffee and shut up, Red,' said Harry. 'Nobody is going to throw you to the wolves. You have my word on that. I'm not logging your charge or punishment. I'm dismissing them. This way, if anyone comes asking, it turns out you couldn't have been that rampaging matelot, because you were already on watch. Mr Harding is going to vouch for it...'

'Is that what he told you, sir?!' yelped Cross, who then suddenly looked horrified, aware he'd just interrupted the captain.

Harry feigned to ignore it, 'No, Cross, but he's going to. You're still going to have your stoppage of rum, though. That is still going to stand... well after this one.' A pause. 'What about your family? You're not married, are you?'

'Oh no, sir,' said Cross, surprised at the idea. 'Just me mum and two older sisters. They're married, sir.'

'You keep in touch?'

'My mum and I write all the time, sir. Sisters too, every now and again.'

No mention of 'Dad'. Harry knew better than to pry. 'Is she proud of you, Red, your mum?'

Cross smiled, 'Oh yes, sir. Says I'm making something of myself, sir. Unlike me dad ever did.' Then he frowned and said no more.

'Well, what would your bloody mum say, if she knew what you were getting up to now?'

'She'd be ashamed of me, sir,' and suddenly Cross looked very young and in despair.

'Well, I won't tell her, Red.'

Cross looked up, and Harry wondered whether he was going to start crying. 'Thank you, sir,' said the lad, from deep in the slough of despond.

'Something's making you like this, lad,' said Harry after leaving a long minute and time for them both to have a slug of their coffees and rum. 'You really should tell me what it is. I want to know. I'm not just coming it the "concerned officer", honest, Cross. I'm not.'

Cross, hunched now, looked at him and sighed, making his decision.

'When I'm at sea, sir. Doing my job. I'm all right. But I get onshore… I been out here in the Med two years now. No home leave. Should've been home by now, but I got sick… sand fly fever… stuck in Bighi when my last boat went home, left without me.' He paused as if considering the enormity of the injustice of it all. '…Did a stint as spare crew then *Scourge*… and there's no sign of us goin' home anytime soon, is there, sir.' He paused again. It wasn't a question he'd just asked, more an acceptance of reality. 'It's the war. It just seems to go on and on, sir. When we was on Malta through the bombing, sir, it was like if we could just get through all that, we'd be okay. Well… we did. But it's not okay. Nuthin's changed! It's all still going on… 'cept everythin's bigger now… bigger and more… on and on. And I'm just wee Billy Cross… a name on a ration bill somewhere… the only thing says I'm still alive… an inky scrawl's all that's between me and nuthin'. The bloody war! Sometimes, I wonder if I'm ever going to see home again. My mum. Family. Sometimes, I can't even remember our street… what it looks like… it just all gets on top of me, sir. And I go… ah, what the fuck… Oh God! Sorry, sir…'

'Red,' said Harry, raising his mug to touch Cross's. 'If it's any consolation, I know exactly how you feel.'

*

Harry had Farrar, Harding and Ainsworth round the wardroom table with Reynolds and Hibbert for a quick orders meeting before getting the two soldiers and their radio ashore.

'Sorry we're going to be late, Sergeant Reynolds,' Harry said. 'It was the gale. It threw us. How badly is it going to bugger up the op?'

'Beg your pardon, sir?' said a puzzled Reynolds, looking even more the dapper grocer than usual.

'Your rendezvous deadline with the partisans,' said Harry, now puzzled himself. 'We're going to be over thirty hours late at last calculation.'

'I wasn't told anything about a deadline, sir,' he replied, looking at Hibbert sitting next to him, the wiry little corporal's face wreathed in his usual inane grin. 'Our briefing officer from Cairo, Major Curley, just said for George here to paddle ashore as soon as, after we arrive, and establish contact. He speaks a bit of Serbo-Croat, his mum coming from that way, sir. They are expecting us but only when we get there.'

Hibbert nodded his assent vigorously.

Harry looked cross. So what was all that guff Shrimp had told him about having to get there on time, regardless? 'Get to sea, Mr Gilmour! There's no time to lose! The mission depends on it!' That guff.

Until it dawned on him that Shrimp had only wanted him out of the way, fast. Just as it dawned on him why. If *Scourge* was halfway up the Adriatic on ops, no amount of squealing from the Bonny Boy was going to bring him back again anytime soon. He was a good man, Shrimp Simpson, always had your back.

'Oh, well I must've got it all arse-to-tit,' said Harry, back smiling again. 'So, Corporal Hibbert. We wait until nightfall to enter the bay, get you and your folbot up onto the casing, and off you go. If you'd speak to Number One to arrange rendezvous times for you coming back... tomorrow night, I take it? Yes?'

'Yessir! Definitely, sir,' said a still grinning, still nodding Hibbert. Then, as if it were a witty, *bon mot* afterthought, '…Aye, aye, sir!' And with that he sat back, immensely pleased with himself.

Dear God thought Harry, but he smiled too.

After it was over, the men all got up, bent over by the curve of the hull above their heads and bumped and jostled their way for'ard along the cramped gangway. Harry gestured for Harding to stay a minute. He wanted to talk about Cross.

'Cross,' said Harry, once Harding had shuffled back into the tight space behind the wardroom table, his face grinning back at him through the insipid light, not a care in the world. 'He's been trouble lately,' Harry went on. 'But I don't think he's a complete King's bad bargain. So, I'm not going to hand him over to the depot ship.'

'No, sir,' said Harding, non-committal. He was curious to see where this was going.

'He is, after all, one of us,' said Harry, letting the thought hang there for a moment. 'And if it's something that's getting to him, and God knows he's not the most imaginative of our souls, then we should be helping him. And asking how many others are starting to fray at the edges too?'

Harding shrugged, 'Me, for one, sir. I'm frayed all the time. Frayed promotion will never come. Frayed Windass will burn the ham…'

'Shut up, Miles. I'm being serious. I was thinking about something those Eighth Army chaps told us about Monty. About how he'd go about chatting to ordinary soldiers then write a letter to their people back home… show the high command cared… cheer everybody up. I think I'm going to write to Cross's folks. Can you think of any others I should write to?'

As Harry was finishing, McCready came sliding into the banquette, balancing a mug of coffee and a huge wedge of toasted sandwich filled with grilled sardines. 'Would you write to my mum too, sir?' said McCready, not noticing the scowl on Harry's face. Captain or not, Harry wasn't sure where stood in telling the young sub to 'piss off, this is a private conversation!' In the Andrew proper, Harry, as captain, would only have been sitting there at the mess president's invitation. A guest. But this being the trade, he wasn't sure what the wardroom etiquette was on a boat.

Harding headed him off by addressing McCready instead, in louche tones, as the young sub bit into his wedge, 'You have a mum, Tom? Well, bugger me! Who'd've thunk it! I somehow never saw you as having a mum. I've always seen you more as a… sort of… naturally occurring phenomenon really… an experiment… something they'd cultivated in the greenhouses at the back of Britannia… that hadn't quite worked…'

'I thought that was you, Vasco,' chomped McCready through an overstuffed mouth.

'Your captain has asked you a question,' said Harry, exasperated.

'No, sir,' said Harding.

'No, sir, what?' said Harry.

'No letters,' said Harding. 'For a start, you're not a general. And, if you write to one family, you have to write to all of them. Which you don't have the time for. And anyway, it just isn't done. The only time you're supposed to write to families is if somebody's dead. And that's only to say "sorry" and "can you send another one". There *is* a war on, sir.'

Harding watched as Harry considered this, which was easy to do, considering there was barely three feet between their faces in the tight little space, each of them looking as if they might be already dead and already embalmed, bathed as they were in the anaemic yellow wash from dinky little wall fittings and their tasselled-fringed floral shades. For a moment, he felt as if he was looking at a fellow passenger in a crowded compartment on the *Brighton Belle*, stuck in a tunnel and fretting over a *Times'* crossword clue.

'Crew morale,' he heard Harry say under his breath. 'I've got to do something about crew morale…'

Five

Harry, on the bridge, was absently aware of the crew on the fore-casing, hauling Cpl Hibbert's folbot aboard. The cheery little commando had gone ashore last night, and right on plan, he'd turned up again tonight. Recognition signals had been exchanged, and here he was. Harding was down there dealing with him, another shadowy figure in the scant wash – from a high, waxing quarter moon – among the little mob of sailors, grunting and muttering.

Harry wasn't paying attention; still lost in thought. He'd been remembering HMS *P268*, his first real command; the new-build S-class he'd been appointed to back in Greenock all those months ago; the one that had never made it out the fitting-out dry dock. All bare steel and unconnected cable runs and the flash of welders' torches and Mr Donaldson, the ironworks manager who never got tetchy or snappy and met every new problem with the merest furrowing of his brow. A short man with a crescent of grey hair under his battered soft hat, economical of speech and profligate in his smoking habits, in his stained charcoal three-piece suit, a knotted bow tie like Churchill and stout black boots that looked like they'd been built on the Clyde too.

How he'd theatrically rise from whatever task he'd been involved in, to pause and address whatever harassing niggle Harry had come up with now. Patient to a fault, but not once failing to make it plain that Harry, the impatient new captain, was doing nothing more than getting in the way. Everything was coming together from scratch, and he, Mr Donaldson, having done it many times before, was best placed to know the order in which to do it, so could he please let him get on with his job.

And Harry, his regular forays from his dockside shack, sometimes armed with rolled-up plans, determined to be master of the challenges ahead. He'd been smiling to himself earlier, remembering the charge-hand electrician they'd called 'Haile Selassie' because of his beard and the fact that he always wore a beret – another pugnacious bantam, with milk-bottle-bottom glasses.

Harry had caught him on board sitting on a bucket with a roll-up cigarette hanging from his bottom lip; Harry was too new on the scene to know there was always a cigarette hanging from his lip. This particular one, however, had been unlit. Harry hadn't noticed that. All he had seen was 'Haile', tool bag at his feet and wedged comfortably over the space where the Asdic dome was going to sit, reading a copy of the *Daily Worker*.

The din on board had been tremendous; drilling, caulkers hammering, men working with steel. Harry remembered shouting at him, more to be heard above the din than in anger. But he was angry. Time was getting on, the boat was falling behind and this son of toil was sitting on his arse perusing communist propaganda!

'…and you know quite well that smoking is completely forbidden on board! Anywhere!' had been Harry's final accusatory flourish.

'Aye, ah do,' 'Haile' had said. His expression half puzzled, half curious.

'You've got a cigarette in your mouth!' Harry had yelled.

'Aye,' 'Haile' had replied. 'And ah've got a hole in ma arse, but that doesn't mean Ah'm' a flowerpot.'

Harry had found Mr Donaldson in the wooden dockside electrical store, where there was a sloping desk to lay out plans, and he had immediately begun to rail at him about communist loafers, slipping schedules and the downright insolence of his workers towards Albion's stout, fighting tars. Harry on *Scourge's* bridge, looking back on that afternoon, reflected on how it was just the sort of guff you'd expect from an overwrought new skipper with a new toy to play with and smirked at his own... youth?

Mr Donaldson, having drawn himself up from the plan he'd been studying, his face as mobile as one of those Easter Island statues, stood patiently waiting until Harry's outrage petered out. Then he'd said simply, 'He was keeping out the way, Mr Gilmour. Not loafing.'

'Keeping out the way of hard work!' Harry had barked.

'They're fitting your torpedo tubes, Mr Gilmour. Big, ungainly and prodigious heavy buggers they are too. There'll have been a squad of platers and a craneman lowering each one into what is a very confined space... as I'm sure you know,' said Mr Donaldson. Then he'd paused as if to consider the full depth of ignorance confronting him. There'd been a sigh, and only then had he begun his exposition, 'Once each tube is in, a welder goes down to tack it in place, so that your Mr "Selassie" can go in after him and start on the wiring... and when he's done a bit, he comes out and waits until the plumber goes in and fits tubing, and when the plumber's done, he goes back and starts wiring the next bit. You found him waiting.'

Harry had remembered frowning gravely, to cover feeling like a gauche schoolboy having to have the subtlety of some great work of art explained to him... in front of the girls.

'Not a bad joke, though, eh?' Mr Donaldson had added with a wry grin. 'He's a helluva man for the wee witty asides, is "Haile".'

It was a funny old game, this command business. You'd have thought command was all about imposing your will. But it wasn't. As old 'Haile' had demonstrated. Sometimes, when you sought to impose, you only ended up making a prat of yourself. Sometimes, things had to take their course. It was the knowing when to do what that was the art. That old, diminutive Irishman who'd been his first cox'n on *P268* had taught him that with their first draft of sailors. A raggedy bunch, tumbling off the back of a three-tonner on the dock on a drizzly afternoon, all flapping navy blue trench coats and huge, bulging, white kit bags and caps crammed on at all angles. God knows why they'd been dumped on the dock, there was no room for them on a submarine still fitting out. Someone was going to have to march them back out again and up to that school that had been requisitioned as a temporary barracks.

What was his name again? That cox'n. An older man, short, jolly face like Staff Sgt Reynolds. Doyle? Dunphy? A country boy long ago, Harry'd guessed, who'd obviously decided potato picking wasn't for him and upped and took himself off to see the world instead.

'There's a few bad deals in that lot,' he'd confided in Harry in that quiet, conspiratorial way he'd always had with him, as if he'd been wanting to tap his nose and wink at you as he passed on his wisdom, except you didn't do that with an officer. Harry had expected him to say he'd already drawn up a work schedule crammed with drill and yard duties to bring them all into line.

'Cut 'em all a twenty-four-hour pass, sorr,' he'd said. 'Let them all go off and get pished. Then we'll wait and see who comes back.'

Harry remembered turning on him, slack-jawed with shock and incredulity, 'What? I need a crew that's ready to go to sea in less than ten days, cox'n. That can take this boat on trials. Not some bloody rabble that only turns to when it feels like it!'

'Oh, I agree sorr. But sorr. With all due respect. You don't have the time to work through them all making sure each one of them is going clap on and pull with the rest, sorr. There's at least three I know I don't want on my… on your boat, sorr. 'Cos I can see they don't want to be here either. Come six a.m. tomorrow, they won't be present. So we lets the shore patrol take care of them, sorr. Quickest way, sorr.'

It was a lesson on how to build a crew. If you've got rotten apples, let them chuck themselves. The ones who remain are always glad to see them go anyway, glad they don't have to carry them and glad they don't have to start the commission having to stand-to while you drag the boat through a tedious round of shouting and charges. Not when you can start with a smile and a wink instead.

Yes, Doyle – or was it Dunphy? – had taught him that all right, the benefits of stepping back, letting them that know get on with the job. You could see the logic if you only stopped to look. Because your subordinate officers also needed to assert, if not impose, their authority too. And as captain, you had to let them and make sure the crew saw you do it. They needed to know you had confidence if they were to have confidence too. Also, it opened out a bit of distance between you and the men, and you needed that. Your very remoteness made your authority believable. Because if the crew really got to know you, they'd probably burst out laughing.

Easier to do when you all started off together though, Harry thought. But that Jerry bomb going right through the as yet unborn *P268's* empty motor room and detonating against the concrete bottom of the dry dock right under her had peeled off her saddle tanks like the segments of an orange, and broke her back. She'd gone in a flash from a brand new submarine, waiting to make her first dive, to a random collection of scrap. Unsavable. There'd be no starting off all together for the captain and the crew of the *P268*.

And now there was this crew, the one Harry had inherited. The *Scourges*. They'd already done their growing together long before he'd arrived. Even so, he'd thought he'd been doing okay with them. But how could he know? He hadn't been through what they had together. And they'd been out here in the Med a long time.

Back in the Lazaretto wardroom, the general feeling was a boat was good for a year. No more. That was as long as you could expect before her operational efficiency began to fall off… and her luck to run out. *Scourge* had been out here a bit longer than a year now. Other boats had been out longer, but then most of them had ended up posted overdue, presumed lost.

Those had been Harry's thoughts since his talk with Cross.

What was his crew thinking now? About the fiasco over their almost sinking the 'safe passage' ship off Vichy and all the scuttlebutt about how the Captain S had had it in for *their* skipper? Had it started more of them – or even all of them – brooding? Wondering if this new boy would ever get them all home?

And what about himself?

The worry that maybe he'd stepped back too far.

He was lost in this reverie when Staff Sgt Reynolds came clambering back up the conning tower ladder, his face all blacked up. He should've been down there helping load parts of his radio set into Hibbert's folbot and getting into his own. That had been the plan. Hibbert coming back meant the rendezvous had been made. Now all that was left to do was to get him and Reynolds ashore, and the link-up with the partisans was all sewn up. *Scourge* could get back out to sea and on with the job of sinking enemy shipping.

'Sir,' said Reynolds, a bit puffed from the climb in all his kit. 'Corporal Hibbert's been sent back with a message from the local partisan commander. For you, sir. The captain.'

The two lookouts kept their eyes on the darkness around them.

Harry frowned, 'Well, Sergeant, let me see it.'

'It's verbal, sir. Nothing in writing in case Jerry...'

'Yes, yes. I understand. So what is it, Sergeant? We're wasting time.'

'The partisan commander, he wants to meet up, sir. He wants you to help him kick Jerry off the island.'

'With a submarine? And anyway, my intel says the island's occupying force is Eyetie...' Harry stopped abruptly. What in God's name was he doing discussing his boat's operation with a bloody pongo sergeant, nice enough chap though he was. And why would a bloody partisan want to speak to him? About what?

Harry looked over Reynolds' shoulder, out to sea. He wanted to just get back there again. But gazing into the opaque darkness, he saw in his mind's eye the petrol dump fireball and the disintegrating Ju 52s on that desert airstrip he'd bombarded, and he knew what the partisan wanted.

'It's your gun he's after, sir,' said Reynolds. Obviously, it was the gun. 'He wants you to come ashore so as he can explain his plan,' he added, at last betraying some of the uneasiness he too obviously felt at this strange conversation.

'He wants me to leave my boat... in the face of the enemy?' Harry let the question hang, more from astonishment than for any dramatic effect. He then went to the hatch and called down, 'Number One, come up and take the bridge, please!' Then he went the bridge front and leaned over, 'On the casing there, stand down and stand by! Mr Harding and Corporal Hibbert. In the wardroom now, please!' And turning to Reynolds, he said, 'After you, Sergeant. Down you go.'

It was one of the things that radio operator Reynolds – never, ever a professional soldier – had found himself liking about this young Gilmour chap; the way he always used to say things like 'please' and 'after you' to everyone. Even though the way he spoke the words, no one was ever in any doubt what he actually meant. But at least he said it, which was nice for an officer and worth remarking on, and likely vital to his mission too. Because Willy Reynolds, a technical man rather than a soldier – just signed up for the duration – had never really liked officers and knew he never would, but here was one you might actually get some sense out of. Which was going to be important because Sgt Reynolds's briefings had all stressed how touchy these Yugoslav partisans could be, and that meant he needed someone sensible on the sub to ensure everything ran smoothly.

*

And now, here they were, the water still sluicing from *Scourge's* conning tower and off her casing; just surfaced into the cocooning warmth of the sudden Adriatic night. Harry had let the lookouts go up first, never really trusting his dodgy night vision, but there was a surprising amount of light still left in the ragged end of this dying moon, and it was already quite high in the sky.

Not surprisingly, Hooper and his little mob of gunners, indistinct in their dark blue work shirts and overalls, were already fussing round the three-inch gun, a round already up the spout. And there ahead, fine on the bow, was the little elbow of a promontory, the pale strata of the cliff glowing dully and the little clutch of buildings atop, their tiled roofs – which Harry knew to be red terracotta from his afternoon look through the periscope – now standing out as black outlines.

And *Scourge*, hanging there in the limpid night, barely more than five hundred yards off, hove-to with over thirty metres of depth beneath her keel, according to the surprisingly detailed local chart Major Drobnjac's industriously serious staff had presented to them. Her silhouette masked from the shore by the shadow of the rising cliff face astern of them that formed the opposite wall of the inlet.

Now all they had to do was wait.

'Thirty of them. That's what we know. We counted them in the days when they liked to stroll our little streets because they thought they owned them,' was what Major Drobnjac had told him when they'd finally met. German army engineers, on the island to refit the harbour so as it could take proper supply ships – ships capable of landing field artillery and anti-aircraft batteries for German defences, not Italian.

That had been two days ago, after a tedious exchange of polite messages, carried out courtesy of Hibbert in his folbot, paddling back and forward. Major Drobnjac had agreed to step aboard *Scourge* if Harry didn't mind bringing *Scourge* to meet him. And to that end, the major had a plan, which Hibbert had eventually delivered after a final paddle through the night.

A local fishing caique would sail out that day and wait for *Scourge* to surface. Harry had been very dubious about surfacing in broad daylight. But Reynolds, wearing his most serious expression, had assured him, and Harry had learned by then that Sgt Reynolds was a most serious man. 'Jerry has precious few aircraft of any type in this theatre, sir,' Reynolds said. 'And the ones he has are all busy chasing Marshal Tito's main force over on the mainland.'

So Harry had surfaced, and a nondescript little woman in a uniform that was too big for her had leapt aboard. The caique had then stood off, its crew and the *Scourge's* eyeing each other with a sort of detached curiosity – sort of, 'So this is what communist guerrillas look like,' and 'Well, well, so these are the capitalist lackeys,' but still waving, friendly, since both sides knew fine well it was Jerry they both were fighting.

Watching the transfer, Harry's heart had been in his mouth, fearing that at any moment, the bloody wallowing tub, which must've have weighed in at over thirty tons, might crash into his starboard saddle tanks and do more than just dent them. And after listening to the little woman-in-a-uniform, he hadn't become any calmer. A local chart had been produced to demonstrate the simplicity of the plan. The man in charge on the island, Major Drobnjac wished the man in charge at sea, Captain Gilmour, to con *Scourge* into the main harbour and secure to one of the stone jetties in broad daylight so that said Major Drobnjac could step aboard over a gangway. Not even the august Royal Navy could expect the regional commander of the Unitary National Liberation Front to absent himself so far from his troops, or indeed risk his neck in a folbot, upon an element with which he was not familiar.

So Harry had conned *Scourge* into the little harbour, tied up alongside the stone jetty – festooned with raffia fenders, which Harry, jealous of his ballast tanks' integrity, had thought a nice gesture – and the major had stepped aboard over his gangplank and then they'd all sat round the wardroom table for their discussion. Even with all the hatches open, the air had been a fug of cigarette smoke.

Major Rado Drobnjac, a tall, spare young man in the same roughly tailored mud-brown uniform every one of his partisan comrades wore – except his had his rank flashes, albeit very subdued ones – had thinning mousey hair and sported wire-rimmed spectacles for reading. He spoke a rather archaic, Victorian English very well, and the accent wasn't too off-putting. It certainly didn't mask his seriousness. Not a jokey fellow, thought Harry. But then how frivolous would Harry have felt if foreign troops were disporting themselves in loud, arrogant fashion around the streets and by-ways of Argyll? Harry tried that thought on and didn't like it. After that, the attitudes displayed by all the partisans he'd then encountered from Vis became completely understandable.

Major Drobnjac had set out a map and explained how his men had secured all of Vis and had the surviving Italians – which was nearly all of them – secured in two compounds in the main town. That left the thirty Germans holding out.

'Here,' he had jabbed his finger at the promontory on the map. 'This is an old fort. They have water from a well in their courtyard and sufficient food for a long siege,' the major had explained. 'The buildings used to house a mounted police detachment, so they make quite a formidable fortress. The road up to it is over rising, scrubby land. A most effective killing field.' A pause, as he pointed out the route any assaulting force would have to take. 'As well as personal weapons, they have a total of eight new MG 42 machine guns.' He swept the palm of his hand over the blank expanse on the map that was the approach. 'That means a total rate of fire of nine thousand six hundred rounds per minute.' Another pause. 'Not survivable.'

Harry didn't doubt him for a moment.

'If they can hold out long enough, on the mainland, soon the Germans will be able to pull together sufficient shipping and E-boats to bring support in. We know they are already assembling shipping,' the major had said. 'When they can free up the necessary aircraft, they will come. The Germans will use mostly Croatian Home Guard. Collaborators, with Nazi hearts. Murderers of children. Using the Luftwaffe for air cover, they will disembark their heavy guns at the stone jetty below the cliff and over the beaches here for their infantry. We have no heavy guns, and we do not have enough men to cover all the landing grounds. We will lose, and the Croats will be let loose to kill us all. But if we can wipe out this foothold… their coming becomes much more problematic for them.' A phlegmatic shrug. 'Maybe too problematic.'

Major Drobnjac had then shut up and confined himself to considering his cigarette between puffing on it. He let it all sink in for Harry – the plan, its necessity, the consequences of failure. He hadn't bothered to ask for help. No point. It was obvious what was needed, and Harry had it, on *Scourge's* fore-casing.

Harry thought maybe he really should deliberate before he answered. There could be implications, political and diplomatic, for a Royal Navy warship placing itself under the operational control of Tito's partisans. But how was he to know, here, up at the fag-end of the Adriatic, with not a friendly Allied face for over six hundred miles?

Serious deliberation was probably called for. Instead, he said, 'When do we go?'

Major Drobnjac had fixed him with his pale, pellucid eyes for a moment before bending down to his knapsack. He placed a large clear bottle of what turned out to be the most throat-scarring slivovitz on the table with one hand, followed by a clutch of chipped tumblers with the other – ones for Harding and Farrar as well.

Harding and Farrar had sat silent through the whole concise, totally unembroidered briefing, mesmerised enough for even Farrar to forget his customary fastidiousness when forced to share his mess space with disreputable-looking foreigners.

When Harry had looked up from the major's gift, he saw an unexpected – stunning, even – boyish grin on the man's face, one that had brought him back with a thump as to how young the major really was.

A whooshing sound echoing back from the cliffs startled Harry back to the here and now; a rocket had gone up from behind the German position. He watched its rapid arc until it was almost overhead the little cluster of buildings, and then a flash dazzled him, and when his eyes refocused, a searing chemical blob was guttering and dangling below the occasional reflection of a tiny parachute as a flare pirouetted slowly to earth.

The light gently bathed the shallow bay, turning it into some magical snow scene, and the first tiny chasing sparkles of light began rising up from inland, startling at first and a little magical, until the sound finally caught up with the image; the chatter of a machine gun. Tracer. It was the signal; the battle had started.

Harry was aware of a shuffling below him, down the conning tower hatch. When he peered over, he could see faces staring up, attracted by the sudden reflected glow from the flare – *Scourge's* machine gunners, waiting in the conning tower space.

Harry gave them a smile, not sure whether they could see it or not in the gloom, 'Stand easy down there, there's nothing to pop off at yet.'

'Aye, aye, sir,' a disembodied voice came up.

When *Scourge* had limped back to Gibraltar to get her bent nose straightened after her inadvertent encounter with the seabed off Cagliari, they'd welded a gun mount to the aft end of the conning tower and presented the boat with twin Browning .303 all-purpose machine guns. 'For air defence,' Harry had been told, although whoever imagined he'd allow his boat to be on the surface long enough to fire that pop-gun if there were aircraft about was never mentioned. Anyway, there it was; they might need it depending on how this fight unfolded, but being able to get the boat down fast if needed was more important. And having to un-ship and stow below two 30lb lumps of gun in a hurry would only get in the way. So, there the two gunners could wait, pending events.

Meanwhile, the rate of fire from onshore was gathering pace. From this angle, the slope of the killing ground in front of the buildings was now being cross-hatched with tracer, and the noise was like Chinese New Year. 'Stand-by,' Harry called down to the casing. He saw Hooper's pale face turn up to him.

'Aye, aye, sir,' he said.

Not yet. They were waiting for all eight of the Jerry MG 42s to be turned on the slope, for Jerry's attention to be fully concentrated down the promontory, then the other flare would go up and *Scourge* would commence firing.

As 'guns as well as torps', McCready was on the bridge beside Harry, up there to observe Hooper's fall of shot. He had his night glasses stuck to his face when he whispered back at Harry, 'There they are, sir. I can definitely see a folbot and a couple of those coracle thingies.'

He was looking at a platoon of Major Drobnjac's finest cut-throats, embarked on local boats of their own, and now led led by Cpl Hibbert, which Harry had thought a shocking risk. They were paddling furiously from the shadows out across open water, heading for a jumble of large boulders that erupted from a sheerer, smoother cliff that was overhung by the back wall of one of the Jerry buildings. This rubble rose twelve to fifteen feet from a tiny shingle beach and was in full view of *Scourge*. According to the major's plan, it would be Hibbert's job to lead a party of a dozen or so partisan sappers, sneaking in under the cover of the all firing, onto that beach, up the slope and through the breach in the wall that Hooper was going to open up for them with his three-incher. But only after he'd started demolishing the front walls of the whole position. Major Drobnjac had been very specific about that; he didn't want the first shells landing at the back of the Jerry position, thus alerting the enemy to someone trying to come in the back door as well.

Between the flare, still tumbling, and the sliver of moonlight, Harry could actually see the little dark smudges on the dark water, stretching out for the beach, if you could call a tiny strip of shingle no larger than his parents' sitting room a beach. He also saw in that moment, the skylight on the building above them rise and a bobbing head, then two, poke out.

Harry turned instantly and shouted down the hatch, 'Biddle! Cross! Up here now! Ship the machine guns!'

The gunners were his main Asdic operator and favourite second helmsman. Up they came, guns and ammo boxes propelled by others unseen up onto the bridge behind them.

The plan was buggered now, Harry knew that instantly, the moment he saw the Jerries stick their heads out the skylight. And all the timings were just as out the window. No question anymore; Jerry knew the partisans were trying to come in the back door. Waiting for the second flare was a luxury they no longer had. He could hear Biddle and Cross mounting and loading the Brownings behind him as he leaned over the bridge front.

'Hooper!' he barked in his most commanding tone. 'Target… the front walls of the enemy position! Commence firing!'

The last syllable had barely left his mouth than the first round was on the way and then the second flying before the first had hit.

Behind him, Biddle called, 'Three-oh-three mount ready, sir!'

Harry spun round, his right arm outstretched back towards the enemy buildings, 'Biddle! Onshore, off the starboard bow… red ten… the building above the rockfall. Do you see it?'

'Yessir!' said Biddle, traversing the Brownings now, looking down the sights.

'The skylight in the roof?'

'…yessir!'

'Smother it in fire, now. And keep smothering it!'

Before Biddle could respond, Harry, looking out towards the beach, saw a tiny line of white spouts ripple along the waterline. Then another line of spouts, then a flash. Two, three flashes, then the rip of automatic weapons followed by the *crack! crack!* of grenades drifted over to them from the beach. The Germans firing down on the landing party, still in their flimsy boats, battling towards the shingle and the safety of the lower boulders.

Burrp! Burrp! Then, *Burrrrrrp! Burrrrrrrrp!*

Right in Harry's ear.

The smell of cartridge smoke as the .303 rounds arced out. But no tracer, no dancing lights to show the bullets on the way. Harry was going to ask about the tracer but then decided not to interrupt a man at his work. Yet, when he put his own binoculars to his eyes and looked, chunks of the building's roof, and then the skylight frame itself, began disappearing in a welter of splinters.

You could see now, in plain view, the small landing force scrabbling ashore. No one was shooting at them anymore, courtesy of Biddle's steady fire on the skylight. It was time to blow the back of the building out. Harry gave the order, and Hooper obliged with two rounds of high explosives.

Harry watched as a couple of huge lumps of masonry leapt, tumbling into the air, higher and higher than it seemed they should; there was a flash below his line of sight, subliminal but there, and then when Harry's eyes began to follow the masonry's trajectory down, they vanished into a powdery billowing smoke rising up to meet each lump. He couldn't work out what had happened. The increasing racket of machine guns and mortar thumps made concentrating difficult.

Figures from the landing party could be seen against the white of the cliffs and the silhouette contours of the boulders beneath the building, spidering upwards. But what Harry on *Scourge* could see, and they couldn't, was the lick of flames now curling from inside the remains of the building. By the time the first climbers were at the base of the shell-shattered wall, they were facing a continuous sheet of fire.

Harry leaned over the bridge front and yelled down to Hooper, still busy, back walking his shells across the front of the barracks now, 'Hooper! What in God's name did you fire at that building!?'

Hooper paused, "T'wasn't us, sir! We're just firing HE. I think we must've set off secondary blasts... white phosphorous, it looks like.'

Chemical bombs, shells of the stuff, very efficient in setting buildings on fire and generating smokescreens. People caught in their chemical fire just melted.

'Aw ...!' was the best Harry could think of to say. He could already see the heat from the blaze had driven the climbing figures back down the cliff to the beach.

The plan had been for Hibbert to lead Major Drobnjac's men up into the back of the buildings – a small stables-cum-barracks – while the Jerry engineers were busy defending the front and for the small team to fire the rest of the buildings behind the defenders, pinning them between the flames and the main assault force, and for Hooper to then continue dropping shells on them until they either surrendered or died. Yes, a fire had started, but it was too far back. There were places left for the Jerries to run. Not that Harry or anyone else from *Scourge* was ever going to see them through all the bloody smoke. Not even McCready with his owl's night vision, all this time observing Hooper's fall of shot for him.

Harry suddenly felt powerless in the action. What in hell were they to do? Then, in the glow of the flames, Harry could see a line of figures, running out across the top of the cliff, crouching low to stay in the dead ground so no partisan advancing from inland would see them. Behind him, Biddle shouted. He'd seen them too.

Harry raised his hand, 'They're running away, Biddle. It's over.' Even so, below, on the casing, there was sharp report as Hooper fired off another round into the now roiling mass of smoke. From across the water, the crackle of small arms fire was slackening. Then one, then another and another two of the running Germans paused and seemed to perform some inexplicable form of one-armed callisthenics. Harry was still frowning at the antics when below the Jerries, on the tiny scrap of beach, a series of silent flashes ripped through the shadows.

Hand grenades. The Jerries had been lobbing hand grenades down on the landing party.

'Biddle…!' Harry yelled, but any further words were lost in Biddle opening up behind him, and the long, sustained burst of .303, the sheer, persistent length of it channelling all the anger and rage at what had just happened.

Harry gazed slack-jawed at the mess on the beach. The Jerries had been running away, so he'd checked Biddle's fire. If he hadn't, if he'd just let Biddle continue his execution… there'd have been no grenades. They'd been running away, and Harry had been content to let them. And look what happened.

But they were running away, he kept repeating it to himself, in his head. *Running away.*

Another *Bang!* From down on the casing.

And another.

Then a flare went up from behind the barracks. He watched it soar. Major Drobnjac. Harry stepped to the bridge front and yelled too loudly, 'Hooper! Check! Check! Check!'

*

They had to put Reynolds ashore, so with Jerry all mopped up, Harry decided they might as well do it from alongside the stone jetty in the town.

It was a hot, cloudless day. The town was arrayed around the harbour in ancient torpor, with its folk going about their business as if no war had ever existed. *Scourge* glided in like a visitor from another planet, and although most folk turned to stare, Harry, on the bridge didn't feel they were exactly causing a stir.

Major Drobnjac and a flunky, another woman soldier with her hair bundled up into an oversized forage cap, were waiting on the jetty, along with a couple of partisans to throw *Scourge* some lines. The boat was secured and Reynolds went ashore where he briefly conversed with the major while his radio set and all his attendant gear was humped off by a couple of sailors who shook the staff sergeant's hand warmly before they stepped back aboard over the plank gangway.

Grieve, *Scourge's* leading telegraphist, had got off with Reynolds too. Now he followed him up into the town with all the radio gear on a handcart, to help him set it up. Harry had told him to be quick; he didn't want to have to send a bloody search party when it came time to go. And if the balloon went up, he was to run like hell. Or they'd have to leave him. And he was 'too bloody important to leave' – that's what Harry had told him.

Harry imagined the friendships that must have been cemented in the for'ard ends between the affable pongo and the *Scourge*, and between them and Cpl Hibbert too. Hibbert now dead. Because the captain had told *Scourge's* machine gunners the Jerries were running away.

Major Drobnjac had followed the sailors over the plank, clutching a knapsack with another bottle of slivovitz in it, and toasts were made round the wardroom table and the crew of *Scourge* thanked. Warmly. Farrar didn't join them, busying himself instead as watch officer and overseeing the loading of fresh fruit and vegetables and local bread. And saving himself the bother of hiding all his disapproval.

It was Harding, with a few slivovitzes in him, who was curious as to why the big boss back on the mainland, Marshal Tito, had made it one of his strategic priorities to grab an island. 'Over there, when Jerry gets frisky, you lot can just disappear up some mountain range,' he'd observed to the stony-faced Drobnjac. 'Out here, there's nowhere to run. They've got you pinned.'

Drobnjac had considered him, as if deciding whether this half-drunk English parvenu merited an answer. It was the look of a man with a lot more moral bottom than you'd have thought someone like Drobnjac might possess.

Which was why, in turn, Harry had begun considering him. It turned out to be an interesting exercise.

The British had only lost Hibbert in the previous night's action. Hibbert, the jolly little commando, who probably knew only too well how to do his fair share of killing, but one of theirs just the same. Hibbert, who Harry'd killed because he'd told Biddle that Jerry was, 'just running away', Hibbert, and the handful of partisans whom the grenades had taken too. But Drobnjac had lost far more men than just the ones Harry had helped kill, and been just as guilty. His ordering his men against a veritable battery of Jerry MG 42s before Hooper's shells could drop in amongst them had been far more deadly.

Drobnjac, Harry had learned from Sgt Reynolds, had been a history teacher in Ljubljana, middle school, fourteen to fifteen-year-olds. Not a natural anteroom to greatness. So Harry found himself wondering how Drobnjac was bearing up under the responsibility? What informed his decisions? If a twenty-something schoolteacher from a hick town in the Balkans could do what he did and live with himself, what were the lessons he could teach Harry?

But sitting there, with the slivovitz warming his insides, suddenly all Harry could see was the death of Hibbert. All he knew was that at the time, he'd felt he was doing a good thing, sparing those Jerries. He hadn't had the remotest inkling of what other consequences might follow from his cavalier gesture. They were, after all, just running away. How wrong he'd been. What a bloody awful thing this war business really was – the whole bloody pointlessness of it all. He wanted nothing more right then than to tell his father he understood now. Was this really the best human beings could do? Poor Hibbert, poor bloody bastard.

But Drobnjac was saying something about Vis and why Tito wanted it. About how Jerry was using small coastal craft more and more to transport vital military stores to avoid all the partisan sabotage on the mainland.

'Did you hear that, sir?' Harding had asked him.

Harry snapped out of his thoughts: 'Is there much traffic…? What size of vessels do they use?'

'Caiques, schooners, anything that can carry a cargo,' Drobnjac said.

All too small to warrant a torpedo, but… In other words, perfect gun fodder.

Harry considered Harding again, sitting across the wardroom table savouring his slivovitz.

'So the crew, Mr Harding,' said Harry. 'You were saying last night, they all like being on bang duty?'

'Like it…?' Harding had said.

80

Six

Well, that wasn't supposed to have happened. Harry shoved his watch cap to the back of his head and scratched. The converted caique *Scourge* had just surfaced to attack was puttering away down the channel on her own now, her entire crew in a daisy chain in the water behind her, all trying like hell to swim for an island foreshore about three hundred yards beyond. In the slight chop, it was obvious some of them were getting into difficulties, and that was before you took into account that the current that was sweeping them all off at angle, which from *Scourge's* bridge, definitely looked like it was going to make them miss the land altogether.

Harry leaned to the voicepipe, 'Get the cox'n up here!'

It was a beautiful morning, with the sweaty heat not yet on full blast, the air clear as gin and the sound of seagulls still loud above the croaky *chuff-chuff-chuff* of whatever it was that was passing for the caique's engine as its wake traced its wobbly course away from them. Beneath him, Harry could feel and hear the burble of *Scourge's* own diesels, but he hadn't even had the chance to order them clutched in yet, never mind deciding what course he was intending the boat to navigate.

Only moments before, he had been watching through the periscope as the little tub turned out of the channel between Korčula and these two islands ahead. Then he'd ordered the periscope down, the boat to surface and Hooper and his gang to gun action, and then he had immediately gone up the conning tower himself as it broke clear. But by the time he'd got to the bridge and stood upright, the target's crew were already leaping over the side and floundering and splashing for the shore. Harry counted five of them. They hadn't even waited to lower a lifeboat – assuming they had one.

Suddenly, Ainsworth, the cox'n, was standing po-faced at his side.

'Sir,' he said, trying not to smirk as he took in the tableau.

'Cox'n,' said Harry. 'Get a team onto the casing. Someone who can swim and a couple of bowlines. And issue a couple of Tommy guns just in case. We'd better pull those two older clowns out the water before they drown themselves. And on your way through the boat, grab as many demolition charges as you think you'll need. Four should do it.'

Ainsworth disappeared back down the hatch with his usual, 'Aye, aye, sir!' and Harry leaned over and rang the telegraph for dead slow ahead together, and ordered, green ten on the helm. The lookouts were all up on the bridge now, and Harry had to turn and give both of them the hard stare to stop them gawping at the pantomime in the water and attend to their duty – looking out for Jerries. He then called down to Hooper, 'Secure! I don't think I'll be needing your services for the time being, Hooper, but hang about down there, just in case.'

'Aye, aye, sir!'

Harry conned *Scourge* sedately towards the closest of their shipwrecked mariners, a balding, stocky figure, thrashing about and in increasing difficulty. As they came up on him, a skinny rating slipped off *Scourge's* extended hydroplanes and wrestled a bowline over his shoulders so he could be hauled aboard. Within minutes, the second one, even older but with a mop of matted grey hair, was aboard too. Off the port quarter, Harry could see the remaining three floundering, treading water and looking back to see the fate of their shipmates. Harry waved his cap at them then he ordered *Scourge* to put on a bit more speed so as to catch up with the runaway caique.

There was quite a party on the fore-casing now. A clutch of ratings in their skivvies and singlets, caps on all a-jaunty, standing around, grinning and gaping in the sunshine, to which they were most definitely unaccustomed. It was already starting to get pretty warm now, and they stood about admiring the rugged, scrubby coast and each other's submariners' tans which really did stand out comically pale compared to the two middle-aged survivors' swarthiness. And the two with their Tommy guns, striking poses like they were seagoing Al Capones. Ainsworth was feeding tots to the two old fellows, squatting on the deck now and being offered a blanket each by another thoughtful Jack.

Harry was smiling to himself, his mind going back to the wardroom after the Yugoslav partisan had left them.

He'd talked to Farrar and Harding about their gun and the use they might make of it up and down this coast, now that they were free to go back on patrol. Farrar had been in favour, but it had been Harding who had rhapsodised about the crew and the morale-raising power of gun actions.

'Lots of loud bangs!' Harding had said. 'Gets them every time. Nothing Jack loves more than blasting away with a big gun. Everybody'll want in on it... there'll be a queue just to pass up the shells. And there will be vice involved. Graft, sir. Venality. Hooper's "sippers owing" tally will grow long enough to keep him drunk until Trafalgar Day.'

Sippers. It was the offer to sip from another man's tot, his daily rum ration, his inalienable right since Jonah beat the whale. And as only a

British sailor could, in his infinite capacity for larceny and corruption, he had turned that custom into a tally to barter, pledge and bet with, until it had become an alternative currency.

The notion of a lower deck bidding war going on beneath his feet made Harry smile even more, the notion of all that excitement among the crew and not bored despondency.

Suddenly, Farrar was at his side. 'I've assembled a boarding party, sir. The TGM and five ratings. Who would you like to lead it?'

McCready led the party. Harry watched them scramble aboard the caique, lugging a gas mask bag crammed with the demolition charges and fuses. Two of their number had Tommy guns slung over their backs. *Scourge* had acquired the weapons back in Algiers, thanks to Harding. When they were kitting out for their jaunt to bump off Kesselring, he'd spotted them in the special forces' armoury and nicked a nice round half dozen, plus extra clips. 'Better to have to ask forgiveness, than permission,' was his excuse when Harry had asked him if he thought he was going to get away with that. Number One had taken a very dim view.

The party spread out over the deck, McCready going directly to the wheelhouse and shutting down the caique's engine. Others went below. The caique was a remarkably smart little boat – wooden, about fifty feet long with a commodious beam, one main mast with a sturdy cargo-handling derrick and small wheelhouse aft. Her clinker hull was all fresh paintwork, white with a deep gunn'l, patterned with painted waves of blue and red. The Tommy guns weren't needed; no one was left aboard. But McCready appeared, carrying three huge salamis and a rope bag with clinking bottles in it and then the TGM, Gooch, emerged from the hold and came to the side to call out to Harry.

'Sir! The cargo looks like it's all lube stuff. Engine oil mostly. In what looks like gallon tins...'

Which explained why her crew had wasted no time in getting off her when a submarine started surfacing alongside.

'…I've set the charges so she's ready to blow when you give the order, sir.'

And a right royal bang it was too. The caique had momentarily performed a lateral wriggle on the surface, like she was some discombobulated duck, then part of the hull on the waterline and another part of her deck had erupted in a welter of timber before the quick ripple of cracks had reached them over the water to where Harry had withdrawn *Scourge*. Harry had been about to comment on what had happened to all that lube oil when there was the most almighty *whummmph!* And the whole lot went up in a roiling mushroom of flame and greasy black smoke that felt like it was singeing your eyebrows despite the distance.

Harry had let the crew on deck remain for the show. When he looked down from the bridge, they were grinning, transfixed, idiot-like. Glee was the word that sprang to his mind. He should've known himself and not needed Harding to tell him; there was nothing like a bit of good old wanton destruction to cheer a crew up. Any more like this and they'll be refusing to leave patrol, he thought. *Well, let's see what we can do,* said an equally grinning Harry to himself.

When he looked back aft, the little dory they'd liberated from atop the caique's hold cover was being rowed back alongside *Scourge's* stern. He watched the two ratings clamber onto the casing and cast it adrift. He'd sent them, with their two survivors, to pick up the rest of the caique's crew from the water and deliver them ashore. He'd learned nothing from the two old crewmen they'd had aboard – no language in common, and anyway, both of them had looked like they thought they were going to be murdered at any moment, even after Ainsworth had plied them with rum. Civilians. He wondered what Jerry would've done with them.

The smoke from the now disintegrated caique was bound to attract someone, so *Scourge* dived and headed into the channel north of the island of Mljet to look for more coastal traffic. Harry thought they would take their time throughout the rest of the day, hanging around between the other islands in the archipelago, Sipan and Lopud, to see if anything ventured in or out of the big port on this coast at Gruz, just behind Dubrovnik.

The chop on the water continued, so Harry held her at periscope depth, not worrying whether any aircraft that might turn up could see them prowling just below the surface. They hadn't long to wait. Harry caught the smoke coming down the channel behind them on his second all-round look. He ordered *Scourge* into a long loop out to sea to come back onto an attacking course and sent the boat to diving stations. The minutes passed. Biddle on the Asdic described the target as, 'A bit of a wheezy old bugger.'

Having been on the surface, breathing the warm Adriatic air, Harry, as he waited to do his next look couldn't help but notice how whiffy the control room team were getting these days; it also occurred to him how the warmer season had brought about a change in the boat's working dress code. Gone were the sweaters, in were working shirts and singlets and skivvies. With all that pasty flesh exposed, jammed up against each other in the sweatbox that was a submarine, you really couldn't avoid each man's reek. He breathed out, directing the air up his nostrils and muttered, 'War is hell,' to himself.

He decided not to start issuing orders on whether he'd carry out a gun or torpedo attack until he took his next look. He wasn't going to waste a torpedo on a tiddler, especially since there didn't seem to be much air activity – just as the major had assured him. It was time. Up went the scope, and there was the target: an ancient

coastal steamer, last century if she was a day. Three castles on her –
the fo'c'sle, wheelhouse and stern, with a towering, rusty natural
draught smokestack belching away. At least between eight hundred
and a thousand tons – borderline for a torpedo, but alas, that didn't
matter right now as unfortunately, the old tub was disappearing
between two of the smaller islands, Olipa and Jakljan, and heading
into the inshore channel.

Harry ordered, down 'scope and a turn to starboard. He hadn't
intended closing Gruz until later in the day and then he'd thought he
would take a look in to see if there was anything worth attacking. But
maybe if he could beat the steamer down the coast… he could bag her
before she got there. To do that, however, he'd need to surface and crack
on – in daylight, and in full view of the coast and not just two uninhab-
ited rocks like he'd risked for the caique. There were farm buildings all
over the shore here. He'd take another look in five minutes and decide.

He stuck the 'scope up again.

Directly on the bow, and just scraping his low horizon, two fully laden
schooners – at least four to five hundred tons each – in full sail, one
heading round past the islet of Grebeni at the entrance to Gruz harbour
and the other coming out. Two prime gun targets. Easily baggable if he
surfaced right now and chased. But when he angled up the 'scope for
an all-round sky look, there it was, a problem.

Buzzing up from the south-east, hugging the coast: a shagbat,
and a weird-looking one at that; flash, more like a sports car than an
anti-submarine aircraft.

Scourge went to sixty feet, and Harry leaned against the chart table,
wondering what to do next. Major Drobnjac had certainly been right
about the coastal traffic. All that shipping, stuffed to the gunnels with
Jerry material, puttering up and down with impunity. It was obvious

now why the partisans wanted to hold onto the island, as the major had said, a base right across the enemy's line of supply. Just like Malta was, and had been, critically, at a turning point in the war.

'We don't have gunboats like you,' Major Drobnjac had said. 'But we have fishing boats, and we have guns to mount on them. It will be a start. And if you really want to hurt the fascists like you say... you have gunboats. Torpedo boats. Tell them to come and join us. You've been to Vis. It's a nice place to go to work.'

The man had a point. Meanwhile, what was he going to do about that shagbat? It was hanging around too long. He took another look and even managed to identify it. A Caproni 124. A single-engined art-deco-designed seaplane, all sweeping contours and go-faster flourishes. A real between-the-wars job, out of date and, he assumed, dragged out of its museum and thrown into second-line defence. He couldn't remember this plane from his plane-spotting magazines, so he had no idea what it carried when it came to bombs, and he was not inclined to do any on-the-job testing. He was going to have to let all three targets go.

'Pass the word for Windass,' he said. When the wardroom steward presented himself, wearing only a singlet between his cap and his skivvies so you could see all his armpit hair, Harry smiled his winning smile, 'Ah, Windass. Lash me up a sarnie from that salami we liberated... and a mug of the coffee too... with condensed milk. There's a good chap.'

No point in going hungry while you were waiting.

Harry let the day drag on, ambling about in the deeper water with barely steerage way on the motors. Then as dusk was drawing close, he crept into the inshore channel between Lopud and Koločep, and when the darkness fell, as it did with some rapidity, he surfaced, bows pointing up the channel, and waited to see what would come down it.

Harry had long got out of the habit of always staying on the bridge at night and irritating the watch on duty, but tonight, he was making an exception.

'Sir…!' It was one of the rating lookouts at the back of the bridge. He was sniffing.

'What is it Addison?' said Harry, turning, catching something in the air… a faint…?

'I can smell funnel exhaust, sir,' said Addison. 'Sure of it, sir.'

That was what Harry could sniff too. That oily whiff. Faint, but definitely there.

But where was it coming from? There was no engine thump they could hear above *Scourge's* own diesels, burbling away mostly on charge as she crawled along. The other lookout was reporting nothing on the bow, and Addison couldn't see anything aft either, nor could McCready who was on the bridge too as officer of the watch. No alert from the Asdic cubby, but then Biddle would be scanning ahead and wouldn't be listening for anything coming out of Gruz. 'Asdic, bridge,' said Harry into the pipe. 'Do a listen astern, Biddle.'

Biddle's voice came up the pipe a moment later. 'HE. Green one seven zero, sir!'

Harry hit the tit twice.

Two blasts from the klaxon and the main vents opened.

Scourge levelled out at periscope depth, continuing on her original heading. You always turned stern on, on making a night sighting on the surface; you never knew who was stalking you, so it let you open the range as you dived until you'd decided whether what was out there was a target or something to the get hell away from.

But once down, Harry decided not to try and turn towards for a look-see. The channel was little more than a mile wide here and not conducive to any fancy manoeuvring. He'd let the target come up on them, and check her out as she passed.

'What've you got, Biddle? Fast? Slow? Big? Not?'

'…it's a merchant ship, sir. Almost certainly. Not fast. Diesel engines. Probably only making five or six knots.'

'Let me know as she's coming up on our quarter, Biddle.'

'Aye, aye, sir.'

Harry didn't like the idea of trying to get into a torpedo shot in these enclosed waters. The track angle and the range would be all wrong. If there was going to be an attack, it would be gun. 'Hooper, you and your lot stand by,' he said, barely raising his voice to call down the control room to the leading seaman gun-layer and his team crouching in the for'ard gangway. 'If we're going to engage, your target will be on the starboard beam. So, on your toes, boys.'

Hooper beamed at him, his teeth taking on a stained porcelain sheen through the red light, on to preserve the night vision of anyone likely to be heading upstairs. 'Aye, aye, sir,' said Hooper.

There was silence in the boat now. So quiet, Harry wondered whether he might be able to hear the splash of the sweat dripping from Windass' armpits even there, in the control room. Then…

'Target coming up on our starboard quarter now, sir.' It was Biddle, in a very conversational tone.

'Up periscope,' said Harry, and as the handles cleared the deck plates, he let it come three feet and then crouched to stop it before turning back to the assembled faces. When he'd decided, a moment ago, he was going to do this, the name on his lips had been Harding's. But he'd stopped himself. Instead, he looked at Farrar: 'Number One. You do the honours, will you Even with the slice of moon we've got, you know how little light'll be coming in,' he said, tapping the slender attack 'scope's tube, 'with all the land shadow in a narrow channel like this… and my crap night vision.'

Farrar stepped smartly forward, not showing the slightest surprise, and grabbed the handles, swivelling the 'scope to starboard.

'Target bearing… that,' he said, matter-of-fact.

And the yeoman, who was doing his periscope assistant, called off, 'Green five.'

'Sir, she's a ferry of some sort. Easily a thousand tons. Range, no more than seven hundred yards,' then Farrar did a quick all-round look, 'No other shipping in sight. Down 'scope,' and he stood back.

From behind him, Biddle's voice echoed from the cubby, 'No other HE, on any bearing, sir. Target is proceeding alone.'

'Surface, gun action!' called Harry. 'Gun crew close up. But at least wait until the tower's clear, there…!'

Hooper was already on the ladder, the hatch wheel half spun open even as the wrecker was still calling the depth as they went up. The two lookouts were already up into the conning tower, and Harry, before he knew it, already had his head almost up the second one's bum.

And then there was water spilling all over him, warm with a salty tang to it, and he was breathing night air and not bodies and diesel, and they were on the bridge, him and the two lookouts, and before he'd even grabbed the bridge front, Hooper had opened fire.

BANG!

Harry's ears were ringing, even as he watched the shadow that was the target's wheelhouse splinter apart.

… and then *BANG!*

Another one, right into the wheelhouse again. *BANG!* And another. *BANG!*

Voices could be heard now, drifting across the water; incoherent shouts. Then suddenly, out of the voicepipe, was Biddle's echoey voice, 'Bridge, Asdic! Target is under helm!'

Harry thinking, *good call young man!*

Harry, was well aware that someone who didn't know what they were doing might not have made that call, might have thought that since there were eyes on the bridge, they could see that the target was turning for themselves and that all he'd be doing would be wasting folks' time stating the bleedin' obvious – but not true! Not at night. In the dark, you could be looking right at a ship and easily miss the start of a turn, especially if the target was showing bugger all bow wave, like this one. And then it might be too late.

'Hooper!' called Harry over the bridge front, calm as a chap calling for a pint. 'Target is under helm!'

It was enough for *Scourge's* gun layer. 'Aye, aye, sir. Target under helm!' All called over his shoulder as Harry watched him traverse his beloved little three-incher aft and after the merest pause, resume firing – this time, the rounds going into the enemy's stern and her steering gear.

When Harry looked back along the hull of the ferry, for that was what she was, he could see now there was a pronounced slew on her, and she was starting to heel over. She was turning away. And speeding up too, from the churn of froth from under her stern. Certainly, she was over enough for him to see the cant of her top deck and the sight unfolding there: shadow figures, pouring up from below like the denizens of a kicked nest – a seething mass of them in what was left of the pale wash of a dying moon.

Soldiers. The ferry was carrying soldiers. And she was trying to beach herself on the opposite shore.

Harry stiffened, but he didn't blink. Wouldn't let himself. He'd sunk a troopship before. As number one on *Nicobar*. On that beautiful morning in the Sicilian Channel. He didn't want to see again that carpet of men, rising and falling on the long undulating swell, drowning.

Hooper fired twice more in quick succession, this time, the rounds going into the hull on the waterline where the ferry's engine room was. Then a flare went up. A pretty raggedy effort, going off at a queer angle, out and aft of the ferry. Harry, everybody, watched it slither into the black sky, its trajectory making it look like it was clawing its way up instead of soaring, until it reached its paltry zenith and ignited, illuminating more beach and rock than ship and surrounding sea. When Harry looked back, he could see men jumping off the ferry and into the water and a lifeboat dangling, skewed from its davits, someone having botched its launch in their panic.

He realised Hooper had stopped firing. Of course he had. The Royal Navy didn't fire on shipwrecked mariners. Then he did blink, except this time, he saw those fleeing Jerries on the cliffs back on Vis, running away, then stopping running away and throwing hand grenades down on the partisans' landing party, on smiling little Cpl Hibbert.

He was about to order Hooper to resume firing when there was a terrific *crump!* and a sudden rearing of the bow of the ferry. She'd run aground. The almost immediate lurch to the side told him her spinning propellers were still driving her hard onto the shore. Then the froth at her stern died; someone had killed the load to the shafts, and the huge dark mass of her just hung there, her bows stove in, up on the rocky beach. Already, he could see the exodus of men from the stricken hull was now really gathering pace.

Harry bent to the bridge front, 'Secure from firing. Clear the casing!' Then he turned to the lookouts, 'Down you go,' and as they vanished into the hatch, he sounded the klaxon to dive the boat and followed them.

While *Scourge* sedately motored up the channel at periscope depth, Harry ordered torpedo tubes one and four ready for firing, shallow depth, and then he propped himself against the chart table, wishing he was wearing trousers and not just his skivvies, so he could thrust his hands in the pockets.

He was looking at Farrar, monitoring the dive board, watching the trim, then he turned to Harding, busy at his plot on the chart table.

He'd almost asked Harding to take the periscope there, and not his number one.

He'd been aware, for some time now, he was developing a certain favouritism for Harding. Yet Lt Nick Farrar, his number one, was a bloody good officer. He couldn't fault him. But equally, there was a bit of the fuddy-duddy about the man. What age was he? Maybe twenty-six, maybe a bit older, yet, there was a staid air about him beyond his years. How he used to turn his nose up at strangers round the wardroom table, especially if they weren't officers, or worse, if they were foreigners. Petty. And he could be precise to the point of pedantry. But Harry would be the first to agree you needed an organised, clear-headed professional to be a good first lieutenant, to hold a boat to its discipline and efficiency. And Farrar was all of those things. It was just that he longed for a spark from the man.

As for Harding? He was just a hooligan at heart. An upper-class one, yes. But with bags of style. And Harry couldn't help but like him. He also thought that one day, he would make a bloody good CO. Farrar? He didn't know. Did he have that necessary flair in him?

Regardless, he couldn't allow himself to show even a whiff of favouritism. Otherwise, the whole boat would go to hell.

And it would go to hell even faster if didn't stop losing concentration like that, having these little reveries to himself inside his head while he was supposed to be trying to conduct submarine warfare in the enemy's backyard.

Like the one he'd been having since Vis that kept recurring, about why he'd let those Jerries go and then they'd killed Hibbert. Going round in circles, wondering what the rule was, the yardstick that told you how to stay on the right side of the line between fighting sailor and bloody murderer?

Was he really going to debate in his head the state of his soul right now? While thirty feet down in a narrow channel off the enemy's coast? Jesus!

'Up periscope,' he ordered. Then, not raising his head, he said, 'Number One. Take another quick all-round look. Tell me if you think the channel's wide enough now to do a one-eighty. I'm minded to go back and stick a torpedo into that ferry, just in case someone thinks it's a good idea to try and float her off again.'

By then, Harry was saying to himself, *all those bloody soldiers will be off her and heading for the hills, and I won't have to worry about blowing their arses off* this *time… the hills where they can get back to killing partisans like Major Drobnjac and maybe even radio operators like Willy Reynolds… where was that rule again? The yardstick that tells you what to do?*

*

Another achingly azure sky, without a cloud. When Harry came up through the conning tower hatch, the heat washed over him like a caress. It would become more like being basted as the day wore on, but for now, it was perfect. He watched Hooper and his team take their time fitting the three-inch gun sight. No hurry right now, the schooner they had surfaced to engage was still on the other side of the headland off their port beam, tacking to clear it.

Harry had heard tell all Jerry U-boat deck guns were fitted with watertight sights as standard, so you didn't have to keep shipping and unshipping them every time you dived. *Scourge's* gun, however, had originally been designed and built to shoot down Zeppelins – in 1917. They hadn't had the technology to waterproof gun sights back in 1917. So if you left its sight still attached when you dived, the outside ERA had to strip it down and dry it out before you could use it again.

Scourge had inherited this one because rifled naval guns took notoriously long to build and any old ones left in stores were being parcelled out to new-builds.

Harry had ordered the .303 mounting up too. This target looked like a good one: five hundred tons at least and heavy laden. And the fact that she was wafting along without a care in the world, or a friend to protect her, told him no one was looking for any enemy submarines this far back up the coast.

Blowing a huge hole in the engine room of that ferry the other night and setting her on fire had stirred up quite a reaction along the coast around Gruz and Dubrovnik – nearly all of it Italian. A clutch of Italian Navy MAS boats had come out and had begun sweeping up the channel. Harry had decided prudence was in order and opted to get out of that narrow stretch pronto. Which had been just as well because as they exited, going like the clappers on the surface, a dark shape had come round the end of Mišnjak Island that had turned out to be one of those Jerry sub-hunters they called UJ-boats, UJ standing for *Unterseeboot-jaeger*, usually a local steam trawler, all gunned up and sprouting depth-charge racks. It had taken *Scourge* just under fourteen seconds to get down – one of their best times yet.

They had hung about most of the next day, waiting for the hue and cry to die down, but it hadn't. In fact, not long after first light, the *art-deco* Caproni had returned, and later, it had been joined by two lumbering Cant Z 501s who just wouldn't go away, like they knew they were being deliberately annoying. And there had been no shipping traffic at all.

Not that the *Scourges* had seemed to be all that bothered; there was a

buzz in the boat… *did you see the mess Georgie made o' that wheelhouse?…
and that second shot into her arse – I saw the whole rudder come off!…*

So they had left the area and gone north again. But not before
they'd deployed a little secret weapon that had been passed to Harry
by Leading Telegraphist Grieve, one that had given him particular
pleasure for the sheer inventive genius of the idea and that it had
come from one of his own ratings. Something so simple and totally
hilarious, he thought Grieve should have his photo on the front page
of *Good Morning**.

(*the *Daily Mirror's* newspaper dedicated solely to the submarine service).

Harry had had no idea what Grieve had wanted when he'd asked for
a 'captain's table', and feared the worst. The L Tel had come before him,
cap on and in the best uniform he could muster this far into the patrol,
just after they had sailed from Vis for the last time. He was carrying
what looked like a metal rod. But it wasn't.

'Bamboo?' Harry had asked after he'd lifted the object off the wardroom table and squinted at it.

It was at least four foot long, and Grieve had sanded smooth its
natural ribbing and painted it with some gunmetal paint he'd scrounged
from the back-afties. Harry could feel it was weighted at one end. The
other end had a little carved screw-on confection that looked like the
head of the attack periscope.

'I had the idea when I was ashore, helping Sergeant Reynolds with
his radio gear, sir,' said Grieve, shifting nervously, which Harry had
thought unusual for a hand like him, who had all quiet confidence of
the technically expert.

'It was their fish traps, sir. When they set them on the sea bed. They'd
mark where they were, using these bamboo sticks. They drilled down
through all the wooden compartments, you see, and dropped ballast

into the last one, so as they floated upright, sir. Like buoys, sir, only a lot cheaper and easier to make. I thought they looked like a periscope, sir. So if I did, I thought maybe the Eyeties would too. I thought if we chucked one over the side and left it bobbing about where we'd been, maybe if someone spotted it, they'd think we were still there and waste a lot of time and depth charges looking for us. Even though we weren't... there, that is... if you see what I mean... sir.' Grieve had trailed off, uncertain whether he was making an ass of himself.

Harry remembered frowning at the thing in his hands. He hadn't meant to leave the L Tel hanging there, wondering if he'd just made the biggest fool of himself, it was just that he was amazed. *Well, bugger me*, he'd thought. But he remembered with a smile, what he'd eventually said.

'Grieve. You're a fucking genius!'

That had put a big smile on Grieve's usually taciturn face, which, of course, had been pretty quickly wiped off by his messmates.

'...*of course, the skipper got the idea from Grieve's dick... when he's 'avin' one o' his Betty Grable dreams, it's wavin' about like Guy Lombardo's baton... so we made a cast of it to frighten Jerry... an' the next thing ye know... "thing?" Aye, that's the right word for it... Hey! Angus! Who'd've thought a cast o' yer porky love truncheon'd become the Allies' secret weapon!*' Every one of them, of course, being as proud as peacocks of Grieve, one of their own, coming up with such a stonker of a ruse.

'Of course, he's one of your lot, sir, isn't he?' Harding had said when he'd heard.

'One of my lot, Miles?' Harry had asked, archly.

'A jockulist, sir.' Harding had smiled back. 'You've all got the badness in you. It's generally accepted.'

Harry watched, as first the long bowsprit and then the hull of the schooner cleared the headland. It seemed to be the pattern of the coastal traffic along here that they snuck in behind every island they passed for fear of what might be lurking outside.

Although he doubted if this one had been worried about anything until they saw *Scourge* and in a panic luffed up and shuddered to halt as if someone had applied a set of brakes.

'Give her a shot across the bows, Mr Hooper,' Harry said. 'See how brave she is.'

Hooper obliged.

The schooner started to drift. She was a beautifully lined craft, rigged fore-and-aft and stately as a swan with all her white canvas set, but a complete scruff when it came to her paintwork – all peeling black and exposed planking. There appeared to be a lot of industry on deck. He could see a figure waving a scrap of material. Harry raised his binoculars. It was a man waving a greyish tea towel. A white flag? Behind him, he could now make out what the activity was about. About half a dozen crewmen were freeing some kind of wooden dinghy when suddenly it shot up off its blocks and dangled from the mainmast jib.

Harry called down the pipe, 'Boarding party to the casing. Bring charges and two Tommy gunners.' Then over his shoulder to the .303 crew, 'Keep your sights on those buggers until I see what they're up to.'

He hadn't long to wait. Quite deftly for a rabble, they righted the dinghy and lowered it into the water. No sooner had the falls gone slack than every man-jack of them were over the side and into her so that the dinghy wobbled so much, Harry thought she'd capsize. Then they were rowing away for Brač, maybe two hundred yards behind them.

Harry conned *Scourge* so as her bows came alongside the schooner, and the boarding party stepped off *Scourge's* casing onto the bow planes and over the schooner's gunnel. Not much of show for Hooper, but the lads would enjoy pirating whatever goodies they might find and then blowing her up with the charges. He looked around him; it was a beautiful, rugged coastline and remote. From where they lay, he couldn't see any settlement onshore. It was early, so once they'd seen off this customer, he thought they'd hang about a bit, see if anything else turned up. When he looked back at the schooner, he could see some of his party emerging from the its hold, shoving up a veritable mountain of booty.

The day had dragged on without even a fishing boat puttering by or an aircraft to darken the sky. So they passed the time on the surface, stowing their haul. The schooner had been carrying sacks of wheat and onions, tins of tomatoes, pallets of soap, olive oil, rifle and machine gun ammunition and boxes of hand grenades. There had also been a couple of cases of French brandy. The boarding party had portered across all they thought they could stow, but with only two torpedoes gone, room in the forward spaces was minimal. Harry sent Harding to conduct a triage on the stuff coming aboard – what was worth keeping and what would have to get tossed. They would have no use for the grenades for a start, and anyway, they'd help the schooner go out with an even bigger bang. Which it did, most satisfyingly, with quite a few *Scourges* up on the casing, snapping away with their Box Brownies. It really had been most amusing how big bangs could put such a childlike smile on the face of the most grizzled stoker. That night, *Scourge* headed out to sea to spend the hours of darkness getting a good charge on. In the morning, Harry thought he'd head down the coast and take a look around the entrance to the Bay of Kotor to see if there were any likely targets there. After all, they still had almost a full load of torpedoes.

Not long after sunrise, with *Scourge* bow on to the coast, Harry took his first all-round look, and there it was: a tiny smudge of smoke on the horizon. Harry leaned back from the periscope to check the bearing bezel himself, then leaning back in, he called, 'Asdic. Do you have any

HE on green two eight?' It was a different rating manning the set this morning; Biddle, *Scourge's* leading Asdic man was off watch, sound asleep for'ard, on his favourite perch above one of the torpedo reload racks. This lad was a bit slower. It took him a few moments to report, 'No HE on that bearing, sir. No HE within range at all, sir.'

Harry ordered the 'scope down and went to look at the chart. While he was pondering it, a voice came from the Asdic cubby, 'Multiple HE on green two zero, sir. It's faint, some of it high speed, but they're only coming on slow, sir.'

'Well done,' said Harry, still peering at the chart. He let five minutes pass, then did another all-round look. The smoke was further above the horizon now, and the range was closing. He issued orders for a course to close the coast ahead of what appeared to be the target's track. The enemy was steaming north, heading to go past, or even into the Bay of Kotor. Also, from his quick look, the smoke smudge appeared to be coming from more than one source, a convoy in other words. Harry sent *Scourge* to diving stations and squeezed himself between the periscopes as the scramble of bodies went past him, but it took only a moment for everyone to be at their stations. Harry let everyone settle down and then stepped to the chart table where Harding, as usual, had already begun plotting all his calls on bearing and estimated speed. He issued another stream of orders and the boat continued to work in closer to the convoy's estimated track.

'The buggers are hugging right in on the coast,' muttered Harry in his usual fashion, so as the entire control room could hear. 'Definitely three steamers... and three MAS-boats, dancing around them... going like the clappers...' another quick all-round look, '...no air cover as yet... down periscope.'

He stepped over to the chart table again. Biddle had given him the mean bearing rate and reported that he could detect no indication that the steamers were attempting to zig-zag. Biddle's usual unhurried voice could be heard easily in the control room, '…the ships, they're a clattery bunch, sir. Real bangers… the high-speed HE, they're scooting about at random, sir. They're all over the place.'

Except they weren't 'scooting about at random', not from what Harry had just seen. These MAS boats were performing deliberate patterns to seaward of their charges – a fancy way of saying they were getting in the way. Systematically and to a plan. The Regia Marina anti-submarine kit had never been up to much, on that, most Tenth Flotilla skippers were agreed. '*Rudimentary*,' was perhaps the most polite description Harry had read in another boat's patrol report. But quite a few of their Italian skippers managed to work distressingly well with what they had. And these three MAS-boat skippers appeared to be at the top end of competent.

He preferred it when the enemy formed a traditional anti-submarine screen when escorting convoys, arrayed in arrow formation, pinging on their echo sounders and listening on their hydrophones, like they were trying to beat any threat away with the sheer volume of racket they'd created, then listening for anything they might flush out. In those circumstances, all an astute submarine skipper had to do was get inside that screen, pick his spot abaft the convoy's beam and bingo! There was your clear shot.

But not with these boys. One of the MAS-boats was zig-zagging apparently wildly ahead of the three steamers, but if you were paying attention, there was nothing wild about it; he was doing high-speed sweeps, positioning himself to go directly at anyone foolish enough to raise a periscope in his path. The other two also had their throttles wide open, but they were staying well back, keeping station always on their charge's beams and aft quarters but ranging out, up to almost a mile – quartering the sea room around the convoy at high speed, their huge wakes like gouts of icing sugar, smothering the sea all around them and getting in the bloody way so you couldn't settle and take your shot. Harry couldn't imagine anything more disconcerting – if you've got your target in your graticules, you've called the bearing and range and you're just waiting on the target's dumb, lumbering bow to cross your DA… and a fucking escort starts coming directly at your periscope at thirty knots.

It was all a matter of keeping your head and concentrating. Of course it was.

The three steamers were a motley collection, none of them more than a thousand tons. Two, with their natural draught stacks aft, belting out black smoke, were easily last-century veterans, the third, and the biggest by a small margin, looked like a scaled-down cargo-passenger liner, with an elongated superstructure that had a row of cabins. All were rust buckets, and all had deck cargo, like giant fruit crates. Was he going in to risk all against a glorified grocery delivery?

He *was* trying to concentrate. Except that from the moment he had started this attack in his head, it had felt different. He was having to think about what he was doing, all the angles and ranges and decisions to be made weren't flowing through his head like they should. It was as if, because all the previous actions had been gun actions, he'd gone suddenly a bit rusty when it came to good old-fashioned torpedoes. Going in with the gun, after all, had only required him to point *Scourge* in the right direction and then his dead-eyed gun layer, Hooper had done the rest. In a torpedo action, however, it was all about him.

That was when the indecision started creeping in. He suddenly discovered, in the back of his mind, he was wondering about whether he should be pressing home this attack at all. Or should he just not bother, just let them pass, don't alert the coast, just move along and wait for the next one. This was the Adriatic. The targets had been coming thick and fast, and he hadn't even ventured over to the other shore. There was no pressure on the boat to press home this one.

Because these bloody MAS-boats weren't going to let him get close easily.

But say he decided to fire anyway a full salvo spread? He'd be bound to hit something. But that would all be down to luck, wouldn't it? In the end, he might just waste six torpedoes. And then there would be the counter-attack. These MAS-boats only carried six depth charges each at most – but it only took one. Was it worth risking it to bag a grocery delivery?

The trouble was, he knew the more he thought like that, the less he was concentrating, and it definitely wasn't him being decisive.

And that was when all the shit he had in his head about the Bonny Boy started leaking in.

The thing was, since the encounter with the safe conduct ship and everything that had surrounded it, the previous reports from the Bonny Boy about Captain Gilmour's 'lack of aggressiveness', there had been a voice in his head, a voice that kept coming back, again and again, these days when he was doing his war stuff, a voice that wondered whether it was true. And whether at some time, somewhere in the future, at some inquiry against him for God knows what, there would be the Bonny Boy, giving evidence, carping on again about how shy that Gilmour character had always been – especially when it came to pressing home his attacks. The boy had been shy before, he could hear him saying it. And who was he to gainsay it?

Harry shook his head; he was supposed to be conducting an attack. But he was getting tired, and he knew it.

Not surprisingly, really. He hadn't had a rest since the bloody war started; he didn't count his two weeks' survivors' leave because he'd 'won' that on his first war patrol. He'd hardly spent any time as a clock-work mouse in the Firth of Clyde – usually every new skipper's time off for practice – and as for racking up lots of shore time overseeing a new-build command, well the Luftwaffe had blown the arse out of that. And anyway, what was he doing having this kind of discussion in his head in the middle of an attack?

Maybe it wasn't his crew's morale he should've been worrying about but losing his own edge, his tiredness, his continued fitness for command. *Concentrate!*.

'Bring all six bow tubes to readiness…' said Harry, back-leaning against the chart table, missing his trouser pockets. Harding, watching him out the corner of his eye, reckoned he wasn't the only one these days thinking the captain was looking… what? Nobody could pin it down… could think of the word. If he was asked to take a stab, what would he have to say? Careworn? Could it really be that? Harry Gilmour, careworn? Didn't seem possible.

'…shallow setting. Ten feet.'

Harry looked at Harding's plot of the advancing track of the little convoy. Harding hadn't even bothered to try and follow the careering about of the MAS-boats. Harry ordered the periscope up for another all-round look, then he turned it back on the targets' bearing.

'Bearing is that,' called Harry, and Dickie Bird, the yeoman, standing by the periscope, read off the bezel.

McCready, on the fruit machine, dialled it in. 'Range is… that,' and Bird read off the minutes. Well over four thousand yards. 'Down periscope!' said Harry.

He went and stood behind Leading Seaman Cross on the helm. 'Steer one eight five,' he said, tapping the lad's shoulder, then to Ainsworth, operating the engine room telegraph, 'Slow ahead together, Cox'n.'

He had placed *Scourge* on a parallel track to the convoy, going in the opposite direction, and when Harding began updating the plot, he could see from their course they would pass at a range of over three thousand five hundred yards. He could see Harry checking his watch – timing himself to the next manoeuvre? But nobody else could tell, because the commentary from the skipper had suddenly stopped, which was unusual. 'Stand by all tubes,' said Harry, then he ordered the 'scope up again. He did his usual all-round look, then, '…We're still shagbat free.' At last, a bit of commentary again. Then, with the periscope pointing almost directly to port so as his shoulders were almost fore and aft down the control room, he began reading off the bearing and range and an updated estimate for the targets' speed, 'Six knots. Down periscope.'

It had all looked very dramatic, with Harry crouching down on the deck plates, holding the 'scope so low to ensure as little of the head was above the flat, calm sea, but his calls and orders were all being delivered like he was dictating a shopping list to the scullery maid. He stood up and reached to tap Cross again, 'Helmsman. Port twenty. Keep on slow ahead together.'

Harding ticked the plot; they were turning in on the convoy's track, and from the look of it, he was coming round to let the leading enemy steamer just pass by. The 'scope went up again, and Harry called the lead target then asked McCready on the fruit machine, 'What's my DA?' McCready called it back. Harry ordered the 'scope down again and stepped to the sound-powered telephone and lifted it. He's doing it all himself this time round, noted Harding, wondering why.

'Mr Gooch, Captain here. On my order, you fire the first torpedo and then all remaining torpedoes on the stopwatch at five-second intervals.

Stand by.' He checked his watch and ordered the 'scope up once more. He called the bearing, range and speed, then, 'What's my DA?'

And McCready called it back.

Harry's face remained glued to the attack periscope's eyepiece. One second passed, two, then… 'Fire One!'

They all felt it go.

Harding started his stopwatch. He looked at the range to the targets. 'Just on three thousand yards. It should be about two minutes to run,' he said. They all felt the next torpedo go, and one by one, all the others. Harry ordered the periscope down, then, 'Starboard thirty! Keep ninety feet, full ahead together.'

They waited until there could be no mistake, until the last torpedo must have finished its run. They'd all missed. Right after, it was pretty certain the attack had failed, Biddle reported more HE from the MAS-boats – they were really going crazy now – then they had heard the first depth charges in the water. But they were a long way astern. Harry secured the boat from diving stations. All he said was, 'Good effort, lads. My eye just wasn't in today,' then he asked for a cup of coffee. Harding and Farrar exchanged looks, and McCready saw them, thinking so it wasn't just him who'd noticed. *Scourge* withdrew further offshore to load her four remaining torpedoes. For the next few days, she cruised the shallow coastal waters at periscope depth down as far as Bar, where Harry conned her on the surface one night, right in behind the port's long, extended breakwater to look for targets. But there was nothing there but fishing boats.

Outside, along the coast, they made several sightings: lone steamers with shagbats overhead for cover, but the sea was too calm and shallow – less than a hundred feet in places – for *Scourge* to even get remotely close before the eye in the sky would spot them prowling through the clear, pellucid water.

The night after their excursion into Bar, Harry had been lying on his bunk, behind his curtain, ostensibly feeding his sleep bank. The whispers in the wardroom were so low he wasn't even certain who was there. And even then, the words were only clear in snatches, '...everybody knows, if it's over two thousand yards, it's pure luck if...' That was all he really heard, the rest was just muttering. But he knew what they were talking about. Three targets at two thousand yards, and him firing a full salvo and missing. With every torpedo. And now, he was eavesdropping on someone making an excuse for him. Harry didn't like that – people thinking they had to make excuses for him. What captain would? But it was true, nonetheless. Yes, he had hit things at much longer ranges. But he wasn't silly enough to believe that was just down to his super-human powers, there had had to be an element of luck. He knew that, just like he knew that luck had been looking the other way when he missed this time. But he couldn't stop picking at it. Then there was the other matter nagging at him. Captain Bonalleck, the old Bonny Boy himself, the man who hated him, who appeared to have a pathological, probably even murderous enmity for him, who thought he, 'lacked aggressive spirit', and the thought that he might just be right.

Even though he knew he was harming himself by doing so, he couldn't stop listening to that voice, undermining his own confidence, putting his crew at risk through his own self-doubts, doing the bloody enemy's job for him.

Was he losing it?

It wasn't that he was scared, that he was a coward. Christ, he was usually too busy in action for the thought to even occur to him. Maybe it was simply that he was just too tired now to be any good anymore? He rolled over, determined to let the fatigue he was feeling engulf him at last and finally shut down that bloody whining in his head. He'd made up his mind, how all this was going to get resolved.

The first thing he was going to do when they docked again in Malta was to go and see Shrimp, and tell him. Everything.

Captain Simpson, the flotilla CO, would be the final arbiter of Harry's fitness. That was how it had always worked in the Royal Navy, and Harry could think of no good reason why it should change now. The next day, *Scourge's* time on the billet ran out. Harry pointed her at the Straits of Otranto, and they headed back to Malta, freshwater showers, clean sheets, long lies and long cool gins on the balcony at the Lazaretto.

Seven

Captain Simpson had travelled by London underground to Swiss Cottage and then walked the rest of the way to the serviced apartment block on College Crescent that now served as the headquarters for Flag Officer, Submarines. Northways was a golden brick edifice that curled around a fountained forecourt and must've been a nice place to live after it first opened its rather grand entrance hall in the 1930s. Now, it had been requisitioned by the Admiralty, its forecourt garlanded with sandbags and its tiers of steel-framed windows starred with blast tape. He'd been shown up to an anteroom with a petty officer, writer at a desk who'd offered him a cup of tea. He had declined.

Then he'd been shown in to meet the new FOS. The old FOS, Max Horton, had decamped to Western Approaches some time previously, and having been out in the Med all that time, Shrimp hadn't had the opportunity yet to meet the new one in his current role. But Shrimp knew him of old.

He was Rear Admiral Claud Barry, and Shrimp had been his first lieutenant in the submarine, HMS *Thames*, back in 1932. He had always remembered a warm man, with a certain quiet power to him, full-lipped and a bit jowly, but that always bespoke a certain presence. All that was still true, but Shrimp hadn't expected the grey parchment look to his fleshy face. The rear admiral didn't look quite well. But needless to say, Shrimp said nothing about that. The handshake was still firm.

'Another few days and I'd have been coming out to meet you,' Rear Adm Barry told him with a laugh. 'Off to see old Harwood at Alex. Which means having to entrust my fragile, corporeal presence here on earth to the crabfats. Bloody flying boats! And you're off to work for Max again. That'll be fun. I've heard he went into the Liver Building like Christ come to cleanse the temple.'

The Liver Building in Liverpool housed Western Approaches headquarters, and it was from there that Admiral Max Horton was now controlling the battle of the Atlantic.

'I'm to be Commodore, Londonderry, so that should be far enough away,' said Shrimp, with a laconic smile. He had worked under Admiral Horton for long enough to know what a terror he could be – but only to those who didn't know what they were doing. If you did know what you were doing, Max Horton was your greatest ally.

'Just make sure that if there are any decent golf courses near you, you get them turned over to vegetable growing instantly, otherwise, you'll never see the back of him,' said Rear Adm Barry, as he thrust a tumbler of gin into Shrimp's hand. 'So, tell me, was it really pretty bloody out there? Actually, you don't have to answer that, George. I can tell by just looking at you. You know, you're never going to pass for twenty-one anymore.'

They talked about the Med, the war, about submarines, about the men, a bit about the future and a lot about the past and then Shrimp got onto a subject that he'd been holding back on because it was delicate; about the Captain S of Twelfth Flotilla, the Bonny Boy Bonalleck, and the bloody mess concerning Lt Harry Gilmour RNVR, the CO of

HMS *Scourge*. Rear Adm Barry said, 'I was wondering when we were going to get around to that,' and then he listened.

The rear admiral had seen the signals; all Bonalleck's ranting about this young skipper, calling for disciplinary inquiries, reprimands, everything short of some official issuing of a white feather. But he hadn't heard the background Chief Petty Officer Gault had supplied to Shrimp during their quiet chat in the Lazaretto. About the ramming of *Pelorus* and Bonalleck's drunkenness. And what the boat's only other surviving officer – the then Sub Lt Gilmour – had told Bonalleck to his face. Barry had laughed at that, no humour in it though, just a dry, sardonic bark. 'I can think of quite a few far more senior officers who'd have jumped at the opportunity to tell him that, even today,' he said. 'What's C-in-C Med's response been?'

'Nothing firm. To date,' said Shrimp. 'He's just asked for clarification. I got the impression he knew nothing about this op to kill Kesselring. Also, I suppose to be charitable, he's been a bit busy guarding Monty's seaward flank.'

Barry didn't look impressed, 'Ah, poor old Henry Harwood. Lovely chap, heart like a lion, but when it comes to mastering the complexities of a fleet command, no one would ever accuse him of being a titan. I'm sure he thinks the paperwork will go away if he stares at it long enough. I'll raise it with him when I get out there. This has all the hallmarks of one of those stinks that can very easily get out of hand if it's not pinched off right away. You were right to raise it, George. This young skipper of yours sounds quite a fellow. And we all know what most sensible folk think about the Bonny Boy.'

'Most. Yes,' said Shrimp with a sigh. 'But the navy isn't a democracy. And Captain Bonalleck has friends who outrank even you.'

Eight

Harry had put on his only white dress shirt and a pair of uniform blue trousers for *Scourge's* return to Malta, and he'd told the rest of the crew to smarten up too.

It was a beautiful day with not a cloud in the sky, and the sun was starting to get hot. The island languished long and low along the horizon ahead, like a bleached stone crust on the blue, blue sea. He was on the bridge with Harding and McCready and four lookouts, one of them being the yeoman, Dickie Bird, to whom fell the honour of tending to the boat's now much-cluttered Jolly Roger. There was a new dagger for all the work with the partisans, quite a few white chevrons for all the small trading craft Hooper had dispatched with his three-incher and a scatter of dynamite sticks with fuses for the ones they'd sunk by demolition charge. But no flat white or red bars for freighters or warships torpedoed.

Everybody had heeded the skipper's instructions, and Harry was quietly pleased with the way they'd all brushed up. Even the stick of five ratings manning the forward casing had managed to scrounge enough sets of whites to fit out all of them. Standing in a perfect row, at ease with hands clasped behind their backs, they actually managed to look proper naval.

Some change from the days of the siege when you had to slink back in between air raids.

There were other changes from the days of the siege.

For a start, the press of shipping arriving and departing Valletta.

The approaches to both the Grand Harbour and Marsamxett, where Harry was conning *Scourge,* had a queue of them: two arriving transports, each of them ten thousand-tonners; a small flotilla of minesweepers coming out and curving round to sortie north, a gaggle of motor gunboats that looked like they might be on permanent guard and the motor gunboat that had been sent out to escort *Scourge* in. Harry had already remarked how far out had been set their rendezvous point, but when he scanned the sky over the island, he began to understand. There were a lot of aircraft around. At least two transports in a holding pattern out over what must be Takali airfield, and when he looked up, two loose-deuces of Spitfires making their standing patrols in long, lazy circles at about ten thousand feet, one almost overhead and the other away to the north. You'd have thought with the war in its third year, the RAF would have got over its fixation for attacking their own submarines, but they hadn't. Which was why the gunboat was here to swat away any over-curious flyboys with itchy trigger fingers.

Even though they couldn't quite see into Valletta harbour proper, you could tell the place was chock-a-block with shipping. Harry could see that everybody on the bridge and on the casing was goofing off at this grandstand view their long approach on the surface was granting them, gawping at the sheer size of the military monster that had dumped itself on their little island, of the build-up now taking place. And it had only been three weeks since they'd sailed. Harry had the sense they were returning to the real war now, from what had just been a sideshow, a playground scrap. It made him feel very small, and all their recent triumphs and disasters up there in the Adriatic seem insignificant footnotes to the big show. Still, it was nice to be back, and he could tell from the tangible frisson running through the boat that everybody else felt the same way.

None of this had changed his resolve to speak to Shrimp.

*

'Call me Hutch. Everybody else does,' said this long, slim, schoolmasterly figure in his immaculate whites, including socks and blanco-ed shoes, lowering himself into the floral armchair next to Harry.

He raised his glass. 'Ice for the gin, eh! We didn't have that last time you were in.'

Harry didn't know him from Adam, but here he was, Cdr Christopher Hutchinson, Tenth Flotilla's Commander S, its second-in-command.

They were on the gallery, which had long served as the Lazaretto's wardroom, and it was jam-packed with bodies. And not just naval officers, there were a lot of khaki bodies distributed about, and it was standing room only. Hutch had had to pull rank to get the chairs, and even though Harry was just in from patrol, he caught a few sniffy looks from out the corner of his eye. Bloody ignorant set of bastards! Who the hell did they think they were? Harry certainly hadn't a clue. He hadn't recognised a single face in the whole throng. And some of the army chaps had looked decidedly dodgy characters. 'Oh they're just special forces bods,' Hutch had explained when he saw Harry looking askance. 'They're billeted just across the yard in the old fort, so they've been given squatters' rights here for the time being.'

He meant Fort Manoel, which was no longer a pile of bomb debris.

All part of the renovations. Just like the Lazaretto, which he'd noticed in the short time he'd been here before getting packed off to the Adriatic. The old building had acquired all sorts of luxuries like electric lighting, more tables and chairs, like the ones they were sitting on, doors and proper walls and cabins again. Nothing was like the old days. Not even the faces. None of these new Tenth Flotilla officers could he put a name to, so not surprising really, that there had been no row of familiar faces lining the gallery to hurl the usual friendly abuse as he'd come ashore across the pontoons. There was one of them there apparently, who was even younger than he was now. Or so Hutch had told him as they'd shoved their way from the bar – the new bar – to claim their seats. 'Johnny Roxburgh, he's got *United*. You're no longer the new kid on the block, as the Yanks say.'

And there had been no Shrimp.

The man who had received him in the flotilla's offices had been a tall, stern figure, with luxuriant black hair and a crisp way about him, in his equally crisp whites. Captain George Philips DSO, Tenth Flotilla's new Captain S. Harry had never met him before but knew about him. He'd won his DSO for sinking the Jerry light cruiser *Liepzig* in 1940, but he was even more famous for being the 'inventor' of the Ursula suit, which took its name from his then command, the U-class boat HMS *Ursula*. Well, fancy that, he was Harry's hero. Oh, how Harry had loved his Ursula suit. However, he stopped himself from saying as much, thinking, correctly, *I bet he's heard that before.*

Harry had delivered his report and handed over Warrant Engineer Bert Petrie's maintenance log which he knew did not make reassuring reading. That Harry had barely been troubled by any technical problems on the patrol had all been down to Petrie's expertise in the good old fashioned Royal Navy lash-up. *Scourge* had been out here a long time without a refit. She was, as they say, knackered. But Bert Petrie was old in the ways of making engines work even if they'd decided they didn't want to anymore.

Capt Philips had taken Harry through his report methodically, asked several pertinent questions and concurred with most of his operational decisions. Including giving him a ringing endorsement of his co-operation with Major Drobnjac. 'It is my understanding that relations with Tito's forces are about to get ratcheted up,' he'd explained. 'When it comes to killing Germans, Marshal Tito appears to be the one killing more of them. So he is going to be our man. Your handling of what could have turned out to be a sticky situation I am sure will have gone a long way to easing that process, Mr Gilmour, and I shall certainly be saying so in my report.'

Which was nice. And a lot better than Harry had had served up to him by the Bonny Boy. But Harry's antenna had not been on receive to appreciate it. He'd come ashore wanting to talk to Shrimp, and he'd got this bloke. Someone he did not know and who did not know him.

They moved on to Harry's list of citation recommendations, topped by a DSM – Distinguished Service Medal – for Hooper, and not a few Mentions in Dispatches. 'I'll pass them up,' the Captain S had said.

Harry had by then been only half-listening. His plan to unburden himself was no longer an option. He felt stumped as to what to do next.

'Now, as to *Scourge's* status with the Tenth,' said Capt Philips, shuffling some notes on Shrimp's old desk. 'There doesn't appear to be any official order here, rescinding your temporary transfer to the Twelfth Flotilla.' He'd looked up, smiling, 'But then Captain Simpson and I missed each other by three days, so we had no time to do a handover. However, from glancing through this,' he said, gesturing to Petrie's log, 'I'd say it was high time you booked your boat in for a spot of dry-docking. By the time you're ready to come out again, I'm sure we'll have worked out whether *Scourge* is back here to stay, or you're back off to Algiers.'

Then Capt Philips had had some things to say about the six torpedoes Harry had fired at that convoy. He had commented on the range: 'Three thousand yards? That was a long shot. You couldn't get any closer?' And he had listened to Harry's description of the MAS-boats handling. 'Given that there was a lot of trade up and down the coast, was it worth it to have gone ahead with the attack?' Capt Philips had asked, then he'd given his hands a little wiggle, 'A fine judgement that, best left to the man on the spot, I suppose. But good for you, you made the decision to go for it. If you'd got lucky, it would've been doubles all round, eh? Now, those lengths of painted bamboo,' said Captain Philips, a fiendish glint creeping into his eyes. 'How did you get on with them? Anybody actually fooled?'

Harry shrugged, 'I'm afraid I can't answer that, sir. We never hung around long enough. But I thought Grieve's idea was worth the shot. I really would have loved to have seen some of those dizzy merchantmen running themselves aground out of fright at the sight of one of his bobbing sticks.'

Captain Philips let out a bark of laughter, 'Couldn't agree more. I see you've put down Grieve for a mention in dispatches. I'll happily approve that.'

'Thank you, sir,' said Harry. The whole boat will be happy about that.'

'And about your last patrol report…'

Harry felt his stomach lurch. What was coming now?

'…Flag officer, submarines passed through while you were on patrol. He asked me to tell he'd been made aware of your recommendation that your navigator, Lieutenant Harding be awarded the Distinguished Service Cross.'

Harry breathed again, 'Yes, sir. It was requested that citation should be verbal, on security grounds.'

Meaning nobody had wanted it known publicly, the background as to why he was putting Harding up for the gong for his little run ashore on occupied Sicily and the deft way he'd managed to nab that Jerry intelligence officer and the entire Jerry order of battle for southern Italy.

'Yes,' said Captain Philips, with a certain resignation. 'Well, the FOS got the details from Mr Wincairns. Interesting chap. The upshot is the award is approved. You can tell Lieutenant Harding the paperwork's on the way.' And then it had been, 'Thank you for a concise report, Mr Gilmour, and it is a pleasure to have you back aboard the Tenth, even if it's only for the time being.'

And then Hutch had taken him into the wardroom for a drink – somebody had to, after all, he was a skipper newly returned from patrol. What was the Commander S supposed to do, leave him standing in a corner studying his fingernails while all these wretched COPP team ruffians commandeered all the sofas? The poor chap looked completely disoriented. In his own wardroom, after all. I mean to say! The next thing he knew, Harry had shot to his feet. 'John!' he was shouting. When Hutch looked round, there was the wardroom steward emerging from a press of officers; that Maltese chap who'd been here forever, apparently.

The steward looked stunned that someone was shouting his name, then recognition and a shout of his own, 'Mr Gilmour!' and he started waving with one hand and trying to balance his tray with the other. In the next moment, Hutch was treated to the somewhat unseemly spectacle of the two men hugging.

*

119

Letters – from the handwriting, he could tell the senders easily. There were three from his mother, two from the last tailor he'd used in Portsmouth, one from old Lexie Scrimgeour, Sir Alexander himself, the Edinburgh financier on whose twelve-metre yacht he used to crew as a schoolboy. And even one from Shirley. He felt the envelope. It was as if there was no substance to it at all. But, all sealed up, he could have no idea what it contained.

He was lying on an old second-hand single bed, tucked into a CO's cabin that had been newly hewn out of the rock at the back of the Lazaretto. The cabin should have been single occupancy, but with the press of bodies now in the wardroom, space was at even more of a premium than when he'd sailed the last time. Hutch had told him he was lucky they weren't squeezing in three to a cabin these days. His fellow skipper in this one, however, was out on patrol, so he had it to himself for now.

The tailor's letters were for unpaid bills for uniforms that now lay shredded somewhere under piles of rubble, probably quite close by. Not that it mattered, he realised; he was still liable for the merchandise. He smiled to himself, considering how alarmed such a missive would have left him if he'd still been a student. Funny how preoccupations change. He certainly didn't grudge the money; if he'd still had a cheque book, he would have posted one off right away. But he hadn't a clue in what bomb crater that cheque book's burnt cinders now resided. They'd just have to haul him off to debtors' prison, which would be a lot safer than here, he reflected ruefully, and probably a bit more comfortable. He did resolve, however, to write the tailor a letter. He was sure he wasn't their first young gentleman to find himself constrained by exigencies of war from settling an account.

He turned to Old Lexie's letter, in his copperplate hand. Fondly asking after his welfare, congratulating him on his medals, expressing pride, confiding his hope that the sextant he'd presented to Harry departing for sea was still rendering sterling service – it wasn't, he'd locked it up safe in his personal trunk back at Fort Blockhouse – and finishing off with an entreaty that, once all this was over, would he, Harry, consider making his civilian career in the Scrimgeour finance empire.

Harry had to pause, with the letter lying on his chest for a moment. The concept of a life after the war was too big for him to get his head round right away. Could such a thing come to pass? Especially one where he would be invited to breathe the rarefied atmosphere of the House of Scrimgeour. The chaps who worked for old Lexie before the war usually ended up being able to afford yachts of their own. He laughed at that. There was a notion to kick about in times of quiet reflection.

His mother wrote like she spoke. Reading the words was like hearing her voice, right down to the quiet inflections and all the pauses she loved to leave. Close his eyes and he could even see her arch looks and her smiles. The letters told the story of home, except it wasn't the home he remembered. The house she talked about was now full of the noise of the three evacuee children, his father's presence on the pages was no longer like some grim cauldron simmering in the background, all that pain of war. The children ran his life now, ruled his moods, or rather had banished them. The bedtime stories, the amateur dramatics, from scripts he'd write for them to the sewing of costumes and building of sets. The banging and the laughter and how his entire existence had returned and been completely taken up with them – especially the little one, Maggie – how everything the children did now appeared to dominate his parents' lives. From their inventiveness in the face of rationing to the visits of the mother, and what his mother didn't say about those or about the woman herself. A whole world going on where he didn't feature, wasn't part of it. The letters evoked a melancholy feeling of estrangement in him, as he pored slowly over each line. The final act of leaving home, he supposed. The letters made him smile too because of the happiness that shone out of his mother's stories. He could tell she missed him and worried for him. But she and his father were obviously having a new life now. *And good for you*, he thought to himself, as he folded the last one and put it away; *good things should happen to good people, at least every now and again.*

Shirley's letter he would leave for later. He didn't want to read it here. He wanted to read with the sky above him and the sun shining down and the sea twinkling all the way to the horizon so that he could imagine she was sitting beside him, no matter what it was she was about to say. The envelope he held was utterly inscrutable. It made him think of the letters he used to get from Janis, doused in Chanel. And all the winks and lewd guffaws in the wardroom every time one was delivered. Now, that had been funny. That cheered him up. That afternoon, another boat returned from patrol, and Harry ambled down to the wardroom for the bash. Another of the new U-class boats, not long out from Blighty, her skipper a proper up-and-down and squared-away RN lieutenant, just in from his latest Mediterranean war patrol – a lot of brisk gun actions and some vandalism to the rail network south of Naples and he was full of it. In the press of bodies, Harry had been introduced. 'Sorry? Harry, is it? Pleased to meet you,' he shouted above the din. 'Haven't seen you here before. You're new. Ah. Well. A word to the wise. Before you go out on patrol, I strongly recommend you get yourself down to the travel section. That last S10 left this collection of inshore pilotage notes for Eyetie yachtsmen... Capitano Massimo's Guido di Mare to Reefs Best Not To Hit, or whatever the title translates as... because whoever did the translation did a bloody good job. I really recommend you have a good read at them. Invaluable they are… if you intend going inshore,' the last words delivered in the tones of one who knew all about 'going inshore'. Harry just smiled appreciatively.

He left it until the hour before sunset to go for his walk. He'd go and see Louis the bookseller tomorrow, after all, *Scourge* was going to be here a couple of weeks while they tweaked her up over at the dry dock, it wasn't as if there'd be any danger he'd miss him. Out towards his favourite café, over Sliema way, he found a stretch between the road and the beach barbed-wire entanglements, and he sat down overlooking the sea to read Shirley's letter.

'*Dear You*,' it started. Harry smiled at that. No endearments. He hadn't expected any. It wasn't as if they were going out together, as she'd spelled out the last time she'd seen him. Shirley, the girl he'd known since they were both at school. Except Harry hadn't really known her at school, she was just the wayward banshee from two years below whom everyone said was using her upper-class pedigree to get away with murder. Then he had come home on his survival leave after *Pelorus* had gone down and discovered everyone had been wrong. It had been Shirley, the apprentice woman with the level gaze and pre-Raphaelite explosion of chestnut hair, who all along had simply just been refusing to suffer fools.

And then it had been Shirley the ambulance driver; and then Shirley, the woman cruelly patronised – by him. And finally, Shirley, his lover; although he wasn't allowed to call her that because she was buggered if she was going to come out of this war another weeping wraith in widow's threads because, as he'd told her himself, the chop rate in his line of work was off the scale.

'After the war, if we're both still here, we'll see!' At least that was what she'd told him, back then.

Her letter opened with brief news of life in wartime Glasgow, driving an ambulance and a line about how the job was a continuing reminder to her of the necessity to keep being a grown-up about everything that happened, in order to cope with it. She thought she was in danger of becoming wise in the ways of the world, which was probably no bad thing.

And then she wrote, '...*and then I go and read something like Emily Dickinson and I think of you. Do you know Emily Dickinson's poetry? Do you know this one?* Wild nights – wild nights! Were I with thee, wild nights should be our luxury! Futile – the winds – to a Heart in port – done with the Compass – done with the Chart. Rowing in Eden – ah – the Sea! Might I but moor – tonight – In thee! *And I don't want to be wise any more. I realise I am getting tired of being wise.*'

Harry sat on the rock, hunched over her letter like some unfinished Rodin, pretending to be reading it again but thinking only about the hardness of the stone beneath him until he noticed the little splash on the paper. There was a moment before he realised it was a tear, before he acknowledged that feeling, that ache in his breast, of the sailor yearning for the land. For home. For his love.

Nine

Harry watched the chart table chronometer as it ticked towards 2400 hours. The hands aligned, and it was, at last, the 10th of July.

'Periscope depth,' he ordered, and up crept *Scourge*, nosing at a steady three knots on 290 degrees. Beneath his feet, he could feel the deck plates begin to rise and fall. There had been a brisk nor'-westerly force seven blowing upstairs when they had dived a few hours after sunset, after fixing their position for the final time, and you could feel the effect of the waves now, even down here at twenty-seven feet. Harry shuddered to think what it was going to be like for all those poor bloody pongos crammed into landing craft on a night like this. *All aboard for the vomit comet!* wasn't in it. And now it was time for *Scourge* to come up and join the bump and grind.

'Asdic. How's it looking up top?' he said, stepping forward, ready to order the periscope up.

Biddle's voice came from the cuddy, 'Same, sir. Multiple HE astern. Some way off and passing from port to starboard. Too many targets for individual identification. No HE from green one one zero through the stern to red zero nine five. The sea is clear from both quarters for'ard, sir.'

'Thanks, Biddle, up periscope!'

Harry wasn't in a good mood. What they were about to do was at once damned tedious and bloody dangerous. They were the designated picket boat and outer marker for the western landing force. And the darker band of a *now-you-see-it-now-you-don't* break in the line between dark sea and night sky that he was looking at right now, was the southern coast of Sicily.

It was a foul night, and once he'd made sure there was nothing but the bloody awful sea state to worry him, Harry called, 'Surface!' And the outside wrecker's hands danced over the dive board to send them up. They had been at red light for an hour now, so the lookouts, when they got up, would have no trouble in spotting anything Harry might have missed through the 'scope. *Scourge* was already bow on to the oncoming seas, and Harry ordered a birdbath to be rigged once the lookouts had clambered up into the conning tower. *Scourge* gave one last lurch, and they were up, and the lump of water that now dumped itself into the control room told everybody the lookouts must have opened the upper hatch and were on the bridge. Harry wasn't going up, it was Farrar's watch, and anyway, Harry knew he'd be able to see bugger all in the pitch black of a near gale.

Harry looked at Harding's plot on the chart for the umpteenth time – the tiny scratch of *Scourge's* progress, five miles sou'-sou'-west of Licata. Their orders lay tucked into the rack at the back of the chart table should Harry need to refresh his memory – highly unlikely since there wasn't much to memorise, and he practically knew them by heart now anyway.

Farrar's tinny voice was in the voicepipe, his first words lost in the bangs of *Scourge's* diesels exploding to life, '…Actually, I think the wind is abating a little, sir. Sea is clear to the south and west, but looking aft, from the top of the wave crests… I can make out the bulk of a mass of shipping… it's pretty bloody dark up here… a lot of muck about, sir, but I think I can see the cloud starting to clear from dead ahead.'

Scourge was running roughly parallel to the coast, and the force seven, or what was left of it, was coming right at them from the opposite direction.

'What's happening onshore, Number One?'

'There are two coastal searchlights doing sweeps to seaward. And away inland, to the north-east, there are flashes along the horizon. Looks like a bombing raid in progress, sir… That's the lights rigged now, sir, you can illuminate them any time.'

Harry glanced at the chronometer; it was too early. Another hour at least before they lit up their line of coded navigation lights, now, presumably garlanding *Scourge's* bridge. Between them and the radio beacon they would shortly switch on, all the ships in the western landing force would know exactly where the left flank boundary lay for their run into the beaches. For that was to be *Scourge's* role tonight, reduced to playing mother hen to the huge clump of ships astern of them that formed the American contribution to Operation Husky – the Allied invasion of Sicily.

They'd all been watching the build-up on Malta for these landings for a few weeks now.

Admittedly, right after they'd come in from patrol and the crew had been packed off to the submariners' rest camp up at Ghjan Tuffieha Bay, that build-up had been no more to them than a dust cloud to the south and lots of noise.

While their boat had been in dry dock on the other side of Grand Harbour having her elastic bands re-tensioned and her bum wiped.

But when she'd come out and they'd all been trucked back to the Lazaretto to work on her and make her ready for sea again, trialling all the fixes and repairs, bedding in the updated Asdics and radio gear, it had been like walking into the middle of Piccadilly Circus. You couldn't step out the main gate at Fort Manoel without taking your life in your hands, not because of Me109s anymore, but all the bloody traffic on the roads. Quite simply, the island was full up. Practically every empty field you used to pass, every spare clump of derelict ground you remembered, there was a tarpaulin-covered dump on it now. Even Valletta's narrow streets were jammed with an endless, slow-moving crush of military uniforms swamping the poor civilians trying to go about their daily business. Harry even had to wait in queues for a dghaisa to row him across the harbour to Valletta when he went to visit Louis the bookseller.

On the upside, however, no one was hungry anymore – you hardly saw a child that wasn't stuffing American chocolate in its face, and the island was practically awash in American PX beer.

The big boys were all here too. Every day, someone in the wardroom was breathlessly recounting a sighting of Montgomery or Eisenhower or even Mountbatten, to the extent that Harry often found himself wondering if any of these top brass were actually doing any work down in that huge bunker that had been carved out underneath the Lascaris battery. And, of course, everyone knew what it was all for, despite all the endless blather about secrecy, where all this mountain of men and materiel was headed. It was Sicily.

The only thing folk didn't know was when. Then one day, the destroyer flotillas and the big US Navy cruisers of the naval gunnery support groups began slipping their moorings and queuing up to leave Grand Harbour, and they had their answer to even that.

In less than twenty-four hours, the Lazaretto wardroom had all but emptied; all the COPP teams and the submarine crews that would carry them were gone. Harry had been reclining in a huge armchair on the wardroom gallery, luxuriating in the warmth of the afternoon, in the peace and quiet, savouring a cup of truly excellent coffee when Hutch had come up and said, 'Harry, can you chase up your number one and navigator and report to the Captain S in ten. He wants to see you.'

And that had been when *Scourge* was handed her sailing orders.

Harry remembered he'd been feeling left out. Over the previous days, he'd watched a daisy chain of Tenth Flotilla officers traipse off down to Lascaris for their briefings, so where was his look at the big wall map with all the marker pen scribbles and all the folders full of call signs and radio frequencies and challenge-and-response codes? But he hadn't said anything.

But his call to action had come, at last.

Capt Philips must have noticed the look on Harry's face. 'I know,' he'd said. 'It's last minute.' And he'd slipped a signal flimsy across the desk to Harry. It was marked '*Western Naval Task Force, Staff of Vice Adm H.K. Hewitt USN, Naval Commander*', and it was from '*RN Submarine LO*', which Harry recognised as being the Royal Navy submarine liaison officer. In other words, one of ours, attached to one of theirs.

Apparently, according to the typed document, Vice Adm Hewitt had wanted an additional tripwire pushed out a bit further on his left flank. Everybody had agreed; they'd feel more comfortable. However, the boat that got assigned the position wouldn't actually be the task force's western boundary marker, more a sort of back-up boundary marker, in case anybody wandered over the real one by accident. Or at least that was what the signal was suggesting. Oh, and they were to act as an outer picket too – in case any nasties tried to creep down the coast and get in among the landing craft. In which case they were to shout, 'Help!' and there were a couple of US Navy destroyer flotillas on hand to rush out and clean up. And maybe the boat could act as 'plane guard' too and be on standby to pick up any fliers who ended up in the drink. Underneath the main blurb had been a handwritten scrawl, '*Request Scourge. She's worked with 12 Flott. covering boats.*' It was signed off, '*SLO*' – the submarine liaison officer. In other words, based on *Scourge's* short, temporary, deployment to Twelfth Flotilla – the Bonny Boy's bloody mob – she was going to be 'it'.

Marvellous.

Harry had felt a cold chill in his belly just reading the innocuous little scrap.

They would be right out at the sharp end of the entire landing force. Right at the point of the threat. Which meant they would not only be the first ones to meet any oncoming enemy, they would also be surrounded by their own side's trigger-happy warship gunners and aircraft, all of them looking for targets, especially U-boats which in the dark, could look uncomfortably like *Scourge*. And they were a last-minute add-on to the main plan.

'Who is the SLO attached to this Hewitt chap's staff, sir?' asked Harry, not sure if he really wanted to hear the answer.

'Can't tell you,' Philips had said, looking even more disgruntled.

'That's a secret, sir?' asked Harry.

'No,' sighed Philips. 'That's an "I-don't-know".'

Philips obviously wasn't enjoying being kept in the dark either. Eventually, he said, 'Look, I wouldn't worry. Now that ABC's turned up here on Malta, and he's running the whole naval end now, I'm sure everything will have been sorted out.'

'ABC', the fleet's nickname for Admiral Sir Andrew Browne Cunningham. The former C-in-C Mediterranean, now back again for the next big show. Of course he was.

And if anyone was going to have to do any sorting out, he was the boy to do it.

The news had made Harry feel a lot better.

Meanwhile, Harding had collected the co-ordinates for *Scourge's* patrol box and Farrar had begun shuffling through all the call signs and radio frequencies to make sure everything was there. There had even been a couple of ship recognition silhouettes, for the USS *Biscayne* and the USS *Monrovia*. He'd shown them to Harry. *Biscayne* Harry had recognised as one of those late-1930s small seaplane tenders the US Navy had – no more than 2,500 tons and now being converted into a command and control ship. But *Monrovia* had looked like one of their big assault transports, except with the landing craft davits replaced by a regular forest of radio masts, another one of these new amphibious warfare command ships the Yanks were turning out.

'*Monrovia* is Admiral Hewitt's flagship and command ship for the whole western task force,' Philips had explained. 'This is so you'll recognise her if you see her. Her call sign and frequency are all in your orders. *Biscayne* is the command ship for JOSS beach, which is the westernmost and so will be nearest to you. All the timings are there… for when you light up your guide beacons and when you switch on the radio beacon. But from what I understand, be prepared to never see a soul. All the assault ships will be lining up on the boat, acting as main guide submarine. She will be *Tobermory*, and she'll be in a lot closer to the beach. You've just to be there like the faithful sheepdog, making sure anyone who wanders off gets swept back again and pointed in the right direction.'

'What could possibly go wrong,' Harry had said, with his old laconic, lop-sided grin, which neither Farrar nor Harding had seen for a while.

'Indeed, Mr Gilmour,' Philips had said, returning his grin. 'What could?'

And now, they were here, on station and watching the clock for it all to begin.

*

Captain Charles Bonalleck RN was now working out of that big villa just back from the Algiers Corniche where Ike once had his headquarters. But Ike wasn't there anymore; he was with all the other brass on Malta for the duration of Husky, chumming it up with Monty and Patton and Mountbatten and Cunningham and all the other truckloads of generals, admirals and air marshals that followed them around, winning the war with their maps and timetables and lines-of-communication schedules. And there too, just for Ike, that knowing little piece of posh Anglo-Irish skirt, Kay Summersby, his British Army driver.

Captain Bonalleck didn't approve of any of them. However, having them somewhere else, halfway down the Med, didn't just suit his easily offended sensibilities, it played so well into his plan.

And right now, his plan was about to unfold.

He was sitting in his office in the big villa, in the dark. Outside, through the wide-open shuttered windows was a garden noisy with crickets and the sounds of vehicles drifting over the high walls. It wasn't long after moonset, and if he swivelled his chair, he could look out at a framed riot of stars. He could feel the caressing warmth of the night seeping into his old bones. A gulp from the brandy balloon and a different heat spread out from his belly. On the table behind him was a flimsy, single sheet of paper, and written on it was the order that would finally fix that jumped up, little wavy-navy wonderboy.

All thanks to the Yanks. It had been so easy to win their confidence. All he'd had to do was flash them his rank and his maroon Victoria Cross medal ribbon, and they'd assumed they were dealing with a big shot. Not just any old flotilla CO. After that, all he'd had to do was always be on hand with the offer of sage advice and a few pertinent suggestions, and suddenly, he was their go-to guy. So that when the SLO billet needed filling, he was the guy they'd gone to. The rest had just been shuffling the paperwork.

He'd never have got away with it though if there had been an actual centralised command for Husky. Yes, they called their command structure 'centralised', but in reality, the actual staffs were dotted all over the Med. The main operation HQ might be in that hole on Malta, but there were subsidiary HQs in all the embarkation ports from Bizerte to here, in Algiers.

And for his purposes, here was the place to be because here was where that spiky little Lt Gen Carl Spaatz had his tent, from where he ran all the USAAF fighters and bombers that would be covering the Western Task Force. And just down the road in Tunis was where that task force had finally to set sail from.

So, HQs here, HQs there, and anyone who knew anything about staff work would know a lot of paperwork could get lost between here and there and the hole on Malta.

He remembered thinking that, while all of this had still been just a notion coalescing, while his own plan was just a germ of an idea.

The other thing he knew about planning: it was such an unforgiving mistress.

For an amphibious operation like Husky, it was all about getting your ducks in a row. One long list after another long list, lined up, all in sequence. And break that sequence and the whole lot falls apart.

Just imagine all those tanks and trucks and shells and ration packs they all had to get loaded onto the transports in the right order. First on, last off. Then all the ships carrying all the different arms had to get lined up so they arrived off the beach in the right order. And before they even got there, all the minesweepers that had to have gone ahead, clearing their paths to the disembarkation areas, and the ships from the shore bombardment groups that would have to be escorted up to their gun lines.

And even before all that, there were the submarines. His job, to see they went in first, there to act as navigation beacons, there to guide the guides, to point the way to each designated beach so that the right battalions went ashore in the right places, and all their follow-on ammunition and k-ration packs and their supporting tanks and artillery too, all having to arrive in the right order on the right beach.

Without the submarines, nobody would know where they were supposed to go.

And if he shut his eyes, he could imagine the beaches as the sun came up and the Air Force arriving overhead. All they'd see was fire and confusion, which, of course, was why they'd have been in on the plan from the start, all those pilots, screaming in at over 200mph, needing to have some idea where they were supposed to be dropping their bombs and where to point their guns and when to pull the triggers.

All those recognition codes that would have to be agreed, the codes tapped out in morse, broadcast in voice, the flares and coloured smoke, all so that when the planes came over, the poor bastards on the ground and on the ships could tell them, 'We're friendlies!' and, 'Don't shoot!' And the pilots, all of them having studied all the codes beforehand for weeks on end, would stay their fire. And, of course, they would all already know their ship recognition charts off by heart, having studied them also, for months on end – pages and pages of silhouettes, our ships and their ships. Or at least, that was how it was supposed to unfold.

Except, someone with Captain Bonalleck's experience knew that it never did, something he was counting on to help his own little scheme along.

But he never said so, when he was touting himself for the job. He'd just let it be known that he understood what it took to make a plan come together. And his ploy had worked.

He got the job as SLO, one of the team, there to make sure everybody got the right codes and knew who everyone was and where they were supposed to be. And he had been meticulous. The quality of his staff work had been obvious from the word go. All his new American buddies said so. This was one campaign he wasn't going to lose because of bad paperwork, he told them.

So that even in the confusion of the final days and hours, in the frenzy of all the last-minute updates and corrections and supplementary orders, he made sure every scrap of paper that passed across his desk got the right stamp, had the right heading and went into the right inbox. All except the one sitting on his desk behind him, that when he finished his brandy, he was going to set light to with the burning end of his cigarette.

'Hey Chuck!' a beery American accent echoed in from the corridor behind him. 'C'mon, man. We're all in the map room. Curtain's about to go up. You wouldn't want to miss it now.' Which, of course, he would not. He reached back and picked up the piece of paper and holding it in one hand, he blew on the lit end of his Lucky Strike, courtesy of the local PX. And then he touched the cigarette to the paper's corner. He watched the flame take hold and creep across, consuming all the words, one by one, until it reached the word *Scourge*, and then he crushed it in the ashtray and strode purposefully to the door. As he closed it behind him, his face met the little name plaque nailed there: '*Capt C. Bonalleck RN… Senior Submarine Liaison Officer, Western Task Force*'.

*

135

At 0030 hours, Grieve called from the wireless cubby, 'That's the radio nets up, sir!'

Until then, radio silence had enfolded the entire task force – the one last exercise in trying to cloak the approach from a prying enemy. Now all the wireless sets in all the ships were turned on, the call signs announced their presence and the airwaves filled with morse and chatter.

At shortly before 0040 hours, Farrar called down to say that he'd sighted *Tobermory's* beacon lights inshore. Harry sent *Scourge* to diving stations, then announced to nobody in particular, 'Rightly ho! Let's switch on the Blackpool illuminations.'

The temporary trips in the control room were closed, and *Scourge's* beacon lights on the aft end of the conning tower lit up. Farrar confirmed it down the voicepipe.

Harry walked back to the wireless cubby and asked Grieve what was happening.

'*Biscayne* and *Monrovia* have both challenged, and I have confirmed we are on station, sir. Even exchanged a quick "good morning" with Warbler, sir. Do you want to say hello?'

Harry frowned, 'Warbler…? Ah. *Tobermory's* call sign. And we're Atlas. Um. No, it's all right, Grieve. Don't want to jam things up with too much chat.'

'Aye, aye, sir. Will let you know immediately if there's any traffic for us,' said Grieve, smiling and looking the very epitome of relaxed, with one earphone off his ear and the other on, signal pads and pencils all laid out before him and the big set and all its dials glowing and humming away on the desk. It was as if he was sitting down to challenge some mechanical quiz machine or some wall-mounted bagatelle in a fairground booth. Not a hint of all those ships and men out there, beyond, in the dark, getting ready to fling themselves at the enemy.

Harry smiled back, wondering why the chap wasn't a gibbering wreck, indeed, why *he* wasn't one. He decided it was time he went upstairs, but not before he'd got Windass to fill him two flasks of that coffee, that brew from heaven they'd bagged in Algiers.

Clutching the flasks in one hand, he climbed up onto the bridge into the warm, humid air and smelled the land in one huge fecund draught. He presented Farrar with his coffee and gazed around him, soaking up the clearing sky. The night was full of the distant thrum of aero engines. With *Scourge's* diesels just burbling along, pushing her at a stately two knots while topping up the charge, it was easy to hear them. Harry put his face to the wind. It was no more than force three now, which would make it less of a torment for the troops sardined into their landing craft, rolling across a beam sea for the beaches. A long way down the coast, a couple of searchlights onshore were dancing around like wands in the hands of someone having a slow-motion fit.

'The moon's just set, sir,' said Farrar. 'You missed it. It was quite a sight. Just one continuous overlapping silhouette of ships, right along the horizon.'

'A bloke in a pub told me there are apparently seventeen hundred of them in the western group alone if you count all the landing craft,' said Harry, cupping the mug he'd decanted his coffee into, and sipping.

Farrar couldn't help a little smile, 'Well, of course the bloke in the pub's bound to know. But not quite accurate, sir, if you ask me. Seventeen hundred and one to be right on the button, if you're counting us, which the bloke in the bloke in the pub wouldn't be, since even we only heard yesterday, and you wouldn't have told him, on account of security. Loose lips sink ships.'

Harry smiled back. Christ, was Number One developing a sense of humour?

Even though the beacon lights on the back of the conning tower were closely shaded, you could still see the beam of them dancing on the rolling waves. But with the wind down now, the white tops had all but disappeared; there were no more foaming crests to reflect the light and cause it to glitter. *Scourge* was bow-on to the shore now, and it was a sudden ripple of flashes from the starboard beam that swung everyone round to look. A wave of rolling thunder followed. The naval gunnery had opened up.

They watched the shells go home in the distance, landing in the huge, featureless shadowy mass that was the land – clumps of blossoming smoke and debris, clustering round their targets in what looked like great vertical spills of black paint on grey-black canvas, and the cracks and booms that followed, and the sudden pressure in the air from the concussions, even at this range. The sight was mesmerising and unreal in the dark, without any contour or the shape of a hill or town or village hiding in the blackness to give it any context. Harry watched for what seemed an age. When he dragged his eyes away and looked further to the east, he could see a band of light now, creeping over the inky line of the horizon. Sunrise was on its way.

Harry turned and dropped down the conning tower hatch. When he hit the deck plates, Harding was at the chart table, minding the plot, making sure *Scourge* kept inside her patrol box. The control room was still in red light, and the smile Harding gave Harry looked like a maniac's rictus.

'Sounds like they're getting busy upstairs, sir,' Harding said. But Harry, as if unable to process what he'd just been witnessing, found himself speechless. He just blew out air and shook his head before taking the handful of steps through the aft door and into the wireless cubby.

A telegraphist, whose name Harry couldn't quite remember, was sitting hunched in the far corner with a headset scrunched over his ears and a pencil in hand. Sitting next to him was Grieve, his headset still had one ear covered and the other clear. He had one hand on the channel knob of the big set, and the other gripped a pencil. He'd obviously been covering a big pad with notes.

'What's happening Grieve? How are we doing?' said Harry, slipping onto a seat beside him.

Grieve turned, a sort of half incredulous grin on his face which Harry found suddenly very funny and at the same time disconcerting, seeing as he'd never seen a grin of any sort on Grieve's face before.

'Nothing for us, sir,' said Grieve. 'Not since the initial challenge from *Monrovia* and we confirmed, "on station". Morton's monitoring the morse frequencies, sir,' he said, nodding to the tensed-up figure at his shoulder, 'and I've been following all the voice traffic, sir. Keeping a note for the log,' jabbing at the pad. 'It's been... well... hectic... incredible, sir. It's been hard to credit that I'm actually here and listening to it all as it happens. Look,' and he pushed the pad across the desk so as Harry could read.

Grieve's dense script was remarkably legible considering the speed he must have been scribbling it down at. Harry began to read the entries, immediately recognising the three main beaches, JOSS, DIME and CENT that extended east from where they were now, off Licata, past the town of Gela. And the names of the USS Navy warships: the Brooklyn-class light cruisers, *Savannah* and *Boise* and *Philadelphia* on the gun line and the destroyers, *Buck*, *Swanson* and *Roe* and others. Grieve's notes started:

0028 – Western Task Force confirmed at assigned areas
0030 – Searchlights from shore probing our movements

0037 – Ancon anchored

USS Ancon, she was flagship for CENT beach landing force

0044 – DIME Force in position in transport and gunfire support areas

0046 – JOSS Force sighted Blue reference vessel light

0050 – JOSS Force sighted Yellow reference vessel light

0055 – Sea state settling, wind now at force 3 to 4

0103 – JOSS beach, first LSTs begin lowering LCVPs

And there it was, at three minutes past one in the morning, the first of the big *Landing Ship, Tanks* beginning to disembark their troops and equipment into their smaller *Landing Craft, Vehicle and Personnel* and them heading for JOSS beach. Harry looked at the innocuous little line of script. Seven pencilled words marking the moment; the first Allied soldiers about to set foot back on the shores of occupied Europe. *Here we go*, thought Harry. *We're on our way.*

Grieve's narrative marched on:

0142 – CTF 86 in Biscayne *anchored midway between Blue and Yellow reference vessels at 5000 yds off beach, Licata bearing 127°*

CTF 86 – commander, task force 86 – that was the JOSS beach boss.

0155 – Biscayne *illuminated by 3 searchlights from shore*

0200 – First waves left rendezvous area for JOSS Blue Beach

0204 – Biscayne *alerts first LSTs: you are anchored too far offshore. LCVP run-in to beach too far*

0206 – Other JOSS beach LSTs late on station

0210 – CTF 85 reports his H-hour delayed one hour at request of commander, transports

0215 – DIME beach, first wave Ranger Battalion begins run-in

0243 – NCWTF orders CTF 85, land immediately

Harry is smiling to himself as he reads that. NCWTF was the Naval Commander, Western Task Force; that would Vice Admiral Hewitt USN on USS *Monrovia*, the big boss. Grieve sees the smile and says, 'The flagship got a bit tetchy there, sir. No mistake.'

0245 – JOSS Beach, enemy MG and medium artillery landing among first waves

0246 – Rocket firing LCTs salvo suppressing fire

0247 – DDs open suppressing fire on enemy searchlights

0250 – Biscayne *reports enemy mobile radio beacon near Scoglitti active, homing in enemy aircraft*

0252 – All CTF 86 first waves landed. Surf reported as 3 ft. Biscayne *advises all units to use blazing coastal towns as navigation reference. Ranger Battalion and first waves of 1st Inf Div landed by CTF 81*

0254 – Philadelphia *ordered to shoot out air beacon*

0255 – USN DDs Swanson *and* Roe *in collision off JOSS beach, both request permission to proceed Malta*

0315 – USN DD Buck *ordered to replace* Swanson *and* Roe *in JOSS Fire Support Area No. 1 and support troops landing at Red Beach*

0330 – USN DDs and rocket-firing LCTs begin bombardment of CENT beach

0400 – NCWTF reports first light

0410 – CTF 85 reports first waves landed at assigned beaches encountering no opposition

0412 – CTF 86 reports continuous artillery and MG fire on JOSS Red Beach and approaches

0415 – Savannah *and* Boise *ordered to open supporting fire on enemy batteries*

Harry shoves the pad back to Grieve and the two men share a long look at each other. There is nothing to say. The scale of the battle out there in the gathering light has silenced them.

'Want to listen in for a bit, sir?' says Grieve, and he plugs in a spare headset. Harry holds one earpiece to his head. He hears staccato voices in matter-of-fact monotone rasping at him through the crackle, an incomprehensible babble of call signs and coded phrases, random cracks that must be gunfire in the background. It is like opening a shutter on a madhouse. Harry can't listen to it. He only realises he's had his eyes closed when he opens them again and sees Grieve is back, scribbling intently. He unplugs his headset. Grieve sees him and says, 'There seems to be an enemy air attack developing over CENT beach…' although he is still listening hard, getting ready to resume his frantic scribbling.

'Carry on Grieve,' says Harry. 'I'll be on the bridge.'

A beautiful day was dawning when Harry got there. But a far from peaceful one. Even coming up the conning tower ladder, he could hear the din of battle, all of it blasting and banging against an all-pervading, sky-to-sky, deep industrial grumbling of aero engines that sounded like it was coming from everywhere, and when he did get up, he could see it was.

The bridge was crowded; while he'd been eavesdropping on the fight, Farrar had ordered up two more lookouts. Harry immediately concurred with Number One's decision; the sheer scale of the shipping that blanked the horizon to starboard needed close watching. Nothing was close, yet. But that could change very fast. Then there was the great arc of sea running from astern to their port bow. It was blank, for now. But if the enemy were coming to interdict this landing, that was the direction they'd be coming from, and it needed watching. And he hadn't looked up yet.

The sky was full, coming from the west and the south, great carpets of bombers. At medium height, USAAF B25 Mitchells, A20 Havocs, all passing overhead, heading inland, and above them, further to the east, he could see three, no four, flights of B24 Liberators. Then he turned right around, and he was looking back west, and much further to the west and lower, where more aircraft, mostly medium bombers, were coming from the land, all heading back out to sea. Definitely Allied, he was sure he could pick out the odd twin tail of a B25. Those must be aircraft who'd delivered their payloads, returning now to the airfields along the Tunisian coast, likely going home only to bomb up and head back.

And when Harry looked back again, over the task force, he could see down at low level smaller, darting aircraft, forming into looping circles over the transports. As they turned and twisted, he could see they were P40 Warhawks and Airacobras, dozens and dozens of them in what looked like continuously moving cab ranks, then peeling off and streaking in over the beaches to drop bombs almost to the shoreline.

Harry had never felt more naked or vulnerable in his life, standing there on *Scourge's* bridge, on the surface in broad daylight now, and he could almost feel his skin crawl. This was not right. Submarines had no business being on the surface amidst such mayhem. He stood on the bridge wing with his binoculars stuck to his face, scanning for threat.

He hadn't long to wait. The tracer curling up from the inshore destroyers alerted him. And there they were, skidding and weaving, two tight flights of Ju 88s coming at the transports, straight off the land. He lowered his glasses in time to see a pair of Airacobras haul back and climb out their cab rank, gaining height to come back and engage. And as he watched, his eyes caught other specks in the distance, way across the Golfo di Gela, beyond Gela itself. The evil, gull wings leaving no doubt. Stukas, a half dozen of them, peeling off and diving in.

The morning wore on without respite.

He commuted regularly to the wireless and Asdic cubbies, checking. The sea was clear to the west, and nobody was shouting at *Scourge*. No Task Force vessels strayed their way.

A thought occurred to him – the crew would be getting peckish. But he was buggered if he was going to secure from diving stations so they could go and eat, not with all bloody hell being let loose round about them. So he ordered Harding to get Windass to start a sandwich production line and keep the coffee brewing and to grab a couple of stokers off Mr Petrie to do the distribution.

On one of his trips down to the radio cubbie, Grieve took a moment, 'Sir! You just missed it! Another station broadcasting from the air net… I didn't recognise the call sign… anyway, some flyboy telling *Monrovia* she had a U-boat on the surface, approaching from the west, and *Monrovia* telling them to shut up and leave it alone, it was one their guide boats. The R/T language was definitely non-standard! Lots of advice about reading operation orders, sir, and doubts cast on aircrew parentage.'

Harry took another brief look at Grieve's log. The boat had secured from red light by that time, and he didn't have to squint:

0448 – CG 45th Inf Div reports Elements from all assault battalions CENT Force have landed. Everything appears to be going well

0450 – USN minesweeper Sentinel *damaged during dive-bombing attack in JOSS area*

0510 – JOSS Red Beach, Beachmaster reports severe shell fire in sector; warns CTF 86 to suspend landing LCTs

0538 – JOSS beach area. Shore batteries in Licata town open fire on Biscayne. *Fire returned by* Biscayne

0600 – CG 3rd Inf Div reports JOSS beach area progress satisfactory on Blue Beach, landings underway at Green Beach, two battalions already ashore on Red Beach

Harry pushed the log back and stepped forward into the control room. Through the press of bodies there, he could see through to the other end and McCready in the passage beyond, backing out of the galley clutching a can of coffee and a gas mask bag over his shoulder with the top of a pile of sandwiches peeking from under the flap. At diving stations, he should've been at the fruit machine in the control room.

'Feeling peckish, Tom?' called Harry, startling the lad.

'Ah! Um, no, sir,' said McCready, turning to see where his CO was shouting from. 'Just taking a moment… something for the lads in the forward torpedo room, sir.'

'Mr Petrie's boys are supposed to be looking after that,' said Harry.

'Ah, well sir, you know. Stokers. They get nosebleeds if they go any further for'ard than number one main battery space.' Poor McCready, he wasn't exactly simpering with guilt, but not far off it. Abandoning his station, with the boat closed up.

From the chart table, he heard Harding's voice, 'I told him to, sir.'

Did you really? thought Harry.

And then he pulled himself up. McCready had committed a grave sin, abandoning his diving station, but not as grave a sin as Harry letting himself get too twitchy in front of the crew. It was time to calm down. He looked around the control room, face grave.

Everyone might look like they were attending to their duty, but you could practically see the entire control room crews' ears flapping, waiting to hear what was going to happen next. It would be bad form for him to let his crew become twitchy too.

And since there was bugger all happening to concern *Scourge* right now, and certainly not a whisper of HE coming out the Sicilian Channel, all he said to McCready was, 'Hurry back.'

Just take it easy, Harry, he said to himself.

But even so, there was too much explosive ordnance flying about in all directions for *Scourge's* captain to be totally relaxed. That, and the fact it was high time for them to receive their recall signal so they could dive and get the hell out the way. With the sun fully up and the day advancing, there was no more need for guide boats to keep the Task Force within the landing area. Somebody in *Monrovia's* ops room must have noticed that by now, surely?

Harry contented himself with issuing a further parting order to McCready before he disappeared up the conning tower hatch. 'And when you've done that, go and annoy Grieve,' he said. 'Get him to show you his radio log and then go through the boat and brief everybody as to what's been happening upstairs. There must be some of them interested.'

It was only when he got to the bridge and the warm sun was on his face that Harry realised how close he'd been to overreacting. *You really are getting tired, aren't you*, he said to himself.

To snap out of it, he began scanning the shore again. The land behind the beach was shrouded by palls of smoke, randomly shimmering with concussions from the continuous bombardment. The minutes ran into an hour, and then another, as he watched the pageant unfolding along the great sweep of the Golfo di Gela. Detached from it, here, then there, along that bay, little incidental swarms of gnats seemed to coalesce, twisting and turning in the clear sky beyond the ranks of clouds, sometimes right down on the sea, sometimes way up to maybe ten thousand, twelve thousand feet, aircraft locked in their own dogfights, coming together for moments then peeling apart again, and then from time to time, one or maybe two of them, falling away in curls of smoke that ended in sudden plumes of water.

Their recall really was long overdue now. That was when his thoughts were interrupted. It was the young stoker covering the port quarter lookout station.

'Four aircraft, red one five zero, right down on the deck, sir. Coming in fast, sir. Right at us!'

Harry spun and saw the specks, growing rapidly in the heartbeat it took to raise his binoculars. 'I have them,' he said. And in that instant, the ragged line of their formation peeled apart and as the four aircraft diverged into two loose deuces, their wings rising into their turns, he could see the distinctive box of their twin booms – USAAF P38 Lightnings. But they were no longer coming straight at *Scourge*, they were moving out to box her. Time concertina-ed. He felt his throat close. This couldn't be happening.

'Sir…! …?' The lookout might only have been a boy, but he knew enough to realise what the P38s were doing. Harry heard him as from down a tunnel. He was looking at the two P38s wheeling right, at the 500lb bombs hanging from their under-wing hardpoints, observing to himself, in a very matter-of-fact fashion, that they were now reversing their turn and were about to start coming back in on him. He looked rapidly to his left; the other two had swung much wider, but they too were now beginning their bank back again. By the time he'd turned back to the two coming in from starboard, he was looking right down their noses and at the two .50 calibre machine guns and a 20mm cannon that nestled in each.

They were setting *Scourge* up for a classic one-two – a simultaneous attack from both beams. He'd known that the minute he'd seen them begin their split but couldn't bring himself to accept it. He'd gone the whole action so far without a single ship or aircraft or bomb or shell coming near. He and *Scourge* had done their job; no vessel had been allowed to stray from the landing area, no aircrew had had to be rescued. And now it was long past the time they should've been sent home, with a nice 'thanks a lot'. Right now, they should've been at sixty feet, heading in the opposite direction.

And he still wasn't reacting. *God! You really are tired.*

But time really was concertina-ing. Bare seconds had ticked away.

'Clear the bridge!' he yelled. 'Number One, dive! Dive!' And he grabbed the young lookout and propelled him towards the conning tower hatch. But there were six of them up there. Four lookouts, himself and Farrar, who was shoving the lookouts down the hole like he was stuffing a last-minute Christmas stocking. Harry held the lookout closest to him back, while Farrar straddled the hole, ready to drop. Something in the corner of Harry's eye; he glanced back. The nose of the lead P38 was sparkling.

Scourge was already on her way down, her bows up past the three-inch gun mount, diving into the welter of foam and spray, the sea rising up to engulf them. Then the *thud! thud! thud!* of blows hitting her. He was already looking aft, but he would never remember whether he saw the gouts of water tripping towards their hull first or whether it was the chunk of aft casing splinter, but he remembered the two vicious puffs that followed, blowing back at an angle out from under the casing and that he'd known instantly what he'd just seen.

He needed to stop the dive. Now.

'Shut main vents! Blow Q! Blow forward main ballast tanks!'

At least two more *thuds!* This time he felt them beneath his feet.

But even his own voice seemed to be coming from somewhere else, maybe behind him, because he was moving so fast he'd left it there, because right now, he was already on top of the crumpled figure of the remaining lookout, jamming him in under the bridge front.

There was a tremendous roar of aero engines, a shadow passed in a draught above his head, so close he could smell the reek of fuel fumes and then a most remarkable, astonishing sight, sailing in slow motion, two bombs in smooth, horizontal flight, over the aft casing. And then water deluged into the bridge and was smothering them, Harry's head shrieking, *Christ! The conning tower hatch!* before recalling he'd actually kicked it shut as he'd shoved the lookout into the corner.

Water engulfed him. Harry felt the pressure in his ears; it meant *Scourge* was still diving.

Bubbles and the noise of water. He daren't open his eyes. He had one hand on his own nose, holding tight against the last gulps of fresh air he'd managed to suck down and the other clamped firmly over the nose and mouth of the young lookout. What was his name again? He was a stoker, Harry remembered that, but his name? The face didn't ring any bells either, but then you didn't often see many back-afties stray as far for'ard as the control room. Even so, he should be able to remember his name. It wasn't as if there were that many of them in *Scourge*. Chapman. That was it. Who would have thought the process of drowning could actually create for you a little quiet moment to collect your thoughts?

Those bastard P38s had shot holes in the pressure hull.

Harry, wedged there, waiting for the water to win, all manner of thoughts came flooding in on him. That sparkling had been the P38's cannon going off. The chunk of casing getting blown off didn't matter, but those seemingly innocent little puffs? Remember them? They hadn't looked like much, but those were cannon shells going into *Scourge's* guts. And now she was diving with holes in her pressure hull.

He could feel the water pressure tighten in his ears. That stupid bastard Harding in the control room, why hadn't he listened to him and stopped the dive?

'Shut main vents!' He'd shouted it loud enough.

But no. And now they were going to lose the boat. There were holes in the conning tower too, at least that was what he reckoned the final thuds had been. *Scourge* could have survived that. Getting back up again might have proved a bit tricky with a conning tower full of water. But there was going to be no way back for them now, not with bloody great holes in the hull, and the boat continuing down, the pounds of pressure per square inch behind the water jetting in, doubling for every thirty-odd feet they dropped. And what about those bloody bombs, flying through the air with the greatest of ease, what the hell were they doing there, like they were sight-seeing? The Yank pilot must have tried to skip them into *Scourge* but dropped them too late and they'd gone sailing over her. Another stupid bastard, couldn't even sink one of his own boats properly. Except, it looked like he had anyway.

Chapman, the young lookout had started writhing, it wasn't going to be long now for him. Harry? He was abstractly wondering how long he'd last before the pressure in his chest defeated his will and he had to gulp for air. Except it wouldn't be air he'd inhale but seawater. It was still remarkably light though, he thought. He could see it through his scrunched-tight eyelids. Shouldn't it have been getting darker the deeper they went? And he was just starting to wonder why the pressure in his ears had gone when all the water sluiced off them, and he and Chapman were suddenly revealed in their contorted embrace, to a deserted bridge, fresh air and sunlight. Looking at his arm, Harry was suddenly aware why the hand on the end of it, holding his nose and mouth, was screaming in pain; the arm was clenched round one of the bridge voicepipes, holding him and Chapman in the boat. But before it dawned on him it would be a good idea to release it and breathe, to release the vice-like grip he had on Chapman's nose and mouth too, the conning tower hatch flew open and Dickie Bird was out and crouched on the bridge aiming what looked like a bloated, ugly, fat pistol at the sky.

A loud *phut!* And reload, and *phut!* And a third. All executed with the speed and sleight of hand of a music hall magician.

And then time stopped concertina-ing.

Other bodies were tumbling up. Number One was there, and Gooch, the TGM, other lookouts, lugging up long metal cylinders. What the…? Smoke pots! Of course! The signal floats submerged submarines released to alert friendly skimmers as to where they were. Harry suddenly noticed Farrar's face, jammed right in his. Farrar was yelling something at him, impertinent bastard!

'Are you all right, sir? Are you all right?' Harry thinking, *Yes, yes. I can hear you,* but looking behind Farrar, to where the bridge was now chaos… which, curiously, had the effect of leaving Harry feeling suddenly, serenely relaxed. He wasn't even registering the screaming roar of aero engines or the yelling from his crew.

Ten

'There is no goddammed submarine on this order of battle in that position,' said Lt Col McBundy Grier, stabbing the desk with his finger. 'Yet you keep saying there was. You keep saying it was assigned to patrol a designated box marked on the map. Goddammit! Look at my operational map! There is *no* goddammed box!'

The USAAF staff officer from Northwest African Air Forces HQ, all the way back in Algiers, was indeed *goddammed* if he was going to let this jumped-up, tri-service, *Allied* kangaroo court hang this snafu around his airmen's necks. And he wasn't the only one who was grumpy in the sweatbox confines of this Nissen hut, out on the fly-blown perimeter of Luqa airfield, Malta, with the noise of all the ineffectual fans inside and the endless, pulsing din of aero engines outside. A gaggle of middle-ranking staff officers, army, navy and air force, British and Commonwealth and US, a hastily convened committee, all sat round an equally hastily flung-together box of tables, sitting there, shirts saturated, unanimous in their verdict that they'd been handed the shittier end of a shitty stick. Their task? To assess all the incidents of Allied forces firing on Allied forces during the landing phase of Operation Husky and to offer suggestions as to how similar incidents might be avoided in future operations. In other words, who do we blame? And how best do we dodge the blame when it happens again?

The US Army stenographer sergeant, taking the minutes of the meeting opted to omit all Lt Col Grier's *goddamms* and *goddammits*.

There were a lot of incidents to go through, dozens of them concerning friendly fighter aircraft being randomly pot-shotted by warships from the covering force over both the Western and Eastern Task Force disembarkation areas; then more seriously, was the systematic anti-aircraft barrage thrown up at the C47 and glider formations passing over Eastern Task Force, carrying the landing's airborne component. A lot of Allied paratroopers had died in the wee small hours of 10 June at the hands of Allied sailors. And then, of course, there was the airstrike, specifically launched from a USAAF airstrip in Tunisia, against His Majesty's Submarine *Scourge*.

That one was different. All the others were the drearily tragic results of inexperience, failure to observe recognition codes, to even bother to glance at recognition charts, lack of training, poor fire control, gung-ho and downright stupidity. But the attack on *Scourge* had been planned.

Lt Col Grier had sat seething through a lecture from that tedious little preppy USN commander from Vice Adm Hewitt's staff, in his razor-pressed khakis that now drooped under the saddlebags of his sweat stains, sitting there, all horn-rimmed spectacles and document-shuffling pedantry, not even looking at Grier. Droning on about the centralised control of the operation, how each arm had been issued with centralised recognition procedures, all the units involved, their approach lanes shared, co-ordinated. But Lt Col Grier had come prepared. He was a career soldier in the Army Air Force, this was going to be his war, and no bullshit fest was going to divert his career-defining mission. He'd been to interview every one of his staff in that ops room leading up to the first missions launching for Sicily, taken note of all the planning that had gone into those ops and quizzed every radioman in the room as to all the radio traffic back and forth to the squadrons involved.

'My crews were told to expect a submarine on the surface to the west of the disembarkation areas,' said Lt Col Grier. Unlike the preppy little USN commander, the rest of the hut was now looking at him, sat at attention, a question over whether the beads of sweat on his scalp you could see through the steel-brush bristle of his haircut were there because of the heat or his anger. He held up a neatly folded air navigation chart, all marked up with pilots' annotations.

'Here is the submarine's patrol box,' he said, jabbing it. '...where the CO of the Three Hundred and Fifty-Ninth bombardment group, medium... among others... among several others... reported a submarine on the surface. And here!' He hit the chart again, in a blank area of water, '...is where they reported another submarine. Directly south of Licata, where there is no submarine patrol box marked up and where no submarine was supposed to be. No Allied submarine!'

Listening to all this was George Wincairns, sitting behind a British Army full colonel, in the hut and at the table as representative of Eighth Army. Wincairns was hidden in full sight among the colonel's pencil case holders. The USAAF officer, for all his belligerence, seemed to be making a valid point, thought Wincairns, who was there to report for a higher master, one who took an interest in *all* inter-Allied vested interest matches no matter at what level they were fought. Despite his fancy dress, pick-n-mix uniform, no one had been paying him the slightest attention, which was how he liked it. Anyway, the Eighth Army lot were used to his unexplained presences by now, and if any Yank were to ask, he'd just say he was lancer in the Submarine Kilties, and how would they know any different?

'As they went over the Western Task Force beaches, several of my crews raised the *Monrovia* on the designated frequencies and alerted them to a potential U-boat in their AOO,' the lieutenant colonel was telling the committee who, Wincairns thought, were mostly thinking, *put a sock in it and take your beating like the pen-pusher you are.* Wincairns was also thinking, *AOO?* Then he remembered, '*Area Of Operations*'. *The military and their acronyms. Dearie me.* But the lieutenant colonel wasn't taking his beating, he was mad, and he was going to be heard.

'…they were told to stay off the frequencies,' Grier continued, '"She's on your operational map", was the reply. "She's the RN guide boat for the JOSS beach left flank approach lanes. She's a friendly".'

All the while Grier was jabbing at his chart. 'But the Three Five Nine group crews weren't talking about *this* boat. They were talking about a *second* boat. Out here. And no son-of-a-bitch on *Monrovia* was giving a damn!'

'Lieutenant Colonel Grier,' the emollient voice came from down the far end of the table, from a US Army colonel who had been convening the committee as its chairman when Wincairns had slipped into the hut. He remembered whispering in the ear of one of the British colonel's pencil case holders, who is this chap? And was told, 'Direct from Ike's own staff.' Wincairns couldn't remember his name now, but if this gathering was going to have any clout in the great Allied edifice, then this would be the man who wielded it.

'Herein obviously lies the confusion,' the US colonel was saying, '*Monrovia* repeatedly advised your crews the western-most submarine on the surface was a friendly. But because its patrol box wasn't on your operational navigation charts, you ignored that advice and laid on your own mission to attack that submarine without clearing it first with *Monrovia*…'

'Begging your pardon, sir,' Lt Col Grier interrupted. Wincairns' ears pricked up. Interrupting your superior was never a good idea, and he was now curious as to how this was going to end up. 'We didn't "ignore" any advice, sir. We could see the western-most Allied submarine because it was in the patrol box marked on our nav chart. We took a tactical decision to launch against this other submarine that Western Task Force was ignoring despite our repeated warnings!'

Ike's colonel let a lengthy silence hang in the hut, and Wincairns wondered how long it might have lasted if another USN officer hadn't butted in.

'Western Task Force ops staff requested the additional Brit submarine as a back-up guard boat as well as extra beacon after consulting with the senior submarine liaison officer,' the USN guy was saying. From where Wincairns was sitting he could barely see his profile. As for his rank, all he could see was one of those US Navy collar insignias that Wincairns could never understand. This one was some sort of silver leaf pin. He could hear the New England glass in the officer's voice clear enough though, 'That officer... an RN officer, I might add... then arranged for the submarine to be deployed and updated the operational navigation chart accordingly. For the entire Western Task Force. Now, it was, and remains, the responsibility of Northwest African Air Forces command to ensure their operational maps are up to date. So, perhaps our senior air force officer could address why his operational navigation charts only show one submarine to the west of the Task Force's AOO? And before he does, I should also like to point out the senior submarine liaison officer's desk was, and is, just down the hall from Lieutenant Colonel Grier's ops room in Algiers.'

Wincairns immediately looked to Lt Col Grier's end of the table.

He half-expected to see steam coming out of Grier's ears. But when the airman spoke, there was an icy calm to his voice. 'If you think you can provoke me, commander, into turning this into some kind of inter-service, Yank versus Limey beef, you are mistaken. My staff have nothing short of total respect for, and trust in Captain Bonalleck's submarine liaison work. If the chart information he supplied to us said there should have been no Allied submarine there, then there should've been no Allied submarine there!'

A siren went off in Wincairns' head. Surely there was only one Royal Navy Captain Bonalleck in the Med? 'The Bonny Boy' Bonalleck and HMS *Scourge* being mentioned in the same breath, again? What was all this about? What was being said here? Had there been some suggestion that *Scourge* getting shot up hadn't just been down to trigger-happy Yanks?

As unobtrusively as possible, Wincairns scribbled some notes on his writing pad. For a moment, the atmosphere in the hut had verged on the bad-tempered, but inevitably, the dead hand of procedure and the heat quietened everyone down. Proper wording to record this incident of communication failure and the committee's considered recommendations on how to prevent it occurring again were agreed and minuted. The meeting moved on to the next item. But Wincairns' attention was still on the implications of what he'd just heard. He'd liked to have left the hut there and then, but his mission dictated he must stay, lest some other potential for Anglo–American discord suddenly break surface. The afternoon wore on, and the heat got worse. Eventually, they adjourned, and Wincairns slid out of his seat and headed for the door. There had been stuff happening in that hut earlier he hadn't fully understood, and that wasn't allowed in Wincairns' world. There were people he needed to talk to.

*

Harry was sitting in the back of Louis' bookshop while Louis served a customer. On the outside, the old shop, up on the top of Valletta old town, was much as it had been during the worst of the bombing, being a half-flight of stairs down from the street, it had escaped the worst of the blasts, and the rubble that ended up half-burying it ended up protecting what was left. Inside, it was still the warm, comforting snug it had been when he first visited, in what seemed like a hundred years ago now; the same dust motes hung in the air, the same oaty smell, the same old creased and burst leather armchairs. The only new smell was from the knocked-off wardroom coffee Harry had brought, wafting up from the little primus stove the pot was simmering on.

Harry was splayed out on one of the old armchairs, looking down on his crisp, new 3Cs – the official rig number for the new, dazzling white uniform that now adorned his reclining frame. He'd made a point of indenting for new kit when *Scourge* was last in, and when he'd sailed back, the new kit had been waiting. It all contributed to his general feeling of well-being.

Louis came back in from the counter, folding some notes. Harry had noticed how much older he was looking. He might have swept all the dust from the rubble out of his shop, but he'd missed the dust ingrained on him. A bit more stooped too, and slower. 'They're charming boys, these young Americans. Not like the English, who are all hooligans,' he said airily. 'And scruffier.'

'The English? Couldn't agree more,' said Harry.

'He was looking for something on the Turks and their siege.'

'So he was after something racy and modern then?'

'Oh, I'd say there are many on Malta today who would say three hundred and fifty-odd years ago would still count as modern, wouldn't you?' Louis paused to top up his coffee and then add a little tot of brandy from the bottle he kept by his chair. He poured another measure into Harry's mug. 'You *are* in a good mood these days.'

It was true, although he was still wondering how he could be.

Yesterday, the ship's company had held the funeral for young Able Seaman Archer, the junior bunts who'd died in *Scourge's* conning tower during the P38 attacks. It had been a sombre affair at the cemetery up at Kalkara. But the atmosphere among the crew had seemed more stunned than grieving. Archer had been a well-liked lad, but what was there to say about a nineteen-year-old who'd never got to be old enough to see or do anything? He was the first man Harry as CO had lost, killed in action. But the death had been so stupid and pointless, Harry didn't really know what to feel about it. He could barely even remember the lad's face or the last time he'd actually seen him alive and kicking, although it must have been on *Scourge's* bridge, before those Yank P38s had strafed them.

He hadn't mentioned any of that to Louis, of course, about the attack, or the funeral, or how hard it had been to write the letter to the lad's parents. You weren't supposed to spread gloom and despondency among the civilian population, and telling stories about the Allies actually shooting at each other wasn't a good message to bring back home.

He did tell him, however, about how he'd had to abort a crash dive and hold onto a junior rating to stop him being washed away, and how the rating, Able Seaman Chapman, was his name, how the lad had approached him afterwards. He could see Chapman now, slight frame, his whites hanging on him, rather than fitting snug like a uniform should and his cap pushing down on his ears.

'Sir. Excuse me, sir,' he'd stammered, holding himself at a smart attention

'Yes?' Harry had said, eyebrows arched in enquiry.

'Sir, sorry to interrupt, sir, but I just wanted to say thank you, sir. For saving me, sir. Haven't had a chance before, sir.'

It had been only then that Harry had recognised him:

'Ah. Able Seaman Chapman. Of course. It was my pleasure. Think nothing of it.'

'Aye, Aye, sir. I didn't mean to… I just wanted to…'

'Of course you did, and it's much appreciated… actually…' Harry had paused then, thinking, then rubbing his chin and smiling, and then he'd said, with one of his winning smiles, 'Actually, Chapman, *do* think something of it. *Do* the same for me one day, please, because, Christ, the way things are going, I'll probably need it!'

And how a grinning Chapman had snapped off a salute, 'Aye, aye, sir!'

Louis had liked that story.

As for everything else that had happened, Harry knew he wasn't going to talk about how Archer had died or even mention the attack, the deliberate attack, how it could have actually happened or the pitiful sobs of the two stokers wounded in the engine room. To himself, the more he'd struggled for the words, the less point there seemed in raking over the whole sorry tale.

'Yes,' said Harry eventually. 'I do appear to be somewhat chipper, although God knows why. The minute the Vice-Admiral, Malta's vultures heard *Scourge* was heading in for damage repair, they descended on my crew. I've lost at least half a dozen to other boats. "Can't have prime hands lolling about the beach while you wait for the dockyard mateys to patch up your boat, Gilmour. Won't do at all,"' he mimicked in gravelly tones. 'And what really hurts is that not one man Jack of them has had the common decency to moan about being shifted.

Most of them bought off with promotions. So much for loyalty. They are quite shameless.'

All of this delivered through an ironic grin.

Louis didn't reply. Harry might look chipper, but the more he went on, the more Louis became suspicious. Until eventually, he knew all this chattiness was smoke and that Harry had something on his mind, and he also knew interrogating him as to what it was would get him nowhere. He was a wise old owl, Louis. Eventually, the real matter in question bubbled up to the surface.

'I've been getting tired lately, you know,' said Harry as if about to meander off on some other subject. But Louis knew he wasn't. 'I don't mean sleepy tired. "A good night's sleep'll do you a power of good, old boy!" No. I mean bone tired. Soul tired. Bloody war, eh? I've been feeling I've been losing my edge. That maybe my luck is running out. That's not a good thought to have in my line of work, Louis. As I'm sure you'll understand.'

'Indeed I do,' said Louis, sipping his coffee. 'I also understand that none of that is likely to make you chipper.'

Harry smiled again, 'No, indeed.' He had a sip of brandy-charged coffee too, 'When we were out there, Sicily, we got clobbered. Something happened.' Harry looked up, directly at Louis, who was gazing back, intently. Harry continued, 'We got caught on the surface by aircraft. I ordered us down, but as we were diving, I could see I was too late. We got hit by cannon shells. Through the pressure hull and the conning tower. Holes in your pressure hull and you can't dive. Because water is going to come in through those holes, and the deeper you go, the higher is going to be the pressure. Water is already filling your ballast tanks. So all that extra water is making you heavier, so you start going down faster. You lose the trim, and eventually you're so heavy you can't come up again, and you lose the boat. So I ordered the dive stopped. But we were already on our way down, and there wasn't enough time for me to get down the conning tower hatch before the conning tower went under. Me and one of the lookouts. So I deliberately shut the hatch and left us both up there while the boat continued down.'

Harry stopped talking, remembering those seconds. Him and the lookout, the hatch already shut on them and the bridge filling with sea and AB Archer on the other side of the hatch, his midriff already splattered all over the inside of the conning tower by one of those 20mm shells that had gone right through the tower's skin.

'The obvious thing to have done,' Harry had started again, 'would've been for me and the lookout to have kicked off out of the bridge and swum about on the surface, waiting, hoping the boat would come back up again soon. Or, if not it, then somebody else would come along and snatch us up. But I think you'd have had to have been in the sea, all alone, well, in this case, two of us, to really understand what a big bloody place it is and how wee and insignificant and so easily un-noticeable two bobbing heads are on it. To know there was a distinct possibility that *Scourge* wasn't going to come up again, and it really was going to be left for that someone else to come along. Except, there was a bloody great battle going on all around us. And all those "someone elses" had other things on their mind... and if they did manage a moment to look for us, what was going to happen?... "oh, and where did we last see them? Where was that tiny little patch of huge ocean they were bobbing about on?"... You see what I mean? So I didn't let go. I held onto the bridge as we went down and pinned the lookout there too. Even though we were both going to drown if *Scourge* had continued the dive. But she didn't. She came up again. Almost right away. The lads in the control room brought her back up.'

Harry turned to face Louis again with a big warm smile on his face. 'And you know the best part? Clinging there with the whole Mediterranean gurgling around my ears, I didn't once think: Will they come back up? Please make them come back up!'

Another pause, for breath? To find the words?

'I didn't think anything, actually. I just concentrated on staying on that bridge. I didn't hope or pray. It was as if I knew, without having to say it to myself. Of course they would've lost the boat if they hadn't come back up, *directly* back up!' A laugh here, to break the melodrama. 'But they didn't lose the boat. They obeyed my order and stopped the dive. And I didn't have to stand over them to make sure they did it. They did everything right, by themselves. I wasn't there, and they still did it right. My crew. Me. Daft wee Harry Gilmour from Argyll. My crew did it. And you know, I've never felt so proud... alive... real... and something else... it's like a weight got lifted. Like I'd felt I'd been carrying them all that time, and now, I don't have to.'

Another pause, a furrow of the brow to collect his thoughts.

'I certainly don't feel so bloody tired anymore.' And another big smile.

Louis smiled back, but what he was thinking was, *my God! Poor Harry, all that nonsense you've just been gibbering, it's just your dull, bashed brain magicking up little epiphanies out of nothing. If that's all you're clinging onto to get yourself through, then you really do need a rest.*

*

Sitting in the dghaisa, getting rowed back to Manoel Island, Harry wasn't paying attention to the other two RN ratings cadging a ride or the battered old dghaisaman. He was composing himself for the task of writing out his full patrol report. He'd already delivered his verbal to a pained-looking Capt Philips, whose only verdict had been, 'You were lucky.'

He'd been right, of course. They had been lucky. They hadn't been a target of opportunity for those P38s. *Scourge* had been on the wrong end of a USAAF mission, and more experienced pilots would have sunk them. But he wasn't dwelling on that right now, he was thinking about Harding's 'unofficial' account, delivered *sotto voce* out on the Lazaretto's wardroom gallery the night they'd got back in. About what had happened after he, Harry, had kicked the lid shut, about how Farrar had gripped the whole show from the moment his feet had hit the control room deck plates. Fussy, punctilious Farrar.

'It all happened so fast,' Harding had said. 'As I'm sure you know, even though you were still upstairs at the time.' Harding had been taking belts out of a tumbler of gin and bitters, between regular, incredulous shakes of his head as he recounted those seconds and minutes.

'I heard the klaxon go,' he said, enumerating the points with his other hand, '…and the bodies started coming down the conning tower ladder. The wrecker already had all the vents open wide and I'd ordered the cox'n hard down on the planes. And then… I'm not sure… whether it was the *clang! clang! clang!* of the twenty millimetres hitting us or you yelling, "Shut main vents!" Because right after that, all this splatter of blood and shite came blasting down the tower hatch, followed by our very own Jimmy, covered in it himself. In fact, right away, I thought, *fuck me! Poor Nick! He's must have a fucking great hole in him somewhere, for all that to have come out of him!* But it was that poor AB that had copped it. And by this time, there's all sorts of screaming and yelling coming from the engine room about how some bastard's turning the pressure hull into a colander. Well, exciting times! And yet there's Number One in the middle of it all, issuing orders like he was just doing a trim dive. And the whole control room just stepped to it. Neither a wasted word nor a superfluous movement. And him just standing there covered in all that gore, like Windass had tripped and hit him with a pail of stew. Who'd have thunk it, eh, sir? Number One, cool as a cucumber. Man of the moment. And then we were on our way up again, and he had the yeoman, Bird, digging out the Verey pistol and the signal flares of the day, and another one of the bunts with an Aldis lamp, and Puttick out his chair on the after planes to grab the chemist shop and see what he could do for the AB in the tower. Although by then, he was probably drowned as well as eviscerated. And then Gooch was queuing up in the gangway with a couple of his mob, clutching all the smoke pots we had.' Harding had laughed at that moment, although his story had seemed far from funny thus far.

'And then, Number One, almost as if he'd planned it,' Harding had said, 'when he opens the conning tower hatch and all the water that's left up there, because bear in mind the tower's got lots of shell holes in it too, and the water's been pouring in, and then out again... what's left comes down, drenches him, and cleans off all the gore. And it was, Tah-rah!' And Harding had executed a mock flourish that made him spill his gin, 'Lieutenant Farrar, ready to go on parade, suh!'

Harry had known the rest, from Farrar's own brief, all the flares Dickie Bird had fired off and all the smoke pots of every colour in the inventory that the TGMs boys had lobbed over the wall and that nice US Navy *Gleaves* class destroyer that had been on the western-most end of the gun line, peeling off and racing towards them, its main signalling lamp going like the clappers, and then the star shells she'd fired over *Scourge*. Even so, the P38s had made another pass, but with all the signal lamps flashing and all pyrotechnics going off, none of them had been able to concentrate enough to score any more hits on poor, crippled *Scourge*, and then they'd got the message and peeled away.

But still, fussy, punctilious Farrar, he'd done all that and saved the boat. Bloody marvellous.

Eleven

'What are you saying about the Bonny Boy?' It was the new base senior petty officer asking and none too pleasant about it, either. The three ratings, sprawled about on the rocks by the torpedo shop's jetty, had been jawing away over mugs of tea on their break from de-ammunitioning *Scourge*, or the *Salt-cellar* as she was now being known on account of all those holes in her.

'Nuthin', Chiefy,' said the surliest-looking one, not even bothering to look like he was impressed by the impressive CPO Gault and all his impressive bulk looming over him. The three were all torpedomen, employed ashore in the workshop, a fact given away by their tanned arms and faces. Fighting submariners were never on the surface long enough to get tans. The three were all in their working overalls, so no rank badges on display and all oil-streaked from manhandling *Scourge's* torpedoes out the forward loading hatch before she went over to the dockyards in Grand Harbour for repairs. The oldest of three, however, didn't want any grief from Gault, who he'd heard could be a right hard horse if you gave him the excuse.

'It was one of the lads off *Tobermory*,' he said, all emollient. 'About how *Scourge* probably copped it off those Yank fighter-bombers. Why she was there.'

'I wasn't asking you about *Tobermory*,' snapped Gault. 'Or *Scourge*.'

'Ah know, Chiefy,' said the emollient one, trying to calm matters. 'But *Tobermory*, she's Twelfth Flotilla, and she's just been in droppin' off COPP teams and shot-down fly boys. They were chattin' about their Captain S and how he's always had it in for *Scourge's* skipper, and…'

'Really,' said Gault, interrupting, whose recent conversation – extraordinary conversation – with Shrimp Simpson about Captain Bonalleck and Mr Gilmour had never been far from his mind. 'And what exactly were these Twelfth Flotilla gentlemen saying about Captain Bonalleck? And *Scourge*?'

'Well, Chiefy, they were reckoning that was why he'd probably stuck *Scourge* right out in the open up there off the Sicily beaches… so as some passing shoot-first-ask-questions-later flyin' Wild Bill Hickock would blast her on his way past. Sounds like that was what happened. Warn't it, Chiefy?'

'You know something?' said Gault. 'For skilled men, you don't half talk a lot of bollocks. And listen to it too… instead of furthering the bleedin' war effort. So it was Captain Bonalleck just took it on himself to order *Scourge* right into the middle of the Sicily landings, eh? Just upped and said, "Bugger me! What a good idea!" Was it Admiral Cunningham told you that? Or Winston himself? When d'you ever hear of a lowly flotilla skipper being allowed to draw up a fleet's order of battle? Eh?'

'Oh, the old Bonny Boy ain't no flotilla skipper anymore, Chiefy. He'd already got hauled off to be the SLO for the whole op ages before…' said the surly one, this time, as if talking to a slow child, '…hadn't you heard?'

SLO – submarine liaison officer – for all of Operation Husky. There was nothing lowly about that berth.

*

'CPO Gault to see you now, sir,' said the young writer in his smart whites as he held the curtain aside for the bulk of the man outside to enter. Yes, S10 could afford to have a writer on his staff now.

Gault marched into the tiny office, his cap squarely on, and snapped to attention in front of Capt Philips's desk. He didn't salute, Philips wasn't wearing a cap. 'Sir! Chief Petty Officer Gault, sir. Requesting captain's table, sir,' he said.

Philips stood up from behind his desk to pull out a chair for the chief; the two men had known each other professionally and as friends for over two decades. That was how long they'd been in the trade together, so it would've been astonishing if they hadn't.

'Hello, Jim,' said Philips. 'Take your cap off, man. Have a seat.'

Gault, still in his working overalls, smiled at Philips, all neatly decked out in his whites. He grunted, 'Sir!' and sat down. Philips, back behind his desk again, said, 'I'd heard you were here, haven't had the chance to look you up yet to say hello. But now you've taken care of that, it appears. Captain's table? Urgent? I can't believe it's because you've missed me so much, Chief, you couldn't wait,' a laugh, to puncture the seriousness filling the tiny room, 'So tell me. What's up, Jim?'

'I want to discuss something with you in utmost confidence, sir,' said Gault, with such gravity that Philips found himself swallowing hard. What was all this formality? This wasn't the man he remembered from the China station. Two minutes ago, Philips had been looking forward to catching up with an old China hand again. Right now, he should've been going into his bottom drawer and getting his gin out. But it was becoming increasingly obvious that Gault wasn't here to catch up, and Philips had gone from surprised curiosity – when he'd first received the *official* request for an 'audience' from HMS *Talbot's* most senior rate, hand delivered not two hours ago – to this creeping premonition he was now experiencing, that what he was about to hear, he wasn't going to like.

'...Of course, Jim,' said Philips, interrupting what had sounded like the beginning of a rehearsed speech. Definitely not the Jim Gault he remembered.

'Hear me out first, sir,' Gault continued, doggedly. 'It concerns a conversation I had with your predecessor, Captain Simpson. I don't know if he mentioned it to you before he left.'

'Our paths didn't cross Jim. He was gone before I got here.'

'Ah,' said Gault. 'This matter I wish to speak of, sir, it concerns another officer, of command rank. If I have your permission to speak, sir, I'd better start at the beginning...'

*

'Now take us to sea, Mr McCready,' Harry said and leaned against the periscope stands with his hands in his pockets as the sub lieutenant bent to the binnacle to line up *Scourge* for her turn into Marsamxett Harbour proper and then out round Tigne Point.

It was all you could expect of a late August Mediterranean day: hot, with a catspaw of breeze on the water and not a cloud to be seen. The harbour was choked with raft upon raft of trotted-up landing craft and victualling craft plying in between, just enough to keep young McCready on his toes.

On *Scourge's* fore-casing, her line of ratings stood smartly at ease, all buffed-up and chuffed with themselves and their boat and her new paint job. She was going on patrol again, free of dockyard squalor and ready to face the enemy. And as everyone had spotted, when he'd sprinted up the gangway or heard the buzz, the skipper appeared to be his old self again, or if he wasn't, he was doing a bloody good impression.

Scourge had been in dockyard hands having her holes patched for what had seemed like an age. But, after doing his rounds and filing all his reports, after Able Seaman Archer's funeral, her skipper, Lt Harry Gilmour, had been nowhere to be seen. The jimmy, Lt Nick Farrar had overseen all the repair and refitting for sea work. Speculation had been rife: the skipper had been relieved, promoted, demoted, caught wearing women's clothing, that bastard, the Bonny Boy, had had him hauled back to Algiers and Twelfth Flotilla to give him thirty strokes with a railway sleeper for refusing to worship at his scrotum pole. Or Harding's particular favourite, from among all the lower deck speculation; '…I reckon it's that ancient bint that did all the singing wots got him… wots-her-name?… Calypso… in that cave o' hers up on Gozo… wi' her thighs wrapped round his ears havin' her evil way with 'im three times a day, four on a Sunday!' – '…'ave ya seen the tits on her?' – '…'ave ya seen the smile on 'is face, ya mean?' The Vasco had been often heard to ponder aloud, after hearing it for the first time, 'Who would have thunk it? Jack. Knowing his Homer?'

Needless to say, all the speculation had been wrong.

Lt Gilmour, after his visit to see his old chum Louis, had returned to the Lazaretto to be greeted by an order from S10 to get himself checked out by the surgeon commander, who pronounced him knackered and sent him off to a beautiful, airy, *fin de siècle* apartment, currently being maintained by the minesweeper boys up north in the hill town of Mdina.

He hadn't the strength to argue, and when he had arrived there, after saying hello to his fellow guests – all junior RNVR officers – he had excused himself and retired to his 'cabin', where he had then proceeded to sleep for over thirty hours.

'You had the odd pee break, of course,' one of the fresh-faced youths had confirmed to him when he'd finally got up. 'But you looked so far gone each time you emerged from your scratcher, nobody had the heart to detain you on your way back, old boy.' All this on the tiny veranda, over a plate piled high with warmed pastries and scrambled eggs and coffee.

'War is hell, eh?' another had observed, reaching for more eggs.

And there Harry had stayed until one day, the phone rang, and it was the S10's office telling him his boat was ready for patrol, and he might want to cast his eye over her before proceeding to sea.

Those had been long, long sunkissed days in Mdina, exploring the medieval town and walking alone through the terraced fields north-west to overlook the sea. The evenings had been spent in convivial company. The apartment had been commandeered as a mini rest camp by the growing flotilla of minesweepers that now shared Marsamxett harbour with the Tenth, and the half dozen or so sub lieutenants and lieutenants up there having a lie-down were happy to share it with a fellow wavy-navy lad 'from the mob up the road'. But they showed absolutely no curiosity whatsoever about Harry's life as a submariner.

'Rather you than me, old boy,' had been the general consensus. Which coincidently, had been Harry's thoughts on minesweeping; all that working in close proximity to all those high explosives put there in your path and designed specifically to blow you to kingdom come had never been Harry's idea of a cushy billet. He remembered his pal from *King Alfred* days; the one whose minesweeper had set off a magnetic one off West Mersea and there'd been nothing left of him but smoking boots. But he'd kept that to himself. Instead, they'd talked about the war in general and what was going to happen once it was won. The whole island was bustling again, this time for the upcoming landings on mainland Italy itself; so how long could it be now? And then there were the girls they'd left behind and the Yanks. Everyone had been agreed: they were amazing. Both the girls and the Yanks. But when it came to the Yanks, it was all the stuff they'd brought with them everybody wanted to talk about.

'They could win this war just by bombing Jerry with Hershey bars 'til he's so fat he can't fight anymore,' had been one strategic option put forward over the late-night brandy decanters.

Harry had decided not to mention things like the four P38s who'd shot up his boat and killed one of his crew, so these sessions had stayed light.

He'd even once ventured back down to Valletta with a shopping list of books to be presented to Louis. 'The ones we've got, we don't need to read 'em anymore,' one wag had assured him. 'We just recite them by heart.' Acquiring new works had become that urgent, so since he 'knew a man', it was the least Harry could do.

'I'm sorry for that bollocks I talked when I was last here,' Harry had said to Louis' back, as the old man had been scouring his shelves for the titles on the list.

'Ah, so what,' Louis had replied. But yes, 'so what', Harry had insisted. Louis had told him to shut up until he was finished and they had some coffee on the go.

'I was just being a big girl,' Harry had assured the old man as he was adjusting the spirit lamp under the percolator. 'And it was an imposition on you. I've no excuses.'

The long walks and the evenings on the veranda had got him out of the habit of chasing all those nagging voices in his head, speculating endlessly on stuff he could do nothing about. He had responsibilities after all, right in front of him, that needed concentrating on. It was a big war, and Harry might have no power over what happened in it and only a small part to play, but it was an important part. Especially for his crew; it was their lives. And for his superiors, for their plans to succeed, it required that he do his bit. Everything else was just noise. That thirty hours' sleep had bought him the time to realise he had to stop picking at the threads of everything and get on with it.

He hadn't actually said any of that to Louis, but looking at him, Louis could work out what had been going on in his head.

'What age are you?' Louis had asked him.

'I dunno. Twenty-four?'

'Twenty-four. It's young for the responsibility,' Louis had said. 'And for the cost. Because I can see now, you know you're going to have to pay for it, don't you?' A long pause followed. 'Make me a promise.'

'Of course. What?'

'When you go home and…'

'…If I get home.'

'*When* you go home and you start to tally it up. Be kind to yourself. Don't count what it's done to you as loss. And remember me, and all the people here… all the people all over Europe… that through your bit in all this, you've given back their future. Don't just look at the cost, look at what you've bought with it, for so very, very many.'

So he had promised, and now he was back on his bridge, heading for a patrol billet that ran north-east to south-west from the island of Capri out into the Tyrrhenian basin, there to form part of an anti-U-boat picket to cover another major US amphibious landing, due for the second week in September and aimed at the beaches around a small seaside resort called Salerno, south of Naples.

Harry had never tackled a U-boat before, while in command. So his head was full of submarine tactics – as it should've been – as they dived to begin their transit up past the eastern shore of Allied-occupied Sicily, heading for the Messina Straits.

Down in the forward spaces, *Scourge's* ratings were getting used to their new crewmates. While *Scourge* had been in the dockyard's hands, a number of ratings and most of the wireless telegraphists had been nabbed by other boats. And two of the new lads had a new job aboard. They were there to operate *Scourge's* latest piece of kit, an RDF set – or range and direction finder – the antenna for which the dockyard mateys had welded to the after ends of the conning tower. It was an awkward X-structure that looked like a parrot's *pied-a-terre*. 'It's there to stop any shagbats creeping up on us, sir, no matter the weather, night or day,' one of the new lads had explained. 'Up to a certain range, it's good for surface targets too, sir.'

'By "surface targets", you mean ships?' Harry had asked when being shown the contraption; he hated all this new technical jargon that was creeping in.

'Or U-boats… on the surface, sir,' the rating had assured him, beaming with enthusiasm. His name was Smith, and he was another of the increasing number of nineteen and twenty-year-old leading seamen technical ratings being thrust on the trade these days. 'The Yanks call it radar, and we're doing the same now, really, sir. Saves confusion, sir.'

Whose confusion? Harry had wanted to ask him, and *what's a 'certain range'?* But there'd be time for that later, once they'd got to sea and settled down.

There was also a new POTel – Petty Officer, Telegraphist – Ken Dandy, and Grieve had been replaced too, by a big-grinning, south London cheeky-chappie, called Leading Seaman Arthur Boxall.

Quite a few of Warrant Engineer Bert Petrie's stokers had been nabbed too, but Harry would leave it to Mr Petrie to see to bringing the new lads up to scratch. It had been a long tradition on this boat that back aft was engineer territory, and Harry was a great believer in not trying to fix things that weren't broken.

Boxall had turned up early to report, before most of *Scourge's* established crew, who had all still been on their way down from one of the rest camps. Sub Lt McCready and the cox'n had seen him onto the boat's books and then sent him for'ard to claim his place. Hooper, *Scourge's* now-legendary gun layer, was already in the forward spaces, having spent the morning helping load all the stores that had been ready to load and had now retired to his hammock for an afternoon nap. Awakened by a clatter, he watched an unusually large amount of kit come through the watertight door, followed by a shortish Leading Seaman 'Sparks' in work rig and sporting an irritating flop of blonde curly hair sticking out from under his cap.

'Wotcher!' said the newcomer and introduced himself. He then plunged into his kitbag and produced a huge glass jar of boiled sweets which he placed by the aft bulkhead and announced, '…a little sumfin' I picked up on me travels, for the comfort of all deservin' souls.'

Hooper's eyes lit up. On account of it being inadvisable to smoke on a submarine while submerged, their lordships had long ago generously began supplying crews with sweets as a substitute: regulation barley sugars by the hundredweight. But this jar had lime ones and red ones and what Hooper could've sworn were butterscotch! Then Boxall had produced a small squeezebox. 'I do trust we like a tune in this mess?' he said, with a winning smile, followed by two swift bars of *Hearts of Oak*, and rounding off with a final flourish of *Mademoiselle from Armentières*. Hooper was already laughing before he'd finished.

There wasn't exactly an official hierarchy in the forward spaces, but it was generally reckoned that Hooper and Biddle, the boat's lead Asdic operator, were the senior rates and were listened to. So, when Boxall asked where he should sling his kit, on a hunch, Hooper decided he could have Grieve's old perch, above the starboard torpedo reloads. There had been a few eyes on that space once it was known Grieve was off, but Boxall was here now and they weren't, and Hooper's gut told him they might have good 'un here, worth looking after.

'Nice one,' said Boxall and slung his kit up.

'I wouldn't unpack right off,' Hooper advised. 'There's usually a couple of boards of fresh bread gets slipped in under you. Makes the lying more comfy while we're still eating our way through 'em!... what's that big lump in yer bag?'

'Oh, that?' said Boxall, giving it a tap with his knuckle. 'An electric iron. I'm thinkin' I might go into business when we gets back from patrol.'

That made Hooper frown, not because, if he thought about it, his 'gut' was wrong as often as it was right, but because he'd already granted Boxall the berth.

*

The Straits of Messina was now the Allies' front line, with Commonwealth and US troops occupying the Sicilian shore and Jerries and the odd reluctant Italian, the Calabrian on the opposite side. So Harry didn't intend hanging about driving *Scourge* through.

It was their second night out from Malta. *Scourge* had surfaced about eighteen miles north-east of Taormina for the run-through. They had come up to a starless black sky, almost slap bang in the middle of the straits' entrance, each shore several miles distant. There was a heavy haze on the water that made the random searchlight activity on each bank look like it was being shone through muslin. But way ahead, Harry, on the bridge, could see the odd star shell going up out of the gauzy night. That would be the straits at their narrowest point. They were going to have to slip through submerged up there, so the sooner they *got* up there, the more night they'd have left to run out the other side.

The threat for the time being, however, was from aircraft. On the Allied side, the air forces should've been alerted that a British submarine would be effecting a transit, but the *Scourges* knew only too well that merely alerting the fly boys meant nothing, and Harry could practically feel the two bridge lookouts straining their senses into the night.

Down below, Harry also had had the two radar lads scanning the sky with their electronic toy from the moment they'd surfaced for the run. However, he wasn't placing a great deal of confidence in them. The previous night's experiments with the new kit had proved patchy to say the least. Harry had sat in as they'd warmed up the set.

'This is the latest Type 291 set,' Leading Seaman Roy 'Smudger' Smith had assured him with a proprietorial air. 'With this brand new PPI display that simplifies everything, sir…'

'I've no idea what you're talking about, Smudger,' Harry had said with a blank smile. He could tell the rating liked him using his nickname. Good. Get him feeling part of the crew right off.

'Oh,' said Smudger, momentarily crestfallen. 'PPI?'

Harry nodded.

'It's the plan position indicator,' said Smudger, now as aglow as the screen in front of him, that he was being asked to explain his pet toy. 'You see the circular screen? The dot at the centre is the radar antenna, and the concentric circles marked on it represent the range and height above sea level. As the radar antenna rotates, the trace on the PPI sweeps round, sending out pulses at five hundred hertz, on a hundred and forty centimetres…'

'To do what…? Harry had interrupted.

'Um! Oh, it's very good, sir. Very good. Any aircraft flying at… five thousand feet… the pulse has the power to hit it at up to thirty nautical miles… we're generating over a hundred kilowatts… and then it bounces back, sir, so we see it right here, sir, as a blip.' And Smudger had tapped the glass screen. 'And we always know the bearing because the lubber line here,' another tap, 'represents the bow of the ship, er, boat… and our heading, sir, and shows us the bearing off.'

Harry, thinking about those P38s, had then asked, 'What if they're flying lower than five thousand? What about right down on the deck?'

'Em, well, the beam is limited by the curve of the earth, sir…'

'So, four, five miles warning then? Same for a small ship too? Or a U-boat?' Smudger had looked glum again. 'Yes, sir.'

'So, only as good as the Mark One eyeball, then?'

And at that, Smudger had regained his confidence. 'Yes, sir. If the eyeball can see as clearly at night or through fog, sir.'

Last night, there had been frequent sounds of aero engines in the starless sky and HE from the Asdic and for most of the night, not a single identifiable 'blip' on Smudger's precious PPI. Every ten minutes or so it seemed, Smudger's oppo, Able Seaman Liam 'Darky' Mularky had the back off it and was jabbing the conductor ends of a megger into its innards or twiddling it with a screwdriver. By the end, they had, at last, been picking up something blipping but had been unable to say whether it was on the deck at four miles or ten thousand feet at thirty.

Tonight, Boxall was on radio watch with the two radar operators squeezed in beside him with their set, all the new boys together. He had just finished listening in on the admiralty band, broadcast from Rugby on sixteen kilocycles, to see if there was any traffic for *Scourge* from home, and was turning the dial up onto the submarine wavelength at 4,900 kilocycles for any morse chatter from S10 in Malta when Smudger began swearing again.

The foul tirade had seemed so jarring at first, coming as it did out of a child's snaggle-toothed mouth, his big, baby-round face and downy-smooth cheeks were too wholesome to spew forth such filth. But out it was coming.

Boxall said, out the side of his mouth, 'I'd say, "why don't you just give it a good dunt," but...' But indeed. As he turned, expecting to see some complicit grins, he was stopped in his tracks by the dark, dead-pan stare of Darky Mularky. Pretty early on, Boxall had worked out the chap's 'Darky' moniker, apart from the rhyming slang, because Mularky was as 'Black Irish' as could be – the pale pudding face topped by a jet, obsidian mop of curls on his head and a five-o'clock shadow that looked like it started growing shortly after breakfast. His piercing blue eyes were normally pretty vacant, but not now. On their short acquaintance, Darky had proved to be a man of few words, never had much to say. And right now, he didn't need to. Not by the look in those eyes. Right now, Darky looked downright dangerous. So Boxall shut up. Here was a man it looked sensible not to piss off.

After a few moments though, Boxall made a peace offering. 'You don't think my set might be causing some interference, do you?'

Smudger and Darky paused to consider this. 'Maybe if we could look at your shielding?' said Smudger.

Twelve

'He's sailed on patrol. Yesterday,' said Capt Philips. 'Bugger!' said Wincairns. The two men were sitting in the S10's office in the Lazaretto. Not much sun was coming in through the open shuttered window, on account of all the high hazy cloud about, but it was bloody hot for this time in the morning.

They'd been sharing their Harry Gilmour/Bonny Boy stories, and both were looking concerned. 'I agree it is time we heard his version of events,' Philips said. 'But what do we do with it when we have?'

Wincairns sighed and rubbed his hands. 'How many guesses do I get?' He had come to see the Captain S to tell him the story he'd heard about the attack on *Scourge* off JOSS beach and to ask him if he could shed any light as to how it might have happened. And in return, he had heard Philips' retelling of CPO Gault's potted history, which had included Shrimp Simpson's account of the existence, somewhere, probably still in the C-in-C Med's in-tray, of the Bonny Boy's report on Lt Gilmour baying for his blood.

'I think we are both agreed that there is something extremely questionable afoot here,' Wincairns had said. And Philips had promptly concurred. 'So I strongly suggest that getting to the truth of the matter should be strenuously avoided. Bury it. That's what I say. But how?'

Philips looked momentarily shocked but quickly recovered. 'We're helped, I suppose, by all the confusion back in Alex,' he said, referring to Admiral Harwood being relieved due to 'ill health'. Poor Henry, he'd proved a dead loss at running a fleet. Their lordships had first hived off half his command and given it back to Admiral Cunningham for Operation 'Husky', and now they'd delivered the order of the boot.

'Your Admiral Cunningham, I'd imagine, has his hands full right now,' Wincairns observed, lighting a cigarette for something to do with his hands. 'It'll get relegated to some staff bugger. We have to ensure he shuts this idiot Bonalleck well and truly up. Seeing as he is the one making all the racket and not your Lieutenant Gilmour, who we know is quite a doughty fellow.'

'Well, I'll help all I can. I don't like the look of what's going on here anymore than you do,' said Capt Philips, 'but if this bastard is up to what it looks like…'

'What does it look like, Captain?' said Wincairns, with some steel in his voice. 'Do you really want to be the one to come out and say what it looks like?' Wincairns gave him a withering look, 'It's your navy, Captain, and its reputation. And history tells us, does it not, that washing dirty laundry in public never ends well. For anyone. It also tells us that "getting to the bottom" of things always requires too many people having to know about those "things", and "too many people" is my definition of "in public".'

'So what do you suggest, Mr Wincairns,' said Capt Philips, now equally icy.

'I refer you to my previous answer, *ibid*, "How many guesses do I get?"' said Wincairns, now sounding utterly deflated.

*

The skies had cleared, so there was a riot of stars going on when Harding came out the conning tower hatch right after Harry to shoot Jupiter and confirm their position on their patrol billet. The two lookouts were right behind him, followed by McCready, whose watch it was.

Scourge had just finished Sunday service. The 'Holy Willy' back-aftie who normally conducted the bible-reading, hymn-singing part had been one of the victims of the Vice-Admiral, Malta's sweep for spare crew while *Scourge* had been laid up, so her captain had done the honours, rounding up all the crew not on watch, in the usual place in the control room, him propped by the chart table and the rest all squeezed in around the periscopes and the diving board valves and the two planesmen, now jammed up against their wheels.

Harry had kept the 'God' bit brief – a reading from Psalm 107, verses thirty-five and thirty-six, ending with God promising to turn '*a desert into pools of water… and there he lets the hungry dwell*', followed by one verse of *Eternal Father, Strong To Save*, all of it sounding suitably reverent and sombre, being delivered under red light because they would be surfacing shortly into darkness. Then with that out of the way, he'd got to the bit they'd all been waiting for: what was happening and where they were going.

'We sailed under sealed orders,' Harry had said, in sonorous tones that got the usual smirks and chuckles from the old *Scourges*. 'Now there's a story you can drive folk to drink with, in bars up and down the nation when you get home.'

There had been a few giggles. 'As for the contents of those sealed orders, well I can only share them if you promise not to tell anyone else… well? I'm waiting.'

Much eye rolling as each had man contemplated the steel hull around them and the fact that they were all sixty feet under the water and a long way from anyone to talk to. 'Ye-ess,' said several silly voices, in unison.

'Excellent. Extra barley sugars for all those who promised,' Harry had said, beaming now. The lads liked him like this, the daft schoolboy they knew he wasn't. More proof the skipper was back on form.

'We're up here in the Tyrrhenian basin for another nice day out in support of our friends and Allies,' he'd then continued in a more serious voice. 'It's called Operation Avalanche, and it is being launched to put the US Fifth Army ashore near a small town south of Naples, called Salerno. Our mission is quite simple, and that is to form a patrol line with *Subedar, Turbid* and *Tulwar*... to warn of any enemy ships or U-boats trying to get in amongst the landing force.'

The line was to stretch west, out along the latitude of the island of Capri and the Sorrento peninsula, with the small town and bay of Salerno at the peninsula's base. *Subedar's* patrol box would be inshore of them, towards Capri, and the other two would be strung out further to seaward. He'd then gone on to tell them that Monty, as he was speaking, was already ashore around the heel of Italy with Eighth Army, so, with a bit of luck, Jerry might not be expecting this second punch. There had been more details about how they would be operating well out from the main landing force, so hopefully, there'd be no repetition of their last outing and that Ken Dandy, their new PO Tel, would be passing out all the call signs and recognition codes for the radio watches and those on lookout duties. Then there'd been some general war updates culled from the BBC about the Eastern Front, what was happening in the Pacific and the stepping up of the bomber offensive against Germany proper, now that the US Eighth Air Force was really getting going.

'And that's it, gentlemen,' Harry had concluded. 'Dismiss. And stand by to surface in fifteen minutes.'

A night of unrelieved tedium followed. Nothing was sighted, nothing heard, and the only events of note were the changing of the watches. No one called Harry to the bridge or to the control room, and as the first light began to creep over the far horizon and swallow the stars, *Scourge* slipped back below the gentle swell for another day of tootling around her own patrol box. In the finest trade tradition of reversing mealtimes – with the dawn now broken above and the boat at watch, diving in the gloom at sixty feet – Windass laid on a splendid 'dinner' of pea soup, roast leg of mutton, roast potatoes and braised onions, followed by tinned pineapple and custard.

It was the same the next day, and the day after. Nothing to report apart from the food was good.

Then, at the end of day four on the line, with the last dog watch about to change over, *Scourge* was at watch, diving with not long to go until she surfaced for the hours of darkness. Harry was sitting on his own at the wardroom table, bathed in red light, drinking coffee, when Ken Dandy popped his head round, 'A signal from S Ten, sir, for CO's eyes only.'

Harry sighed, got the code books out and settled into decode. He was expecting more bumpf regarding 'Avalanche', which he knew from the now infamous 'sealed orders', was supposed to launch later that night, but what he read made him exclaim, 'Well! Bugger me!'

McCready, who had joined him only a few minutes before, all gummy-eyed from sleep and getting ready to go on watch, looked up from his coffee and bacon-and-egg sandwich. 'Sir?' he said.

'It's the bloody Eyeties,' said Harry. 'They've just surrendered!'

And there was more.

Harry had Harding woken, and when he too had slid into the wardroom benches, Harry had told them the signal was also alerting their patrol line to a sortie by major Italian Navy units sailing from Genoa and La Spezia.

'It's the *Littorio, Vittorio Veneto* and *Roma*,' he said. 'Our old battleship chums, I believe. The ones we *didn't* bag because I let them get away. Except this time, they're not coming out to fight but to surrender. This says they're heading for Bone in Algeria. There's no specific course detailed, but we're to let them proceed unchallenged if they come our way and help defend them if they come under attack by Jerry. Fancy that. Maybe they'll sell us some ice cream on the way past. That'd be nice.'

Harding said, 'Aw, sir. You didn't let them *get* away… they *ran* away.'

And Harry said, 'Shut up, Miles, and go through the boat and brief everyone about Italy's throwing in the towel.'

As Harding left to spread the word, he said, with an arch wistfulness, 'We could've had a spaghetti dinner tonight, to celebrate, if it wasn't for Windass and his stupid ban on Axis grub.'

Which was true; you'd never have found a frankfurter or anything at all schnitzeled in Windass's pantry.

Then they'd not long gone to middle watch when Ken Dandy summoned Harry to the radio cubby again. The 'Avalanche' frequencies he'd been listening in on had all just sprung to life. 'It's all crash, bang, wallop over there, sir,' he said in his thick scouser twang, holding onto his headphones so they scrunched down what was left of his thinning pate. The landings had begun.

With the middle watch about to change, it had again been, 'Captain to the bridge!' And when Harry got up there, the eastern horizon had been glowing and pulsing.

Windass's 'dinner' that dawn had been based around oxtail soup and veal & ham pie, rounded off with apple pie and cream. Afterwards, stuffed full and distracted by his thoughts about what must be happening on the beaches away to the west, and in Jerry southern command, Harry found himself knocked out of the wardroom versus the POs' mess uckers tournament. Bugger!

The next night, this time two-thirds of the way through the middle watch, the call came again: 'Captain to the bridge!' Harry had been sound asleep on his bunk, but he was out of it and up the conning tower ladder in seconds.

Harding had the watch, and he was scribbling frantically into a notebook as one of the bunts who just happened to have the middle was dictating to him, eyes still jammed into his night glasses. Harry followed the young signalman's line of sight to look directly astern, and there, he could see a blinking light, brighter than the residual starlight through the high haze and blinking to a beat.

'…signal ends, sir!' said signalman.

'Thank you, bunts. Well done. Carry on,' said Harding, looking at Harry. 'It was *Subedar* signalling, sir. She's picking up E-boat HE on her Asdic. Quite a few of the buggers, apparently. Coast hugging round Point Campanella. Heading into Salerno Bay. She's shadowing but doesn't want to break radio silence in case they take fright.'

A swarm of E-boats could be decidedly fatal for a submarine to tangle with on her own, but down Salerno Bay, there was a US Navy destroyer gun line. They'd be more than capable of dealing with them, so they needed to know.

Harry leaned to the voicepipe, 'Yeoman to the bridge, and tell him to bring his Aldis!'

Within seconds, Bird was there, and Harry had Harding re-dictate what the bunts had decoded for him while Bird flashed the Aldis signal lamp to raise *Turbid*, the next boat on the line. 'Tell them to on-pass to *Tulwar*,' he said. 'She can raise the USN on the tactical net and let them know. She's so far away, Jerry won't twig it's someone's spotted them.'

The flurry of activity was soon over. Everybody had got quite animated for a moment, something to do for a change. Then it was done. Bird went back below, and the lookouts went back to scanning the dark horizon. For this patrol, Harry had doubled the watch roster so that lookouts spent only one hour on the bridge with their binoculars stuck to their faces before receiving a break. It ensured they weren't peering into the night for too long, lest their minds start to drift or their eyes became so tired straining in the dark that they'd miss something.

Harry said to Harding, 'Well I suppose that was our excitement for the night.' Then he went below himself with the next flip of the lookouts. But despite this coddling of them, it turned out not to be one of the lookouts who triggered the next alert.

'Captain to the radio room!' It was the new boy, Boxall, shouting.

Harry's head was round the cubby door in seconds, 'What's up, Boxall?'

'It's not me, sir. It's Smudger, sir. He thinks he's got something.'

Harry looked down and saw, to his surprise, the two radar operators perched low on a pair of tinned fruit boxes right under his nose. The 'Black Irish' one was in the process of giving Boxall the evil eye, obviously resenting him making the call and not letting his boss, Smudger Smith, do the job.

'Smudger,' Harry said. 'What d'you have?'

'I didn't want to alert you, sir, in case it wasn't…'

'Smudger, on this boat I decide whether it's worth it or not,' said Harry. 'Now, what *is* it?'

'The set's been coming and going, sir. Playing up more than…' Smudger was saying. But Mularky was watching the expression on Harry's face. The skipper wanted an answer.

'It's a U-boat, sorr,' Mularky butted in, in his ripe brogue. 'On the surface. Range four miles. Bearing green seven zero. Course one four zero, speed approximately fifteen to seventeen knots, sorr.'

'Show me,' said Harry, leaning over the PPI.

'...We've had a quite a few false traces, sir,' said Smudger. 'Aircraft that...'

'It's a U-boat, sorr,' interrupted Mularky again. 'I've seen one before, on a set like this.'

'Good show, Mularky,' said Harry brushing off Smudger's caveats and leaning back to yell into the control room, 'Diving stations! Close up the forward torpedo room! Gun crew close up in the well!'

On his way up the ladder, Harry ordered a turn to starboard. Bodies tumbled down the passage behind him; it was a complete scrum, but the diving stations order was carried out without even a mutter, just the pounding of feet on the deck plates and then silence. *Scourge* was only moving at three knots, so she was making next to zero wake or bow wave. When Harry reached the bridge, he addressed the lookouts, his voice quiet and measured, like they were all twitchers in a bird-spotters hide, 'Target on the starboard bow. What can you see?'

A pause, then, 'I can see a bow wave, bearing green ten!' yelled the lookout, just a black lump on the bridge because Harry's night vision was still acclimatising. 'So can I,' called Harding, straining through his own night glasses. 'It's not *Subedar, Turbid* or *Tulwar* is it?'

'Can't be,' said Harry, not bothering to look yet, knowing he'd still just be seeing black, dark nothingness. 'Their patrol areas are to port and starboard of us, not dead ahead. No other Allied boats in the area.' Then he turned to the other lookout, 'Put me on the bearing.'

The lookout grabbed Harry's shoulders as he bent to the binnacle. 'That's you fine on, sir!' he said, steadying his captain on the line to the darkness. And yes, Harry could now just make out the glimmer of phosphorescence. He peered back at the binnacle, 'I estimate target's true course to be one five five degrees. Call it down to the fruit machine, Mr Harding.'

Harding got McCready on the voicepipe and told him enemy course 155 degrees. The range was going to be tougher for Harry to call, with nothing but a vague black shape to gauge against a black background and right down on the water, as a U-boat would be. What he could see was that the shape was a couple of points below the night horizon, not right on it. And since he knew *Scourge's* line of sight to the horizon, to the yard, he simply subtracted.

'Range, four thousand yards!' he called down the voicepipe now, talking directly to McCready. 'Estimated speed, twelve knots!'

The bearings began coming up to him from Biddle on the Asdic set, '…target bearing, three five zero.' And from Smudger on the Type 291, and they were concurring. Harry ordered all six bow tubes readied. Full salvos were the standing order for U-boats, they were considered such high-value targets that they were worth it. Although convention dictated that he should fire them to cover one and a half lengths of the target for safety, one just ahead, one just behind, Harry knew that simply wasn't going to work. Not here, not with where he and the Jerry were fine on each other's bow.

He needed an edge. Then, out the corner of his eye, Harry noticed the poor glimmer of phosphorescence in the water below the bridge wing, curling off *Scourge's* saddle tanks as they made the barest of way. Not nearly enough to reflect their presence at this range.

At this range, the night was shielding them, while the bubbling phosphorescence of the U-boat's bow wave, coming on at twelve knots, was lighting *him* up.

But *Scourge's* torpedoes, once Harry had fired them, if the phosphorescence was this bad, Jerry would see them coming like horizontal rocket trails. If Jerry was keeping a good watch, he'd have time to turn and comb them and dive away to safety.

He bent to the binnacle again and began calling the latest bearings and the target's estimated speed. Then he called, 'Range eighteen hundred yards!' In the time it had taken him to think and call his orders, the U-boat had already travelled more than halfway towards where he wanted his range on firing to be. The bugger was coming on too fast. He needed to be closer before he fired so as the U-boat would have less time to see his torpedo wakes.

The gun! That would do it!

'Hooper!' he called into the voicepipe. 'Close up for gun action!' And seconds later, as *Scourge's* magic gun layer came tumbling onto the casing, Harry was leaning over the bridge front, calling out the bearing and range.

The words had just left his mouth when an insistent voice was in his ear: the port lookout. 'Target's under helm, sir! Lots of wake, sir!… She's turning away! Her helm's hard over, sir!'

Harry already had his night glasses up. Indeed, she was turning away. Even he could see the welter of foam the U-boat was chucking up as it heeled around. The bastard had spotted *Scourge*.

'Commence firing, Hooper!' Harry was yelling now.

BANG!

But before Harry had even time to think, *that was quick, even for Hooper!…* a tiny green thread of light came jerking out of the night, like little occasional stitches, one bounding behind the other as if the next one was pushing on the first, until the stitches, as they crept closer, suddenly speeded up to racing flashes, and then they were ending in a running gout of tall pillars of exploding water, acutely angling in down *Scourge's* starboard beam. Tracer. The bastard was firing on them, using its bandstand 20mm anti-aircraft gun. And then the stitches suddenly stopped, like a tap had been switched off, the last two continuing to arc towards them out of the night.

'Target is diving!' It was Biddle's tinny voice out of the voicepipe, who must be listening to the din of the U-boat flooding all tanks.

BANG!

Harry turned his night glasses in time to see the first shell hit the water where the U-boat had been as it had gone into its turn. A second or so passed and then… an explosion… sparks… had the second round hit? Had that been the back end of the Jerry's conning tower? But where Jerry had been a moment before was now all tumbling water and more glowing phosphorescence.

'Check fire! Clear the casing!' And as the bodies vanished into *Scourge's* bowels, Harry hit the tit twice. The klaxon almost drowned out his shouts of, 'Clear the bridge!'

Harry's first U-boat while in command, and the bastard was getting away! Well, not if he could help it! A jumble of images ran through his head from his time in *Radegonde*, the Free French submarine he'd been appointed to as British Naval Liaison Officer, and their encounter with a forming wolf pack in the north Atlantic. And what they'd done to attack all those massing U-boats. He held those thoughts as his feet hit the control room deck plates.

'Keep periscope depth! Slow ahead together. Maintain heading!' Then, 'Mr Harding, start a plot,' he said it as he stepped aft out the control room door to the Asdic cubby, and as he passed the fruit machine, he added, 'Mr McCready, continue to update on the target.'

Biddle was hunched over, gently moving the big dial on his set.

'Right, what have you got, Ken?' said Harry. Him using his first name told Biddle *we're playing now*.

'He turned stern on to us as he dived, sir,' said Biddle. 'But he's come back onto his original course. I think he went quite deep at first, but from the noises in the water, I think he's coming back up again. But he's not running, sir. He's going dead slow, sir… I think we winged him… he is noisier than he should be.'

'Excellent,' said Harry, and he leant against the door jamb. Biddle gave him a glance as he called out the target's new bearing and speed. The captain's hands were already thrust into his blue drill trousers. Very un-officer-like. And his ratings' drill work shirt didn't immediately pick him out as an officer either; only the sets of two wavy rings wrapped round the epaulettes and his favourite bashed watch cap gave the game away. But hey, it was only on board, and nobody gave a bugger here. But his crew gave a bugger; it was great to have the old Harry back.

Harry called the bearing and speed to McCready and Harding as he took the four steps to the chart table to inspect Harding's updated plot, the pencil lines on it standing out stark in the red light. A scratch of the head under his cap, hands back in pockets. The control room crew couldn't keep their eyes off him. Oh, it felt good. The skipper was home again.

'What d'you think the range is now, Mr Harding?' he asked. 'After all that up and down and turning?'

Harding tapped the space between *Scourge* and the Jerry. 'Twelve hundred yards,' he said. 'On the button.'

'You're certain?' asked Harry, smiling.

'I feel it in my water, sir,' said Harding, smiling back. *A cheeky bugger*, thought Harry, who was seldom wrong when it came to his job. Anyway, Harry knew what Harding meant to say: Bearings on a plot never lie. Harry knew what Harry knew what

Harry, mumbling to himself, the crew hanging on every snatched word. 'He's thinking if he hangs about, he can bag us as we scoot by, chasing him.' Then more mumbling, to nobody in particular, just like in the old days. 'And he's not deep?'

Biddle must've thought Harry was asking him a direct question, because he replied, loud and clear, enough so that Harry could hear the helpless shrug in voice, '...I can't tell with this kit, sir... but he was definitely making a lot of pumping and blowing noises... and one of his screws is "singing"... I'm hearing something... definitely.'

Biddle's reply was interrupted by stifled snorts of laughter from the wireless cubby next door.

Boxall, thought Harry, *thinking smutty thoughts again*. He started sucking in his cheeks to stop himself giggling too. 'Periscope depth,' he said, finally, but not as an order. 'That's where I'd be. What's the periscope depth of a Type Seven U-boat? They're about the same size as us, so, what do we say? Twenty-seven feet, keel to surface?'

'Twenty-seven feet, sir,' said Farrar.

Harry glanced at the plot. 'Rig for silent... helm, steer starboard fifteen... engine room telegraph to stop together.'

He stepped back to the Asdic cubby and gave Biddle a reassuring wink, 'Ken, keep singing out the bearing...'

And so *Scourge* commenced her slow turn. He was no longer engaging a high-speed target on a tight bearing. The track angle was opening out now, and so was the chance of lining up for a bloody good shot at this bastard.

'Aye, aye, sir,' said Biddle.

'...and Tom,' he said, leaning back into the control room to where McCready sat in front of his fruit machine, 'keep dialling in the plot's solution and updating the D/A... fast as you like... when I call for a D/A, I'll want it fast.'

Aye, aye, sir,' said McCready.

There was utter silence in the control room.

Harry leaned back to the chart table and Harding's immaculate plot. From there, he told Farrar, 'Number One. Get on the blower, and tell TGM to set the torpedoes in tubes one, two, four and five to run at twenty-five feet. Fire on my command.'

'Aye, aye, sir,' said Farrar.

Biddle called the latest bearing.

Harry watched the little repeater compass behind the chart table showing *Scourge's* heading.

A few seconds passed. Biddle called again.

Harding marked his plot deftly. *Scourge* was steering zero seven nine degrees.

'I have range seven hundred and twenty yards!' called Harding. 'On bearing red one four, speed three knots.'

McCready was next, bare seconds behind with his dialling and solution, 'D/A is red five!'

'Asdic!' said Harry, in his most even tone, 'Sing out, please, when our chum's bearing is crossing red five.'

'Aye, aye, sir,' said Biddle, calmly reflecting his skipper's *sangfroid*.

The Asdic was going to have to be Harry's periscope for this attack. Because on this attack, there'd be no looking at the target as it steamed past your periscope's graticule, that you'd set on the director angle to tell you it was time to yell 'fire one'. Because you weren't going to be able to see your target if it was submerged like you, were you?

No, Biddle was going to have to sing out the bearings as the target came on until it crossed the magic line...

...and that was exactly what he was doing... until he wasn't...

'...target is speeding up, sir! ...turning away... bearing red seven now, sir!'

Bugger, bugger and damnation! thought Harry with one part of his brain, while the other collapsed the triangle in his head.

'Helm, port twenty, half ahead together!' said Harry, still keeping it calm.

Biddle kept calling out the bearing...

Biddle's last bearing and Harding's last best solution, their numbers crunching through the big box in Harry's head, and *Scourge*, in there too, in the pellucid water, a gently swinging long, slim shadow. And in his head, a steady pointer coming round until in his head, he knew it must be pointing with mechanical certainty, and then he yelled, 'Fire one!'

Harry watched closely *Scourge's* heading on the little repeater compass, above the chart table, as the torpedo, being blown out, checked the turn slightly, then as *Scourge* came back, he called, 'Fire two,' in a more measured tone. Admirable, since all the certainties of Harding's plot and McCready's fruit machine solution had gone out the window the moment Jerry had had the ill manners to move fast to get out of *Scourge's* way. From that moment he'd been winging it, all the angles calculating in his head.

Then, in quick succession, '...Fire four... fire five.'

Harding had his stopwatch in his hand, saying nothing, his lips mouthing the seconds. The range wasn't far, then '...Aaa-nd... ten seconds to run... five... three, two...'

BUDDUDDUMMM!

The first torpedo hitting...

But Biddle's voice was echoing in his ears through the crash, 'One of our torpedoes's gone rogue, sir. Circling back...!'

'Zero bubble! Keep one hundred and eighty feet!' Harry was listening to himself before he realised it was him shouting. But his voice was being all but drowned out by terrible tearing sounds filling the hull. Then through it, came the shrill, dentist-drill whine of their torpedo coming back.

You got down faster if you ordered the telegraphs to full ahead together and the planes on hard dive, but Harry had yelled, 'Zero bubble!' He didn't want their arse up as they went bow down, for their own torpedo to clip it as it went past... and kill them all. He could physically feel *Scourge* sink rapidly beneath his feet now, on an even keel... and hear their torpedo go over the top... everyone could... its noise setting your teeth on edge, like tearing linen, and then the sound of it disappear again into the steel death screams of the U-boat they had just destroyed.

'I don't think anyone's done that before,' said Harding, sounding laconic, like he was practising his lounge-lizarding. 'A submarine, sinking another submarine while they were both submerged.'

Harry turned and gave him a look, and somewhere, there was the sound of someone being sick.

'It's Leading Seaman Smith, sir,' it was Boxall's voice from the wireless cubby. 'I think he's all right now though, sir.'

And then there was the whining of that damned, bloody torpedo coming back again.

The torpedo circled back twice more in the following minutes, everybody wishing it away, yet still straining to hear the sound of it come taunting back until its fuel must have run out somewhere at the other end of its lethal orbit, and it had sunk without trace.

Scourge surfaced immediately, into the sickly reek of diesel fumes, all that was left of the German submarine and her forty-odd officers and men. Harry, on the bridge, noticed the high haze had cleared and

197

the night sky was a riot of stars again. He ordered the battery charge to be resumed and that the forward torpedo room crew start reloading tubes one, two, four and five.

Boxall, still on watch, was pleased. He wouldn't have to lie on those bloody uncomfortable tubular torture devices anymore. And Farrar ordered Windass to rustle up a celebratory order of coffee with condensed milk and toasted sardine sandwiches for the entire crew. As they munched and slurped through it, more than a few contemplated those other poor bastards who'd been just like them an hour or so ago – submariners on patrol. Who, if they'd been here now, would probably all have really enjoyed the coffee and sardine sarnies too. Except, now they couldn't. And wouldn't, ever.

Radio traffic over the next few days told them the Salerno beachhead was coming under serious Jerry air attack. Harry frequently listened in or read through Ken Dandy's transcripts. The chatter revealed several ships from the covering force had been severely damaged by Jerries using some new secret bomb device, including the light cruiser HMS *Uganda* and the battleship HMS *Warspite,* which had been crippled by one of the damn things and had to be towed back to Malta. The US cruiser, *Savannah,* that the *Scourges* remembered from the Western Task Force off Sicily, had also taken a hit from one and had been almost sunk.

Then came the recall order, and Harry ordered *Scourge's* bows pointed back towards Malta.

On the way, one of the world news round-ups, broadcast to submarines at sea from the big Admiralty transmitter at Rugby, reported a signal that had been sent to London from the C-in-C, Mediterranean, Admiral of the Fleet Sir Andrew Cunningham. It had said, '*Be pleased to inform their lordships that the Italian battle fleet now lies at anchor under the guns of the fortress of Malta.*' Harry had the report typed out by one of the telegraphists and stuck up outside the galley. Everybody gave themselves a pat on the back, especially for the '…under the guns…' bit because they might all be trade on *Scourge*, but they were still part of the Mediterranean Fleet, and hadn't they done a good job?

Thirteen

Scourge came to periscope depth an hour after first light. They should have been, by Harding's dead-reckoning, fourteen miles nor'-nor'-east of Qawra Point. That was their rendezvous point. Harry ordered the main search 'scope up for the usual all-round look, and there she was, less than a quarter of a mile away, right on the starboard bow – a bouncy little Fairmile D Motor Gun Boat, all one hundred lovely feet of her, and that jaunty little white ensign fluttering from her stubby mast: their escort back into Marsamxett Harbour and a reserved berth on one the Lazaretto's pontoons.

'Diving stations!' called Harry, as he stepped back from the 'scope, and for a moment, you could see the sunshine on the surface reflected through the eyepieces onto his face, like some kind of comic mask. 'Stand by to surface,' he said, slapping up the 'scope's handles. 'Down periscope. Blow all main ballast.'

On the roster, it was McCready's watch, so Harry let him go up and crack the lid, followed by the two lookouts. There was a *whumph* and a sudden rush of air upwards that told him the hatch was open – pressure exiting the boat – and then a couple of solid little lumps of Mediterranean came cascading down. 'Ring for half ahead together,' said Harry to the rating on the engine room telegraph and then to the fore-end of the control room and the man on the wheel, 'Steer one nine zero, helmsman,' then, 'Pass the word for the yeoman!'

Dickie Bird came barrelling down the passageway, clutching their ensign and their Jolly Roger.

'Do the honours, Dickie,' said Harry.

There was a huge *bang*! aft, and suddenly a gale of wind came down the conning tower hatch; the diesels had burst into life and were now sucking down the pure, clean tang of sea air.

'Aye, aye, sir,' said Bird. 'And I thought I'd add a nice little flourish, seeing as that one was a first, according to Mr Harding, sir.'

'Go on then, Dickie, give me look,' said Harry, stepping to the yeoman's side, all curious now. With a little fumble, Dickie folded out the place on the black flag. There, sewn on, was the usual symbol for a U-boat sunk, but above it, there was a thin wavy line of blue thread.

'Shows she was under when we bagged her, sir,' he said, grinning.

'You're an artist, Dickie,' said Harry, grinning too. 'You've missed your calling. Up you go and get it hoisted.'

Harry stood aside and ushered Bird up through the hatch. Then he turned, 'Number One, join me on the bridge.'

There were waves and greetings exchanged with the motor gunboat. 'Good hunting?' came a cry from over the water.

'We got a U-boat!' Harry called back.

'I say! Bloody good show!' they said.

Farrar offered Harry a cigarette, and the two leaned against the bridge wing and puffed away contentedly in the warming sunlight. There were a number of aircraft about, mostly away to the west. Harry told the lookouts only to sing out if they were actually coming at them.

They could see Malta and Gozo clearly now, off the starboard bow, a little ragged tear of white rock above the horizon that was growing by the minute.

'Two single-engine aircraft, bearing red ten, at two o'clock, approaching,' said one of the lookouts. Harry turned. They were Spitfires. And they were closing fast, until one, then the other reared up, showing their plan view, their dun-coloured sand camouflage, their big red and blue roundels and the unmistakeable curve of their unique wing shapes. One continued to climb, but the other peeled off and came tearing in not much above the waves. Harry felt his throat tighten, but immediately he could see the Spitfire's nose wasn't boring in but pointing to pass. And in an instant, the aircraft was up with them, zooming past *Scourge's* bridge at practically the same height. The air was solid with the full-throated roar of its Merlin engine as it went by, waggling its wings, and Harry could plainly see the cockpit hood slid back and a grinning pilot, his oxygen mask un-hooked; grinning and waving right at him. And then he must have hauled back on his stick because the little aircraft suddenly reared up and climbed away, the wings still waggling. Until the two formed up again and banked away to the south-west and were streaking for the horizon again.

Harry and Farrar were grinning too, as they watched them go.

'It used to be the only things flying about when you were trying to return to Malta were Me 109s,' said Harry. 'Makes a nice change.'

Farrar said he was going below to get the casing party squared away and to make sure the clean-up was in full swing. 'Send Harding up,' said Harry. 'And if Mr Petrie's engines are behaving themselves and he can spare a moment away, tell him he can come up for a goof at the scenery if he fancies.'

Harry was scanning the shore with his binoculars. Comino had separated herself in the channel between Gozo and Malta, and he could see the Qawra Tower clearly. Harding was smoking, and Mr Petrie, looking particularly pale, was gawping at the sea and sky like a schoolchild. He might have cumulatively spent more years of his life at sea than both Harry and Harding put together, but as most of that time had been in a submarine's engine room, from slipping, to coming alongside once more, being in the offing, heading home, was a sight he'd rarely beheld.

It was what he could just pick out beyond the Qawra Tower that stopped Harry. He couldn't make it out for a moment, and when he could, he realised what he must be looking at: a forest of masts. It must be what Cunningham had said in his signal – the Italian battlefleet. They really were 'anchored under the guns'. And here he was, about to actually see them, close up, not through a periscope, racing away into a spray-lashed night.

'Pass the word for the camera,' he said into the voicepipe.

It took an endless time, it seemed, to come up on the mass of warships where you could see them properly, to actually open the bay where they lay at anchor. Not all the Italian battlefleet, however, you could see that right away. At least three of the battleships weren't there, nor were most of the surviving cruisers, nor any of the flotillas of destroyers and torpedo boats. At the surrender, the Italian Navy must've still numbered over two hundred ships, but here was just a half dozen or so. But, my God, didn't they look impressive! Anchored, fore and aft, bows angled towards the shore, like a long row of half-chevrons.

Harry detailed them off, and one of the lookouts scribbled in a notebook: a *Conti de Cavour*-class battleship and two *Caio Duilio* class, two *Abruzzi*-class light cruisers, a *Capitani Romani*-class cruiser and the seaplane carrier, *Miraglia*. And was that some submarines too, trotted up together at the far end of the bay? It was.

And there they lay, beautiful ships, huge, majestic and very real, between the bluff topped by the squat, stone, seventeenth-century St Marks Tower, and to the south, the gun battery next to the coast's other seventeenth-century watchtower, the Madliena, all presided over by the guns inland at Fort Pembroke. That beautiful, sun-dappled bay that for centuries had been used only by colourful fishing caiques and more recently, the odd ferry to Mġarr, now dwarfed by these great, grey steel behemoths, squatting there like the mobile castles of some conquering horde.

Scourge's crowded little bridge all looked on, dumbstruck, even the lookouts, unable to take their eyes off what had been the might of the enemy. Harry felt a tumult of emotions in his chest. So this was what victory felt like.

With the motor gunboat off their port beam, *Scourge* was now coming up on the first ship in the line: the *Cavour*-class battleship. He'd ordered the helm to nudge *Scourge* a little closer in so they would pass within a few score yards of the anchored stern, so the Italian's quarter deck was now rising like some city tenement above them. Aboard the battleship, a sailor, then half a dozen more, came to the rail to look down on them. One of them, then all of them started to wave and call out, 'Ciao!… Inglese!… Amici!…'

Harry stepped to the voicepipe, 'Mr Ainsworth… casing party to the casing now, I think, if you please.' He stepped back, raised his cap and waved up at the grinning Italians. 'Well, well,' he said to Harding, who was frowning at them instead. 'Our enemy at bay.'

'Uh, what? Oh, yes, sir,' said Harding who'd obviously been thinking something else. 'Cheeky bastards though. Look at 'em. It's like they never caused all that bloody bother.'

'Beautiful ships though, Miles, their battleships. You've got to agree,' said Harry, looking thoughtful. 'When you see them up close, it would have been a shame to blow holes in them.' And for a moment, he could almost see the battleship through his periscope, engulfed in flame and smoke, all mutilated steel, a capsizing hull with a blanket of running men covering her as she rolled. 'I'm glad she made it... that they all did,' he said. 'Her and her scruffy crew. At least someone's getting to go home... as Shrimp always used to say, "It's not as if they've actually done anybody any harm."'

Harding laughed, 'That's not what I'm seeing, sir. I'm seeing a whole row of prime targets. I'm seeing us sticking three torpedoes in each one of the bastards, right into their guts. And what a sight it is. And then I'm seeing Dickie Bird sewing three lovely battleship-shaped strips of red cloth onto our Jolly Roger.'

Looking up, it was apparent that there was now quite a crowd round the battleship's stern rail, and when he looked down the row of ships, there were sailors starting to gather on the other quarterdecks. Immediately below, coming out the gun well, the half a dozen immacu-lately uniformed casing party was spilling out, dazzling in their whites, with Ainsworth himself as their senior rate. Obviously, curiosity had got the better of even him – a chance to see the enemy, or a former one least, at close quarters.

Scourge was now passing the first battleship. Harry could read the name on her stern – *Ceasare*.

'Attention on the casing,' he called down. The line snapped to. 'Three cheers for the Eyeties... stand by!' he cried, then, aside to Bird, 'Yeoman. Dip the colours!' then back to the bridge front, 'Caps off!... Hip, hip!...'

Then in unison, the casing crew and everybody on the bridge yelled a throat-tearing yell, 'HOORAY!'

And again... and again.

The Italian sailors, manning their stern rails, went crazy. Jumping up and down, cheering, whistling, laughing, slapping each other on the back and blowing kisses.

Harry called over the bridge front, 'Stand easy on the casing!' The *Scourges*, all of them laughing now too, just stood grinning at each other and at the slab grey walls passing and waved their caps back.

Harry turned back, and all he could see was the crazy battle light in Harding's eye and that evil grin of his.

'...We could still do it, sir,' Harding was saying, all malevolent smiles. 'We could, you know... pretend we never heard the signal... we just say we turned up off the coast and thought they were trying to invade... just a thought, sir.' This from the man who'd refused to allow a mob of cut-throat commandos to 'murder' out of hand a lowly Luftwaffe Gefreiter because it 'wouldn't have been British'. Harding then gave a chuckle, and he went on, 'A naughty thought, of course. But you know me, sir. What about you, sir. What d'you see?'

Harry looked back at the Italian ships and their waving sailors, cavorting like children. What he saw was a lot of young lads, all going home... to their mums and sweethearts, wives and *bambinis*, to their own beds and lives... and futures.

He said, 'I see a lot of sailors, just like you and me... well, maybe not quite like you, Miles. ...But a lot... and it's all over for them... all this nonsense. It's done. And beautiful ships too, of course.'

Miles, still gazing at the ships, shrugged and said, with all the insouciance he could muster, 'Only if you're a big soppy Jessie, sir, and wished you'd married Mrs Miniver.'

'But only if she was played by Betty Grable instead of Greer Garson though,' said McCready, the official officer of the watch, who'd been so completely silent until now that Harry and Harding had forgotten he was there.

'You're a dirty little boy, Tom McCready,' said Harding, 'and the captain should subject you to regular underwear inspections.'

Although he was laughing, Harry's attention was drawn to a commotion on the quarterdeck of the second-but-last ship, the second of the *Duilio*-class battleships. There were several glintings on metal. He tensed. But in that instant, the milling mob on the deck parted, and there stood, in un-serried ranks, the ship's band – the glinting had been the sun on their polished trombones and tubas. The band members had obviously all just tumbled up there on deck, but what in God's name was going on?

As he watched, Harry ordered another three cheers. Looking down on the casing, he could see the *Scourges* were obviously warming to their celebrity now and enjoying their audience's appreciation. They hadn't yet spotted the band.

Until out of the blue, it struck up, and the unmistakeable strains were belting out across the water at them, and bloody professional they sounded too, the band of the Italian battleship *Andrea Doria* playing *Lillybulero* loud and clear, like it was being played by the Royal Marines on the parade ground at Guz.

Everybody on the Italian ships and on *Scourge's* casing were waving and cheering like mad now, and all to the strains of *Lillybulero*.

*

Captain Philips didn't rise to greet Harry. He was sitting behind his desk, looking grim and distracted. Harry snapped to attention. Oh, God. What had he done wrong now? Surely teasing Eyeties hadn't suddenly become contrary to naval discipline? And anyway, how could the news have got back here so fast?

'Sit down, Lieutenant Gilmour,' said Philips. Harry did as he was told. Philips continued, 'Leave your patrol report on the desk,' Philips said, gesturing to the small folder Harry had been carrying. 'Right. Your verbal report please, and keep it brief. There is someone here waiting to speak to you after we have concluded.'

Harry did as he was told. When he was finished, Philips stood and with his hand, gestured for Harry to rise too. 'Cap on. The officer here to see you, Lieutenant Gilmour, is Captain de Launy. He is from Admiral Cunningham's staff, which is to say now, the First Sea Lord's staff, just so as you appreciate the gravity of the interview about to take place. This man is not your friend, Mr Gilmour, and you should remember that. He is here to ask you questions on a matter the admiral has insisted be resolved. I recommend you be concise and frank in all your replies. Remain standing, Captain de Launy will be using this office for the interview.' And with that, Philips placed his cap on his head, saluted Harry, paused for Harry to return the salute and then left. A moment later, a tall, slim officer in his late thirties/early forties entered. Salutes were exchanged.

'Lieutenant Gilmour? Please take a seat.' And the officer, all tanned golden in his immaculate whites, removed his cap and sat too. Dark hair, swept back like a cruiser's bow wave. Even on this short acquaintance, Harry could see he exuded all the qualities of a steel hawser. A small dossier and a notebook was placed on the desk in front of him.

'I have here a request from the Captain S of the Twelfth Flotilla to C-in-C Mediterranean requesting you be court-martialled,' said de Launy. The voice was quiet, and Harry formed the impression that it was never used to saying things it didn't mean. He felt his stomach lurch. Bonalleck, coming back to haunt him again.

*

Outside, at the far end of the Lazaretto's wardroom gallery, Wincairns was leaning over the rail, watching the *Scourges* hand over their boat to the base personnel. He was smoking like he meant it and halfway through a lung-bursting drag when Captain Philips joined him, carrying two large gins.

'Well, he's in there with him now,' said Philips, passing a gin and receiving a cigarette in return. He lit up.

'Do you know this chap?' asked Wincairns. 'You navy lot all seem to know each other from somewhere.'

Philips shook his head. 'No. He's a skimmer. A destroyerman, which I am assuming is why Cunningham appointed him, him being one himself. A very cool customer indeed.'

'Indeed, as you say. When he came to buttonhole me, I felt like I was being measured for my coffin.' Wincairns took a belt of gin. 'Did he give you any indication of what he's got?'

Philips laughed a sardonic laugh. 'Given that he's had communications with everyone, I would guess he's got *everything*. Whatever that might be, in all its glory. He's got statements from Shrimp, Sam Bridger, Bonalleck's Commander S Twelve, Admiral Barry too. And even from Horton. Needless to say, our Captain de Launy wasn't giving anything away about what was in them.'

'I know what's in them,' said Wincairns, 'or at least I've a bloody good idea.'

'You do? How's that, George?'

'Do you know what I do out here, George?'

Philips gave another of his sardonic laughs and not just because they both had the same first name. 'No,' he said.

'Good. But since it's you, I'll give a little teaser. I'm not military, but then you've probably realised that. I'm more Foreign Office. The *what's-going-on* department. All that intelligence bumpf that keeps coming in from London... out here, I'm the spigot from which it spouts. Here to make sure the right people at the sharp end get to know what they need to know. I also keep my ear to the ground because the person I report to, back in London, likes to know what's actually happening at the sharp end, especially the stuff that doesn't make it into all the official flummery that flows back to him. So, I've been making inquiries of my own. Ignoring my own usually sage advice and predictably coming to regret it.'

'All this nonsense between Bonalleck and young Gilmour? Is that what you're talking about?'

'Yes.'

'And?'

'Bonalleck has been trying to kill him. At least that's what it looks like. I don't think the evidence would pass any legal test just yet, but I can't imagine anyone, least of all my boss or even Captain de Launy's wanting it to ever get that far.'

Philips stared at him. 'So what Chief Gault told me... and I told you... it really is worse?'

'Oh yes. It wasn't difficult to flesh it out when I decided to look. De Launy has talked to all the big players. But it's all there too, in the correspondence files and the Twelfth Flotilla's logs, and it's also all the talk of your lower deck. I believe that is the expression for the common Jack Tar? Yes. It's amazing what you can find out just by opening a file cabinet or listening to what the chat is in the gin joints.'

'Kill him?' said Philips at last.

'Oh, it didn't start out like that. Just a little doctoring of the files, knobbling medal recommendations...'

'He must have done that under Admiral Horton's watch,' said Philips. 'That wouldn't have been a good idea. I bet that backfired on him.'

'Thus stoking the fire more, if you get my drift,' said Wincairns. 'It's like Gault says. It all goes back to *Pelorus*. She'd just sunk a Jerry cruiser and ends up sunk herself... rammed by one of our own coastal convoys on her way home in the dark. Our hero, the Bonny Boy, is skipper.

Philips said, 'A few of us thought he would bag a bar to his VC for that.'

'Except that his luck ran out that fateful night... or at least that is the story he puts about,' said Wincairns. 'His heroic works have had all the burnish taken off them by the cruel mistress of fate... at least that is the story he wants put about. Unfortunately, among the survivors is Gilmour... popped up like a bad penny... and he has a different version of events. One that says that Bonalleck was lying drunk when his crew torpedoed the Jerry. And that he was still drunk when he was hurrying home to court-martial said crew for their zeal in showing him up, and that was why he blundered into that convoy. And the young Gilmour, full of righteous indignation and dripping wet straight from the lifeboat, apparently had the effrontery to tell him as much to his face. But being a good chap, Gilmour didn't go blabbing to teacher. Some might call it loyalty... I'd call it the first indications of wisdom by young Gilmour. Telling tales against a senior officer? Who'd want to listen? Anyway, Bonalleck doesn't see it as loyalty... and the seeds of loathing are sown in the Bonny Boy's breast. There's someone out there who knows the truth.' Wincairns paused to consider, then added, 'And I gather, within your service, Bonalleck has never had the reputation of being a forgiving soul in the first place.'

'Correct,' said Philips.

'What happened next, all the petty stuff, I'm sure de Launy must have it all in graphic detail. Where it gets serious though, is when Bonalleck's pestering gets him a sea job running a flotilla in the Med... and bad luck and trouble sends Gilmour back into his clutches. Our Chief Petty Officer Gault is pretty short on the specifics from here on in, but it's obvious it's now that the potential to do real damage presents itself to our man. And damned cunning about it, our Bonny Boy has been too, I can tell you. The first thing he does when Gilmour's boat comes under his command is to send it inshore to the Franco–Spanish border to disrupt the blockade runners, telling him intelligence says the coast is clear when we know it isn't. However, Gilmour, being a good skipper, has told his crew their mission, and when they get back, sailors being a chatty bunch, they tell their chums on the depot ship, especially all the office scribblers... who see all the signals and hear all the chatter... and Gilmour's crew discover nobody's ever heard of any new intelligence reports and that the coast is still heavily mined and patrolled. They also learn about safe conduct ships... there are such ships? Is that right?'

'Yes. We allow special ships passage. If they are carrying medicines, Red Cross parcels, that sort of stuff, we promise not to sink them. It's all very regulated,' said Philips.

'Well, one was on its way through when the Bonny Boy sent Gilmour onto that coast, and although a warning it was coming was to be flashed to all submarines in the area, the Bonny Boy didn't flash it to Gilmour. There is a big hole in the Twelfth's log listing signals to *Scourge* where the warning should've been. I don't even want to think about what would've happened if the intrepid Lieutenant Gilmour had sunk that ship... to Britain's reputation... to the navy's reputation. Nobody would've cared that nobody had told our Mr Gilmour what she was. And that's when Jack Tar starts wondering... has the Twelfth's skipper got it in for the

Scourge's skipper? Which is how I know about it. It was the talk of the mess decks back in Algiers. The Bonny Boy next gets active against Mr Gilmour by cosying up to the Yanks. Suddenly, we see there are memos flying... him bending over backwards to facilitate our new Allies. Especially when he learns, from me I regret to say, where Field Marshal Kesselring is going to be on his holidays. The paper trail shows him become a veritable font of helpful ideas. Like, why not nip in and bump him off? I've got just the sub and just the skipper to take you there. And guess what? His offer comes right at the moment the Yanks' cloak-and-dagger mob have splashed ashore with this idea about using the local Italian mafias in Sicily and the mainland as off-the-shelf guerrillas... and they're lugging a sack full of loot and free guns to snag their interest. So the Yanks say, "Yes, please," and Bonalleck is told to round up a few of those commando cut-throats that are always hanging around sub operations... and now they have a mission. Except Bonalleck hasn't told anybody at C-in-C Med. And this is where we disappear through the looking glass. A Royal Navy captain, holder of the Victoria Cross and the officer commanding a Mediterranean Fleet submarine flotilla... freelancing his services... offering to carry out ops for a foreign power... okay, well, the Americans... but still without telling his own side what he's doing... because it lets him get his favourite sub skipper tangled up in a highly risky mission... to do something wholly un-gentlemanly and distinctly un-British, all without the official sanction of their lordships. I think it's safe to say that at this point, the man has gone mad.'

'Good grief,' was all Philips could manage.

'Then there was the Americans shooting up Gilmour's sub... *by accident*... convenient accident. Well, I don't believe in accidents, especially not convenient ones. Have I found any proof though? Well, my answer to that is I said he was mad, not stupid. But I tell you what I do know

now… he's not going to stop unless someone stops him. I sat through a liaison committee discussion about that incident, and it was plain as day something was up. When I started asking afterwards, what do I find but a whole trail of signals lost down the backs of the sofas and subs being where the shouldn't be, and at the very centre of the whole tangled web, guess who's there? Captain Bonalleck. And do you know something else? I think your Mr Gilmour knows it too. I think he knows what Bonalleck has been up to all this time and hasn't known what to do about it. What could he do about it? It's an utterly preposterous, fantastical tale. Who would believe him? Well, I do… now.'

'What d'you think is going on in my office right now?' asked Philips, absently contemplating the rainbow swirls of oil on the water below him, so as not to think on how angry he was. It wasn't just that Bonalleck had been out to bring down this one lowly lieutenant, he'd actively worked towards and intended to sacrifice a king's ship and her crew and the good name of the service in the process. It was beyond comprehension.

'I've no idea, but I'd bet Lieutenant Gilmour is not having a happy time of it,' said Wincairns, staring, ditto, into the water. 'We both know none of this is his fault, really. Even if he'd kept his mouth shut from the start, foreswore the pleasure of telling the Bonny Boy that he was a not-so-bonny drunk… it probably wouldn't have made any difference. Just by the very fact of his surviving… a nutcase like Bonalleck was probably going to come after him anyway. That's the trouble with these big bombs, when fate fires one of them into the ring, you don't have to have had anything to do with how it got there to get blown up by it.'

'So what happens now?' asked Philips.

'What happens for me is I have to report up the chain of command, preferably with a sensible recommendation attached.'

'Doesn't it depend what the first sea lord decides to do about it?'

'The first sea lord will do what my boss tells him to do. And I know what I'm going to recommend to my boss. Which is I go back to that liaison committee I was mentioning earlier and tell the Yanks that the attack on the British submarine was all our fault. *Reus sumus*... breakdown in communications... our officer in charge an old man... time he had a well-earned rest. And that's what we tell Bonalleck too from the other end but with a bit more vim in it. Stick him on a homeward-bound tramp steamer and hand him a pair of carpet slippers when he gets off... and an order that nobody is to ever hear from him again... if he knows what's good for him.'

'Scot-free, in other words. I think we should shoot him, personally.'

'Don't be silly, George. You can't shoot a VC without giving a good excuse. People might talk. And how do you think all this would look on the front page of the *Daily Express*? Where would you start, trying to talk your way out of this one?'

'Uh-oh,' said Philips, and Wincairns looked up to see him squinting down the length of the gallery. Wincairns turned, and there, walking in the other end was Lt Gilmour, face looking like he'd seen his destiny.

'Well,' said Wincairns, pushing his bulk upright, 'here's one thing we can do right now. Go and cheer that young man up.'

*

The first thing to flash into Tom McCready's head after he'd charged into *Scourge's* torpedo stowage space was, *Rule One for junior officers: Never directly approach drunken or fighting ratings, always summon senior rates to intervene first.* It was a sensible rule, tried and tested down through the three hundred years of unbroken naval tradition because usually, when violence erupts, or there's at least the threat of it, the person first intervening can normally expect a punch in the mouth too, and if that person happens to be an officer – no matter how junior – everybody ends up getting court-martialled.

So he bellowed, 'Mr Ainsworth! To the...'

But the cox'n was already there. He'd heard the yelling and the actual scream and the thumping and crashing too and was barrelling past McCready, even as he yelled, with Gooch, the torpedo gunner's mate, right behind him.

The tableau before them in the space was Hooper, their gun layer, sprawled against the stacked torpedo reloads, breathing in pained gasps and clutching at his right breast, with wisps of smoke from his white vest eddying up between his fingers. Before him, rolling about the deck, was Boxall, the new telegraphist, and one of the new radar lads, Mularky, who was punching seven bells out of him. The fight was taking place in amongst a scattered pile of over a dozen or more ratings' uniform white shorts and shirts. There was also an electric iron, still plugged in and sizzling, and the debris from a makeshift ironing board smashed.

'Get up, and stand to attention!' yelled McCready. However, Ainsworth and Gooch were bent on their own intervention and that didn't involve using words. The two of them bundled right in and in one great heave, had Mularky off his victim and on his feet, but it took them a few more grapples to stop the big Irishman from continuing to windmill his fists in mid-air.

Meanwhile, Boxall was struggling to get off his back. A sudden torrent of abuse and absolute filth suddenly burst forth from the bloodied Londoner's burst mouth, and he went to push himself up from his elbows. Gooch's right leg shot out and kicked him onto his back again. He kept his boot on the man's chest and pressed down hard. 'Shut your fucken mouth, boy!' he said equably.

McCready, standing stock still and open-mouthed, watching it all, noticed Ainsworth trying to make eye contact with him. The cox'n's face was still tight with the effort to restrain Mularky, but he managed to arch his eyebrows and give the briefest of nods back towards the space's watertight door. 'I think we have this now, sir,' he said. 'I will report to you in the control room directly.'

In other words, *fuck off, sir!*

*

McCready had sent for the first lieutenant right away, and he was tracked down to the Lazaretto's wardroom easily enough. So Farrar was back aboard now, and none too happy, sitting with McCready in *Scourge's* wardroom, while elsewhere in the boat, the watch left aboard and some of the harbour crew continued to clean up and make her ready for the turnaround maintenance team to start work and mess everything up again.

'Apparently, Hooper, being the old-fashioned type he is, took exception to new-hand Boxall skimming cash off some of the more junior hands, sir,' McCready was saying with a weary sigh. Fisticuffs on board was not a common occurrence in this boat.

'Explain,' said Farrar, pleased despite everything, that McCready had summoned him, the number one, and not the captain.

'Boxall had come aboard with his own electric iron, and when we got in, he started offering to press everyone's whites for a price… a few pennies per item,' recounted McCready. 'He fancies himself as a bit of a businessman, I'm told. Anyway, Hooper confronted him… told him making money off your fellow crewmen wasn't proper. And he *was* making money, sir. More than a few of the younger lads were coughing up. Although they didn't like it much, their natural tendency towards idleness overcame any scruples. And when Hooper went to tackle him about it, Boxall was well into a big load. So he told Hooper to mind his own business and go forth and multiply. Hooper grabbed him, and Boxall jammed the hot iron into his chest.'

'Ouch!' said Farrar.

'Indeed, sir. It's a nasty burn. Dispensary has sent him over to Bighi for proper treatment.' Another sigh at the stupidity of men, then McCready continued his tale. 'Mularky, who was still on board, heard Hooper's yelp and intervened. A confrontation, I'm told by the cox'n, that was coming sooner or later. Wireless and radar share the same cubby as you know, and our cheeky chappy Boxall has been irritating our mercurial bog-hopper since they both joined.'

This time, it was Farrar's turn to sigh. 'Righty-ho. I'll arrange a defaulters' parade ashore as soon as I can set it up. Tell the cox'n to keep Mularky and Boxall under arrest until then. I'll speak to Hooper myself. Stupid bugger. A man his age should know better.'

'It's all about the boat's good name, he says, sir.'

'Yes, well, I refer you to the captain's favourite rejoinder on all such matters… bollocks!'

Oh dear, thought McCready, *Number One saying a bad word… whatever is the world coming to?*

Fourteen

Another bloody autumnal storm. Harry could feel the deck plates rise and corkscrew beneath his feet, even here, at periscope depth, and the splash and spray from the short, choppy seas made seeing anything out of the main search periscope all but bloody impossible, even with the bloody thing fully raised.

There was nothing around in the dark. All the Asdic was picking up was the churn of shingle on the shore ahead, and there was nothing at all to see upstairs, not a ship, boat, little island caique nor shagbat, not even an insomniac seagull; just the dull, looming mass of the island and the glimpse through the flying spume of a nasty band of surf where their landing beach should be. He was aware of their tame pongo dancing underneath the gun tower hatch. Every time Harry leaned back a little from the 'scope's eyepiece, he could see the young soldier's face, all blacked-up and looking oddly detached from his body in the red wash of the control room lights. He was itching to go, but to Harry, going didn't look much of an idea from here. Maybe things might look different on the surface.

'Down periscope!' he ordered and stood back as the tube slid back into the bowels of the boat. 'Surface! Blow all main ballast tanks! Maintain heading, slow ahead together!'

And up went *Scourge*, into another warm, wet Aegean night.

This time, Harry sent Harding up first, then the two lookouts, then Bird, the yeoman, with his infra-red optics. By the time Harry's turn came to go up the ladder, when he got there, everyone on the bridge's shirts were pasted to their bodies by the driving rain. Harry estimated it was blowing a good force six, and from the land too, causing the short, stubby waves to pile up on their way shoreward; bloody awful conditions if you were trying to paddle a folbot onto that beach, somewhere dead ahead in the dark, that Harry's night vision had yet to settle down to. He wiped the rain and spray from his face and asked Bird if he'd spotted anything yet.

The yeoman, who was already busy flashing *Scourge's* identification signal over the bridge front on his infra-red light, said, 'No response from the beach yet, sir.'

Harding was wiping off his night glasses. He'd just finished taking bearings on the headland off to starboard and two of the peaks off their bows. 'Well, that's definitely the island of Kos,' he said – in his usual '…as if it could be anywhere else?' tone – '…and we're exactly where we're supposed to be,' as if he was having to 'state the bleeding obvious… again'.

Harry ignored him. Sometimes Harding's languorous affectations really got on his nerves, but not so much as he was going to waste a bollocking on him in front of Jack. 'Stop together,' he ordered down the voicepipe, and in the engine room, Mr Petrie disengaged the engine clutch and turned *Scourge's* two big diesels solely over to battery charge. Then Harry added, 'Send Sergeant Probert to the bridge.'

With the way off her, *Scourge* began pitching in irritating jerks, her bow pointed directly at the beach half a mile away. Probert shot out the conning tower hatch like a scalded cat and was at Harry's side in a blur of movement. 'Suh!' he said, managing to make his whisper still carry all the bang of a shout.

Harry had already had several conversations with the young sergeant since they'd sailed from Malta three days ago, and he'd come across as a precise and articulate young man. Certainly, he'd come aboard highly recommended, but it was by some crowd of hooligans based on Cairo that were calling themselves the Special Boat Squadron that Harry had never heard of. When he'd asked around, one of the Malta pongos had told him there was apparently a whole mob of them back there in Cairo that had grown out of the original Long Range Desert Group, all dedicated to special ops. 'SBS must just be the latest,' the pongo had reasoned. 'But it's all just the same behind-the-lines, hit-and-run stuff. Winston loves it, apparently. Otherwise, they'd never be allowed.'

And now, here was a real live specimen.

The sergeant had proved to be a nice chap, all open-faced and easy to get along with, if a little quiet. A lot like a few of the other commando types they'd encountered, the good lads, anyway. Or so Ainsworth had told Harry when he'd asked how their guest was fitting in. 'He's got a harmonica in his kit, and he can hold a damn good tune,' the cox'n had said. 'Although if it t'were otherwise, I wouldn't like to tell him to his face. He's a right wiry little bugger. And the way he's always cleanin' his weapons, especially that knife of his… it gives you a queer twinge in your puddings, sir.'

And here they were to deliver Sgt Probert, right on time and onto the right beach. Except the conditions were bloody awful.

'Take a look yourself, Sergeant,' Harry said, tucking his chin in against the warm rain. 'You'll never make it. It makes sense to hold off twenty-four hours.'

But Sgt Probert was having none of it. The whole operation wasn't going to get held up just because he was frightened of getting his hair wet. He was ready to go, now.

'We're still getting no responses from the beach,' said Harry. 'There might be nobody there to meet you anyway.'

A whole litany of scenarios were then recited by the sergeant – full of ifs and maybes – all perfectly plausible reasons for the friendlies being there, but just not being able to say, 'Hi!' back again. Better to take the chance and go, sir!

It was only because he thought the wind was veering and falling off that Harry relented, and Sgt Probert was down the hatch again to get his folbot.

The mission, as briefed to him in the Lascaris bunker, had been straightforward and urgent. And George Wincairns had been there to offer encouragement and nod sagely at the intelligence assessments as they were delivered by the briefing officer, an RN staff commander from C-in-C Med. George Philips hadn't been there, however, because *Scourge* was no longer a Tenth Flotilla boat as of the start of the briefing. She was being transferred, officially, and would forthwith be under operational command of First Flotilla, based on Beirut. *Well*, thought Harry, *at least the runs ashore will be more fun.*

A major operation was about to get underway, the commander had revealed. The Allies were going to grab the Dodecanese Islands from the Axis. Until now, the archipelago between Turkey and Greece had been occupied by the Italians mostly, but since Italy had surrendered, it was thought best if the British stepped in and secured them... before Jerry did. Especially since Jerry had already got his mitts on one of the biggest: Rhodes.

'As we speak, a small squadron of specially converted caiques, very similar to the local trading craft of the region, is carrying a raiding force to the island of Kos… here!' And the RN Commander had given a chart pinned to an easel a martial swipe. 'They are V-Force!'

Wincairns had given Harry a knowing look while the commander's back was turned, as if to say, 'Ooh! Fancy! V-Force!'

Harry had tried not to laugh.

The caiques were to drop V-Force off in secret and sail away. V-Force were then to proceed across the island to Kos's commodious airbase, sneak in under the cover of darkness and plant bombs on all the Jerry aircraft there, and in the bomb dump and in amongst the fuel tanks, thus preventing the Luftwaffe from launching a rapid counterstrike against all the British landings scheduled for all the other islands to the south.

'You're probably wondering why we don't just bomb the place,' said the commander.

Harry hadn't been.

'Well, it's because we want to use the airfield ourselves. So cratering the runways and smashing up the hangers wouldn't be the smart thing to do, what?' And at that, the commander had given a bark of a laugh before moving on. 'You're job, on *Scourge*, is to get inshore while V-Force's raid is going on and wait until they've made good their withdrawal from the airfield then snatch them away from this beach…' another swipe, '…before Jerry can get them.'

Yes, the plan did eventually include the British landing on Kos and grabbing the airfield for themselves, but the way each landing up the chain was scheduled, they wouldn't be able to get there for at least another few days, and since nobody fancied V-Force's chances having to hang on until the cavalry arrived, *Scourge* was to be on hand.

After extracting V-Force, Harry was then to rendezvous with a scratch

Royal Navy squadron – sent to cover the several, disparate landing forces – and remain under the local command of its senior naval officer for the duration of the campaign, or until recalled.

'A couple of weeks should see the whole show stitched up,' the commander had concluded. 'Piece of cake, as the crabfats say, what?'

And that had been that. *Scourge's* turnaround in Malta had been expedited; as her presence was going to be crucial to the success of the whole op. Or so he was assured. A nippy little S-class boat like her was just the job. Nearly all First Flotilla boats were T class – and they were just too big. And the U and N class didn't have the endurance – or the room for a decent stick of commandos.

It made sense. Harry had seen that. But he could also see that *Scourge* was overdue for a rest. Her hull and engines needed a proper refit and her crew a long lie-down. A year was the rule of thumb, and she was past that.

'It'll be after this patrol,' Captain Philips had said as he shook Harry's hand goodbye. 'The recall signal will be waiting, and it'll be back to Pompey for a good rub down.'

All delivered with a reassuring smile that Harry hadn't quite managed to share. He'd taken comfort in one thing, however: the threat of his getting court-martialled must've been kicked down the road. Even so, the memory of Capt de Launy still made him feel queasy.

Probert was on the fore-casing now; you could see his dim shape wrestling with his folbot. He had brought its collapsed bulk up through the gun tower, and now, on the pitching, wave-swept casing, he was trying to put it together... in the dark.

Two ratings stumbled onto the casing to help him, and then the thing was over the edge, bouncing on the saddle tanks, and Probert was in it and away, his arms punching the air as he strained to paddle. The two ratings sat, crouched against the *slap-slap-slap* of waves hitting them as they rolled over the bows. Probert's folbot had leapt to the side and now, before Harry's eyes, was being swept backwards by wind and sea.

Harry on the bridge, rolled his eyes and leaned to the voicepipe, 'Half ahead starboard, slow astern port, port thirty on the helm.' He turned to Harding, 'We better go back and get him before he's blown all the way back to North Africa. He's never going to make the beach in this crap.'

By the time they'd got Sgt Probert back aboard, he was exhausted and could barely speak. Harry ordered a double tot fired into him, and then he was tucked up and ordered to sleep; an order, which this time, he obeyed in a matter of seconds.

The next day was spent lounging around at sixty feet, with a big Windass dinner followed by a few tunes in the forward torpedo room provided by Probert on his harmonica and Boxall's squeezebox. The succeeding watches in the Asdic cubby made sure nobody was sneaking up to hear them. Then Harry ordered *Scourge* surfaced, and up went Dickie Bird with his infra-red gizmos into an altogether calmer night. Bird was flashing away for less than twenty minutes when the first response came back.

'Question and response tally, sir,' said Bird. 'It's them all right. They want to know if Sergeant Probert's still got 'that damn mouth organ' or whether we've... err... can't repeat that last bit, sir.'

Probert was practically dancing to get going. But Farrar, who was on the bridge with Harry this time, intervened. 'I have an idea, sir, I'd like to try,' he said. *Farrar, with an idea?* thought Harry, who was suddenly all ears. His staid Jimmy wasn't usually one for innovations.

Probert, eager to get the folbot assembled and on his way, was furious and curious in equal measure.

Harry listened patiently then said yes, and *Scourge*, very slowly began to nose towards the beach, with Harding and his chart on the bridge, taking bearing after bearing until *Scourge's* bow was little more than thirty yards off the rising beach, when it was as if she suddenly stumbled, and Farrar ordered, 'Stop together!' and then a few more squirts of seawater into the already partly flooded number one ballast tank, to settle her on the sandy bottom. They were now aground, just.

'All we have to do now is rig the grass rope to the shore,' said Farrar, trying to hide a certain feeling of triumph that his idea had worked without wrecking the boat, 'then when V-Force come rolling up, we can daisy-chain them from the shore and have them stowed in minutes. No rowing and paddling to and fro.'

'You're in charge, Number One,' said Harry, all stern-faced for effect. 'Make it so.'

And even Sgt Probert was left standing, quietly rubbing his chin in admiration before he managed to gee himself and get off, paddling the few short yards to the beach to meet up with his pals, now coming out of the scrubbery to see what was happening.

*

At that moment, on the other side of the island, two goatherds were crashing through shrubbery, trying to look like they were scrambling to herd their goats and not actually chasing them. Watching, from behind double-height rolls of barbed wire was a lowly Luftwaffe Gefreiter in khaki shorts and a sleeve-rolled shirt, with a rifle slung on his shoulder, peeking out from under his oversized coal-scuttle helmet. He wasn't quite convinced.

In the warm, balmy night, the amount of starshine from the clear vault of the heavens was quite remarkable and easily illuminated the two scrappily dressed locals' antics. The German shouted at them to clear off – in German, which wouldn't have been much use if both of the stumbling, cussing men had been local. But one of them wasn't.

In fact, Lt Col Oliver Verney – Irish Guards, and latterly founder and officer commanding V-Force – could, courtesy of his previous diplomatic career, actually speak German.

'He's really pissed off and telling us to get away from the wire,' he hissed to his Greek guide. 'Yell something Greek at him.'

Dimitrios, the local dentist, who was proud of his amateur dramatics ability to get them both costumed-up as peasants, yelled, 'How much for your sister!' twice, in Greek. The goats, obediently, continued to scamper up to the wire.

The German produced a torch and fumbled to shine it at them. Verney scrunched his eyes shut. He didn't want his night vision blasted. Dimitrios shielded his eyes and pointed at his goats, who were now scampering along the line of the wire fence. Vernay stumbled away from the German and up a little rise, as if moving to head the goats off. The German un-slung his rifle and holding it with the torch shining, began pointing it at both men, one after the other while continuing to curse them, loud and furious. Dimitrios had two of the goats now by their horns and was pulling them away, all the while shouting back, in Greek, accusations as to the nocturnal philanderings of the German's wife, none of which, needless to say, he even remotely understood.

But it kept the German occupied long enough for Verney to get a look at the airfield down the reverse side of the slight slope. He'd been expecting only to see a scatter of dark mounds to give him a sense of where the aircraft lay... but there were lights! Dim, down-pointing, floodlights, dotted across the field. He could make out the fuel dump, the bomb dump, and he could see every single aircraft, in lines, not dispersed at all. Two Fieseler Storch recce kites, then up close to what must be the control tower, a row of three Junkers 88s, and across the dispersal pan, twelve Ju 87 Stukas. Clearly, Jerry wasn't expecting any Allied air attack. Why should they – the nearest RAF base was a good 1,200-mile round trip away.

He immediately grabbed at a couple of goats himself and succeeded in chasing several others away from the wire. The German audibly calmed down. The two goats, Verney sent off with his boot in their rumps, and then he began theatrically halloo-ing the rest away and down the rise. Dimitrios and the German shared a few more parting volleys of abuse, and as suddenly as they had arrived, the two goatherds were away and stumbling back into the night.

'Bugger me,' whispered Verney to his comrade. 'They must think we don't have any aircraft with the range to strike this far up into the Aegean. Otherwise, there'd be no Blackpool illuminations like that lot back there. That is useful to know.'

Because the RAF did now have aircraft capable – a couple of squadrons of B24 Liberators were now operating from airfields 'somewhere in the desert'. A trip up to Kos would've been a milk run for them.

Verney fumbled out his notebook while what he saw was fresh, and began to scribble a rough map. But it was what else he'd noticed that was mainly on his mind. There had been the stick shadow of a guard, sometimes two, at each aircraft and two searchlight towers which probably held MG 42 machine guns as well. But also there were the huge patches of shadow the sparse lighting created, like oil slicks. It put a grim smile on his face; they'd be able to use those.

*

'They're doing the close-target recce tonight,' said a breathless Probert, sitting hunched over his mug of coffee in *Scourge's* wardroom. 'Then they'll go in tomorrow night.'

Probert was newly back from the beach, where he'd been doing his liaising with V-Force's rear TacHQ – which amounted to two corporals with their own infra-red signalling kit, a spirit stove and large quantities of tea, tins of bully beef, hard tack and two large bottles of arak.

'So, how many are we to expect when they return?' asked Harry.

Meanwhile, on the bridge, Farrar, on watch, was conning them back out to sea after their brief sojourn in-shore to establish contact. Getting away had been even easier than he'd envisaged in his plan. *Scourge* hadn't even needed to go full astern together to shake herself free. Farrar had merely ordered number-one ballast tank blown, and she'd just floated off.

'Ten, altogether, including the TacHQ,' said Probert.

Harry's brow furrowed. What was going on with these clowns? A TacHQ – Tactical Headquarters – made up of two corporals and a mini Naafi. And V-Force – a motley gang of scruffy hooligans that couldn't even muster half a platoon. Somebody was taking the piss here. And he said so to Probert.

'Sorry, sir,' said Probert, half embarrassed and yet still half amused himself. 'It's the lieutenant colonel, sir…'

'A lieutenant colonel? V-Force, all ten of them, is commanded by a lieutenant colonel?' said Harry, eyes rolling as if *you expect me to believe any of this?*

'He's a bit of a flash Harry, sir… the boss,' said Probert, more serious now. 'Likes his mickey-take, sir. It's all one big hoot for him, sir.'

*

Lt Col Verney picked two of the team to remain at the rally point, about half a mile from the airfield perimeter, atop a gully that eventually led to the tracks that led south to the beach. The rest of V-Force was split into two teams of three, each with a local Greek guide to steer them over the goat tracks through the scrubby hillside to their points of ingress.

Each man was equipped to fight light, armed only with a Browning 9mm automatic pistol or a Webley .45 navy revolver and an F-S commando knife. But in their webbing satchels were four Mills bombs each and a clutch of Lewes bombs – home-made-looking explosives made up from a pound of Nobel 808 plastique, mixed with a quarter pound of thermite and a couple of squirts of diesel oil and steel filings. The devices were each primed with a two-ounce wad of dry gun cotton to act as a booster and a detonator with a thirty-second fuse. The whole sticky mass would cling to virtually any surface and had to come wrapped in greaseproof paper, which could be awkward in tense, close-quarters situations because of the scrunchy sound it made when you peeled it off. Each had a canteen of water on their hips.

The teams set off shortly before ten p.m., going at a fair clip over the rough terrain, the guides keeping them away from gullies, sudden drops and skylines. It was dead quiet. Not an insect chirrup. Close and warm, with a high haze gauzing over the stars and cocooning them in the dark. Each man closely followed the moving lump of shadow in front of him, keeping up the steady pace. They had their plan; Olly Verney always believed in keeping it simple. Team Two would go in at the main gate end and deal with the fuel and bomb dumps. Anything left over, and they could take a pot at any Stukas close at hand. Team One, Verney's own, would go through the wire halfway along the southern perimeter and make straight for the Ju 88s. They'd tackle the Stukas next. Two searchlight towers were in their path – any spare Lewes bombs, they could slap them on their legs as a parting gift.

The teams had been lying up all day and were hot, sweaty and eager to get at it. A dishevelled bunch in a fashion catastrophe of gear, loose fatigues and local garb, the odd beret, mostly bareheaded and all blacked-up like West End minstrels – a regimental sergeant major's vision of the seventh circle. If, as was often said, the British Army was nothing more than organised hooliganism, then these were its poster boys.

Team Two was led by a callow youth, Second Lieutenant Boyd. Nicko, his guide, brought them just beyond the corner, where the paved road turned into the main gate and a perimeter track continued on round the wire. They could see the guardhouse clearly, nestling beneath its little clutch of down-lamps. The weak wash of their light had created deep shadow all around, and Team Two lay secure in its spill, watching. The guardhouse was little more than a shack, and its door was flung wide so you could see several Luftwaffe ground crew on guard duty sitting inside smoking. The noise of their talk and the crackle of a sentimental song on the radio were the only sounds around.

Boyd shrugged at Nicko, smiled, shook his hand and stood up. His two comrades followed, patting Nicko as they went, and they walked slowly, so as not to scrunch the gravely surface, up to the wire. Nobody bothered crouching or crawling; what was the point? Jerry was decidedly not paying attention tonight. The soldier behind Boyd knelt, produced his wirecutters and began to attack the wire just as *Lilly Marlene* came on the radio and the Jerries in the shack began to sing along, their maudlin caterwauling drowning every single snip. Nicko watched as the last of Team Two disappeared through the hole they'd cut and then he withdrew back up the track he'd brought them down and further into the dark.

After the guardhouse, sitting in its little puddle of light, the next buildings were much further into the airfield; a long barracks, and what looked like a small office structure beneath the control tower, which only rose about two stories, but enough to lift it above the pools of surrounding light, giving anyone up there perfect vision of what was moving below. And it being up in the gloom, Boyd couldn't make out if anyone was actually up there, looking down.

Stretching in a line away from these buildings was a row of bell tents. On the other side of the perimeter road from them was some kind of motor pool with lorries and a petrol bowser, and beyond all of that, rising like some kind of Greek Ayers' Rock, all in shadow, a hanger.

Those weren't his prime targets, his prime targets were much closer to hand, behind earth berms that sat squat and massive either side of the road leading into the base, shadows too like they were the Greek Ayers' Rock's stunted offspring. The first one was right in front of them and the other on the opposite side of the road. That was the bomb dump; you could see the sandbag piles and the protruding ends of stacked lumpen cylinders through the open entrance gap in the berm. So the one dead ahead must be where they kept the aviation fuel.

Boyd waved the other two towards him for a quick brief. He was going to take the fuel dump, and Sgt Rabbett and L Cpl Miller could do the bomb dump. Boyd peeled away round the corner and in through the entrance gap to the fuel dump.

Rabbett and Miller peered into the dark like sprinters on the blocks, ready to dash across the road to their target. They hesitated too long, or maybe their hesitation saved their lives, because almost as if on cue, round the far end of the bomb dump's berm, came the figure of a Jerry sentry, being led by an Alsatian guard dog into the edge of the guardhouse light, obviously completing his round. Rabbett and Miller reverse crawled further into the shadows, so the rise of the fuel dump berm swallowed them.

'Shite and abortion,' whispered Rabbett. The two waited… and waited. Then a shout from round the end of their berm and into the light, from their side of the road, walked another guard, led by his dog. The guard opposite was already getting his ciggies out; it was obviously going to be chatty time. Did these thick square-head bastards not know you shouldn't smoke near fuel dumps! Let alone effing bomb ones!

Miller whispered, 'I thought they were supposed to be the fucking master race.'

'Any more brains,' whispered Rabbett, 'and they could be British officers.'

They were going nowhere.

Meanwhile, Boyd was into the fuel dump and running. He heard the voices but thought nothing, it was as if he was a kid in a sweet shop. Stack upon stack of fifty-gal oil drums, three high. He kept running until he was in the middle of the rows and then dropped to one knee and broke out the first Lewes bomb. He leaned as far into the nearest stack, peeled the paper off, stuck it to the lowest drum and snapped the fuse.

All but two of Boyd's Lewes bombs had been fitted with longer, two-minute fuses, same for the rest of his team, given that the bang they were supposed to set off was going to take a lot more running away from than a thirty-second fuse would allow.

Within fifteen seconds, he'd placed all his bombs and was sprinting towards the entrance gap. He heard the voices just in time before he blundered into the open, the two guards, diagonally across the road, chatting… and *smoking?!* Boyd dropped to his knees and peeked again. The dogs were grizzling. Did they sense him there, even among all the vague fuel stink?

One Jerry shushed his dog, then so did the other. Jesus Christ! When were they going to move? Boyd had a vision of himself in the second before immolation and wondered what he'd be thinking. He slipped out his Webley. Maybe in all the confusion after he'd shot these two arseholes, he might just make it to the hole in the fence. He refused to think about where Rabbett and Miller were, not because he didn't care but because he was completely helpless to do anything for them. He was about to cock his gun when the guards slapped each other's arms and went on with their patrolling. He felt himself breathe as if for the first time in hours. And then he was up and moving, and just as his run was gaining momentum, he cannoned into Miller, lying face down in the dirt.

A stifled grunt from the heap he'd just hit, then a 'Fuck's sake… is that you… Boydie?' It was Rabbett. V-Force didn't ever use the word 'sir' or salute officers, the lieutenant colonel – Olly to his men – insisted on that. Nicknames or first names only. You never knew who was listening or looking when you were in the field, so best just get into the habit before you got there.

It was obvious to Boyd that the two troopers hadn't made it onto the bomb dump. Well, it was too late now. He was about to say so when they heard the first crack of a pistol shot from way deep in the airfield. Nobody was in any doubt it must be Olly's lot, come to grief.

Behind and off to the side of where they lay, the guardhouse was emptying. There was the pounding of running boots… and, of course, the yelling. Searchlights snapped on all across the field, near and far. Boyd raised his head; he could see all the Jerries from the guardhouse were running up the road towards the main buildings. Only one was left, standing, holding onto the door, jiving about like he had ants in his pants, craning to see what was happening. They'd obviously left him to hold the fort. Boyd had an idea. 'Up!' he hissed, and Rabbett and Miller followed him.

*

'Once through the wire, keep moving,' Verney had told them. 'The only reason you stop is if a searchlight pans your way. Then you freeze. Don't even think about dropping to the deck. It's movement that catches the eye. So freeze.'

So that was what he was doing, following his own advice.

The searchlight from one of the central towers between the runway and airfield's hard pan was slowly creeping across the field. Verney and his two chums, Sgts Dickerson and Meikle, had fanned out for their run across the field to the parked aircraft – Verney for the Ju 88s and the other two for the Stukas. Verney was first in line to be hit by the beam. He kept his face tucked down and eyes tight shut, and he stopped breathing lest even the rise of his chest catch a Jerry eye. The light bathed him... and moved slowly on. He breathed again. His eyes flicked to his right, to see whether the other two were going to get caught in the open as he had, and he froze again. The light was panning over a figure in shorts and a Jerry helmet with a slung rifle, walking the line of a taxiway. The light stopped on the figure, which was less than ten yards away and walking towards him, and the figure raised his arms.

It was one of those moments when time collapses, when you know what you have to do, even as you know you really don't want to do it, and you know there is no time to debate the difference. The memory of the last time he'd killed a Jerry with an F-S knife rose up in his mind, and just as quickly in his mind, he killed the thought. The knife was in his hand, and he was running.

The Jerry had turned towards the beam with one hand shielding his eyes while with the other he was waving. The light paused only for a moment, then began panning on. The Jerry began to turn back, bringing his arm down from his eyes. He never saw Verney before he ran straight into him like a freight train, Verney's left hand shooting by his ear and grabbing the back of his neck and pulling, and Verney's right hand coming up from waist height at sixty degrees exactly, as he'd trained to do. Did the Jerry see the glint of the blade? And even if he did, did he know it for what it was before the steel went up under his jaw and straight into his brainpan, before Verney's left hand came back to shut off his mouth and kill any residual scream from a body that was already dead before it hit the ground?

Verney could shoot Jerries all day long, plant bombs or throw grenades and see them blown sky high. But killing up close, with your hands still on the breathing, living man's body and his death grip still on you, as you took his life, it sucked something out of him too. He *hated* it. He could feel the tears pouring down his own face as he struggled to disentangle himself. But he couldn't think about that now. He'd think about it later, whether he wanted to or not. He knew that. But then he'd have gin for company. For moments like that, there was always the gin.

He was up and running again; the Ju 88s just fifty yards ahead. The first one was deserted. Not a figure near it.

The brief from the Greek locals had been specific – the Jerries always had at least one guard per aircraft. Because they feared local partisan action more than anything the British might do. And there were at least a hundred and thirty-odd Jerries on the base at any one time. All Luftwaffe ground crew. The aircrew slept in the nearby village. Verney remembered thinking that was a pity; chucking a half dozen grenades in amongst all the sleeping pilots as well would really have fucked up their air defences. Backup was a one hundred and eighty-strong company of Panzer Grenadiers, based on the island's main town, with a clutch of Hanomags and two armoured cars. The Greeks even had some Box Brownie snaps of them. Verney had identified them immediately as Sd Kfz 232s. Nasty. But they were all a good ten minutes away, long enough for his lads to make a mess and leg it.

So where was the first Ju 88's armed guard? Sod it! He slowed to a halt by the first aircraft's undercarriage. Nobody there. Jerry guards bunking off, whatever next! He fished one of the Lewes bombs out his satchel, stripping off the paper and stepped up onto the undercarriage wheel. With a lunging reach, he slapped it up into the wheel well, right against the main wing tank, which should, with a bit of luck, be topped up with fuel and ready to go. Verney's bombs had replacement minute fuses; he snapped it and dropped down onto the pan again and started racing for the next Ju 88 in the line. Again, no guard. He snapped up another Lewes bomb, stripped it and slung it up into this one's wheel well. It was only when he jumped down again that he noticed the oversized bundle clustered between Ju 88 number three's main undercarriage. He froze in the shadow of this one's main wheel and peered into the space between the other's. It looked like some sort of cover had been stretched... a blanket? It was then he could hear the muttering, and if he just offset his eyes... was that a faint glow? What on... earth? And then it dawned on him. The Ju 88 guards were playing cards... and maybe some of the nearby Stuka ones too. There was a vague whiff of tobacco smoke in the air. Jesus Christ, if they'd been in any of his units, he'd have had their hides flayed off them.

What to do? He was aware he was hesitating, which broke Rule One in *The Olly Verney Guide to Raiding!* – *keep moving*. The other Rule One was *concentrate on the target*, so he did, and he decided was he was going to bag that bloody Junkers. And the only way to do that was to kill those guards... he had his Browning 9mm in his hand now and was fishing for a grenade… when one of the guards suddenly stood up, pointing away from Verney, back towards the main buildings. The Jerry shouted a challenge. It wasn't very loud, like he wasn't sure what he was seeing. Verney followed the line of his sight… and there was Dickerson and Meikle, dodging in and out the far end of the line of Stukas, just fleeting shadows to the Jerry, but Verney knew all right exactly who they were.

The figures went to ground. And the Jerry raised his rifle. The other Jerries stood up too… five of them. Another challenge from the Jerry with his rifle. Inexplicably, his comrades just stood there. The Jerry was yelling he was going to shoot. Verney heard a breech block. And that was it. Decision made. Verney shot the Jerry with the rifle in the back of the head, and raised the grenade, intending to pull the pin. The other four, all of them Luftwaffe ground crew… engine fitters and airframe riggers, just like their dead pal lying there on the ground with his helmet leaking blood and brains… all of them immediately threw up their hands and started shouting, 'Kamerad! Kamerad!'

'Bloody hell!' yelled Verney, aloud, out of incredulity and frustration. What did these idiots think he was going to do with four prisoners? Stupid bloody… and then he saw they were all edging apart, and one of them was edging further than the others, towards the dark. 'Kamerad!' the Jerry shouted, once more for good measure. Verney stared at him until he realised he was hesitating *again*. He turned his pistol on the Jerry, and as he did, the one at the other end of their group ducked in behind the tapering rear fuselage and started running, keeping the tailplane between himself and the crazy Englander's gun. When Verney swivelled to try and get a shot at him, the other three fanned out and tore off into the blackness as well.

'Thank you, Fritz,' Verney muttered to himself, relieved not to have had to shoot them all in cold blood. There were things you had to do sometimes, even if sometimes you'd've preferred not to. Meanwhile, behind him, all hell was breaking loose. He saw Dickerson and Meikle emerge from behind the line of Stukas, heads up, one of them shouting, 'What the fuck?!'

'Use up what's left and head for the wire!' yelled Verney and then he turned and started running… towards the searchlight tower and under its sweeping beam. On the tower, spits of light appeared… an MG 42 had opened up and tracer arc-ed, and the rounds, as they hit, bounced and toppled across the hardpan between the last Ju 88 and the line of Stukas. No one was there, Jerry was firing blind. Verney heard a bang, like a grenade going off, but quite a way away. He blanked it – too much to think about right here. And then a flare went up with a whoosh. Verney didn't look, he just kept running through the dark. And then the whole world was bathed in a sickly, chemical light that turned it into one vast frieze of moving shadow. But Verney was already under the view of the machine gunners in the tower. Two more Lewes bombs, stripped and fused and stuck to the tower's legs. Thirty-second fuses this time.

And then, *BOOOOM!… BOOOOM!*

Great billowing mushrooms of flame and oily smoke billowed from the two Junkers in quick succession, so that between them and the parachute flare, the whole airfield seemed fixed in some awful artificial daylight. Both aircraft had collapsed on their sundered wing roots and were now blazing furiously.

*

Boyd, on his feet and running, began yelling, 'Achtung! Achtung! Alarm! Alarm!' and started pointing wildly into the dark maw of the airfield.

'Bunny! Dusty! Start yelling too, you soft bastards!' he hissed, much lower. Rabbett and Miller, also up and running now, caught the drift and obliged, 'Achtung! Alarm!'

The Jerry at the guardhouse was suddenly aware of these three dark figures appearing on the road, coming from behind the fuel dump. Who? What? But they were heading towards the gunshot... and shouting warnings... in German. He thought no more about them as he turned and began winding the field telephone for a connection to the Panzer Grenadiers' barracks in the town.

The three raiders were running towards the two Storch recce kites, and Boyd was fumbling in his satchel for the Lewes bombs with thirty-second fuses. He kept pulling bombs out to check the coloured tape marker, but he couldn't make out any bloody colour in the dark. Every time he checked, he slowed, so that Rabbett was racing ahead. Rabbett reached the first Storch before Boyd and simply pulled the pin on one of his four grenades, popped it in the cockpit, and ran on to the next.

The Storch was an ungainly excuse for an aircraft to say the least; all struts and wire with a high monoplane wing all propped up and looking like an overgrown balsa kit flung together by some enthusiast in his shed.

Boyd stopped in astonishment, and before he'd remembered to start running again – remember Rule One of *The Olly Verney Guide to Raiding*! – the grenade went off and was enough to reduce the middle of the Storch instantly to a pile of kindling. Then there was a flash, and its petrol tank went up, scorching Boyd's eyebrows.

This was the grenade Verney heard as he ran towards the searchlight tower.

An instant later, Boyd could see Rabbett clear as day as he reached the next Storch and repeated the exercise.

Because suddenly, as if from nowhere, a huge parachute flare had appeared almost directly overhead.

The *BANG!* from Rabbett's grenade, however, was drowned in a big, one-two yellow flash and blast out in the middle of the field as Verney's Ju 88s went up.

Everything was total confusion now. And everything began happening at once.

Verney's team and Boyd's, from their different angles, could see the avalanche of figures pouring out of the barracks hut, in various stages of dressing, clutching rifles and sub-machine guns, holding helmets on, struggling with their webbing. All the airfield's lights were now blazing and the searchlights probing wildly around the perimeter. Some of the Jerries were making for the trucks directly ahead of Boyd's lot, but he urged Rabbett and Miller to keep running towards them. Shots filled the air, and the chatter of machine guns, though it was obvious to the two British teams nobody knew what they were shooting at. Certainly, nobody was shooting at them, not yet.

Another flare went up. And as it did, in a regular *BOOM! BOOM! BOOM!* the line of Stukas started to explode, like a row of fireworks in a closely choreographed display. Seven of them, in quick succession, turned into collapsing bonfires. And as they did, two more *cracks*! And the central searchlight tower's beam began to spin wildly through the sky, jabbing up into the haze, as the tower itself, in slow motion, toppled its full length to the ground.

Verney, standing behind the two back struts of the tower, stepped deftly aside as they too, split and splintered, and he stood motionless as the whole structure crumpled onto the ground. The platform that had once been its top, spilled four figures, sprawling onto the rough gravel, each of them landing hard and bouncing. And as they did, Verney was already running towards them with a grenade in one hand, pin already out. He threw it, checked his pace momentarily and shielded his eyes as it went off. When he turned back and started running again, he could see one of the Jerries had taken most of the blast. His disrupted body lay to the side, unrecognisable as a person now. The other three were all conscious and moaning. One got to his knees, and Verney shot him twice. The other two, especially the one with the spectacularly broken legs, just lolled, so he left them alone. It was their MG 42 machine gun he was after and its belts of ammunition. He swept it up; he'd fired a Spandau before – beautiful device! He flipped down the bipod and threw himself to the ground. The enemy was firing everywhere, but not at him. With the second flare guttering away furiously above them, Verney knew he was in plain sight now, but nobody was going to distinguish his prone figure from the other Jerry ones lying around him. He checked the belt, cocked it and then systematically began pumping tracer rounds into the still intact Ju 88. One of its fuel tanks detonated almost immediately.

This had all been planned as a sneak-in-sneak-out-again op. We just cut through the wire, mark the spot, then creep through the shadows to the aircraft, plant our charges and then run back to the holes and away before the balloon goes up. Funny how all these raids always went to shit, one way or another.

But none of the six British commandos tearing across the airfield that night was worrying about that. It was the speed of it all that was consuming them, and that they were feeding off it too. That old Verney dictum again: *keep moving*. The rush, the sheer excitement, the no time to think.

He was still in his early twenties, but this thrill was Boyd's drug of choice now, this was what he craved, where he could feel the fitness of his body sing back to him after all those months of training, carrying knapsacks full of bricks for hours and hours in a running crouch round that track, or out over the desert for fifteen miles and back, the endorphins pumping through him. And the action, the unalloyed joy of explosions, destruction, mayhem, power. Everything else in life was just killing time until he could be back here, right here, in this very moment, living. Fear was just something he'd heard about.

Two trucks, now loaded with a scrambling mob of Jerries, suddenly started up and shot out of the motor pool area. A couple of Jerries, hanging out the back of the second one, saw the three commandos running towards them and never for a moment realised who they were. They just assumed the obvious and waved for them to 'Come on! Come on!', thinking the three were Luftwaffe, just like them. But the lorry was tearing away too fast. The commandos waved back. But it was the bowser Boyd had his eyes on. He ran straight to the cab and jumped in. Miller came up to the door behind him. Boyd turned the ignition, and the engine started.

'Slap a couple of Lewes on this, and open the outlet valves,' he yelled, but his voice was almost drowned by the Stukas blowing up, one by one, on the other side of the row of bell tents.

Miller nodded and did as he was told. When he banged the cab door, Boyd slammed the petrol bowser into gear and drove it across the perimeter road and directly into the row of tents, spewing fuel as he went. He ran over three; from the crunching and clanging coming from beneath the wheels, the tents were obviously workshops, as he'd been hoping. Then he yanked on the handbrake, jumped out and ran before Miller's Lewes bombs blew the lot into a flaming pyre.

He was back on the other side of the road when a series of flashes dead ahead almost blinded him. The Lewes bombs he'd planted in the heart of the petrol dump were going off now and turning their enclosing stacks of oil drums into even bigger bombs. The noise was tremendous; huge *whumphs!*... and thundercracks too, like the sound a giant redwood tree might make being snapped like a cocktail stick. And then there was the display, the drums that hadn't detonated, where the heat and blast only sundered their base plates, going off like huge barrel-rockets, the burning petrol roaring out of their ends, sending them soaring in gigantic fiery parabolas into the night; and the heat, the roiling, rolling waves of furnace heat.

The two troop-laden lorries reached the centre of the field and stopped. Any further and they might have run Verney over. Verney, who was still prone behind his MG 42 Spandau. He was trying to decide whether it wouldn't be a good idea to start firing at them when there was a huge *BANG!* and a mushroom of yellow flame billowed out from behind the lorries, then a line of flame, like a theatre curtain opening out, and Verney could make out the tent line behind, each bell of canvas crinkling as it was consumed.

It must have been that bowser he'd seen. Boyd and his lads must be busy.

That was when Verney really was stunned, physically, because of the blast, but also by the sheer biblical conflagration of it as the flames erupted over towards the main gate, as the fuel dump went up.

He turned back to see the lorries begin disgorging strange, jerky, stick-like figures, all silhouette limbs and rifles dancing in the glare of those flames and flares. The figures fanned out across the field as if without a plan and began firing as they went at God knew what. Verney watched a wave of them stumbling directly towards him, all of them, half-blinded – thankfully – by the glare. He shuffled himself round until he had the MG 42 facing the other way, and then he began shooting randomly into the night. As the first of the running Jerries impinged on his peripheral vision, Verney began yelling in his diplomat's excellent German, 'Draussen! Tommies! Schnell! Ausschwärmen!' And the Jerries went scurrying past him, at the crouch, rifles at their shoulders, firing too.

And look who was creeping up behind the Jerry line? Verney'd know those rumpled, shady, moving heaps anywhere: Dickerson and Meikle.

'Where's our hole?' hissed Verney. He'd long ago lost his sense of direction, thus breaking that other Rule One of *The Olly Verney Guide to Raiding*: concentrate.

'Buggered if we know, Olly,' said Meikle. 'We've both lost the marker points too. None of the terrain makes sense in all this light. We've still got the cutters though.'

Over on the other side of the burning tents, Boyd, Rabbett and Miller stood admiring their handiwork but only for a second – remember Rule One: *keep moving*.

It was obvious their work was done. Everything they'd come to blow up was burning, except two of the Stukas that neither they nor Verney's team had managed to get at. Too late now, there were too many Jerries running about.

'Head for the gate,' hissed Boyd and set off at a run. Rabbett and Miller looked at each other, did he mean for them to just walk out the front door? Well, okay then. Off they jogged after him down the perimeter road. Until Rabbett shouted, 'Oi!'

Meanwhile, on the other side of all hell, Verney was scanning the tableau before him. He thrust his hand directly towards the mid-point in the one, immaculate black and untroubled stretch of perimeter. 'Right there. Off we go,' he said, as if suggesting a stroll down the pub, and his team took off at a jog after him. Dickerson, on the outside, noticed as they went past, two pale, frozen faces following their progress.

The Jerry lorry drivers were still in their cabs, and they had both just looked up to see three commandos loping through the shadows less than ten yards away. Their expressions were a sort of pastiche of incredulity and terror. Neither of the two Jerries uttered a sound, nor, it seemed, dared move a muscle; frozen, except for their rigid stares which seemed to follow the three without a blink. Dickerson winked back at them over his shoulder, but he couldn't tell if they saw, so he just turned and jogged on.

Boyd had been concentrating on trying to see what the Jerry left in the guardhouse was up to when Rabbett's 'Oi!' had brought him up short. He turned to look where Rabbett was pointing, and out beyond the fence, tearing down the town road at great speed and perfectly lit by the fuel dump blaze, was a Jerry armoured car and three Hanomag half-tracks.

Leaving by the front door was no longer an option.

It was one thing after another.

'Right, back the way we came,' sighed Boyd, and he turned until he was looking into Miller's troubled expression. He stared at it just long enough to think, *Fuck me! Get a move on!* and then, *…what's up with him?* when Miller yelled, 'Get down!'

Boyd turned and looked where Miller was looking. Maybe three hundred, three hundred and fifty yards ahead of them, a moving, burning tributary of fuel was well into the process of seeping across the road from the fuel dump and was eddying around the bomb dump's berm. Its advancing, flaming tendrils must already be probing through the berm's entry gap. Getting down sounded like a good idea. But maybe putting a bit more distance between them and the dump might be a better one.

'Run!' yelled Boyd. Rabbett and Miller didn't need telling twice.

Verney's team got to the wire fence, and Meikle bent to start snipping through. He went fast and was quickly crouched inside the lower roll, holding back the cut wire. Not a word had been spoken. Dickerson went through first, and Verney was halfway when an angry, challenging shout came from the centre of the darkness, slightly above and off to their left.

'Halt oder wir öffnen Feuer! Hände hoch! Kommen Sie undiden-tifizieren Sie sich!'

'He says, "Kommen-sie outen, mit yer hands up!"' whispered Verney. 'I think we should do as we're told.'

The three commandos came out from the tangle of the wire, and as they did, Verney began shouting at the Jerry like he was punching him.

He started off with a good haymaker of a 'Dumbkopfs!' And then, as far as Dickerson and Miekle were concerned, a torrent of violent gibberish followed, but each bark was landing home like the Jerries might have wished Max Schmeling should've done against Joe Louis.

When Dickerson and Meikle looked up, they could see the Jerry, a dark shadow with the muzzle and magazine of a Schmiesser machine pistol protruding, standing on some sort of parapet that, now they were looking, they could see were sandbags. Twin gun barrels... really quite substantial gun barrels... peeked skyward behind him. It looked like there were other heads peering over the sandbags too.

The Jerry's pose had stopped being aggressive immediately Verney had begun his tirade; now the figure stood as if he'd come to attention. The words that came barking back out the night from him were larded with contrition.

'Mein Herr! Ja, mein Herr!' The Jerry was shouting back, the way you do when you repeat your orders to show you've understood.

'Die Englischer fallschirmjäger sind im Umkreis! Das Feuerunterdrücken, mein Herr! Jetzt anfeuern, mein Herr!' Verney yelled and pointed into the night.

And the twin gun barrels behind him depressed and disappeared for a moment, only to appear the next, and begin firing, the steady *bump! bump! bump!* of a 20mm cannon, pumping out at unseen targets in the middle of the airfield. By the time the reeling and chastened Jerry looked back, Verney and his men were gone.

'I told him the perimeter was full of British paratroopers,' wheezed Verney as he ran. 'And then I demanded to know why they weren't gunning them down!'

Dickerson and Meikle wheezed with laughter too as they ran. The boss was always pulling stunts like this, shouting at Jerry as if he was an idiot… and it always worked… which always made it funnier. And thinking about it as they ran – since they had nothing better to do, pacing it out into the night – they shuddered, each to themselves, at the system of discipline and command that must prevail in the Wehrmacht to get those poor bastards, just like them, to jump like that. I mean to say, the British Army always did a good line in bullshit-baffles-brains… but the Huns? Christ, almighty! And then there was a flash like the opening of the fabric of the universe followed by a roar louder than the last trump and a wall of blast that made them all stumble and reel like they'd been slammed by the side of the world.

The bomb dump.

On the other side of the airfield, Boyd and his men had been running too, after his order to run, run for their lives. But it felt to Boyd, right then, that they'd been running for far too long without anything going *bang!* yet. It must be right now, it must be now that it was going to blow.

Running, thinking – the bomb dump had been on Boyd's mind since they'd all gone charging through the wire fence – how Jerry getting in the way had meant they'd had to swerve, stopping them getting their own bombs into the bomb dump. But funny how events change stuff and how now, all bloody mayhem was breaking loose, and they'd turned to start running for the door themselves. Why not, on the way past, just chuck the last of their Lewes bombs in amongst all that Jerry ordnance by way of a parting gift? Just the job. Except, as he was running towards the bomb dump berm, it had never in a million years occurred to him that the fuel dump across the road – and all the leaking, burning fuel spewing out of it – might be about to do the job for him before he got there.

Because when that bomb dump went up... you didn't want to be around. So it was good to turn and be running away, to be putting the distance between them. God knew how many tons of shite was in there. And it must, *must* be about to go any moment now...

Then he saw something that made his heart sing. He was looking at the edge of the perimeter road as it began to curve and the little drop beyond it.

'Ditch!' he screamed and launched himself through the air in an amazing diver's arc. Rabbett and Miller tumbled in behind him, and as they hit the dirt at the bottom, each wriggled and pressed against the shallow lip of it, trying to insinuate themselves into the very earth, contemplating solemnly the minutiae of the tiny pebbles and gravel their noses were pressed into as they waited.

And then there was light.

It came as a physical thing, but not as physical as the thumping, crushing ripples of the blast wave that came seconds later and raced and rolled over them, sucking the air from their lungs and, it felt like, the very pulp from their eyes. It had been the bomb dump's berm and their pitiful excuse for a trench that had saved them from the full lethal effects of that terrible, levelling blast, although the steel debris that began raining down in the seconds that followed threatened to get them in the end. Which was why, even though scorched and winded, they got up and started running again. They didn't wait to see the mess the blast had made of the Jerry flying column that had been coming down the road.

Fifteen

Harry was on the bridge, leaning against the aft periscope stand, gazing into the night. It was crowded up there but strangely silent. *Scourge* had a full charge on now with no need to run the diesels, so she was gently wallowing in the slight swell as she waited for a signal from the beach, which was why Yeoman Bird was up there with his infra-red look-a-scopes, along with four other lookouts and Harding doing his Vasco stuff, making sure they were exactly on station and ready to run in when V-Force's TacHQ started flashing their call sign with their own infra-red Aldis lamp.

The very mention of 'V-Forces' and 'TacHQs' brought forth another snort of derision from him. Bloody idiots. But he couldn't help smirking to himself too; three and half years of war hadn't quite knocked all the schoolboy out of Harry Gilmour either.

It was exquisitely warm, with a high-vaulting sky, bursting with stars from horizon to horizon, and now, so close to the predicted time, *Scourge* was at diving stations. Pretty soon it would be time for the torpedo loading hatch on the forward casing to open and Number One to emerge, leading Sgt Probert and his folbot and then the casing team and their coiled grass hawser.

The plan had been thrashed out round the wardroom table earlier, over cocoa. When Bird got the agreed signal, it meant V-Force was going ahead with the op, which 'wouldn't take long', Probert had assured them. V-Force would sneak in, give it lots of flash, bang, wallop and then leg it hell-for-leather back across the island, with the fair chance that Jerry might not be far behind. So everything had to be ready for them on the beach. On the other hand, they might manage to sneak away in the confusion, then there'd be more time to disembark. But best to be prepared for all eventualities. Which was why Harry had ordered the twin .303 machine guns up. The weapon was mounted and manned now by a gunner and an ammo tray feeder, right beside him on the conning tower's aft bandbox. Bloody right the bridge was crowded tonight. He shuddered to think of the carnage trying to get down that conning tower hatch if he had to give the tit a double hit. Hooper and his three-inch gun team were waiting below in the gun tower.

But it was very quiet. And there were a lot of eyes on the horizon, watching in case it stopped being quiet. Below, Biddle was on the Asdic set, listening for the slightest propeller sounds out there in the deep, and those two new ratings had the radar going too, its boxy cage aerial raised on the stand above him, scanning the sea's surface and the skies. Smudger Smith and Darky Mularky, them and their set in the wireless cubby with that new leading telegraphist. What was his name again? Boxall, that was it. Number One had told him all about Boxall. And Able Seaman Mularky.

'I changed the watch list to make sure they are both on duty now in the wireless cubby together as often as possible,' Farrar had told him. 'There will not be any private grudges aboard this boat.'

'And they understand that?' Harry had asked.

'Oh, I've left that to Mr Ainsworth, to ensure they both fully comprehend the level of conduct expected of them while serving aboard *Scourge*, sir,' he had replied, with the faintest of evil grins. 'So I'm sure they do. Now.'

Boxall had still to come before Harry on his charges. Captain's report, nothing else would do. After all, he'd inflicted a nasty wound on the *Scourge's* darling with that scullery maid's iron of his. Their ace gun layer, Hooper, wasn't the type to bear grudges, but the fact that the rest of the crew were 'somewhat sanguine' on the issue, according to Number One, led the two of them to conclude that Hooper must be playing a long game when it came to settling with the now notoriously gobby Boxall. And, they also concluded, everybody knew it.

Ah, all life is here, said Harry to himself, as he contemplated Number One's deft handling of it all. And that made him smile because hadn't he been the clever one, deciding to look beyond all his earlier doubts about Farrar's fuddy-duddyness and look to his qualities as an officer instead. Yes indeed, Mr Farrar's conduct these days had definitely justified his writing that letter, currently sitting in Captain Philips in-tray, seven hundred and fifty miles back in the Lazaretto base, recommending Farrar sit his Perisher. If that didn't call for a smug smile, what did?

Thinking about long games, as he waited, his mind drifted back to a very old friend indeed: CPO Gault, who'd turned up on Malta while he'd been at sea, as HMS *Talbot's* senior chief. He hadn't been able to believe his eyes when he'd seen him after getting back from that last patrol. There had been old times and news to chew over, like how Ted Padgett sent his best, how, with his sea-going days over, the old warrant engineer from *Pelorus* had conned his way into a berth on the training staff at the new Royal Naval Engineering College at Manadon, above Plymouth, so he now caught the bus to work every day. How he had insisted his new grandson be called Henry, after Harry, and how he, Harry, hadn't had the heart to tell Gault that his name wasn't actually the common short form but a reference to an Inner Hebridean island. *All life*, indeed.

Then, he recalled, they'd talked about the Bonny Boy.

'It was Shrimp Simpson who first asked me about you and him,' Gault had said. Harry remembered he'd just nodded, not knowing where this was going. But Gault had continued, 'Then the rumours started, and I told Captain Philips what I knew, then that bloody captain from C-in-C Med turned up like bloody Torquemada… they're onto him now, Mr Gilmour. They must be. Whatever he's been up to, he's not going to get away with it anymore. Jesus! What a fucking madman!'

Harry wasn't so sure about the Bonny Boy not getting away with it anymore.

He's not your friend Capt Philips had told him about the C-in-C's Torquemada. How their 'interview' had rolled out certainly gave the truth to that:

Capt de Launy: *Who issued you the orders for those patrols?*

Lt Gilmour: *The S Twelve, sir.*

Capt de Launy: *How did he communicate them?*

Lt Gilmour: *He told me, sir.*

Capt de Launy: *Was this customary? Normal? In your experience, was this how other flotilla captains did it?*

Lt Gilmour: *Normal, sir? Um. What is normal, sir? Captain Simpson used to issue railway dockets with just the billet square and recall date scribbled on it, sir.*

Capt de Launy: *But there was always a written document?*

Lt Gilmour: *Yes, sir.*

Capt de Launy: *Yet there was no written document for your orders to patrol off Port Vendres?*

Lt Gilmour: *No, sir.*

…and the same for the op to dispatch Kesselring and for the billet as guard boat at the scrag end of the Sicily landings. *No. No. No written documents.*

On, and on, meticulous, unrelenting, back and forward, question after question and the scratch, scratch of de Launy's pen – for there'd been no writer in the room to take it all down. No witness, just the two of them.

And yet, throughout the whole process, not once had de Launy asked him if he suspected Captain Bonalleck of actually being out to get him. Or even if he wondered why he was being asked all these questions? Harry remembered with a thin smile, resolving at one point to actually ask de Launy what all this had been about, but only after he'd finished.

He didn't get the chance. The last question came and went, and then it had just been, 'That will be all, Lieutenant Gilmour. Dismiss.'

And you don't argue with a four-ringer when he tells you that.

Isn't that right? He silently asked the stars, head right back, gazing up at them now, suddenly thinking this is much how an ancient Greek must have seen this sky two thousand years ago. What it must have felt like to have been one of those to whom the world was so new.

He gave his head a shake, his mind was drifting off on another reverie instead of keeping his eye in. That was the bloody trouble with this waiting. Your mind rattled on if you weren't busy. He always used to try to keep it on track, going over the plan, trying to come up with everything that could go wrong and what to do in each eventuality. Sometimes it worked, but other times, like now, it didn't. Maybe some chaps had the mental steel, patrol after patrol, like the old aces, Bryant or Tubby Linton, or Wanklyn, except Linton and Wanklyn, the greatest ace of all, were now dead. So maybe it was a godsend Harry Gilmour wasn't one of them; a good thing that keeping his eye in felt like he was trying to ride a penny-farthing at 90 mph across an oil-and-water skid pan with marbles randomly scattered on it.

'Jesus!' It was a soft utterance, from behind him, but delivered with emphasis.

Then, 'Wow!'

Then, 'Sir!'

He was already turned and stepping to the bridge front for a better view when the stretch of skyline between the two peaks off the port bow really lit up and the first roils of flame could just be seen tipping above the base of the 'V' between.

'Wowser, indeed,' Harding was muttering, gazing open-mouthed at the spectacle. 'That'll teach someone to light their farts.'

Then the thud of the explosion echoed over the water.

Harry leaned over the voicepipe, 'Tell Sergeant Probert it's time to get his folbot up and get going.'

The business ashore was obviously now well underway.

*

Tom McCready was standing on the beach with nothing to do. His face was all blacked-up, and he was feeling particularly stupid, especially because of the way the little group of Greek civilians were looking at him and sniggering behind their hands.

First, there'd been all the excitement when the first fireball on the horizon got massively bigger and just kept burning, then there had been the flash and then moments later, the thunderous boom that had been like a volcano going off and the fact that, despite the distance, even they had felt the pressure of the blast wave.

It had all made Tom think getting blacked-up was just the start of something big that he was going to be part of, and then Probert had rowed him ashore with the grass hawser's bitter end in his lap. When they'd scrambled up the beach, it had become apparent that none of those civilians were blacked-up and neither were the two commando lance corporals waiting with them. What were those civilians doing there anyway?

And now, Probert had disappeared into the scrub at the head of the beach with one of them, the tall, distinguished-looking young chap who should've been sitting on a tavern veranda discussing *The Iliad*, not out gallivanting in the middle of the night like one of Daphne du Maurier's smugglers. So now he, Sub Lt Tom McCready, had been left with nothing better to do than watch these two pongo non-coms fiddling with their blasted primus stove, trying to get a brew going.

He went over to check the hawser again, where it had been made fast to a boulder the size of a saloon car. The hawser hung slack as it snaked away into the water, with life jackets tied at regular intervals along its length to help keep it afloat when the weight went on.

Because when the time came, the idea was for all those on the beach to hand-over-hand out to *Scourge* and then get hauled aboard by Cox'n Ainsworth and his party on the casing. He and Probert had also brought along a stretcher when they'd rowed ashore, in case there were any wounded to transfer, although that was going to be awkward. The stretcher, with a casualty aboard, wouldn't lie lengthwise on a folbot, so they would have to ship it athwart, with one man rowing, and the other in the water, keeping it close to the hawser and making sure the stretcher didn't tip one way or the other and the patient end up in the ogin.

He went back and plonked himself down by the two lance corporals, and began to sullenly eye the civilians.

'I wouldn't worry about them, mate,' said one of the lance corporals.

Mate! thought McCready. *Mate!* He'd give him bloody *mate!*... then he remembered what Probert had told him earlier, that the commandos didn't say 'sir' or salute when they were in the field, so as not to identify officers... and get them killed by any nosey sniper in the vicinity.

'Naw,' said the other pongo. 'They're here because they hate Jerry more than we do. Nobody on this island's going blabbing. And they're also here in case we need a hand.'

'Good,' said McCready, for something to say.

'Yep,' agreed pongo one. 'They're a lovely folk, the Greek islanders. But a cross-grained, ugly shower if they don't like you.'

'Too true, mate,' added pongo two. 'Even more bloody-minded than a bloody Jock!... ohh... that's us... brew's up. Fancy a cup?'

It was like bloody Margate on a bank holiday, thought McCready. And that was when a long line of stumbling figures suddenly appeared where a moment ago there'd just been the scrub, all being led out of the night by the lanky Greek chap he'd seen go off earlier.

*

Harry sat, watching the grubby figure of Oliver Verney, with his right leg impossibly bent up beside him and his bootless foot on the wardroom banquette while he leant over it, rubbing his ankle with some smelly embrocation from *Scourge's* medicine chest. Both men were smiling inanely.

Scourge was dived now and heading south-west away from the mayhem V-Force had wreaked on Kos well behind. They'd had to leave it perilously close to first light for the wayward Verney to eventually turn up on the beach, hobbling in, using some hapless Jerry's rifle as a crutch and being helped along by some teenage goatherd with an old-fashioned crook he'd bumped into along the way.

'I've got to stop kicking next door's cat,' was all he'd said by way of explanation to McCready for his turned ankle and late show, to McCready, who'd been anxiously pacing the beach, feeling like he was ready to have kittens himself, so fine had they cut it to wait for this clown.

Well, he was aboard now, and they were on their way.

Harry had recognised the name right away when he'd demanded to know who this clown was that he was endangering his boat for and why the other members of his unit were so sure he'd turn up. Oliver Verney. How could he forget those warm Mediterranean nights they'd spent together? Wrecking trains on the coastal line that ran from the toe of Italy up to Naples. And how Verney had known him from a time before, even though Harry hadn't known Verney from Adam, because Verney had watched him lighting and placing a ciggy in the gob of a wounded sailor in the rain, on that stone jetty up in Shetland after *Trebuchet* had come in from off the North Cape, already sinking beneath them. And Verney's little story about how just watching Harry, with his dashing wound dressings on show, going about ministering to his wounded crew had inspired him to join up. How could Harry not be smiling, meeting a chancer like that again?

'If I rub it with this on the outside,' said Verney, applying another cupped handful of the stuff and rubbing briskly and then nodding to the tumbler of arak in front of him, 'and then with that on the inside, I'll be right in no time.'

'Serves you right for going back,' observed Harry, taking a sip from his own tumbler of the white spirit.

'The hun was otherwise engaged, old chap, and it was just too good to miss,' Verney said, looking up at him, grinning.

The reason Verney had been late, a jumbled tale told by his Sgt Dickerson, and the likelihood vouched for by his deputy, Second Lieutenant Boyd.

'We were goin' like the clappers for our first rally point,' Dickerson had blabbed, while pleading for Harry to give his boss just a bit more time. 'When we passed our original 'ole in the wire... where we'd gone in. "Hang on a minute chaps," says Olly, and off he goes...'

'Let me get this straight,' Harry had said. 'You'd been into the airfield, set your charges, they were going off, and Jerry was after you... and Olly decides to go back in through the wire?'

'There was a couple of Stukas left we didn't get,' Dickerson had said, like this was a rational reason to go running back in when the enemy was running your way, looking for you.

'He does that sort of thing,' the other sergeant, Meikle, had said. 'And anyway, that Jerry anti-aircraft gun we'd passed, they were shootin' up everything that was moving inside the wire, which was mostly other Jerries...'

'Yes, and your Olly had just gone back in there,' pointed out Harry.

'Ye-es,' said Meikle, 'but did he look like a British paratrooper? See?'

Harry had given up at that point. Which was when Boyd had said, 'Give him time, Captain Gilmour. Please. He's always popping up again when you least expect it. We've got until first light. Wait and see. He'll be here.'

So they'd waited, and here indeed, he was.

'...and all without incurring a single casualty... unless you count you,' said Harry, gesturing with his glass at Verney rubbing his ankle.

Verney stopped for a moment and seemed to look a million miles away. Then he said, 'We were only up against a mob of Luftwaffe erks. It'd have been a different story if it'd been the German army. Still, job done, eh?'

*

Harry had Harding plot him a big circle course away from Kos, on a sou'-westerly heading, so that *Scourge* could make a long, direct run into the island of Thirios from the west. They remained at periscope depth for the entire run, despite the clear calm weather making them highly visible from the air, a big black shadow slinking silently through the crystal clarity of the Aegean. No hiding place down there. But then, thanks to his new pal Olly, there were no Jerry aircraft around to be in the air today.

Harry let Harding do most of the periscope work since it was him navigating them through these shallows, never much more than three hundred feet beneath their keel and the waters littered with islets and reefs.

After retrieving 'V-Force' from the beach, Harry had opened the second packet of his orders. The papers were headed '*Operation Hoplite*', after ancient Greek light infantry? Harry wondered. He'd never heard of any British military mind ever being imaginative enough to actually devise an operation name that had any relevance to anything like the what, why, where or when. Somebody must've sneaked through.

Anyway, it was a landing force made up of a random mob of Combined Operations specialist troops – they of the 'Wings, Anchor and Thompson Gun' shoulder flash – two companies of the Parachute Regiment and an entire battalion of the Staffordshires. There'd be signals and engineers but no artillery. The troops would be put ashore by a Royal Navy task force made up of the Hunt-class destroyers HMS *Alconbury* and HMS *Howsham* and five motor gunboats from Coastal Forces, supported by the 'Levant Flotilla', a rather large ragbag collection of local caiques – a *very* old eastern Mediterranean wooden boat design that the loonies at Combined Ops had converted as *very* makeshift troopships, transports and gunboats and operated directly themselves. From what Harry had heard of that lot, they were much more deserving of flying a Jolly Roger than even the submariners.

'Winston says we're to, "Set the Aegean ablaze!", or some such guff,' Verney had told him, right after he'd told him, how come V-Force. '"V" for Verney, of course,' he'd said, with a winning smile. 'And all my own work too!'

'Isn't that utterly childish, if you don't mind me saying?' Harry had asked, remembering not to call him 'sir', even though military discipline dictated he should've – Harry being just a lowly lieutenant and Olly a lieutenant colonel.

'Got it in one, Skipper!' said Olly. 'And me? Mind? Don't be silly!'

But Olly was still a lieutenant colonel and that meant Harry felt it better if he refrained from reminding him the term for a Royal Navy vessel's commanding officer was 'Captain'. Some habits, he decided, died hard.

They heard the landings on Thirios long before the saw them.

The island was located at the tip of an almost perfect equilateral triangle with Tilos to the north and the northern tip of Karpathos to the east. It had been chosen as the forward base for Operation Hoplite because of its deep harbour with its long bar that reached out to the south-east and enclosed an extensive anchorage. Thirios was mostly mountainous, with two large volcanic outcrops and a jagged range that ran to the sea in the west. The north-east was relatively flat and cultivated, but everywhere else, the numerous fishing villages and a small monastery all clung to the steep hillsides and rocks.

There was no space for an airfield, but then they were going to land on Kos soon, after they'd taken Symi to the east and finally cut off the big Jerry base on Rhodes. Or so Harry's packet of orders informed him.

Where he and *Scourge* actually fitted into the big picture here, however, was vague. His orders merely stated he was to place himself and his boat under the direct orders of the local senior naval officer, who was apparently to be one Commander T.A.G. Pleydell RN, *Howsham's* CO.

Harding ordered the periscope up for his latest all-round look, and eyes fixed to the search 'scope's eyepiece, he announced, 'We're here.'

Harry had a look, and what he saw across the glass-calm sea was like a little theatrical show, with the two Royal Navy destroyers lying off the bar, signal flags fluttering in a light breeze, the blue of the sea dappling on their hulls, guns turned shoreward.

Suddenly, one of the destroyers fired, its main battery delivering a broadside to some target inland. He could also see the masts and bridge tops of the gunboats and a forest of caique masts, all inside the bar. Two gunboats now emerged from behind the bar and were running down slowly towards the furthest-away destroyer.

The problem now was to surface and join without the destroyers turning on them, thinking they were a U-boat, and blowing them to pieces; just because a packet of orders said to expect a submarine didn't always mean everybody had read them.

'Pass the word for Mr Ainsworth,' said Harry. 'And Yeoman Bird. And tell him to bring an Aldis.'

While remaining submerged, he would launch two smoke pot recognition buoys to get their attention, as per colours of the day. Then he'd extend the search 'scope to maximum, point it at the nearest destroyer's bridge and then have Bird jam his Aldis to the eyepiece and start flashing the day's recognition codes and *Scourge's* number up it. That ought to do the trick.

*

Cdr Pleydell was a nervy bugger, Harry decided. Middle of stature, thinning tobacco hair, his recent Middle East tan was scant cover for a skin that was naturally pale, stringy of arm and knobbly of knee in his Number-Thirteen whites. He populated every sentence he spoke with 'right', 'yes', 'well', all in a cut-glass accent, and he was perpetually drumming fingers or shuffling papers. Their SNO.

Harry was with all the other COs, navy and pongo, sitting penned in around *Howsham's* wardroom with Pleydell nearest the door, behind the wardroom table that had been dragged there and covered with bumpf for his use. The table was also effectively barricading everybody in, which Harry didn't think was a good idea, and from the expressions on other faces, he wasn't alone.

But none of this could blight his unalloyed joy at spotting the face opposite him; a blast from the past that had him grinning from ear to ear. It was Kit Grainger. He was waving and winking at him every time Pleydell buried his nose in a document. Kit Grainger, now a lieutenant commander and HMS *Alconbury's* captain. Grainger, who'd commended his humming of *All The Nice Girls Love A Sailor* while they were being depth-charged back on the old *Bucket*; Grainger, who'd been his Jimmy aboard that 'boat of the damned', *Umbrage*, with its martinet skipper Clive Rais, dead now, through nothing else than his own stupidity. And here was Grainger again, out of the trade now, but back at sea and at last with his long-coveted dream, a command of his own. From the moment Harry had filed into the wardroom and spotted Grainger's curious scowl of recognition, he couldn't wait to pump his hand and buy him a large one.

He'd always been an awkward bastard, Grainger, Harry remembered that much at least. How he'd used to bait their former CO, Rais, to the point Harry thought he might be endangering the boat. But Harry didn't really care about that anymore, not if he was asked to put it in the balance, not then, not now because Grainger was always going to be a special chum, one to be forgiven anything. What else could you accord the man who'd come back for you when everybody else on *Trebuchet* had thought you were dead, that night in the Soviet fjord with *Trebuchet* and *Trumpeter's* deck guns blowing holes in those Jerry transports and the tracer criss-crossing the black night like braiding on a black satin sheet, and Harry, last seen lying there on that shattered Russian tug, his brain addled by blast and his forearm opened by splinters and the petty officer from his party swearing it was too late to go back because he was already 'a goner'. Grainger hadn't listened then, just like he never did, and he'd come back for him when he shouldn't have. You didn't forget that.

Kit bloody Grainger. Well, who'd've thunk it! As Harding might've said. Operation Hoplite was getting to be quite a reunion, what with Olly Verney sitting there next to Pleydell, looking like he was about to nod off.

But Pleydell and the pongo brigadier sitting on his other side were all about the plans and where Hoplite was going next – the island of Symi, apparently, for all those who were listening – and how *Scourge* was to play a key role.

'Our orders are to deny the Germans the Dodecanese,' the brigadier was intoning from behind his moustache. His name was Plomer, and Harry wondered if he was any relation to the Great War general, He looked antique enough to actually *be* him, demoted now for pockling the mess fund, maybe. 'And to achieve that, we must first take Symi,' he was droning on. 'Doing that will put a noose around the German's main garrison on Rhodes and leave us free to push on up through the entire chain.'

Plomer was obviously another of those chinless skeletons who pre-dated modern warfare, with a shiny, bald pate and crescent of hair to top his luxuriant 'tache and a swagger stick on the wardroom table, set in front of him like a form master's cane. Harry sighed to himself; their ground commander had actually brought a fucking swagger stick to an amphibious landing!

Bad enough, but Harry had thought their orders were to 'set the Aegean ablaze', or at least that was what he remembered Lt Col Verney telling him. Whatever that meant. Was this different? This 'denying' and 'putting nooses round' Jerry's neck? Did it mean the pongo top brass couldn't make their minds up? And what the hell did '…putting a noose round…' mean anyway? He never liked it when orders got mixed up with all that, '…*into the valley of death…!*' and '…*once more unto the breach dear friends…!*' bollocks. That was how you introduced confusion – to your own side. It didn't augur well.

Sixteen

If Harry could've paced on his bridge, he would've. He was seething, and he wanted to step it out. But the bridge was too small and too crowded, which he hated in itself. There was him, Harding at the binnacle – taking constant bearings, trying to make sure they kept on station – the two ratings on the mounted twin .303s behind him and the four lookouts, needed especially tonight because of the surprisingly luminous newly waxing moon.

His was not any sudden flash of anger. It was a rising, cold fury at the systematic cockups that were dogging this stupid operation in which the exceedingly valuable strategic asset that had been placed under his command – namely HMS *Scourge* – was now being pointlessly, farcically, endangered.

His mouth was pinched shut, creating around him a serenely scary silence that all the *Scourges* on the bridge had seen rarely, but knew to beware.

Lt Gilmour being angry was bad joss.

Harry stepped again to the bridge front and looked down for the umpteenth time on the two huge flaccid black shapes draped across the fore-casing like collapsed whales. McCready was standing over them as he had been for the past hour or more, still looking as despondent. The shouty

Parachute Regiment three-pipper, whom Harry had previously warned about his shouting, had gone all silent now and was sitting cross-legged, way forward, just underneath the jumping wire, as innocent as a Buddha.

'What a fucking mess,' Harry mouthed to himself, or thought he had. He heard a muffled snort of amusement from right next to his ear. Bird, the yeoman. He'd forgotten about him when he'd been doing his bridge body count a moment before. Bird was up here too, night glasses stuck to his eyes, waiting for Olly Verney's little flashing torch from the beach to tell them he was back and had come up with some brilliant wheeze that'd get them out of this fucking mess.

Scourge was stuck to the glass-flat sea, less than a quarter of a mile off Symi, waiting to discharge her cargo, except she couldn't. So the cargo – almost seventy soldiers, mostly from the Parachute Regiment – sat, stifling and sweating and not daring to swear or curse under the eye of the cox'n, all kitted up with nowhere to go.

It had been a long day. Two days if you took into account nobody had got any sleep the night before.

There hadn't been any time to catch up with Kit Grainger after the planning meeting on *Howsham*, just a passing, 'bugger me!' each and a shake of the hands and a promise to tell all later, over 'refreshments'. For there had been work to be done. The entire squadron had got under way and entered Thirios's anchorage, except *Alconbury* because her captain had informed the SNO he was experiencing problems with his anchor mechanism. Knowing Grainger of old, Harry had suspicions about that.

More than likely Grainger hadn't wanted his command stuck behind a sand bar, her room for manoeuvre severely constrained if something untoward turned up. Like an enemy air attack. Or E-boats. The anchor problem was more than likely all eyewash. Harry smiled at the thought his friend hadn't changed much.

Once inside the anchorage, however, *Scourge* was ordered to go alongside the largest of the transport caiques, open her torpedo loading hatch and offload all her torpedo reloads. She could keep what was already in her tubes, but the rest had to go. It had been backbreaking, sweaty work under an unrelenting Aegean sun, and it had lasted into the night, hauling the one-and-a-half ton monsters out and over on the caique's creaky system of derrick and pullies. But space had to made for the paratroopers and all their arms and ammo, V-Force, all ten of them, including Lt Col Verney, the two Royal Signals corporals, with their big radio set, mini-generator and coils of aerial and the six Royal Engineers with all their kit to get Symi's stone wharf going as a military port.

And, of course, once the torpedoes were out, the pongos and all their paraphernalia had to go aboard – and be stowed! All in a space less than two hundred and nine feet long and twenty-four feet wide – a lot less when you considered all the submarine stuff already in there, not to mention *Scourge's* thirty-nine crew, including her captain.

'It won't be for long,' the brigadier's utterly indifferent staff officer had told Harry while handing over his orders. 'Symi's only a hop, skip and a jump away. A nice afternoon for a Med cruise, what! God, it's hot! How do you stand it in that tin box of yours?'

'We're usually underwater,' had been all Harry could bring himself to reply.

A surface passage would be quicker, he was told. He was expected to sail there on the surface, in daylight. He'd been psyching himself up to actually refuse that order if Pleydell did actually write it, when the whole idea got kiboshed first thing the next morning when a Feisler Storch came puttering over, sounding like a flying lawnmower, way up in the sky so it was only a gnat against the impossibly clear blue.

'Where has that come from?' Harry had said, craning his head up and shielding his eyes to see it, already snappy and irritated after a long and snappy and irritating night. 'I thought your lot were supposed to have blown them all up,' this last to Lt Col Verney, standing on *Scourge's* casing with him.

'Rhodes,' had been Verney's reply. It turned out that Rhodes had airfields too, more than one of them. 'But last intel said there was only three Junkers transports and one of those jobs on the island,' he'd explained, jerking his thumb skywards. 'Them, and around ten thousand Axis troops.'

Harry frowned. 'How come if Rhodes is Jerry's main base and it has more than one airfield, Jerry put all his bombers on Kos, in one bag for you to blow up?'

Verney smiled. 'Most of the ten thousand troops on Rhodes are Italian. And what with them surrendering and all that, I suppose Jerry thought his air support was better off on another island in case the Italians decided to cut up rough and come in and nick them. Anyway, once we grab Symi, the Jerries on Rhodes will be surrounded by us as well as all those reluctant former chums. Hopefully.' A big grin had followed.

'Hopefully?' was all Harry had been able to bring himself to say.

'I know,' Verney had replied, still grinning. 'You couldn't make it up.'

'Well, with that little bugger about up there, we still go submerged. At least during daylight,' Harry had said. 'Presuming you want your arrival on Symi to be a surprise.'

'Definitely a good idea,' Verney had said. 'We're not *exactly* sure who's there.'

That had been the first of several conversations he and Verney had had on the mechanics and the wisdom of the whole operation.

The plan had been simple enough. Grabbing Symi gave the British force a base astride the lines of communication between Rhodes – Jerry's main base in the Aegean – and mainland Greece and the German army in Yugoslavia. And so, unable to be re-supplied, Jerry on Rhodes would then wither on the vine. All *Scourge* had to do was get the initial occupation force ashore on Symi, then the island could be built up as raiding centre for the armed caiques, and eventually, for the flotillas of MTBs and MGBs that had also been promised as reinforcements by C-in-C Med in Alexandria.

'Wouldn't it be smarter for us to be going back to grab Kos right now, instead of Symi?' Harry had asked. 'Seeing as Kos has an airfield… for these Spitfires that are supposed to be on their way… Symi's just a volcanic pimple.'

This conversation had taken place round *Scourge's* wardroom table as the boat was inching its way, submerged, east-nor'-east towards its objective. The table, like everywhere else on board, had been crowded, Harding, listening, all ears, with a mischievous grin on his face, two para second lieutenants, one lolled back, sound asleep with his mouth wide open and gently snoring and the other hunched over the table, oblivious to all around him, scribbling endless lists in his little notebook with a stubby pencil. And, of course, Verney, who, like Harry, was nursing a mug of coffee.

'You'd've thought so,' Verney had replied. 'But who knows what wonders are working their way through the brigadier's mind?' He'd paused to muse for a moment. 'It could be because the Spitfires aren't coming now, of course. Last guff I heard, they were going to throw an ad hoc group together from leftover Tomahawks instead. Better fighter-bombers than Spits. Could make more sense. And meanwhile, best for the rest of us not to sit about on our arses for too long, eh? "Best to be up and doing, what!"' This latter in his best brigadier impression voice.

Everywhere you went on board, you were stepping over bodies, lying down or propped up. And you had to bend because every inch of *Scourge's* deck space and passage was covered, so you were walking on a layer of boxes of stuff from ammo and grenades to rations and radio batteries.

'How are they doing?' Harry had asked on one of his frequent tours, making sure none of these pongos was breaking his boat.

Ainsworth had cast a mean eye over the sprawled humanity. 'Have you noticed, sir, how none of them ever take their damned berets off?'

Harry looked again, and indeed, did see nothing but a sea of maroon.

'I think they go to bed in them,' Ainsworth had added. 'Apart from that, I've got 'em quiet. Can you be imagining the racket, them all going jabber-jabber, whinging and moaning. I told them the sea's full of Jerry U-boats, and their secret listen-o-scopes'd hear 'em five miles off, and ka-boom, we'd all be fish food. I've got the other boys all along, fo'rad to aft, watching, so as they don't touch anything or pull the wrong lever. So we're all right, sir.'

Of course they were, the para three-pipper had assured Harry. In fact, not long now 'til his chaps would be off his hands. Just a matter of getting the troops up on deck and into those two huge inflatable rafts the Americans had given them. The manuals proudly boasted each one could carry a dozen fully armed men! It would be a milk run.

The heat had been bloody and the air had got fouler by the hour, putting everyone's mood on edge. Harry made sure a daisy chain of ratings kept the drinking water flowing among their guests.

Then another chat with Verney about the relevance of the whole campaign. It had been the two huge, black rubber rafts, collapsed and stowed where *Scourge's* torpedo reloads should've been that sparked his train of thought. All the kit he'd seen at Gib, in Algiers and Malta for

Husky and then for the Salerno landings – new, just out the wrapper, the latest technology, nothing spared. That was the real war.

And now there was this sideshow.

What with the Spitfires being diverted away, then the news that the more MTBs and MGBs that had been promised were definitely coming, but not yet. And no landing craft, just ancient, wooden local workboats – cobbled together lash-ups. And a frontline submarine having to be used to launch what might end up as an opposed landing with nothing more than two inflatable dinghies capable of carrying less than a dozen fighting troops at a time and supplied not even with the outboard motors the manuals said they came with because 'the noise might alert the enemy'. He couldn't even remember what idiot had told him that. It meant that the soldiers were going to have to actually paddle ashore, knackered before they even started fighting... the ones who actually did get to go ashore, that is, because some of them would have to stay in the raft to paddle it back for the next load.

Harry had said as much to Verney, this time on the back of the bridge just after they'd surfaced at sunset, with not much longer to run now that they were cracking along at twelve knots.

'You're sort of right. It is a sort of sideshow,' Verney had said. 'But what are you going to do? Tell Alexander to fuck off?'

General Sir Harold Alexander, Britain's overall theatre commander.

No, Harry hadn't thought that a practical idea. But he hadn't liked the idea of his crew, his boat, even himself being frittered away on a sideshow when the real war against Germany was being waged a couple of hundred miles to the west in Italy. Were they really going to risk British lives for nothing more than a bit of tidying up round the edges? The answer was, obviously, yes. He remembered the feeling of impotent anger rising in his craw.

And then this had happened. This fucking mess on the forward casing.

When they'd arrived off Symi, Harding had navigated them in close to the island, marking off each bearing from all the hilltops and headlands he'd picked out and studied from the army's maps and the PRU photographs, to make sure exactly where they were. Once hove-to, the torpedo loading hatch was opened and Verney's folbot was hauled up. He and Sgt Probert were going to paddle ashore and flash the all clear if it was safe for the rest to follow.

The collapsed rafts were already being hauled up behind them, and Verney and Probert were getting ready to cast off when all industry on the casing abruptly ceased. All Harry saw was McCready, who had the deck, in deep conflab with the cox'n and the para three-pipper – Captain Tolland, his name was; he was in charge of the airborne contingent. It was Verney in overall command of the ground forces.

McCready suddenly held up both hands in a gesture of frustration and headed towards the bridge, obviously on his way to break the bad news. Harry could see immediately the young sub lieutenant was shaking with fury. Down on the casing, Harry had seen that Verney had got back out of his folbot and was now getting into it with the para captain.

'What is it, Tom?' Harry had said, slowly, trying to keep McCready calm.

'It's the air line adaptors, sir,' McCready had replied, swallowing hard. 'The pongos have *forgotten* them, sir.'

The American inflatable rafts had come aboard as army kit and, therefore, not the Royal Navy's responsibility. However, having had his cox'n, Chief Petty Officer Ainsworth, inspect them anyway before he loaded them, Harry had discovered that being US equipment, the air valves for inflating the rafts wouldn't accommodate the Royal Navy's air line nozzles. So Harry had asked the para captain before they'd sailed, did he have adaptors that would match up *Scourge's* low-pressure air lines to the raft's valves? Yes, the para captain had replied, he was certain. Being army kit, it was the Royal Engineer team that was responsible, and he'd been categorically assured that they knew exactly what was required. Harry had pointed out that 'knowing what was required' and 'having what was required' were two different things, which was when the para captain had become quite sniffy and had practically told him to stop flapping. Yes, everything was under control! Which had made everybody happy, until two minutes ago, with the boat riding off an enemy coast and the troops ready to go, when the senior Royal Engineer warrant officer was asked for the adaptors, and he had replied, 'What adaptors?'

Verney was now ashore. Before he'd paddled off, he'd told Harry that he'd had, 'an idea', and would be, 'back shortly'. And with that, he and Probert were gone into the night. That had been several hours ago.

If Harry had been able to see what Verney was up to ashore at that very moment, he might have succumbed to apoplexy. For the lieutenant colonel and his sergeant were sitting at an outside café overlooking the island's main harbour, drinking ouzo with a gathering of half a dozen or so local worthies.

*

It was not long until first light when Probert turned up alone, paddling his folbot with all the slow deliberation of a man knackered. One of the lookouts had spotted his flashing torch from the beach, but it had taken an age for the man himself to be half-hauled out of his seat and onto the port bow plane. He'd looked in no shape to negotiate the conning tower ladder, so Harry went down onto the casing to speak to him, if Probert's breathless, staccato gasps counted as a conversation.

'It turns out Lieutenant Colonel Verney has had an idea,' Harry had later informed Farrar and Harding, back on the bridge.

The plan, in short, was that Harry should forget about getting the paras ashore by inflatable raft. Instead, *Scourge* should abandon the designated landing beach, cruise round to the island's main harbour and unload them directly onto the town's stone jetty. Verney'd be sending a local man out in a boat to guide them in once they'd got themselves round to the other side of the island.

Harry's first question had been, 'Is there a garrison?'

'Yes,' Probert had wheezed. Mostly Italian, but a platoon of Jerries, pioneer troops or engineers, he wasn't sure, there to operate the harbour. 'It's used by E-boats,' he'd added, 'sometimes.'

'So we're looking at an opposed landing?' Harry had asked. 'From my submarine?'

Probert had shaken his head. No. Verney had had an idea about that too. All would be revealed later.

Really? Harry had thought to himself. As far as he was concerned, the whole thing was still the 'fucking mess' he'd first identified, whether Verney was having ideas or not.

Harry had then said, 'If we're still talking about the element of surprise, we'd need to do our transit submerged, and I'm not sure there's enough amps left in the box.'

Although *Scourge* had been on the surface all night, she hadn't been charging, lest the racket from her diesels this close inshore woke the whole island.

Then there was the question, what do we do with the rafts? Broken open and ready to be inflated, it would take hours to roll them up into the same compact shape they'd arrived in, so as to get them back down the torpedo loading hatch. And they didn't have hours. The eastern sky above the island was already lightening.

'Dump them,' Harry had said.

When Probert had heard, he'd gasped, 'No! The boss says we have to keep them, sir!'

And even though the para captain was staying way back in the shadows, for obvious reasons, even out the corner of his eye, Harry could see him visibly agitated at the suggestion his rafts were going to get jettisoned.

'And even if we do get there without being spotted,' said Harry. 'How do I know there's enough depth alongside this wharf to accommodate a boat this size? And fenders. Any suggestion of any fenders? So as I don't collapse my saddle tanks when I bang up alongside the stone walls… and then can't dive anymore? Hmmn?'

With Probert finally capable of speech, the whole story had come out.

He and Verney, having hidden their folbot in the scrub, had fast-marched across the shoulder of the island, folded map in hand and moonlight above, between the peaks of its precipitous interior and down into the small town that surrounded the harbour. There hadn't been an Eyetie or a Jerry in sight, just a gaggle of old fishermen sitting about outside a café, who had spotted them immediately, and known just as immediately who they were, and so invited them over for a drink.

Verney, with his seriously imperfect Greek, had got the drift of their questions pretty quick. Was this the liberation, and should they wake everyone up and start celebrating? Not quite, Verney had said, but if they could spare some fishing boats, it could be.

It wasn't possible. The Eyeties only doled out the fuel for their engines by the cupful and demanded to know when and where each boat was sailing. Which was when Verney had noticed the stone wharf and the rusting relic of a small steam-powered crane. He hadn't been able to make sense of the answers he got when he kept asking how deep was the water. So, said Probert, he'd just jumped in and dived to the bottom.

Well over fifteen feet, maybe as much as twenty had been the answer when he'd finally coming spluttering to the surface. The old Greeks had been delighted at this performance, and it appeared Verney'd been instantly made an honourable islander.

'Small inter-island steamers use the jetty, apparently, sir,' Probert had assured them. 'The sponge trade. It's where they load them for transport to the mainland… from all the islands around.'

Harding, who'd been looking at the chart and working out distance against the feeble charge they had left, had added, 'I'm sure if we switch off all the lights and go dead slow, the batteries will hold out.'

'It still leaves the matter of the garrison,' Harry had added. 'What if they decide they want a moonlit stroll tomorrow night, and are there to meet us when we arrive off the stone jetty? Then there are these bloody rafts!'

'Leave the rafts to me, sir,' said Number One. 'Leave the garrison to Olly,' Probert had said. And then Probert had paddled back to the beach, intending to run over to town with the news that the sub would be there the following night., Farrar, who, when everyone had got squared away, then motored *Scourge* right into the two-fathom line, had Ainsworth buoy both the rafts and had then ordered them shoved over the side into the shallow water, to be collected at Captain Tolland's leisure another day. *

Just over sixteen hours later, in the dark, with the moonlight dancing on the water, *Scourge* lay hove-to at periscope depth off Yialos, Symi's tiny harbour town. Harry had made no attempt to surface because up there, lying close in to one of the harbour's headlands, was a vessel of some sort – small, but he couldn't tell what. The shadow of the land destroyed any sense of its full outline or true size. A right idiot he'd look if it turned out to be an Eyetie MAS-boat, or worse, one of those 'sometimes' Jerry E-boats.

Now that they were here, Harry had been expecting Verney to come out and guide them in. But Verney wouldn't be so daft as to approach, flashing recognition signals all over the place if there was a strange boat hanging about, intentions unknown. So, Harry was waiting. For what? Who knew? Bloody hell! Was there no end to the fuck-ups and the calamities?

Biddle hadn't heard a peep on Asdic out of the stranger, not even a clashing pan in its galley. And McCready, on account of his night vision, was on the periscope, whipping it up every ten minutes for a quick all-round look and then down again. Nothing. It was almost ten p.m., long after dark, if you could call that moon-drenched bay up there dark.

The air in the boat by now was truly fetid, and *Scourge's* ratings not on watch were handing out barley sugars with their tin mugs full of water and refilled water bottles to try and help with all the coughing; and with all those bodies, the stink was pretty ripe too – bodies and piss. Because getting about along *Scourge's* jammed gangway also meant lots of the soldiers weren't bothering trying to fight their way to the heads anymore and were just pissing into the bilges when the urge became too much. Squalor didn't even begin to cover it. And pretty soon, tempers would start fraying. Where the bloody hell was Verney? And even if he did turn up, what were they going to do about that bloody boat up there? A milk run. It was just supposed to be a milk run.

And then McCready piped up, 'Light, on…' and leant back to read the bezel, '…red ten, sir… flashing recognition signal. Flashing…' and he turned the periscope slowly to starboard, '…he's flashing to our chum hiding behind the headland now, sir… heavens! The lights are on! It's a fishing boat, sir. He's just switched on all his lights…'

'HE!' called Biddle from the Asdic cubby. 'Bearing green one three zero. Someone's just started a small engine… petrol one by the sound of it, sir.'

Harry relieved McCready at the 'scope. Indeed it was a fishing boat, one of the local caiques. He swung back, and there, not far away, a mere lump in the water and someone flashing a torch, the letter 'V' in morse, all around the horizon. V-force. Bloody Verney, at last. The clown! He wanted to kiss him.

'Surface!' called Harry. 'Gun crews stand by to close up!'

Unfortunately, Verney's arrival provoked more mayhem. The strange vessel had been one of the town's fishing boats that had stayed out that night on purpose, waiting for *Scourge*.

'The Eyeties scream blue murder,' Verney had said, once his little dory – with Probert on the oars – the fishing boat and *Scourge* had all trotted up. 'But nobody pays any attention… the fishing boats are always skiving off, dropping anchor off the other smaller islands all the time… because the fishing's good or they fancy a party. The Eyeties might not like it, but they're used to it. No, I needed that boat out here waiting because I want to collect my V-force boys. We're the surprise attack! Oh, and by the way, this is Alex.' A tall, tanned man who'd come from the fishing boat stepped forward, once handsome but going a bit to seed now; a local, of course, in his duck trousers and pyjama shirt. 'He used to be deep sea, but he's come home again for all sorts of reasons you don't want to ask. He'll be your pilot getting into the harbour. Lay you alongside the wharf smoother than Fred Astaire.'

Most of the V-force had bunked down aft with the stokers, so it was just a matter of getting them up out the aft escape hatch. A lot of their kit, however, was for'ard. And what a palaver that turned out to be, finding it behind the torpedo reload racks, getting it over the piles of paras, up out the torpedo loading hatch and onto the fishing boat. Over two sweaty hours, with lots of swearing. Then they were off.

'We'll fire a flare,' said Verney. '…a green one!'

And so it was just a matter of waiting, again.

Hours passed. Then there was a burst of fire. Then nothing. And then, with barely an hour to go until first light, a flash, like a grenade going off, some more firing – rifle shots – then bursts of automatic. A real fight. And then silence. Until the green flare went up in a spluttering chemical *whoosh!* The tall Greek, who'd been 'deep sea' turned, smiled at Harry and gestured towards the harbour entrance.

Oh well, what the hell, thought Harry. 'Slow ahead, together,' he said into the bridge voicepipe. 'Helm. Steer two six zero.'

*

The sun well up, Harry sat outside the same café Verney had been drinking at with his new-found local cronies two nights ago, regarding, with a mixture of curiosity and resignation, the small clutch of Italian soldiers squatting on the stone stand in front of the wharf. With them were two sullen German soldiers, barefoot and in their uniform trousers and singlets only. Verney's prisoners.

Behind them, the paras were still hauling themselves up through *Scourge's* torpedo loading hatch, being assembled by one of their captain's subalterns and then parcelled off in penny packets into the town, lugging their kit, all of them in crushed, stained desert battledress, smeared with oil and God knew what, but all of them with their maroon berets still spick and span and firmly in place.

'We had to drag the Italians out of their charpoys,' said Verney, sipping arak from an ancient tumbler. 'A lot of shouting and bawling at first, but a burst from Rabbett's Tommy gun shut them up. We had to fight the Jerries, though. These two eventually put their hands up, but there's a few dead ones up there and one that soon will be. But another lot legged it into the scrub. Can you believe it? I mean to say, it's an island! Where do they think they're going to run to?'

'I suppose you'll be expecting me to haul your catch over there back to Thirios?' said Harry.

'You don't mind, do you? You're a pal,' said Verney, toasting him. 'I'll be coming too though, so me and my lot will keep an eye on them for you. We'll be no trouble.'

Harry was resigned by then, he shrugged and smiled and just started looking around to pass the time.

The little town was timeless. If Socrates had come strolling up in his sandals and introduced himself, he wouldn't have been surprised. The houses, bathed in that fierce Aegean light now, all heat and shadow, were mostly small stone boxes, some of them two or three stories, rough-hewn so that it looked like the stones had merely been slotted together, no plaster or cement, and they rose in ranks up the steep, rocky cliff faces of the harbour which sat like a stopper on the end of the long channel that led in from the sea.

There were no streets as such, just steep alleys that climbed up between the houses, front doors right onto the cobbles. And one road that led directly from the wharf, out of the town and over the hill behind it.

A few civilians were starting to show their faces, emerging from the doors, laughing and curious and slapping and cheering the little bands of paras as they marched up the alleys to their positions surrounding the town. Harry couldn't help but notice how skinny and starved the people looked. But of course they were; neither the Jerries, nor Mussolini's mob were ever going to waste space on their transports to ship in food and medicines for a local population who so obviously must have hated their presence.

So he supposed *his* presence here now, and all these grumpy paras must've seemed like a victory to these poor people. A thing to make them happy again. Just like his sailing past the Italian battle fleet that day off St Pauls' Bay. He'd been happy for those Italian sailors that day, happy not to have to kill them anymore, for them all to get to go home.

But he didn't feel happy right now. This didn't feel like victory.

Right now, the utter pointlessness of what had happened here just overwhelmed him. What on earth were these Jerries and Eyeties sitting over there actually doing here in the first place, in this unspoilt nowhere, wrecking these poor, inoffensive people's lives? Why? What was it about fucking Adolf Hitler's so-called fucking worldview – his *Weltanschauung* – that made it necessary for these idiots to come all the way down here and starve these poor souls half to death?

He suddenly felt heartsick and for a moment, he wondered whether he was going to start crying.

For a moment, he wondered about feeding these poor people, a sort of gesture to show compassion hadn't totally passed from the world, getting the crew to distribute food from *Scourge's* mess stocks. But he dismissed the idea instantly. It would be some time before they'd be re-victualling again, and he could imagine the looks he'd get from the crew if he ordered them to start throwing their tins of ham and fruit salad to the locals, no matter how hungry they were. His crew had to eat too.

When he looked back at Verney, he saw him gazing around as well. Sanguine, the killer's poise, no longer clinging to him. He almost looked like an ordinary bloke, apart from that dirt-ingrained battle smock and the weaponry draped about his person.

An idea suddenly occurred to Harry, a sort of experiment he could conduct to see what kind of man might live inside the Olly Verney who now sat before him.

So he started talking; a stream of consciousness about everything that had just been going through his mind. All of it. Including the bit about wondering whether he was about to start crying.

Verney looked surprised at first, then, chin cradled in his palm, he began to listen without interrupting, rapt, in fact, right to the end. When he said, 'So, you too, huh?'

Seventeen

There was a pall of smoke rising above the harbour on Thirios; you could see it from miles away. And now, as *Scourge* rounded the headland into the big bay, Harry could see both *Howsham* and *Alconbury* were now anchored outside the bar. He'd known about the air raid long before he'd sighted the smoke. *Scourge's* radio room had picked up the island's base transmitter, alerting the SNO who had been at sea, that it was under attack two days ago, and then the SNO's signal from *Howsham* to C-in-C Med in Alexandria.

The damage hadn't been much, or so the signals had said. Nobody had said why. They were going to have to get back to find out all the grim details. But that had taken a lot longer than anticipated.

Scourge's trip back to Thirios had been dogged by a series of failures and breakdowns – lots of stops and starts – and a grim Bert Petrie's face being seen too often in the control room.

The oil-spattered warrant engineer had first turned up in the passage opposite the wardroom to report to Harry that there was flooding in the engine room and they were going to have to heave to.

'It's not your fault, Bert. The boat needs a refit. It's needed one for a long, long time now,' Harry had told him.

When Petrie had finished his report and was heading back aft, Harding had leant into the passage to make sure he'd gone then turned back with a smug smile. 'Well, that's it then, isn't it? You owe us all a drink, sir.'

'What's he talking about?' Verney had asked.

'Oh one of our ancient rights,' Harding had said, looking mock studious for Verney's benefit. 'From back in the mists of time. True throughout the Andrew and ever has been. A rating in your division comes knocking on the wardroom door… seeking you out… on a business matter… you pay the forfeit… you have to buy the wardroom a drink.'

Nobody had felt like laughing; of course, they'd been worrying about what they were going to find when they got back to Thirios, and anyway, Petrie's face had sucked any remaining cheeriness right out of the boat.

What had happened was the gland packing around the port diesel exhaust muffler valve had failed and water was just running through the valve stem and thence into the bilges. The bilge pumps had been running hot, and there was a danger that allowing time for each of them to cool off in sequence might let the flooding reach the electric motors. So *Scourge* had to stop while Petrie effected repairs.

But that sort of thing wasn't supposed to happen. Not on *Scourge*. Because the way things had always worked on *Scourge* was things didn't go wrong in Petrie's engine room. If ever anything looked remotely as if it might, he'd always had it stripped down and fixed before it did. Up until now.

Then they'd hit one of those inter-island currents – eddies flung off from the masses of water at play between the Mediterranean and the Black Sea, far away to the north. And they took the hit beam on which had caused *Scourge* to roll and the rising bilge water to splash the port armatures, putting a full earth on them and putting the port motor out of action. Petrie had tried to cure it on the go, but after several hours hove-to again, he'd concluded they'd need to go alongside to effect a fix, which meant they were down to one motor, the starboard one.

Having repacked the port diesel exhaust muffler, they dived just before first light. They'd only been down a few hours when the starboard motor main bearing began running hot, then 'wiped'. All the power to the propeller shafts stopped, and the number one and the wrecker had to bring the boat to stopped trim at sixty feet, which was uncomfortable even on a good day; and after he'd stripped it out, Petrie had even brought the offending bearing to the control room to show Harry. It had been clear to see the bearing surface was scoured and torn and blackened from heat, with patches of lining material torn cleanly from the steel backing. 'Wiped', in other words.

Petrie said, '...Dirt contamination aggravated by concentrated loading.' And then he'd added sullenly, 'We need a new one.'

Without motors, *Scourge* could not make any headway submerged. The rest of her journey would have to be completed on the surface, on her diesels. At that point, not knowing what type of aircraft and how many had attacked Thirios, Harry was reluctant to go up in daylight. So, more hours' delay, dived, wallowing at stopped trim and relying on emergency lighting just to see. And no galley stove until they could rig it to the emergency generator.

It was only after they'd navigated in through the bar on their main engines, not as handy as doing it on motors, and secured alongside one of the town jetties that they learned the raid had just been three Ju 52 transport aircraft, probably with a couple of Gefreiters in the back, booting the bombs out the door. Not a serious raid, hence the 'no significant damage' signal.

'They were the ones left on Rhodes, I expect,' said Verney to Harry later, when'd he'd wondered why had Jerry bothered. 'Jerry sending a message. Whatever he was planning before, he is never going to let us get away with this. They'll be back. They'll get more aeroplanes and more ships, and they'll be back. They've already got the troops, after all. There's the ten thousand still languishing over there on Rhodes. And its just twenty-five miles that way,' gesturing towards where that enemy stronghold lay over the horizon.

'Less quite a few Italians,' added Harry.

Verney smiled, 'Indeed. Less more than a few Italians.' A little laugh, then, 'You should've been there on Symi when we rounded the ones there up... just how keen they were to carry on the fight for Fascism!' And then he really did laugh.

*

Scourge was creeping along her patrol line between the islands of Andros in the west and Samos over towards Turkish territorial waters. It was well into the last dog watch, and she was on the surface, her radar raised and on, cruising along at just eight knots, cramming charge in and looking for any Jerry reinforcements coming south from the Adriatic.

'Bridge, Asdic. Multiple HE bearing red two zero.' It was the bridge voicepipe talking, Harry couldn't place the voice. Not Biddle, one of the other ratings.

'What do you make of it, Asdic?' he said into the pipe.

A long pause. 'It sounds a fair way away, sir. Not heavy. Lots of light engines.'

'How many? Can you tell?'

There was an even longer pause, then, 'Can't tell, sir.'

'Control room, bridge. Pass the word for Number One.'

He didn't want to go to diving stations right away; he'd get the gun crew closed up first and then tootle over and see what they were dealing with. No point in getting everybody up and running about just for a mob of fishing boats out for a night's work.

Working this patrol line was the first sensible job *Scourge* had been given since being assigned to this operation, and Harry wanted to ease her back into her old ways, doing what the *Scourges* did best: hunting down the enemy and sinking him.

The downside, however, was they weren't heading into this patrol fully armed. When the signal traffic after the Ju 52 raid had said, 'No significant damage,' it wasn't strictly accurate, certainly from *Scourge's* point of view. The caique she had discharged all her torpedo reloads into had been sunk. Shrapnel from a bomb hit on one of the stone wharves had riddled her hull, and she was now lying in twenty-six feet of water at the head of Thirios's port. The torpedoes were still intact, or so divers had found. But how to get them back up again? A problem for another day. In the meantime, *Scourge* would have to sail with only the torpedoes already in her tubes: seven altogether, six bow and one stern.

But before all that, Petrie and his men had gone to work on *Scourge's* engines while Harry had set off to report to Cdr Pleydell.

And there, on one of the jetties, had been Kit Grainger, heading back to *Alconbury* on the destroyer's launch. He'd offered Harry a lift.

'Been negotiating with some local cut-throat over the possibility of another quiet consignment of the local rotgut,' Grainger had cheerily informed him. 'It's surprisingly palatable for something that's closer to paint stripper than a Grand Cru. After you've presented your home-work to his nibs, come for lunch and sample a tipple. You know where to come,' Grainger had said to him, jauntily jabbing his thumb at

Alconbury riding at anchor, back again out beyond the long spit of sand that separated the anchorage from the bay. 'We're at the bar.'

The meeting with Pleydell had been perfunctory; the SNO had listened to Harry's report on the near fiasco at Symi, drumming his fingers and turning corners on document stacks. 'Well, there wasn't enough time to train the troops before we had to go on this one,' was how he'd dismissed Harry's verbal report, as if he was anxious to get onto what new thing was happening. He had lots to tell and appeared pleased he'd someone to tell it to.

He and his two destroyers had been transporting a 'substantial force' to Kos while Harry had been away – and, luckily, while Jerry's flying lorries had been over, 'Otherwise, they might have had something more substantial to aim at, what?'

Something between a self-satisfied and a self-conscious bark of laughter had followed.

Anyway, the thrust of Pleydell's resume of events was that Kos was now occupied and they were looking at Leros next. But until the air support arrived, he was concerned lest Jerry start trying to infiltrate down the island chain and disrupt his and the brigadier's plans. Which was where *Scourge* was to come in. Detailed orders and co-ordinates for a patrol box were passed to Harry and polite inquiries were made about when he'd be ready to put to sea.

'Apparently, there's intelligence Jerry might be preparing to act,' Pleydell had said vaguely. 'Nothing concrete, as far as I can judge. Probably just inter-island troop shuffling. We've got some of those armed caiques patrolling among islands to the west in case anything is coming out from Piraeus, but we want you to keep an eye on the Adriatic, where Jerry has all those divisions up there, busy containing that bloody communist Tito and his gang.'

And that had been it. No mention of what exactly the intelligence was, or if there were any informed assessments – by anybody. No 'well done, despite the problems' for Symi, no 'sorry about your torpedoes'.

And then Harry had taken the launch over to *Alconbury*, and lunch.

'I was on my back for weeks, or I should say my front, and when I was recovered and ready to come back to work... everybody got very sniffy,' Grainger recounted, pouring another hefty belt of the local retsina, so chilled it was almost cloudy, to accompany a plate of truly sublime fried lampuki, freshly caught that morning, he was told, off the quarterdeck by the afterguard.

'...as if I'd been skiving. You got all the glory for that one, Gilmour. Even if you did get your dickie shot off in the process... Ha! Ha!'

That final patrol on *Umbrage*, after their skipper, Rais, had got washed off the bridge, and Grainger had fallen down the conning tower hatch, concussed himself and broken his shoulder blade. And all of it happening while an Italian cruiser squadron had been bearing down on them, two of which Harry, as the next senior officer with a damaged boat under him, had gone on to cripple.

They'd given Harry a Distinguished Service Order for that – a DSO – that being the acronym for Grainger's crude allusion. But Grainger hadn't seemed jealous; in fact he'd looked really rather happy these days, even pleased with himself as Harry, in turn, had been pleased to note.

'I was told there wasn't even a Jimmy's berth going for me,' Grainger had said. 'Well, sod that, I thought. It was like they didn't want me back. So I cast my eye around, and guess what? Turned out the escort boys were panting for officers with actual sub experience... you know... poacher turned gamekeeper sort of thing. They practically bit my hand off. First lieutenant's berth right off the bat, and mere months later there I was... with my own command. She's not a fleet destroyer, but by God, she's a beaut!' And he'd raised his glass and toasted himself – which was very Kit Grainger, 'To the master of all he surveys!'

They'd had a long talk, that afternoon; one of those talks where the world doesn't end up looking any better but you come away feeling better able to deal with it.

Back on the bridge, Harry's reverie was broken by another voice echoing up through the pipe. It was Darky Mularky from the radar cubby, reporting he had multiple contacts on the same bearing as the Asdic's HE. Seven altogether but including one bigger than all the others. Which suggested not a fishing fleet. Range, just over five miles. The set must be performing well tonight, he thought, before he hit the general alarm and brought *Scourge* to diving stations.

He watched as Hooper and his mob tumbled out onto the casing and had a shell up the spout ready to go and edged out the way as the two .303 gunners lugged their cumbersome weapon up through the conning tower hatch and mounted it. And there was McCready, grunting and cussing, bringing up the TBT just in case Harry wanted to try a surface shot with what torpedoes they had. It was almost like the good old days, he thought.

He noted the time: 2108 hours. Moonrise in less than ten minutes. The moon was just past full, so it would be practically daylight when it rose. Perfect for a night gunnery action, especially as *Scourge* would be down moon and not silhouetted and plain for the enemy to see. Mularky and Biddle, back at his diving station on the Asdic set, were agreeing on the targets' estimated speed: nine knots, which was even better. He leaned to the voicepipe and asked Harding – down in the control room, leaning over the chart table and starting his plot – for a course and speed for interception.

Back it came, and engine telegraphs were rung and a heading passed to Leading Seaman Cross on the helm.

HMS *Scourge* began standing in to engage the enemy more closely.

The moon, when it came up, was a huge opalescent ball with a slice out of its lower starboard flank and its splash unfurling across the obsidian smooth sea like a carpet of light. Almost immediately, the port lookout was calling, 'Enemy in sight, bearing...'

And there they were. All Harry could make out were a series of blobs dancing on the moon's splash just below the horizon line. But McCready was counting them.

'I've can see five... definitely caiques, sir,' he said. 'Quite big ones... lots of deck clutter... cargo? And this other bugger, sir. Like a big box lying on its side... with a hut at the arse end... and guns... gun barrels... yes... that's what they are. But too many...'

'Artillery... carried as deck cargo?' offered Harry, peering through his own night glasses.

'Of course, sir! That's what they are... and I reckon it's another one of those bloody F-lighters.'

An F-lighter was bad news. *Scourge* had come across them before. They were Jerry's equivalent of a tank landing craft, except bigger, about a hundred and sixty feet long and could carry up to a hundred and fifty tons of any cargo you cared to mention, including – if what McCready was seeing was true – field guns. These wouldn't be of any use to Jerry in a fight here and now, but the other thing about F-lighters was, they tended to be armed to the teeth, usually with a 75mm cannon of their own and a scatter of those damned 3.7cm flak guns. They were also of very shallow draught, even when loaded, and so almost impossible to torpedo, as any torpedo fired at them usually just carried on underneath.

This changed everything.

Harry ordered the engine room telegraphs rung again; it was time to slow down and think about this.

'So, troops on the caiques and a bloody great F-lighter riding shotgun, as they say in the Westerns,' said Harry aloud, for all the lookouts and the .303 crew to hear. It was the captain's running commentary again. Everybody had a quiet smile. Mr Gilmour was back in harness. 'Mr McCready,' he said. 'Yell... immediately... if anything changes,' and with that, Harry disappeared down the hatch and into the Hades-red gloom of the control room. He put his elbows beside Harding's on the chart table and squinted at the chart and then the plot.

The Jerry convoy was obviously heading to navigate to the right of the Fournoi archipelago of small islets that lay between Samos and the next biggish island to the west, Ikaria. They must be bound for the next big, Jerry-held islands to the south: Leros or Kalimnos. Both were only a few miles from Kos. And those were quite a few troops on those boats out there, and artillery.

Tangling on the surface with that bloody F-lighter, however, was going to get them sunk.

Unless...

Harry stepped through the control room for'ard door and went up the gun tower. He took Hooper completely by surprise when he stepped onto the casing behind him.

'Hooper,' he asked. 'What's your best rate of fire? And how fast can you get down that hatch if I have to dive in a hurry?'

*

'Steer green two zero,' Harry leaned to speak into the voicepipe and then straightened again, watching as the stern of the F-lighter, now a mere six hundred yards or so away, slid round towards *Scourge's* bows. Any minute now.

'Down you go, Hooper,' he said. 'Give me a thumbs up when you're ready to commence firing.'

'Aye, aye, sir,' said Hooper, and he and his loader disappeared over the bridge wing and down onto the casing and their three-inch gun. It was just Harry and two lookouts left on the bridge now. He said to them, 'When I shout go, I want you down that hatch.'

Both of them, in unison, replied with an, 'Aye, aye, sir.'

The F-lighter, like any good broody hen, was sweeping her charges along from behind, ushering them into the channel dead ahead. Harry could clearly see six caiques now. In McCready's original sighting, one must have been masked by another.

For this all to go wrong, all it would take would be a conscientious Jerry lookout deciding to look aft – well, one with sharp eyesight at least.

But Harry wasn't too worried. *Scourge* was trimmed well down – which was why Hooper and his loader had been standing on the bridge and his gun tower hatch safely shut, and why he and his loader had wet feet now as they sighted the gun.

All that would be visible now from the deck of the Jerry was the narrow fin of their conning tower, one slim shadow, way beyond the carpet of moonlight, only to be seen against a sea of darkness. Also, it was amazing how lookouts never tended to look behind them. Enemy ones at least. In the Andrew, a lookout not looking behind would get his bum felt in no uncertain terms.

Harry continued to study the target. There was no movement around the F-lighter's flimsy wheelhouse, and he could see no figures manning the 3.7cm twin flak mount abaft it.

'Stand by on the dive board,' he almost whispered down the voice-pipe. Yes, even conversations could be heard over silly distances at sea but not above the clatter of the F-lighters' ex-truck engine. No matter, he wasn't taking any chances.

Harry had *Scourge* running silently on motors right now, for the quiet, and so there was no delay in de-clutching diesels when it came time to get down.

The plan was to close the F-lighter astern to at least five hundred yards and then start firing into her steering and wheelhouse and engine room, catch the Jerry completely unawares and keep firing until it looked like someone might be about to start firing back – and then dive in a hurry. If they moved fast enough, they'd escape the torrent of heavy calibre fire an F-lighter was capable of throwing out: shells, any one of which could shatter *Scourge's* pressure hull and end her career there and then. With a bit of luck, however, if Hooper could fire enough shells of his own into the damn thing, they might cripple her before she could bring any of her guns to bear. Especially that bloody 75mm.

Well, now was as good a time to start as any.

'Righty-ho, Hooper. Commence firing!'

Barely were the words out his mouth when, *BANG!… BANG!… BANG!… BANG!…*

The flashless powder meant there was no flash. Nobody aboard the Jerry would see where the firing was coming from. He'd forgotten about that. So sweet!

The rounds were fairly pumping out. Christ! Any faster and it would be like a machine gun! *A double tot for you, Hooper*, Harry was thinking as he watched each three-inch projectile blow another lump out of Jerry's arse end with unerring certainty.

…and then silence!

Harry leaned over the bridge front. It was a jam.

For gun crews, standard procedure for a gun jam was you let the shell cool before you reopened the breech and tried to clear it, in case the un-ignited propellent ignited in your faces.

Harry looked back at the F-lighter. Figures were emerging from cover... his hand went to the voicepipe... time to get under... he bent his head forward...

He could make out a figure, and another – the ubiquitous coal-scuttle helmets, one sliding into the aimer's seat on the 3.7cm, and then from right under his nose... *BANG!*... *BANG!*... so that the recoil concussions from *Scourge's* own three-incher, right below him, practically rippled his eyeballs.

As far as Hooper had been concerned, letting a jammed shell cool was standard *peacetime* procedure – in war, you did what you had to. And right now, what he'd had to do was get that flak mount. Harry was watching, face frowning, leaning on the voicepipe as Hooper's next shell detonated right under the enemy gun. Its aimer went one way, like he'd just bounced off a trampoline, an elegant parabola over the side. Harry watched him splash into the sea. By the time he looked back, the entire twin mount was already slowly pirouetting the other way, with its barrels protruding at angles that definitely weren't right.

Behind where it had been, the wheelhouse was already a ruin, but when Harry looked at her hull, something else was happening; it was elongating. The F-lighter was slewing to port. Now it was time to get down.

He hit the tit twice, and the klaxon blared.

'Hooper! Now! Clear the casing!' When Harry turned, the two look-outs had already vanished down the hatch. He followed, slamming it shut behind him.

The Jerry might be damaged, badly , or even crippled, but she was still afloat, and she still had that bloody 75mm. Harry didn't think it would be smart to hang about assessing the damage they'd done if there was a chance some disgruntled Jerry wanted to get one last shot off… from that bloody 75mm.

'One clip on, two clips on,' said Harry as he secured the lower lid, and then he hit the sloping control room deck plates as *Scourge* continued down. 'Periscope depth,' he said. And *Scourge* started creeping gently back up again.

Everybody in the control room was beaming. Harry ordered the periscope up and told McCready to take a look. Although the moon was bright, it really wasn't daylight, and McCready was more likely to see more than Harry ever would. McCready gave a running commentary. The F-lighter was still underway, but she was having hell's own job steering. There was a fire somewhere below, with odd flickers of flame coming up through a hatchway and billows of black smoke. A lot of Jerry sailors running about mad on her deck. And she was very low in the water, aft, said McCready.

Harry jammed his hands in his pockets. He'd been intending to sneak off after the caiques, which were racing off south as fast as their lawnmower engines would shove them, catch them up, surface alongside each one and have Hooper lob shells into their hulls while the .303 boys raked their decks. But McCready was saying the F-lighter was low in the water. He decided to have a look himself; it bloody well was!

He asked Farrar what he thought. Farrar only took a moment, peering through the scope, then he leaned back, 'Yes, sir,' he said simply, nodding.

'Yes?' said Harry. 'Yes, what?'

'Yes, it's worth risking a torpedo, sir.'

Harry laughed at that and said, 'Start the attack!'

The F-lighter might not be moving fast, but she was erratic, and the fire had been quickly brought under control. McCready sat at the fruit machine, dialling in all the data that Harry called as he manoeuvred *Scourge* at dead slow ahead together back round to line up for a ninety-degree track angle – the range, the bearings, the speed, the target's heading.

The control room seemed preternaturally quiet for some reason. This wasn't a big target and was really a sitting duck, but the tension was there . Harry ordered the rating on the sound-powered telephone, 'Tell Mr Gooch, ready tubes one and four, shallowest setting. Firing on my orders.'

Then, for McCready, 'The bearing is… that!… Range, that!'

The rating behind him read off the bezel, and the range: seven hundred and fifty yards. The target couldn't be making more than three knots now but looked to be falling off her course again.

'Range opening,' called Harry, 'she's veering away… what's my DA, Mr McCready?'

'Red zero eight, sir.'

'Place me on,' Harry said to the rating behind him, who then eased Harry a fraction to his left.

'Torpedo room… sta… ahh… and… by… Fire one!' And Harry, face still stuck to the 'scope's eyepiece, counted to five in his head, then, 'Fire two!'

It would only be seconds to run. He could see the bubbles now of the first and then the second torpedo as Biddle called from Asdic cubby, 'Torpedoes running.'

And then the first one vanished. It had been dead on target, the bubbles showing it streaking towards the crippled Jerry, straight and true, aimed right at a point two-thirds of the way down its hull.

Gone under, thought Harry to himself, and he'd just had time to say it out loud when there, in the eyepiece, a gout of water shot up right in front of where the wreck of the wheelhouse had been, and the aft part of the hull snapped up like the bar on a spring-loaded mousetrap, and at least twenty feet of the rest of the hull vanished. Torpedo two hadn't gone under.

Then they heard and felt the *boom!* in the control room. *

The caiques, when a now-surfaced *Scourge* had them back in sight, had scattered into the Fournoi archipelago, two down one channel, three down another and obviously the fastest of them running pell-mell straight west for Agios Kyrikos, the small port town on Ikaria. Harry ordered full ahead together on the diesels and went after the fast one.

Harry told Hooper to pick his moment to open fire, and he waited until they had closed to eight hundred yards before the first rounds were on the way. Some of these wooden inter-island craft were next to bloody impossible to sink, their stout timbers soaking up the shells. But this one was ablaze from stem to stern after only six hits. God knows what she'd been carrying apart from Jerry soldiers, but it burned well. She was never going to make the safety of Agios Kyrikos now. Figures were jumping into the sea, lots of them. Too many for *Scourge* to 'rescue'. Harry ordered *Scourge* to turn away; he'd seen scenes like this before. Maybe boats might come out from the port once they were gone.

The group of three, they caught up with halfway down the gulf on which the town of Fournoi itself sat. When Harry looked at the chart, right at the bottom was a tiny narrows, less than twenty yards across. The caiques could squeeze through, but a six hundred and seventy-ton submarine couldn't. They were obviously hoping to shake off *Scourge* there. But going flat out at almost fourteen knots, *Scourge* was too fast for them.

Hooper began engaging at 1500 yards, just to make sure every shell counted. He and his crew had got three rounds away when everybody froze – Hooper and his gun team and Harry and the rest of the bridge crew – everybody.

They'd been watching the second and third shells hit the stern of the hindmost caique. Harry had been aware of the twinkling out the corner of his eye from one of the other boats but had thought little of it until the little trail of waterspouts came walking down the starboard side of *Scourge*, landing about twenty degrees off the bow and passing ten to twelve yards off the beam.

He knew what it was immediately, and so did everybody else. And then, drifting over the flat sea above the clatter of their diesels, came the distinctive rip of an MG 42 machine gun. Nobody imagined they had such an effective range. But everybody knew it wouldn't take long for the gunner to correct his fall of shot, and it stood to reason there'd be more than one of the bastards on this little clutch of glorified bath toys.

Hooper instantly switched targets and fired another three shells into the caique that was firing on them. It was enough to silence the gun, but not before the next burst had been on the way, and its rounds, obviously fired in a spray, walked in off the water and started tinging on the for'ard casing. One of Hooper's loaders suddenly sat down, clutching his right buttock, and Harry, looking at him, saw the young rating's mouth open in astonishment, like a cavern, and then he yelled, 'They got me!'

So loud that Harry, to his shame, actually laughed out loud before composing himself, before shouting, 'Get that man below!'

They got me! Just like in a Tom Mix western. Silly bugger.

There was a lot of blood pumping out between the lad's fingers, however. One of the older hands on the gun team quickly had him in a fireman's lift, and Harry recognised one of the senior rate's heads in the gun tower hatch waiting to grab him.

None of this made the slightest difference to Hooper's rate of fire.

301

Harry was about to order him to switch targets again, but before he could shout, Hooper already had. So Harry shut up and smiled a little self-satisfied smile to himself; *his* gun layer didn't need telling to start dropping suppressing shots on all the caiques now, to discourage other MG 42s from getting into the game.

As *Scourge* started coming abeam the first caique she had engaged, Hooper swung the gun again and fired another two rounds at close range into its hull, right down on the waterline where its engine space would be, and there was a secondary bang and a huge puff of smoke that wafted up like solid shadow in the moonlight. The caique lurched and slewed her bows towards *Scourge* as she swished past in a glittering surge of phosphorescence. Close now, so that Harry, on the bridge, could quite clearly see the crush of Wehrmacht grey on its deck, some clinging to anything that looked solid as the caique wallowed.

Rapid tattoos of tinging began hitting *Scourge's* bridge wing. Harry could see little tornadoes of flaked paint dancing away. Small arms fire. Jerries on the sinking caique were actually shooting at them.

Harry turned to see the outraged faces of the two ratings on the .303 mount behind him. Jack could be a fearsome warrior when his dander was up, but he could also show a rare compassion for fellow seafarers in peril. Even an enemy, if the vessel they were on was foundering. But it was obvious to Harry right away, that as far as those two able seamen were concerned, that bloody shower, in that tub over there had just crossed a line. The two of them were looking Harry straight in the eye. So Harry said simply, 'Return fire.' And they went to work with a vengeance.

The other two caiques were both now in considerable states of disrepair, courtesy of Hooper's attentions, and obviously sinking. When Harry studied the furthest one, he could see most of the soldiers on board had already jettisoned their kit and were either in or in the process of getting into the water. He only had to shift his night glasses a shrug to see why; the beach was close and eminently swimmable.

'Check fire!' he ordered. Then into the voicepipe he ordered, 'Slow ahead together. Starboard fifteen.'

As the way came off *Scourge* and she turned stern on to her former targets, everyone could see the spreading slicks of German soldiers in the water, all splashing and stretching out for the shore. It was immediately obvious to everyone on the bridge and the casing that all of them were likely to make it.

The firing from the first caique had ceased, and so had the firing from *Scourge's* .303 team, seeing as there was no longer any enemy fire to return. Its soldiers had further to swim, but they all looked like they were going to give it a try. Many of them were clutching lifebelts and one group had torn off a hatch cover and were clinging to it as they too kicked for the beach.

Harry was aware of Farrar standing next to him, as he'd been since the start of the action.

Suddenly, there was a question hanging in the air. What was the captain going to do about those German soldiers?

As it had been up in Yugoslavia, so it was down here in the Dodecanese; a nasty little war where civilians were just as much a target for the Germans as partisans and Allied troops, where the objective wasn't merely to pacify the conquered territory but to create a wasteland, with no mercy shown in the process. And as everybody knew on *Scourge's* bridge and in the hamlets and villages ashore, as far as these survivors in the water were concerned, the minute they got back on land again, they'd be soldiers again, and it would be business as usual.

Harry looked at the floundering figures, the bobbing heads and flailing arms, hundreds of them and said nothing.

*

Scourge was running north again, back to her patrol billet. It was halfway through the morning watch with less than an hour to first light. There were just two lookouts, Harry and Farrar on the bridge, and the two of them were standing right aft beyond the .303 mount, gazing at the wake.

Harry had been up there all night and had watched the watch changes come and go. He hadn't felt like going below, hadn't felt like eating. But he had been accepting piping hot flasks of Windass' coffee. And seeing as he was up here anyway, he'd spelled the rostered watch officers and let them get some sleep. So he couldn't know the mood in the boat.

Farrar had come up to join him about ten minutes ago. There had been a silence since.

Then Harry had said, out of the blue, 'Our old chum Verney doesn't think this is a sideshow, you know. This Greek Islands show. Well, maybe a sideshow for this war. But not for the next. He says his diplomatic nose tells him so. He used to be a diplomat, you know. A Foreign Office type... before he became a full-blown nut job.'

Farrar didn't reply; he sensed he wasn't expected to.

'There's no getting away from the fact that what we're doing here is still "noises off" though, is there?' Harry continued. 'We're a long way from the main thrust going up through Italy. We don't need these islands to win. The Yanks obviously think that too, which is why we're conducting this out of a shoebox. There's no big kit being diverted our way. No landing craft... anything that even looks like proper air support... no carrier. But it's what happens next that'll make here the frontline in the next war, or so Verney says. That Uncle Joe might be our big pal now, but after we've won, it will be back to business as usual. Tsarist Russia, communist Russia, the Great Game goes on. And if the Red Army coming from the east gets as far as Greece, Joe Stalin will have achieved what no Romanov ever did… a friendly opening into the Med. Verney says it's a certainty that's what Winston's been telling the Yanks… why it's important. And he reckons the Yanks have been telling Winston, "Nonsense, Uncle Joe's our friend now," and Winston's telling them back, "We don't have friends, we have interests," …and that's why he wants us here before Stalin… before the Greek communist party and their partisan army hands the whole caboodle over to him.'

Harry paused, then turned to look at Farrar, 'And I look at all those poor, starving islanders we've been seeing, and I think, "You poor bastards. Even when it's over, it won't be over for you." We'll all go home, and a new lot will come in. A change of shift, and it'll all keep on going. I think I'm getting tired, Number One. And I don't mean sleepy.' And he gave a little laugh. 'How about you? Are you getting tired?'

'Crete,' said Farrar, deciding it was time to get to the point.

'What?' said Harry.

'It was while Jerry was consolidating his position on Crete and they were "cleaning up" on the surrounding islands… a rather unfortunate metaphor, sir, considering the mess they were making everywhere they went. That was when Lieutenant Commander Bayliss ordered a spot of "cleaning up" of his own. I'm talking about what happened when we were evacuating troops from a raid on Karpathos. You'll have heard, sir.'

'I haven't,' said Harry, although he was aware there was some kind of story about Bertie Bayliss 'only doing his duty' somewhere in the Greek islands. Whatever that meant. He'd always tried to stay away from the rumour side of the Andrew, where it was all nods and winks and suggested allegations about God knew what. It just depressed him and usually signified nothing in the end.

'Coming out, we met a small reinforcement convoy… mostly local craft like tonight, sir,' said Farrar. 'Stuffed full of Jerry troops on their way to help out with the work their pals had already started and we'd just experienced. We shot up the craft, like tonight, and the soldiers went into the water, like tonight, with the beach less than a hundred yards away,' Farrar paused, 'Bayliss ordered the crew to continue firing on them until there weren't any left, sir.'

'And you think I should've done the same thing?' said Harry, his voice very cool now.

'When those soldiers got ashore, we all knew what they were going to be doing, especially since the commandos we'd been carrying had given the Jerries already ashore a pretty hard time…'

'I won't do it, Number One,' said Harry, interrupting. 'I don't care what your old skipper might have done, or why. I don't care about what the consequences might be. All I know is I've thought about it a lot. I know it's war… I know there could be, will be times when people on my side will likely die as a result if I don't… but I still won't do it. I will not order my crew to fire on survivors in the water. And d'you know why? Because, if I live through all this, I don't want that in my head. I don't want it to be my first thought when I wake up every morning and my last thought when I go to bed. That I am a man who has ordered the killing of unarmed survivors. Am I selfish? Damn right I am. I don't presume to answer for anyone else. But not me, Number One. Call me squeamish, call me spineless, call me anything you like. But if I get to go home after this war, I'm not carrying that back with me. I won't do it.'

Farrar gave a slight shake of his head and a smile. For a moment,

Harry thought he was mocking him for a weak fool, and he started to feel the anger rising.

'So we saw, sir,' said Farrar, now meeting his burning eyes. 'Bayliss ordered it. You didn't. And what I am saying, sir, is that I don't think you'll find a man aboard this boat who isn't grateful right now for not having had to pull the trigger again on Jerries in the water. For not having to have that in *his* head again... because you wouldn't order it.'

Eighteen

When the petty officer writer got back to his desk, Admiral Cunningham's office door was closed, which was unusual, and there were voices coming from inside. He recognised Captain de Launy's voice. There was no shouting, there never was with the admiral, so no major row, but when he listened carefully and began to pick up the gist, he could hardly believe what he was hearing.

It was a typically gorgeous Malta afternoon outside – warm sunshine, rays of it flooding in through the blast-taped windows. The PO writer could remember a time when there was barely a pane of solid glass left on the island, and the orderly clack of typewriters echoed everywhere, a smoothly functioning staff machine at work in a rational world. Which made all this stuff they were discussing, about Captain Charles 'the Bonny Boy' Bonalleck VC, the S12 back in Algiers, all the more disorienting. Could such things have actually happened in this world?

'I still cannot get to grips, sir, with how it all had got so far,' the PO writer recognised de Launy's voice. 'But there are the transcripts of the interviews I conducted… the other documents… the blocking of the DSO… the binning of the recommendations for gallantry awards from *Scourge* while was she detached to Twelfth Flotilla… and the evidence of all these orders he was issuing without telling anybody… of what he was up to with the Americans, sir. It's a building pattern, and it's all pointing in the one direction.'

'Yes, indeed, how did we let him get away with it?' It was the admiral speaking now. He heard paper being shuffled. 'He got away with a lot of it, I imagine, because poor old Henry was never actually on top of things…' Henry? thought the PO writer, he must be referring to Admiral Harwood, '…but let's face it… if someone had come to you with any of these stories, would you have believed them? I know I wouldn't. I barely do now, except it's you Gillie, who's telling me, and you've got all the paperwork.'

'A court martial will be bloody, sir,' it was de Launy now.

'No court martial. Not yet, anyway. I've already cut orders relieving him, but I want to you to present them to him personally. Then I want you to get him out of theatre, Gillie, pronto, you understand? And take a couple of regulating petty officers with you. With side-arms. I want it plain there's to be no negotiations or appeals. There's an RAF ferry flight for Algiers going from Takali, my driver will take you out there.'

'D'you want me to charge him with anything, sir?'

'If it were up to me, I'd have you take him behind a sand dune and shoot him. No, no charges, Gillie. I'll have him have no rights in this matter. Get him back home, and we'll decide his fate then.'

And with that, the door flew open, and the PO writer was to be found at his desk, diligently cataloguing a signals file.

De Launy swept out the door. Admiral Cunningham stood on the threshold watching him go, then he turned to look at the PO writer. The admiral was a slight man, not very tall, with thinning grey hair, who could've been mistaken for the owner of a small-town haberdashery. But the look he gave the PO writer sent a chill into his heart.

'Wragg,' he said, 'Did you know we have a PNO stationed at the docks in Murmansk?'

PNO – Principal Naval Officer; and Murmansk, the Russian end for the dreaded Arctic convoys.

'Yes, sir,' said PO Writer Wragg, swallowing.

'He has a small permanent staff to help him effect the smooth turnaround of our escorts on that run. He's always on the lookout for replacements. I make it my business to always keep an eye out for likely candidates for him. Carry on, Wragg.'

Nineteen

'You're joking,' Harry said to Kit Grainger while lounging in the floral-patterned easy chair that dwarfed Grainger's captain's cabin aboard *Alconbury*. He swirled his tumbler of pink gin once more, just for the luxury of being able to do so.

'Au contraire, young Jock,' said Grainger, with his own pink gin, but perched on his desk chair. 'I thought it rather a good idea, actually. Since everybody is sitting around here on their arses with bugger all to do.'

Harry had already been to see Cdr Pleydell to report on his patrol; the F-lighter and all the caiques they'd sunk early on and then the eight hundred-ton coaster they'd torpedoed off Kokkari at the entrance to Samos harbour itself. That the coaster hadn't expected them to be there had been obvious. Because what had also become obvious, after several days of encountering nothing on their patrol line, was that Jerry must have had some system for reporting sightings of *Scourge*, as she plied among the islands, and was routing any convoys through one end of the chain while *Scourge* was at the other.

'Couldn't you have stayed dived so they wouldn't see you?' Pleydell had asked.

Harry explained that it didn't matter; even if they had, they'd still have had to come up at night to recharge their batteries, and in those confined island channels, someone would always hear their diesels thumping away. But he had explained to Pleydell that he'd tried other ways to confuse the enemy, and that was how they'd bagged the coaster.

'We still had a few of these silly fake periscopes we'd mocked up from our patrol to the Adriatic, sir,' Harry had explained. 'So we popped a couple off Mykonos to confuse their spotters and then headed back up to the other end of our patrol line to see who we could surprise.'

Pleydell had heard him out like a man just waiting to say what *he* wanted to say, and that was that the patrol line idea was scrapped, and *Scourge* was needed to act as a taxi for the brigadier's raiding parties.

After Harry had been dismissed, he'd headed over to *Alconbury* to see if he could find any sanity there. And that was when Grainger had begun by telling him about the stasis that was now afflicting Operation Hoplite, the plummeting morale and eventually, his idea for arresting it.

But first, there'd been the matter of events.

'There's still a load of Jerries dug in round the western end of Kos,' Grainger had told him. 'And every morning, us and *Howsham* up anchor, tootle round and spend a leisurely day bombarding targets for the pongos, and when it's time for sundowners, we tootle back here.'

Confronted by the fact that there were Jerries still holding out on Kos, their ancient brigadier, had apparently run out of ideas, according to Grainger. After failing to budge the two companies of Panzer Grenadiers from their holes at the other end of the island by naval gunfire, he'd just hunkered down. All plans to push steadily up into the rest of the archipelago, taking islands as they went, rounding up the surrendered Italians and sweeping out the few Germans left had been sacrificed to simply holding a line across the island, and whatever troops not being used for that, he'd just been sending off on random raids, hitting all the nearby islands in order to 'strike fear into Jerry's heart, wherever he's lurking' and then pulling back again. Not surprisingly, leading that charge had been Verney's V-force.

Everybody else had been left to just sit about and wait on Thirios, including all the RAF ground crew that had arrived on two Fairmile D motor gunboats from Alex, who were waiting for the two squadrons of P40 Tomahawks that were supposed to be on their way, before moving up to Kos' airstrip.

'Our only excitement since you left is a nightly sweepstake on whether the two Ju 52s Jerry's got left on Rhodes will come over to drop supplies to their foothold. And as for what happened to the third one, well since you're asking...'

Grainger paused theatrically to grin, '...Let me tell you. He came over a little too early one night, while we were just coming off station and there was still light left, and one of my Oerlikon crews bagged him... boom! boom!... wing off... into drink. Double tots all round. The entire command now talks of little else.'

And then he laughed, not out of fun, but at what the operation had been reduced to.

'Your pal, Verney, has been away regularly, island hopping, cutting throats,' he'd continued, 'so you'd think he'd be happy enough. But not so. He is definitely of the opinion Jerry isn't going to let us get away with this. And I agree. Hence the idea. We might as well. It's going to get a lot grimmer here before too long.'

The idea, that Harry had thought was a joke, was to stage a Sods' Opera on *Alconbury's* quarter deck for the evening after next.

'So that's what all the sawing and banging is,' Harry said. 'You're building a stage.'

'Absolutely, old chap,' said Grainger. 'So you have to get your chaps to put their acts together. I'm expecting a strong contingent from *Scourge*, and if your lot don't have any ladies' underwear to hand, I'm sure my stokers will be able to help them out.'

*

Harry didn't like the idea, not this close to Jerry. Admittedly, there was no credible threat from the air right now; you couldn't really count the two Ju 52s or the Storch, even though it was apparently overhead nearly every day now. And what light forces Jerry had – an unknown number of E-boats and *Raumbooten* – were not likely to be more than double figures and less likely to come out with two Royal Navy destroyers about, and the navy's seriously dangerous little fleet of MGBs.

But just because nearly all his air force was otherwise occupied over a thousand miles to the north in the Soviet Union, that didn't mean the Luftwaffe's operations in Yugoslavia couldn't spare a geschwader or two of Stukas to pop down for a long weekend. With the RAF Tomahawks still a no-show, they'd encounter no real opposition. Because let's face it, the dead-eye dicks on Grainger's Oerlikon wouldn't really count as a proper air defence if Jerry turned up mob-handed.

Grainger had said there'd been, and continued to be, a lot of signals traffic between Alex and *Howsham*. 'It all looks like intelligence stuff,' he'd said. 'Coded, for grown-ups' eyes only. And the brigadier and Pleydell aren't sharing. The likes of us aren't getting a look at the raw material. But I'm sure if it all looks like it's about to get sticky, I'm sure even those two would tip us the wink.'

All Harry could think was, *yes, but only if they knew what they were looking at.*

What did look certain was that their brigadier must've been warned about something because on his trip ashore to try and chivvy up the Royal Engineer detachment into helping recover his torpedoes, Harry discovered they were all too busy preparing defences for the main town and port.

His lads had managed to find a motley collection of buoys to help lift the one-and-a-half-ton monsters out the caique's hold, and they could use the destroyers' launches to drag them to a wharf, but they needed a crane to lift them out the water and then into *Scourge*, and there was no one available with the necessary tools and bits of machinery to jury-rig one, apart from the engineers. Because, given their daily bombardment sorties, neither *Howsham* nor *Alconbury* could spare anybody from their engine rooms to do the job, and Mr Petrie didn't have the materials.

Frustration everywhere and uncertainty. A fertile environment for sapping morale and laying on the strain. He could see why Grainger thought the Sods' Opera would be a safety valve. The lower deck's version of what might be described as a concert party, except these things were nothing your grandmother or auntie would recognise. A Sods' Opera was an irreverent, bawdy, crude and depraved parody involving music, songs (filthy), jokes (even filthier) and drag, and all of it thrown together with the single-minded aim of plumbing the absolute stygian depths of utter obscenity.

And didn't Jack just love them.

There had been much excitement aboard *Scourge* when Harry had returned, although how the news of it had beat him back on board, he had no idea. He really was reluctant to let anyone out of the boat while there was even a remote chance of Jerry turning up. But he could see playing the strict dad might not be a good idea. Permission for the off-duty watch was granted. There was a lot of grumbling among the rest, but everybody could see there was a logic to keeping *Scourge* at operational readiness, just in case, given Jerry was just over the horizon.

He was firm on one thing, however: his officers were staying on board. So, it had taken a lot of cajoling and begging, with segues into sweet reason and bathos on Harding's part to get his pass. With McCready, the answer had remained firmly, no. Harding, jumping into *Alconbury's* packed pinnace with the rest of them, had winked at poor McCready. 'If the captain changes his mind, Tom, we'll be at the bar, you know,' and grinning evilly as he jerked his thumb at the destroyer riding beyond it, just to rub it in.

Meanwhile, *Scourge* just had two torpedoes left in her forward tubes and one in the stern tube. But more worrying for Harry was that her three-inch magazine was almost empty, and there were no other ships in Pleydell's little squadron that mounted the three-inch gun and so no more three-inch shells.

So, while they waited for the big night, *Scourge* topped up her fuel tanks and her fresh water from *Howsham* and scrounged some extra rations from the destroyer's galley stores.

Then Verney returned from one of his raids. He had casualties who were all immediately loaded aboard *Howsham* for her surgeon lieutenant to patch up.

When Harry eventually spoke to him, he said, 'Pleydell tells me you weren't sure how many Jerries were managing to sneak through your patrol line unobserved.'

Harry had nodded, 'Yes. They were spotting us.'

'Well, I can clear that up for you,' Verney had replied, with a wry smile. 'Lots. As you can see, we bumped into some of them,' and he gestured to the casualty transfer going on from one of his caiques alongside *Howsham*. 'Lots and lots of Jerries. They're on the move.'

Twenty

Capt Bonalleck collected his mail on his way to breakfast, which he usually took on the veranda of the US staff officers' mess. Being the senior joint western Mediterranean submarine liaison officer certainly had its privileges. He acknowledged several friends on his way to his usual table. His US officer buddies and the mess stewards alike knew that when it came to breakfast, the old captain preferred to dine alone. Among the post was a copy of *The Times*; an old chum at the Admiralty sent him one regularly, not for the news, for the crossword. This edition was only eleven days old.

It was another stunning morning on the Algiers Corniche. It was already hot from a cloudless sky, with the turquoise water sparkling in the light. Not so much shipping these days; the war was moving on. But he'd miss the view when they finally transferred up to Palermo. He ordered Arab coffee, French-baked croissants and scrambled eggs. No rationing here. Then he opened his paper and prepared himself to enjoy the start of his day.

All the more reason for the fury that exploded in his chest, almost choking off his airway, when he saw that someone had already started on his crossword – seven words crossing seven rows of boxes. He felt his fists crushing the newsprint, *What did bloody...?* And he'd almost said his friend's name with a curse when what those words were hit him like a punch.

SOMEONE–BIG–IS–AUDITING–YOUR–SIGNAL–TRAFFIC

He read it again to make sure he'd understood. And a voice in his head started up.

The voice, more in sadness, than in anger now, began its prating, '...prying... there are lots and lots of little people out there who just love to pry... to pry and tell... rummaging around in the dirty linen, looking for little stains... like you're no more than some sordid little prep-schoolboy whose personal hygiene is in doubt... and they're doing it again... siding with that jumped-up little oik of a grammar-schoolboy, spreading his little poisons...'

So, of course he had acted. What decent man wouldn't? An honourable man has to act... to shut down sewer pipes like that sanctimonious little Jock. Except, these days, how can an honourable man act honourably with all those little people, all holier-than-thou, looking on, judging, when they don't know the whole story. Don't want to know it. All the mediocrities. Everywhere. That was why he couldn't do it above board, couldn't shut him up by just slapping him down, why he'd had to go in dived and silent-running.

Because all the good people had gone, and it was just the drones left who cared not a jot for a good man's name.

That type had been after him all his life. That was why he'd been constantly superseded all his career by lesser men. It didn't matter that he'd won a VC, that if anyone had bothered to look, they would have seen his new tactics, seen how they would change the face of submarine warfare. But the enemy had listened, had understood, hadn't they? That was why they were winning the submarine war, because they'd adopted his ideas, while the mediocrities here, they wouldn't listen. Refused to listen. It didn't matter that the facts had spoken for themselves, that he was ahead of his time. And right!

And oh, how they hated it when you were right. The cardinal sin, the uttermost heresy for you to be right and them to be wrong. That was why they all wanted to listen to the poison, to deny an honourable man his right to silence his enemies, why they were coming for him to humiliate him and erase truth from the world. Well, he wasn't going to sit here and wait for them. He was better than all of them, and he'd show them how much.

Twenty-one

There was the little bastard: a tiny speck against the seared blue of the sky, with the midday sun making you squint 'til it hurt just to see it, the Storch performing a lazy circle away off the port bow, like some drunk gnat. It was easily 15,000 feet up, way above where any weapon carried by *Scourge* could hope to hit her. And it was obvious they'd been spotted, plunging ahead on bearing zero four zero, the bows pointed directly at Symi and both diesels driving them on at fourteen knots, the boat's churning wake unfurling a glittering ribbon over the deep blue sea like an arrow back at them that the Storch pilot and his spotter couldn't miss.

Boxall, down in the radio cubby, had reported the radio chatter right away; it was a miracle he'd been able to manage even that, given the severity of his hangover. From the bearing of the signal and its proximity, it could only be the Storch, reporting their progress.

There were only a few more hours to run.

The signal from the para detachment on Symi had come just after first light. For that was when their observation post on the highest peak had first spotted two Jerry Siebel ferries – disgorging all those troops on a beach on the opposite side of the island to the town – and the three artillery pieces that they could see. One of the paras had identified them as 7.5cm mountain guns, the sort used by Alpine troops; small – the barrel, not five feet long – and light – just over 1,500lbs – and a lot more firepower than the paras could field. Not to mention the flock of Jerry-flagged caiques milling about that beachhead and another one down south. Number of troops coming ashore? Possiblly as many as a thousand.

The brigadier and Pleydell had been impressively nimble on receiving the call, as if they'd been expecting it. And especially since there had been another message, passed to them by local fishermen, about all the Jerry water traffic up Leros/Kalimnos way. Big stuff, Siebel ferries too and F-lighters. Right out of the blue, just one narrow channel away from the north shore of Kos.

Everybody had been shaken from their hammocks, hangovers or no. *Scourge* was to head for Symi, to 'support' the paras. Harry read it to mean 'evacuate', especially as Pleydell had told him to forget his sunken torpedoes and how much room did that leave him on board without them? Pleydell's two destroyers, meanwhile, were heading off early on their bombardment patrol, except this time, they'd be going north about Kos, to 'investigate'.

Harding was on the bridge with Harry, feigning to take the odd bearing from the island peaks that dotted the horizon around them, just to 'make sure of our position', but really, just for the fresh air, lungfuls of which looked like they might be necessary to stave off a full nervous breakdown.

There were lots of cigarettes involved too and mugs full of coffee from the flask Windass always kept topped up for the captain.

Although alcohol at the event had been strictly rationed – three bottles of beer per rating, to be topped up by a limited supply of locally purloined wine – two of *Scourge's* crew had discovered other seams. For Boxall, it had been all the reward tots, and as for the vasco, he'd made a pig of himself in *Alconbury's* wardroom.

For Grainger's Sods' Opera had been a soar-away success and *Scourge's* part in it, the most successful, apparently.

Now it was the morning after, and Harding's description had had *Scourge's* lookouts, the three who hadn't been there, twisted in agonies trying to hide their laughter and make it look like they really were minding the horizon. Harry, trying to appear the responsible skipper, was trying not to laugh out loud too.

There had been the usual parade of offerings, including an Andrews Sisters tribute act, who'd changed all the songs to dirty lyrics, and the inevitable Sods' poet laureate with endless renditions like, '*There was a young lady from Leeds, who swallowed a packet of seeds, a big blade of grass grew out of her arse, and her muff was a garden of weeds.*' Then there had been *Hitler Plays George Formby*, taking the piss out of everybody from Churchill and Eisenhower to *Alconbury's* surgeon lieutenant and his sexual hygiene lectures. But the triumph had been *Scourge's* own wireless operator, Arthur Boxall.

'It's difficult to do him justice,' Harding had said, sucking on his cigarette. 'He came on with his face all painted up with ink… red for his lips and blue round his eyes and flour all over the rest of him… and these blonde ringlets made out of unfurled bandage for a wig, that he kept flouncing. He had this bedsheet wrapped round him, with a split up one leg to his hip, to show a lilac frilly suspender belt holding up a single stocking with more ladders in it than a fire engine… and he kept flicking the split wide open… which he said was so any passing matelot could cop a feel. And all this foundation garment ensemble was complemented by a pair of French drawers two sizes too small for him so that every time he did the flick, you could see he'd stuffed an inside-out Arctic glove down the front of them, so there was all this fur hanging out of it. And there he was, mincing round the stage, so the sheet kept slipping, so you could see this lacy brassiere… and every time it did, he'd go all gravel-voiced, and coo, "…Call me torpedo tits, Jack" …and start plumping up all these old socks he'd stuffed in it. Anyway, his act started with this big drum roll and the master of ceremonies camping it up at the top of his voice… "Here she is! By popular demand! Saucy Seaman Boxall! She says she's got a box for *all* the seamen!" and out he minced… galleon in full sail… a vision. He had his squeezebox with him and he was pumping it away between his legs. You couldn't hear yourself think for all the whistles, cheers, offers to indulge in unnatural practices… he really is bloody good on that box of his, isn't he? And dance? If he'd shave regularly, there'd be a place for him in the Folie Bergere. Brought the house down, he did.'

There had been one particular song, '…Pure filth… hard to imagine a mind could be so depraved,' Harding had rhapsodised. He couldn't remember all the lyrics, he'd been laughing so hard.

'The opening line went, Here's *to the cut that never heals, the more you tickle it, the better it feels!* I can remember that. And then he'd strut around thrusting that furry glove about. In the end, he had the whole lot of them singing along… in between all the offers of marriage getting yelled at him. How did it go? …*You can wash it in soap, you can wash it in soda…* and, …You *can rub it and scrub it and hose it as well…* and the squeezebox is going ten to the dozen and he's high-kicking that laddered stocking.' Harding stopped and began shaking his head at the memory, and the lookouts were grateful because it was hurting so much.

They saw the smoke plumes before they raised the island, and the persistent chatter of small arms fire began wafting out to them on the light breezes and the occasional dull booms of the Jerry 7.5cm guns. Sgt Probert was with them again to offer soldierly advice on how best to get the troops off the island in an orderly fashion while under fire.

Harry had already explained to him that it was out of the question he'd be risking *Scourge* anywhere near those 7.5cm guns, so whatever plan the sergeant was contemplating better take that into account. Sat at the wardroom table, Probert had looked blank and pale as he stared at the map of Symi. 'It all depends on the paras' positions when we get there,' and he'd jabbed at Symi town and its port. 'And whether we can get in or not.'

The more Harry thought about this, the more it seemed a hopeless case. 'A thousand Jerries are going to swamp them,' he said and shook his head. He ordered *Scourge* to stand off until someone could tell him what the state of play was ashore. He was buggered if he was going to motor into that little harbour only to see some pile of fishing nets at the end of the jetty whipped aside and a battery of Jerry mountain guns ready to start blasting away at point-blank range over open sights.

Radio contact wasn't established until after dark. For a force of under a hundred, the paras had put up a more than creditable defence.

Probert made sense of the para's signals on the map. The island was all rough terrain, and the only easy approaches to the main town, Ano Symi, were along two valleys, one short, to the north-west, and one long, to the south-west. While their artillery was all mountain guns, the Jerry troops were all Panzer Grenadiers – motorised infantry but without the motors. And according to the para captain, until now, the Jerry approach hadn't included any mountain-goat tactics. 'He says they're just coming straight at them up the roads, and so far, their roadblocks are holding.'

The thing was, said Probert, as more Jerry troops got organised after coming off their boats, the more they'd start to infiltrate, and then the game was up. The para captain was hoping to hold out until the next night, and if he could, then he had a plan, if the Royal Navy would agree.

Scourge spent the next day at sixty feet, off the long inlet that led into Pedi beach. He wasn't going to let that bloody Storch alert Jerry to the fact that the enemy submarine was still hanging about. Harry told Windass to lay on a slap-up feed for the crew and then ordered everyone not on watch to get a good sleep. He spent the time studying the chart and the slim finger of Aegean sea that poked into the eastern cliffs of the island, and the longer he looked at it, the less he liked it. Long and thin and brooded over by high, rugged slopes, it ran in for almost half a mile, and he was supposed to steer *Scourge* up it. He was eyeing its narrow throat and was doubting *Scourge's* ability to turn in it. Once in, would he have to come out going astern?

That he was going to try was never in any doubt. He thought back to Shrimp Simpson, his Captain S in Tenth Flotilla; he would have roasted him alive for thinking what he was thinking, for daring to risk a strategic asset as important as a submarine for a hundred soldiers' lives. But what the hell. Either he was going to pluck these lads off that beach or they were going into the bag, and there were terrible stories now about what Jerry was doing to Allied island raiders when they caught them. And anyway, there was bugger all left for a submarine to sink down this end of the Med these days; they'd done too good a job. So how strategic were they now? Weighed against the lives of a hundred British soldiers? Bugger it. The evacuation was going ahead. They were going to get them out or get sunk trying. What had Admiral Cunningham said? '*It takes three years to build a warship but three hundred to build a tradition.*' No bloody pongo was ever going to say the Royal Navy left them behind while Harry Gilmour was on watch.

At the changeover from the last dog watch, Harry ordered *Scourge* up, and in they crept on their motors. Progress was dead slow, but at least there was no diesel thump to alert the shore. What was left of the moon, when it rose, shone directly down the damn inlet, casting *Scourge's* long shadow along its beam. But no alarm was raised.

The bridge was crowded; Harry, four lookouts, the .303 gun team, Yeoman Bird, to spot for the signal from shore, and Probert, to make sure the pongos, when they came, did what the matelots told them. Harry also had Hooper's gun team up, but he was refusing to think on how few three-inch rounds were left and any good they might do if things got sticky.

And there, in the wash of moonlight, dully shone the beach, dead ahead, and not a sign of the paras. *Scourge* hove-to. The sound of intermittent firing could be heard in the distance, in the stillness that followed.

The para captain's plan had been for his lads to continue putting up a stubborn resistance around their positions on the roadblocks and around the town until well after dark. Meanwhile, the minute the sun went down, an advance party of the signallers and engineers would double over the neck of the peninsula between Ano Symi and Pedi Bay to be there when *Scourge* showed up. It wasn't far, less than a mile and not particularly steep terrain, but they'd be carrying the wounded.

Some time after 2200, the paras would start to disengage; the town defenders first, because they were the ones who were going to have to carry the inflatable rafts – the ones they'd recovered from where Farrar had buoyed and sunk them when the whole mob of them had first arrived. And the rafts were going to have to be already inflated because there'd be no time to inflate them by foot pump once they'd got to the beach.

For a moment, Harry thought: did they need the rafts? What about Farrar's grass hawser? But from the chart and the evidence of his own eyes, he knew immediately that the shallow, barely sloping beach stretched out too far. Any attempt at grounding *Scourge* close inshore so the paras could haul themselves out was just not practicable.

'The disengaging is the hard part,' Probert was whispering in Harry's ear as he studied the pale beach for any sign of life. 'Trying not to let Jerry know you're pulling back, in case he decides to follow you. You can't turn and run and stand and fight at the same time, if you get my drift.'

'I get your drift,' said Harry, trying not to let his impatience show. It wasn't Probert's fault the bloody pongos weren't there. How many times had he sat off a bloody beach waiting for bloody pongos to show up? He was about to say something when he heard one of Hooper's gun crew down on the casing, shouting, 'Who the fuck are you?'

The next thing he knew, two of the gunners were leaning down over the saddle tanks, dragging a sodden figure in singlet and skivvies from the water.

'It's a bloody pongo, sir,' Hooper shouted up from the deck. The soldier had obviously swum from the beach, two hundred yards off. He didn't look in any fit state to climb the bridge ladder so Harry dropped down.

The soldier's story was simple. Right after dark, the Panzer Grenadiers, supported by two of the 7.5cm guns, had outflanked the para position in this ancient Byzantine fort on the road to the main town called the Kastro. With the paras pinned down there, Jerry had started infiltrating round the back end of the town. So the British party with the three stretcher cases had had to go to ground on the saddle because there was a platoon of Jerries now swarming all over it.

'What time is it?' wheezed their visitor, a Royal Signals corporal who looked about fourteen years old.

Harry looked at his watch and told him.

'In twelve minutes time, our lot are going to start fighting their way through,' said the corporal. 'They've been working down round a gully, and they're going to come out of it and try and pin the Jerries up against this scarpe… so as the rest of us can run through… rafts… wounded… everybody…'

'Where?' said Harry.

'Can you see that line of boulders… and then what looks like a camel's hump and the head is turning back to look at you?'

Harry called Hooper over to listen and look. They could.

'…they're going to try and jam Jerry up there 'til everyone's through…' said their still-breathless visitor.

'They're going to need help, Hooper,' said Harry. 'What d'you think? It's in range, but can you drop some rounds in there without hitting our lads?'

'I can if I light them up,' said Hooper.

Back on the bridge, Probert said, 'Not until everyone's through, sir. Dark's their best friend.'

So they waited again. But not for long.

Harry didn't bother with night glasses; with the moon and the flash of white phosphorus grenades and the billowing smoke, it was pretty clear to see. The chatter of automatic fire rose into a continuous tearing sound, echoing off all the slopes. The noise of the fight quickly built into something truly terrible, like armies clashing. And it went on, and on.

But Harry could also see what Probert had meant. With all the flashes and tracer now – green stuff, Jerry, likely an MG 42 – little lakes of dark were being created. Harry decided there was something he could do to kill the gut-wrenching tension of all this waiting. He stepped to the voicepipe and called down, 'Engine room, bridge. Stand by to answer telegraphs. Control room, bridge. Stand by to get under helm.'

There was a loud explosion aft and a gout of dark smoke – the diesels coming to life. Then the steady, comforting thrum of them, echoing through the hull and coming back off the cliffs through all the noise of gunfire, like the rising of hope.

Harry, with a long steady gaze, measured by eye the distance to the far shore, and then he rang for half ahead port, half astern starboard. As *Scourge* began to stir under him, he bent to the voicepipe and called the turn. And slowly, *Scourge's* bow began to swing. Mere moments passed, the bow edging round, then he rang for stop together, then half astern together. And slowly he nudged his boat around, 180 degrees until her bow was pointed at the open sea, far too many hundreds of yards away for comfort. There'd be no need now for Hooper to light up any target on the hills; or risk dropping shells so close to friendlies. He could put his precious few shells away now, his gun was pointing the wrong way. If *Scourge* was going to offer any fire support now, it would be from the .303 mount. Meanwhile, onshore, the firing never ceased.

'Here they come!' shouted Probert and one of the lookouts together, and Harry turned to see a gaggle of shadowy figures staggering out the scrub with three stretchers slung among them. The gaggle turned to a flow, many of the men walking wounded, white bandages glowing in the moonlight as they scrambled down to the water's edge.

Then came the rush, a huge commotion in the scrub at the top of the beach, heads bobbing. And then out onto the sand came the raft carriers at an ungainly stomp, with the huge black slugs being half-carried, half-dragged between them, the carriers stooping with exhaustion, tripping over their own feet as they lurched the final yards towards the lapping waves, the rafts collapsing onto the sand and being dragged now, into the water.

Harry was aware of a lull in the firing. He scanned the rising ground leading up to the saddle. When his eyes dropped again to the beach, it was to see it crowded – thirty, maybe forty-odd figures in a crush around the now floating inflatable rafts. But he could see it wasn't a mob; disciplined hands had already loaded the stretcher cases into the first raft, and the walking wounded were being seated in orderly rows.

Down on *Scourge's* casing, Farrar had taken charge. The torpedo loading hatch was open, and half a dozen ratings were lining the side, ready to secure the rafts once they'd rowed the two hundred yards to them. When Harry looked back, the first raft was coming, paddles and oars of various descriptions propelling it on in rhythmic strokes, its black rubber hull all but disappeared under the crush of the bodies it carried.

Renewed firing made Harry look back to the beach. It was closer now. The *Crack! Crack!* of two grenades going off blasted a flurry of debris skywards, close to the scrub's edge.

Christ! he said to himself. There were Jerries right on their tail.

Puttick, the second cox'n was on the .303. Harry turned to him and said, 'Did you see the blasts there, in the bushes?'

'Yessir!'

'Drop suppressing fire on it, now!'

The twin guns started juddering enough to make his teeth shake; the din was so loud it was as if he was feeling it rather than hearing it. He watched the tracer reach out in a lazy arc, scything into the vegetation. Two short bursts for ranging, then a longer one, until Harry saw a figure at the shrubs' edge, a familiar figure, waving wildly.

'Check fire!' said Harry. The figure was the para captain, the side of his head plastered in his own wound dressings. Four soldiers burst from the shrubs at a run, and the captain turned and limped off with them. Two stopped to heft the captain off his feet, and the entire group jumped a small parapet of sand where two other soldiers lay stretched, one with a Bren and the other a Thompson sub-machine gun. The staggering group went past, and the two on the ground began peppering the shrubs.

Harry could hear the captain yelling above the din, 'Go! Go!'

The second raft pushed off, paddles biting the water as the group carrying their officer splashed through the tiny waves, and with one heave, they lobbed him in, scrambling after. The Bren gun and the Tommy gunner were charging in now too. As Harry watched, Probert was suddenly there, shoving him aside, hissing, 'Sir! Sir!' There was a para beside him from the first raft, and he had a Bren gun too. The para immediately dropped, flicked down the gun's bipod and began firing at the beach. Harry saw Probert's eyes boring into his, understood, and nodded, and Probert took command of *Scourge's* guns. Barked, clipped single-word commands, his hands pointing, muzzle flashes from the bushes now, lots of them, like twinkling fairy lights, and spurts of water running through waves, and little bursts of metallic tinging as Jerry rounds hit *Scourge's* casing and conning tower. Harry felt himself trying to shrink his torso behind the periscope stands. The battle was taking place with him as a bystander. He stepped back to the bridge front, ordering all the lookouts below as he went.

Below him, there was only Farrar and the para captain on the casing now, the captain rising after casting off the second raft – the other was already floating away. Harry bent to the pipe and yelled, 'Full ahead together!' And when he looked back, the water was already churning as *Scourge's* twin screws bit into the water. He had to yell the course down the pipe twice, his orders being drowned by all the automatic weapons fire pumping out three feet away over his shoulder.

He saw Farrar standing half in the torpedo hatch, but when he looked for Tolland, he couldn't see him. Then, out the bottom of his eye, he saw him on the aft casing, in the act of throwing a grenade, then another. Why? Then as he turned to run back, his left arm suddenly shot up and out at a wrong angle. He yelped, almost thrown off the casing, then staggered on into Farrar's arms and was bundled below, the hatch being yanked shut behind him.

Harry was aware, behind him, of the firing petering out. Then two cracks as the grenades detonated, shredding both rafts and whatever was left in them.*

Scourge had cleared to the open sea before Harry decided he should take a turn below, leaving Harding on watch on the bridge.

Soldiers filled the boat's gangway, and going for'ard from the control room, Harry had to pick his way between the tangle of legs and slumped bodies; nearly all of them had some wound or scratch. Earlier, Farrar and Tolland together had taken a headcount. One of the Royal Signals corporals hadn't made it, cut off with his transmitter up in the Kastros fort. But all the Royal Engineers were there. And of the three under-strength para platoons who had gone ashore, thirty-four men had made it off, three of them seriously wounded. Capt Tolland told Farrar they'd been lucky.

The wounded who needed space were all laid out on the forward torpedo room deck plates, and up on the empty reload racks. When Harry stepped into the space, the smell of blood was winning against the smell of feet and diesel and bilges. Ainsworth was in there, but two para medics were doing nearly all the ministering, wound cleaning and dressing. They had a drip into one of the stretcher cases. Propped right by the watertight door was Capt Tolland, his floppy, mousy hair all caked and brittle now with dust and blood. He sported a big, wadded wound dressing taped to his right cheek and covering his ear. From the livid welts round the edges, Harry could see it covered a nasty flash burn. His shirt was in shreds, and there was a hole in his arm, seeping blood; from the way it dangled, the bone was obviously shattered. For some reason, all Harry could think of was all the stiff-upper-lip war film scenes he'd ever seen at the cinema and truly what a load of bollocks they all had been. He wanted to say something, but all that came out was, 'Fuck me.'

Tolland looked up at him, as if just noticing him, then he looked round his men and the carnage that was filling the torpedo room. 'You took the words right out my mouth, Captain Gilmour,' he said.

Harry took a step further into the space and tapped the stooping cox'n on the shoulder. 'Mr Ainsworth,' he said. 'Open the spirit locker. I think there are a few of our Parachute Regiment guests here who could do with a drink.'

Twenty-two

Captain de Launy had managed to borrow a Riley staff car from the PNO (Principal Naval Officer) for Algiers port for the short drive down the Corniche. The two leading seaman regulators he'd brought with him sat in the front with the PNO's driver, smart as pins in their whites, with their lanyards and sidearms in webbing holsters on their hips, caps on straight and socks pulled up. Their destination was the requisitioned pink stucco villa, all garlanded in bougainvillaea with the big wooden sign outside saying, '*ETOUSA*' – meaning European Theater of Operations, United States Army – '*Staff Offices: Authorised personnel ONLY*', and below that, all the acronyms in a descending list that said who else lived there. It included NAAF, the Northwest African Air Force's headquarters staff, and finally, in small print, SSLO, the Senior Submarine Liaison Officer, meaning this was where Captain Bonalleck had his cupboard he called an office.

It was mid-morning, and de Launy felt himself getting sweaty in the back of the car, despite all the windows being wound down. That, and the building anger in his chest. That he was being forced to carry out this outrageous duty infuriated him. It wasn't that he didn't want to do it, in fact, he was looking forward to it. It was the affront itself that this madman, this degenerate, had perpetrated against the service he loved, that he should have to clean it up.

He had phoned ahead to the villa's guardroom to alert them he was on his way, so the Riley swept in past the white-helmeted American MPs on the gate, both of them snapping off a smart salute as the car went through.

He checked for directions at the door, and then he and his escort marched purposefully down polished corridors in tight V-formation to Bonalleck's little den. When they got there, Bonalleck was nowhere to be seen. Heads were sticking out other office doors, alerted by the measured steps. A young US Army Air Force officer, buzz-cut hair, wearing wire-rim glasses and lieutenant's bars on his shirt collar was leaning out a door with a sign above it announcing, '*NAAF Ops Room*'. He said, 'You guys looking for Charlie? He's not turned up yet. He usually has breakfast at the staff officers' mess. If you want to try, he might still be there.'

Some sixth sense told de Launy something was seriously wrong.

*

Two days later, in HMS *Maidstone's* wardroom, a steward walked the length of it to whisper in Capt de Launy's ear; there was a phone call for him in the commander's office.

When de Launy took the receiver, an American voice said his name. De Launy said, 'Yes,' and the American officer, in a nasal southern twang, introduced himself.

'I understand you have been trying to reach one of your officers, a Captain Charles Bonalleck, who is the SSLO for the western Mediterranean? I have some information for you.'

De Launy's sixth sense sent alarm bells ringing again.

'Captain Bonalleck boarded a US Army Air Force C54 ferry flight to Casablanca on Tuesday afternoon,' said the American officer. 'We know this because we have the carbon of the NAAF travel docket he forged in order to make the trip. Have you any idea why he might want to travel to Casablanca, Captain? The reason I'm asking is our MPs want to speak to him on another matter too.'

'Really?' was the best de Launy could manage by way of innocent response while his mind raced.

'Yes, sir. Our staff officers' club safe is missing a substantial sum of US dollars. In fact, all the petty cash they use to fund purchasing local produce. Somebody palmed a set of keys, and your man is the only member we haven't accounted for yet. The guys at the club are pretty steamed.'

Twenty-three

Harry shifted in the camp chair and accepted another cup of sweet, thick Greek coffee which was really rather fantastic. He'd been waiting outside the tent for ten minutes, and this coffee was the only reason he hadn't been getting impatient.

On the bridge, as *Scourge* had come back round the Thirios bar, he'd been handed a radio signal that he was to report ashore immediately to Brigadier Plomer's TacHQ, which was a small collection of bell tents on one of the few patches of level ground coming out the town. And now he was here, looking at the sublime view down to the sun-bleached jumble of flat-roofed stone houses that made up the town, across the harbour and anchorage to where one of the MGBs rode on a mooring, and out beyond the bar, to the sea, the azure water all ruffled by breeze and dappled in the sunlight. Missing from the view, however, were *Howsham* and *Alconbury*.

'They went off last night,' one of the brigadier's staff captains had told him, offering him the camp seat and asking him to wait. 'Jerry started dropping paratroopers on Kos yesterday. They've gone to try and stop any landings from the sea. We're on full alert here.'

Which had explained why the captain and everybody else around the TacHQ were wearing tin hats.

Harry had come wanting to know what he should be doing with all the wounded left aboard *Scourge*. All the walking wounded were already off down the gangplank the instant *Scourge* had come alongside the town's wooden wharf. But his intention had been to decant the serious cases aboard the destroyers, where their sick bays would be the best place to treat them. And the last thing he'd wanted to do was start moving them around from pillar to post for no good reason.

He was also curious as to why the brigadier had needed him so urgently. Or, as it appeared, actually not that urgently. Maybe it was just a case of the army being just like the navy; all 'hurry up – and wait!' At least now he understood *why* he'd been kept waiting. Jerry paratroopers. Suddenly, Harry didn't want to be there, halfway up a bloody mountain while his command lay tied impotently to a wharf, a sitting duck down below. He needed to be back on board and getting sea room around him right now!

'Have you any idea why the brigadier needs to see me right now, sir?' asked Harry with an edge in his voice.

The captain said, 'He wants to know the state of your ammunition and fuel and to discuss how best to deploy you in the coming action.'

'Discuss? …Sir?' said Harry standing up. 'Tell him I have three torpedoes, six rounds of three-inch and my three-oh-three is all but exhausted. I really must be getting back to my boat now, sir. Pass on my…'

Both Harry and the captain looked up into the cloudless sky. The sound of aero engines. They scanned round. A lot of engines.

Then high up, maybe ten thousand feet, to the north-west, a cloud of what looked like gnats – two dozen? More? And as they drew closer, the telltale gull wings began to stand out. Stuka dive-bombers. At least thirty of them.

A soldier was already running to a siren sitting on its steel frame behind the tents, and he immediately began to wind it, bringing forth a mounting wail. Harry ignored everything happening around him and started running down the hill. His pounding heart and the blood in his ears and the pumping of his breathing made it feel like he was running under water as each bounding stride took him into the start of the town, and he could feel the lumps of the cobbles punching up through his plimsolls.

Until, through all that sub-aqueous pulsing in his head, there was infused the beginnings of a scream, louder and louder, the tearing screech of a diving Stuka ripped away as it pulled out of its dive, only to be replaced by the whistle of a bomb… and then the rip of high explosives. When he looked up, he could see the Stuka had been aiming for the wharves and the harbour, but the sheerness of the surrounding terrain meant it hadn't been able to hit the right angle of dive and have any hope of climbing out again without hitting the opposite hills. Its bomb had gone into the town. The town Harry was running into. Yet he had to get through it to get to *Scourge*.

He could see the MGB, figures on her fo'c'sle slipping the mooring and the tiny jets of smoke around her gun mountings as she pumped up shells into the path of the next diving Jerry.

Noise was everywhere now, again and again, the curdling scream from the Stuka's *Jericho Trompetes* – those wailing sirens mounted under their wings, the Nazi terror sound signalling death from the skies. It really did shrink your skin, thought Harry as he charged on down alley after alley, dimly aware now of the civilians scurrying for cover too.

They must have come from Rhodes, he thought, absently, as Verney and Grainger had both predicted. Jerry'd found the spare aircraft and now they were all here, clapping a stopper over Tommy's little caper. They must've sent more Ju 52s too, for the paratroopers. As he continued running, Harry found himself wondering, how many?

And then there was the second cox'n, Puttick, stripped to the waist, leaning over AB Windass, propped against the corner of another alley. Strange, he remembered thinking, as he was about to automatically speed past, what were they doing here? And at that, he jerked to a halt. There was bread and smashed wine bottles spread around the two sailors and the stink of explosives in the air and shattered stone and debris.

Puttick had his shirt pressed tightly against Windass' upper thigh and the material was already staining red. With his other hand, he was trying to tear an arm off the shirt. Harry, without a word, dropped to one knee and took over, ripping both arms off the shirt and using them to tightly bind it to Windass' wound. Windass just sat, unflinching, staring at the hole in his leg and then all around him like a dazed child who's just fallen off his bike.

They must've come ashore to buy stuff, the bread and wine. And been caught like him, thought Harry. The noise was too great, too indiscriminate to talk. He and Puttick hefted Windass, and together, they resumed their headlong flight, staggering and lurching towards the harbour.

The next thing Puttick was aware of, was he was lying on the ground, dust choking his mouth and nose and stinging his eyes. He couldn't hear properly, like his ears were listening from down the end of a tunnel, and Windass, randomly flung, was lying against the far side of the alley, and there were two civilians pulling on them. And rubble, a lot of rubble. He shut his eyes, and when he opened them again, he was on a bunk in the PO's mess space on *Scourge*, and everything was still, not even the sound of her diesels, and Dickie Bird was sponging dust off him.

Dickie Bird in the control room, face ashen, interrupting Farrar and Harding at the chart table.

'Pardon me, sir!' Dickie was saying, breathless, 'It's Captain Gilmour, sir!'

'What about him, Bird?' said Farrar.

'Puttick says he's copped it!'

Scourge was on the sea bed, eighty-two feet down at the bottom of the harbour, safe from the Stukas. It had been the major saving grace for Harry, forced to bring *Scourge* in here in the first place, that the steep sides of the place carried on down to a sandy bottom, so that in the event of an air raid, all *Scourge* had to do was dive, like they used to do in Marsamxett harbour at the height of the Malta siege.

The lesson hadn't been lost on Farrar, so when the Stukas had come over, down went *Scourge*. During a lull in the raids, having spotted their two wounded shipmates through the periscope, sprawled against bollards on the wharf, up they'd come to collect them, and down they'd gone again. As for Captain Gilmour, everybody assumed he'd be safe enough up the hill, sharing a slit trench and probably a ciggy with the brigadier.

'What d'you mean copped it, Bird?' said Harding, voice hard, not the usual light touch.

*

That night, on the wharf, a big confab. *Howsham* and *Alconbury* are back, so Pleydell and Grainger are there; Farrar and Harding are there too and so is the brigadier.

Jerry is closing in; holding Kos is doubtful. Plans are getting discussed for the destroyers to evacuate troops from up there. Someone has to tell the RAF not to send the Tomahawks; the airfield has already been overrun. Will holding onto Thirios still be viable? Big debate on that. Grainger has been delegated to brief *Scourge* on her part in the coming fray. It's to be transporting wounded, a job less fitted for a submarine it is hard to imagine.

Harding, Farrar and Grainger are standing at *Scourge's* gangplank.

'We've given you all the three-oh-three we can spare, but with nothing left in your locker for that pop gun on your casing, you're really no good to us,' Grainger is saying. 'So Plomer wants you to take all the serious cases back to Beirut, clear our sick bays for the ones that will inevitably follow. When can you sail?'

'We've got to go and find our captain first,' said Farrar.

Grainger already knows what has happened to his friend. 'How long d'you think it's going to take to find him, for Christ's sake? You know there's rumours Jerry's already infiltrating troops in here.'

'Sorry, sir,' says Harding, 'I don't think you quite understand what's happening here. We're not coming back without him.'

Grainger sighs. It's no more irresponsible than he's been himself. 'When you get him, bring him to us,' he says, pointing at his ship and her sickbay, riding beyond the anchorage. 'I'll see you at the bar.'

Down in the control room, a press of sailors. Harding is picking his team, except it's turned out most of the choices have already been made for him. 'I'm going, sir,' says Leading Seaman Billy Cross. Able Seaman Chapman says, 'And you're not going without me, neither, sir. Not a chance, sir!'

The bloody cheek! Harding is thinking, but he knows what they mean. That's how he's thinking too. 'And me too, sir,' says Darky Mularky, the new boy.

They find him in a half-demolished house, just before dawn. An old Greek woman and a child are tending to him. There are multiple wounds, but it looks like he's already received some medical attention – a local doctor, doing rounds, patching up who he can after the bombing. Locals had had to dig him out from where the wall of a house had collapsed on him. The bomb that had blasted Puttick and Windass in different directions had buried Harry. Nobody had come to raise the alarm down on the wharf because the British soldiers had imposed a curfew.

In the end, they don't take Harry to *Alconbury*. Her surgeon lieutenant does a house call to *Scourge*. He removes the shrapnel from the chest wound and the wound on his right side, but he thinks there might be more in there, maybe in his liver. But he's not going in there to look, not here. He could kill him. Their skipper will need a proper operating theatre to do a proper job. He drains, packs and sutures what he can and sets the fractured leg. And *Scourge* sails with her full cargo of broken and shattered for Beirut, just after first light, diving the minute she clears the bar.

*

The city of Beirut sits right on the Mediterranean in a near-perfect amphitheatre of mountains. And the Third NZ General Hospital was located in an old French Army barracks on one of the foothills that ring the city to the east.

The First Submarine Flotilla, to which *Scourge* now belonged, had dibs on dock space down in the port, so it was no chore for her crew to come up the hill to visit their former CO, Lieutenant Harry Gilmour, and many of them did. The cohort of Kiwi girls who formed the core of the nursing cadre at the hospital didn't mind, they quite liked Lt Gilmour – a couple of them more than liked him – so they were happy to entertain the stream of submariners who were always passing through to say hello. After all, it cheered Lt Gilmour up, and God knew he needed it. The poor fellow had been lying there under strict orders not to move for a couple of weeks now, prostrate after some pretty heroic surgery to save his life: one lung lacerated and collapsed, his liver scarred by shrapnel and recurring infection and a tibia that wasn't knitting as it should.

Despite the pain, Harry couldn't remember the last time he had luxuriated in such sleeps and each time, waking to all these gorgeous girls, each one a picture of rude colonial health and cheerfulness. They could tuck him in any time they wanted, even wake him in the middle of the night to do it, he didn't mind. But the pain was always there, and all the senior surgeon had said he was, 'Buggered if I'm giving you any more morphine, or you'll end up a dope addict. Grin and bear it, lieutenant.'

Scourge had a new skipper now, a lucky replacement CO from First Flotilla's pool, to take her back home to Gosport and HMS *Dolphin*. The *Scourges* he'd talked to about him seemed to think he was okay, not that they wanted to talk about him much. They wanted to talk about all the leave that was getting flung about, the boat being mostly in the hands of the dockyard, tightening up the lash-ups, covering all the multitude of sins she'd racked up with licks of paint, getting her ready for her voyage back to Blighty and a proper refit, a long time overdue after seventeen months of continuous operations. But Beirut! What a town! He'd better get himself better and get down there before they drank all the beer and wine and arak and all the available women got taken.

And now, on this particularly beautiful morning with the sun streaming in the windows, there was Harding, walking down the ward alone. Harry didn't spot him until he was halfway to him – two of the beds on this side of the ward had screens round them, very poorly young men behind them. They blocked the view.

It was unusual for Harding to come alone.

'Wotcher, Miles,' said Harry, no 'sirs' or 'Misters' anymore, he was no longer captain. 'Have we won yet?'

Harding handed Harry a signal flimsy. 'A present for you, from their lordships. And guess what? I got one too. And so did Hooper.'

Harry opened it. It was a notification of a bar for his DSC.

'Fancy that,' he said. 'And you too, eh?'

'I don't know about you, but I intend to always keep mine about my person in case any girl wants to touch it,' said Harding with his usual evil grin.

A bit more chit-chat, then Harding came to the point.

'We've got our sailing orders,' he said. 'Tomorrow morning.'

'Going home. The lads will be chuffed rotten.'

'No. They're not,' said Harding, wearing a peculiar expression that told Harry he wasn't joshing him. 'And they've told me to tell you so.'

'What...? Why not?' Harry looked even paler, with his face all blank incomprehension.

'They don't feel it's right to be going home without you. Number One's told them if he gets another delegation telling him to get you back aboard, he's going to start charging them with mutiny.'

Harry snorted then winced with pain, because it hurt. 'Bollocks,' he said.

'You don't get it, do you, sir?' said Harding, using the honorific on purpose, even though he no longer had to.

'Get what, ya daft bugger?'

'What they thought about you after you came aboard. After Bayliss,' Harding paused, to regard him, lying there, chest swathed in bandage, skinny as an anatomy class skeleton draped in white crepe. Frail. 'But right from the start, you made it plain. You weren't Bayliss. Ordering the forward watertight doors open again and sod the mines... *If we're going home, we're all going home together.* Then, when you missed those Eyetie battleships with a full salvo. It was, I *made a right bollocks ...*

not, *you lot* …not even, *we* …it was, "*I*". And when you took the time to sit and chat to Red Cross after his drunk-and-uncatchable antics instead of throwing him to the wolves on the depot ship. And you still don't get it, do you?'

'Get what, Miles?'

'That crew. They'd follow you up a dead bear's bum. Even if it was on fire.'

After a brief silence to let it sink in, Harding asked him if he had any letters or parcels for *Scourge* to carry home for him, but Harry had had no strength to write and certainly no chance to shop. So, eventually, Harding got up and said that he'd see him back in Pompey one day, once he'd stopped leaking. Then it was a handshake and they both said goodbye, and Harding was striding back down the ward, not looking back.

Harry watched him go and felt his chest tightening. It wasn't his wounds, it was the realisation that Harding's had probably been the last familiar face he was going to see for a long, long time.

The end.

CPSIA information can be obtained
at www.ICGtesting.com
Printed in the USA
BVHW042207130223
658290BV00026B/966